STANLEY SOUTH
&
THE HUSTLEDOWN SNIPES

Carl Barton

First published in Great Britain as a softback original in 2022

Copyright © Carl Barton

The moral right of this author has been asserted.

Editing, design, typesetting and publishing by UK Book Publishing

www.ukbookpublishing.com

ISBN: 978-1-915338-76-1

For my family

Carl Barton was born in Stanley, Co. Durham, and lived there until his late twenties, when he packed up and headed West, six miles, to Consett, where he has lived for the last 35 years. This is his first novel. He would love to hear from readers on facebook.

/Carl Barton Author

"I just can't listen to any more Wagner, you know... I'm starting to get the urge to conquer Poland."

Woody Allen

Chapter 1

1994

From the path outside the Post Office, Norman Bembrage looked across the road at the backs of three soaking wet workmen, standing like fence posts in the gloomy late November mizzle, as they watched the last smashed bits of the pub they'd just torn down being dragged about by the grabbing yellow arms of the wrecking machines. He was there to watch what they were watching, but the reflective strips on their safety jackets kept catching his eye. It might have been the way they flickered like broken lamps in the headlights of the homecoming traffic that made him think about the people in the cars, or the way the workmen seemed completely indifferent to it all, that made him think of how little the flattened pub would mean to anybody now. Whatever it was, it awakened the sadness he carried in what he couldn't forget, and the squealing, clattering work of the giant croupiers, calling him back to watch them raking in the spoils of what the past had lost, made him remember what was breaking his heart to see.

A blaring car horn brought a sideways glance from the middle of the three workmen to see the little old man who'd caused it. He saw him stepping awkwardly back onto the kerb and went over to help. Stopping the cars heading up the hill with a Nazi salute and those coming down with a left arm barrier, his nodded invitation to Norman was accepted, and he passed underneath the mucky sleeve to the other side. Standing with his back to the splashy noise of the re-flowing traffic, he looked down the slope of the bulldozed car park, and could see the carcass of the village pub having its brown and red furnished guts pulled out by the metal scavengers. The traffic cop workman watched him take his cap off and lower his head, but not far enough to stop him thinking how easy it was to tell the difference between raindrops and tears. He wanted to put his hand on Norman's shoulder but didn't, and didn't know why he couldn't. Elsa Carr, an old-looking 59-year-old care assistant from Tipton Grange Nursing Home, didn't share his reservation. She bowled across the road holding a tartan blanket like a matador to a bull, and swept it around Norman's shoulders with well-practised ease, gripping it under his chin with a prize-fighter's fist:

'What on earth, Norman?' She began, lifting her free hand to the silvery satin plumes turning slowly in the orange street light. 'You've given us all a fright wandering off like that. Come on, let's get you inside. You'll catch your death of cold in this.'

The traffic cop workman smiled at her equally well-practised caring tone struggling to hide her annoyance from them, and watched her change from rain and cold protector to store detective, as she jammed the old man's cap on and tried to turn him to face the road. Without speaking, or making any obvious effort to resist, he made it clear he still wanted to look at the fallen pub, and with the irritated resignation of a dog owner at a lamppost, she let him. Norman knew his time would be brief, and went to his cardigan pocket. The moment she took her eyes off him to let the workmen know with a shake of the head, how much she had to put up with, he flung something away without looking at it, not caring to see where it landed. Whatever it was, it seemed to take his resistance with it, and the workmen watched him being led away forlornly by Elsa, at the end of her tether.

'Alzheimer's,' said the first of the three.

'Aye,' said the third with a smile, but thought he'd better come up with something else about mental illness to make sure he knew he'd got it:

'The old fucker'll be thinking he's Clint Eastwood in that blanket.'

'Aye, with a fistful of Werthers,' added the first.

The middle traffic-cop workman didn't hear them because he'd walked away looking for what the old man had thrown. He found it sticking on its edge, poking out just above the caramel slop slowly filling the muddy clay casts of the Caterpillar tracks. Cleaning it as best he could between his finger and thumb, he stepped into the headlight beam of one of the machines. The shock stopped him in its tracks when it lit up a Victoria Cross.

Chapter 2

Pressing the white buzzer button for the second time brought a familiar face to the reception window in the neat neutral foyer of Tipton Grange Nursing Home.

'Hello there,' said the hesitant traffic cop workman, thinking she didn't recognise him, 'it's just that the old lad you came across the road for yesterday dropped this.'

'Oh, right, sorry, I didn't recognise you without your work gear on,' said Elsa Carr, looking at the medal. 'What is it?'

'I think it's one of them old military service medals they all got from the war,' he lied.

'Oh, right, just put it in the tray there and I'll see he gets it.'

She could see he didn't want to and waited for the reason.

'I don't suppose there's any chance I could give him it back myself, is there?'

'Well...' she began, raising an eyebrow to let him know she'd be doing him a favour.

'It's just for a bit crack really; about the war, if he wants to, that is, I like all that stuff and thought he might like a bit company.'

She smiled at his kindness, told him how to get to Norman's room and buzzed him in. By the time the lock on the security door clicked shut, she was getting ready to leave. Standing at the end of her directions, with no response to his polite taps on the half open door, he went in and made his way up the short passage to look into the dimly lit living room. He saw Norman sitting forward on a fat-armed, dark green leather chair, staring into the burning brightness of the gas fire, and coughed before saying, 'Hello,' in his friendliest voice.

4

The old man heard the voice calling him to leave the far-away place in the fire and come back to his room. He returned to look at his visitor.

'Hello there,' said the workman, stepping into the room with his hand held out.

Norman lowered his head and made his elbows tremble as he pressed the chair arms to help himself up. They shook hands – one doing all he could to make a proper grip and the other doing all he could not to; it was like a prop forward shaking hands with a child.

'I'm Brendan, I was working across the road, there, yesterday, when you came over.'

'Yes, I remember. Hello, I'm Norman.'

'It's nice to meet you, Norman. I just wanted to give you this.'

He gave him the freshly polished medal and he looked gravely at it in the palm of his hand.

'Thank you,' he said slowly.

'Not many of those about,' said Brendan to break the growing silence.

'No.'

'You must've been very brave to get it.'

'No,' he said distractedly, putting it in his cardigan pocket. 'Please, have a seat, I'll make some tea.'

Brendan smiled at his teatime dictator heading for the kitchen, and sat in the chair he'd been pointed to at the other side of the fire. A beautiful old rosewood bureau, standing painfully out of place in the drab magnolia room, drew his eye to the framed photographs standing on it. He went over to look at them. The largest, in prime position, was a black and white picture of a Glenn Miller type big band. He smiled again as he looked at the portly little band leader, standing proudly in front, dressed the same as the others in a white tuxedo jacket and black bow-tie, holding his trombone vertically on the pivot of his hand so the mouthpiece pointed straight up. 'Stanley South and the Hustledown Snipes, August, 1939' was engraved on an elegant silver tab fitted to the bottom of the frame. He noticed the top of the pub they'd just pulled down in the background. Towards the back of the bureau was a small, faded colour photo of a young man with fine fair hair, pink lips and ice blue eyes, wearing a very dark coat that highlighted the white dog-collar. He picked it up to check if it was the same person now making him tea.

'I gave it up after the war.'

'Oh,' said Brendan, thinking he'd be better not ask why.

Seeing the tired old wooden tea tray, stacked with cups, saucers, teapot, milk jug, sugar bowl and a plate of Garibaldi biscuits, being set down on an oval coffee table between the two chairs, he knew to replace the photo and take his seat. Norman lifted the teapot lid and gave it a good stir before he sat down himself:

'We'll give it a minute to mass,' he said.

'My grandmother was just the same.'

Norman smiled.

'I see the old pub's in the background of the band photo, there,' said Brendan.

'Yes, it was their local.'

'Were they friends of yours?'

The old man shook his head slowly as if to say it was more complicated than that. Brendan waited and Norman poured the tea. Pressing down on his chair to stand up again, he went to the bureau and unlocked the cabinet doors with a thick little key. Pushing them wide open let Brendan see the Air Force blue bindings on the tightly packed notebooks filling both shelves; he pulled one out and went back to his seat.

'Here,' he said, handing it to Brendan, 'it's all written down, the work we did together, the band and me during the war, it's all written down.'

Brendan opened the notebook and looked at the graceful handwriting. He thought of school and his first fountain pen with the wide gold nib, the smell of Quink ink, and how he liked the smell of old books better than new ones.

'Is this your diary, then?' he asked.

'Sort of. At least it was until a friend of mine thought to write it up like a story; to get more detail in, you see. But it's all true all the same.'

'Sounds fascinating.'

'You can take them if you want; it's nice to think someone might be interested in them.'

'Are you sure? Is there nobody else you'd rather have them?'

'No, no. I've no family, or friends either, for that matter… no, you have them.'

Before Brendan could say anything else to make sure he wanted him to have them, Norman left the room. He came back with a dirty old dark brown kit bag and knelt in front of the bureau to fill it with the notebooks. It looked like a child's coffin when he'd finished.

'There, take them when you go, but please, have your tea.'

Brendan felt the first light touch of something that didn't feel right, but easily brushed it off with his curiosity:

'So how did you come to be working with the band, then?'

'It was through the Church; I'd been recommended to do some work for a new department that had been set up, nothing very glamorous, you understand, just working on ways to keep morale up, you know.'

'A government department?'

'Yes, but as I say, nothing very grand.'

'And that's where the band came in?'

'It was, yes.'

'So were you their manager, sort of thing?'

'No, they worked abroad mostly and I was based here in England, but you'll see when you read the books. Would you like another biscuit?'

Brendan took one to be polite.

'So what were they abroad for then, like a Vera Lynn thing, playing for the troops?'

Norman half smiled and raised an eyebrow, but didn't reply.

'So what did you get the medal for?' tried Brendan.

'It isn't mine.'

'But it's linked to the band, though?'

'It is, yes. As I say, you'll see for yourself.'

Realising he wasn't going to get anything out of him, Brendan turned to a more chatty track. He made him smile with a story about a young lad at work they had believing Garibaldi was the patron Saint of alopecia, but it was hard work and he was pleased to spot an opening to take his leave politely. Norman seemed just as pleased to hand him the bag. Brendan took it like a parent rescuing a struggling child from a heavy suitcase, and offered his hand to say goodbye.

'Oh, there is one small thing,' said Norman, as though he'd just remembered something he hadn't forgotten: 'I'd be ever so grateful if you could do this for me.'

He pulled a glossy Sunday supplement magazine from under his seat.

'Put my story on this,' he said, tapping the cover image as he handed it to Brendan, 'on the world wide web. You need a computer like that, you see, and I haven't got one, but you just need to type it into one and send it to the web, and then anyone can read it, if they want to, that is.'

Brendan smiled. 'I'm just thinking of my wife saying you'd be better off giving a fish a bicycle.'

'But it tells you how to do it,' said Norman, missing the humour.

'Right,' said Brendan cautiously.

'Good man, that's very kind of you, thank you. Oh, and would you be sure to use this as the name of the website.'

He pushed a piece of paper into Brendan's coat pocket.

'It will seem a strange name, but please don't use any other.'

Although he'd managed earlier, now Brendan couldn't brush off the feeling that something wasn't right anymore. When they said their goodbyes he was more relieved to go than he ever thought he would be.

Chapter 3

'And you've got a spare computer handy then, have you?' said Brendan's wife, Janet.

'No, but I know a man who has,' said Brendan with a smile.

'Oh, Christ no, not Charles.'

'Needs must, sweetness, needs must. I'll give him a ring and see if he'll pop over after tea.'

'Oh bloody joy of joys, and he'll have "Mrs Charles" popping over with him then, poor bugger. Well, that'll be me away up to our Shirley's.'

Brendan smiled at his wife. 'He isn't that bad. And don't make out you don't like Gloria, she's a lovely lass, a bit numb I'll grant yer, but harmless, and I know you think the world of her, so don't try and say you don't.'

'I know, she's a lovely thing, but all that sickly, bloody lovey-dovey stuff, Christ, it's the way that sackless little sod's got her.'

'It's just the way he is, Pet. Mind, she does seem to like it though.'

'She does, bless her, she does, but it's still hard work; the pair of them.'

*****

'So, Charles, that's the top and bottom of it,' said Brendan, pouring the coffee.

'Sounds like there's a good bit more to this than he's letting on, mind; provided he's not doo-lally-tap, like?'

'No, definitely not, he's as sharp as a tack. But, to be honest, I came away thinking there was more to it as well, mind.'

'There has t' be, or he wouldn't have had it all written down in the first place, never mind gettin' it made into a story and keepin' it all these years. I'll bet he's jumped at the first chance that's come his way to get it out there, on the web, like.'

'No, there's bound to have been others he could've given it to.'

'Couldn't be, or he wouldn't have collared you, a complete bloody stranger, he must've thought it was the end of the line, eh.'

'Maybe.'

'He must have, I mean, just throwing that medal away says he must have, Christ, collectors'll pay a bloody fortune for them.'

'Well, I've said I'd do it, so we'll have to now.'

'Aye, but there's a canny bit work involved in this, mind; building a website and getting it registered and what-not, never mind getting it typed onto a computer for a start, although Gloria can do that, can't yer, Sweet Pea. Thinking of which, it'll be better if I take the books home and do it on mine.'

'What's that face for?' demanded Janet, looking straight at her husband.

'No, nothing. I just thought if we did it here I could help a bit, y'know, reading it out for Gloria.'

'Then just come round ours.'

'You know he won't,' jabbed Janet, 'he's gettin' worse for thinkin' he's botherin' people if he's in their house – he's the one that's doo-lally-tap.'

'I'll sort something out.' Charles smiled.

'You're a good'un, Charles, lad. So, is this the right disc thing, then? The lad in Woolworths said it was.'

'Let's see, a 3.5 floppy, it is. Pity you're not still at Woolworths, Sweet Pea, you could have pinched one, eh,' winked Charles.

'I didn't know you worked at Woolworths, Pet,' said Janet.

'In the office,' said Charles proudly.

'It was when I left school, but I wasn't there very long though.'

Gloria looked uncomfortable as she headed on to tell the truth because she didn't know how to lie: 'They said I was too slow.'

'At typing?' asked Brendan innocently.

'Well, they didn't say it was that...'

'No, but that's what they'll have meant, Pet,' said Janet, picking the disk up to say there was no more to be said.

******

'And before you ask,' said Charles, looking at Brendan who obviously wasn't going to, 'it's a good one, it's a 486 DX. I was humming and harring over the SX, but looking into it a bit more, I couldn't see where the extra 80 quid was going, so I went for the DX.'

'Eighty quid! Bloody hell, Charles, how much did yer pay for it?' asked Brendan, shocked by Charles the tight.

'One thousand, one hundred and forty-one pounds,' answered Gloria because she knew the answer.

'Christ, Charles.'

'Had to be done,' was the heroic reply.

'Not for this stuff though, surely?'

'No, no, I needed one for the shop and what-not. Anyhow, that's not desperate, so we can set it up here and do this first, eh. You want to think about one of these for yourself, Bren, dead handy and things are all heading this way now, mind.'

'Aye,' said Brendan, knowing what his wife was smiling at.

'Right, that should be it,' said Charles, crawling backwards from under the table.

'Come on, Gloria, Pet, yer on,' said Brendan playfully.

Janet noticed the nervous tremble reaching Gloria's fingertips as they hovered over the keys, and looked her warning at her husband not to read too fast. Brendan waited and smiled at Gloria's little nod to say she was ready for his steady 28 words per minute to start. Ten minutes later the silence of the keys came with Janet and the coffee.

'You're doin' a grand job, sweetheart, absolutely fantastic, Pet,' said Brendan honestly.

Janet saw Gloria's shoulders relax, and rubbed her back without the others seeing. Gloria looked at her with the thankfulness of an overlooked child being noticed. Charles put the right milk and sugars into the three coffees and passed Gloria her dilute orange. One sip was all she needed to nod for the steady tapping clips to begin again.

******

'You did, you did, you did. Yes, you did say you'd got one,' recollected Charles. 'This old noggin of mine's on the slide, I think, I even forgot to put the price on an invoice the other day, didn't I, Sweet Pea.'

'Oh, but anybody could do that, Bunny.'

'When did you realise…' began Janet.

'It was in bed,' answered Gloria like a quiz show contestant.

'When he woke up screaming?'

Brendan smiled at his wife refusing to be knocked off her one-liner, but Gloria spotted a mistake:

'Oh no, it was before he went to sleep, Janet, it was when…'

She stopped as quickly as Janet's joke had gone over the big pink bow on her flamingo hairband.

'When we were having our hot *choc-o-lat*,' smooched Charles comically.

'Is that right, Gloria? When he was doing naughty things to yer, Pet?'

Gloria went a colour that showed the flamingo of her hairband was an albino.

'Take no notice, Pet,' said Brendan kindly.

Janet rubbed her back to make her smile her relief.

'So what do we have to do now then to get it on this web thing?' asked Brendan.

Gloria clapped her hands, bounced on her chair and beamed at her husband. They smiled at her excitement and looked at Charles.

'Well,' he began, loving the attention, 'there's a canny bit to it, mind, but I think I've got it sussed.'

Janet braced herself for his give-up-the-will-to-live computer speech, but, mercifully, Gloria scuppered it:

'It's web sight, isn't it, Bunny. It means you can only see the web through a computer.'

'That's it, Sweet Pea,' said Charles, taking her hand, 'our website will be there for anybody in the world to see – well, anybody with a computer connected to the internet that is; that's what they call the world wide web, y'see.'

Janet liked this kindness in Charles.

'And can you do it for this stuff then, Charles?'

'I think so, and if I get stuck there's this fella who gets into the shop who's well into all this. Christ, he was in this mornin' looking for a refurb axial fan – I know, a bloody refurb! They're only four quid new, and he wanted less than 80db with a shutter timer, which isn't a common fan, mind, I mean, for the money he'd have been lucky to get an 83db, which in this case…'

'But the web, Charles?' interrupted Janet.

'Aye, well, the upshot is, I'll give it a go, if you want me to, that is.'

They could see she'd huffed him.

'Of course we do, Charles,' said Brendan sincerely, to compensate for his wife's lack of fluff.

'And any problems you can catch that fella?' checked Janet.

'Aye, but even if I can't, I'll be alright with the magazines.'

'Them in the box at the back of the wardrobe, Bunny?'

'No, no, they're, er, more specialist: electricals and things, Sweet Pea,' lied Charles.

Janet coughed.

'Have you come across any of the computer ones you'll need though?' asked Brendan.

Janet coughed again.

'Oh, he has,' said Gloria, who hadn't a clue about any kind of entendre: 'he was thumbing a thick one on Saturday morning in WHSmiths when I was in the queue to get one over the counter.'

Janet coughed and Brendan choked back a laugh. Luckily for Charles, Janet caught sight of the lovely wide eyes looking at her from under the big pink bow and held her fire. Gloria took it as her cue to go on:

'I was getting my favourite one, Janet, '*Make and Do*', it has lots of things in it to do and make…'

Janet resisted.

'…and I'm nearly finished making your Christmas present from one of them, but it's a secret surprise, but I think it'll be nice for cold mornings.'

Janet laid her tongue to rest and smiled with a mother's heart at the 15 stone child who was older than her, looking at her honestly, and thinking she'd never guess she was making her another woolly hat. She leaned over and kissed her forehead. Gloria felt the draught of heaven touch her neck.

'So, anyhow, all we need to do now is come up with a name for the website,' said Charles.

'No need,' said Brendan, giving him the piece of paper, 'the old lad said it had to be this one.'

'"Gretchin Odontoceti",' read Charles. 'Christ, that's a name and a half, sounds like a mafia wife.'

'She might have been his one true love,' said Gloria shyly.

'Sex, sex, sex, Gloria; that mind of yours, honestly, Pet!' Janet couldn't resist.

******

'So it's done, then?'

'It is,' said Charles, 'it's out there for the world and his dog to see.'

'So there you go; what the old man asked you to do, you've done, eh.'

'We have,' said Brendan with a smile. 'But there's still that other problem, though…'

A line of worry settled above the thick lenses of Charles' unfashionable gold navigator glasses.

'… y'know,' continued Brendan, 'the one for me and Janet to work out where to take you and Gloria for a nice meal, and one or three bottles of the old vino du rocket. And before yer say a thing, we are, because I'd have been stuck without you both – well, without all three of yer if the truth be told.'

'And long before you got yer hands on that old man's bag,' poked his wife.

Gloria clapped her hands, pressed them over her mouth and bounced her happiness on the chair.

----

www.Gretchin.Odontoceti.com

Norman's Notebooks

Chapter 1

April, 1939

The big black telephone was the only thing on the lonely little desk shoved into a corner of the largest office of the German counter-intelligence services at 76/78, Tirpitzufer, Berlin, and it started ringing. Oscar Klemp, the operations manager, showed his watching staff a sickly smile that didn't want to be there as he lifted the receiver and directed the call through the loudspeaker:

'Bonjour, Programme d'echange de musique en euros, comment puis-je aider?'

'Bonjour. Is that Mr Fromelle from the Music Exchange Programme?'

'Oh Anglaise, yes, this is I, Marcel Fromelle,' said Klemp.

'Hello, Mr Fromell. Je suis Denny Foreman here, pour le Hustledown Snipes grand band,' said the matter-of-fact pit-head baths attendant from Firstwood Colliery. 'Do you est parlez-vous English, pour I am non so bon at the Francaise?'

'Oh, yes, I can speak in English.'

'Champion, aa'm phonin' about gettin' one of your exchange lads t' come over and play with us.'

'Oh, yes, very good. I have good musicians on our programme. They are most young but have all their studies completed and wish to first travel and see more places. How did you have heard of us, Mr Frogman?'

'Pure chance, Marcel, and it's Foreman, aye, it was a new music rep mentioned it when he heard one of the lads was sick of standin' in on the drums…'

'He happened t' mention that bands offerin' a place got paid as well, like,' interrupted a different English voice.

'Yes, that is correct. And so you would like a drummer to come to you, yes?'

'Aye, but only if he can play with groove and vibe, and gets that swing thing, mind,' said a different third and younger voice.

'Oh yes, I see, let me look at my list. Ah, here is one who has studied here in Belgium and in Vienna, and he has England for his first choice to go to also. That is good, yes.'

A muffled muttering came over the loudspeaker.

'So how much does the band get paid then, Mr Fromelle?' asked the second voice.

'Let me see,' said Klemp, 'from his grant of 80 English pounds, the band will receive 32 pounds, and the rest is for his room to stay and money to spend, which we are told is enough for him to be six months with you.'

'Thirty-two pound cash?'

'Oui, yes.'

'Champion. When can ee come?'

'If you will be kind please to give only one minute you can ask him for yourself.'

Klemp passed the phone to the waiting staff member standing by the desk.

'Hello, I am William.'

'Hello, son, it is Lester here, now. I am the baritone sax and treasurer of the band. I will speak slowly for you. How is your English, lad?'

'Yes, I think it is good, thank you…'

The well-trained gentle voice worked well as a winning start. '… but it is good to learn the tongue in England, yes.'

'Oh, hell aye, son.'

[Sniggers come over the speaker.]

'So have you played in a big swing band before, William?' asked Lester.

'Yes, I have played many times in this kind since when I passed out from the Conservatoire of Vienna…'

['What the hell's him bein' pissed in a Conservative club in Italy got t' do wi' 'owt?' crept out of the speaker.]

'...and I will be very much happy to come as a big swinger in England.'

[Sniggers.]

'Fair enough, son. Can yer put Mr Fromelle back on and we'll sort the money out to get you over for a try-out, eh.'

And so arrangements were made for one of the German Abwehr's agents to be sent to England as a Belgian exchange drummer called William Leplanc, to play in a swing band from a pit-village in County Durham.

******

'Is he ready?' asked Count Otto von Leibernitz, head of OKW, German Counter-Intelligence.

'Yes, sir,' replied Klemp, handing him the file. 'He passed his drum training and playing assessments with moderate proficiency.'

'I see. And when does he go?'

'Midnight, Friday, sir.'

'Good, let's hope he'll be in time.'

Klemp looked puzzled and the Count smiled his contempt.

Chapter 2

In the dead of night on Saturday morning, Wolfgang Bundt parachuted into the wood behind the Co-op, in Oxhill, about a mile and a half from the Townley Arms pub. Quickly cramming his parachute back into its bag and hiding it under the jutting roots of an ancient tree, he unfastened the holdall strapped to his chest and took a small torch, compass and map from a side pocket. Stumbling through the tripping traps of nature, he got to the main road he wanted, and set off as if to make up more time than he thought he'd lost.

Seventeen busy hours later, when the last of the eight clangs of the Church bell sounded, Bundt felt the first heavy drops of rain touch his face, before the heavens opened and joined together the early spotted little wet dots on his holdall. Ten minutes later he was in the Townley Arms, being introduced to everybody in the hot, noisy, smoky pub as Billy, the new drummer from Belgium, who'd come without a raincoat.

'Ee's a big bastard,' said Wilf to Colly.

'Best Belgian beef on the bone, eh,' said Lenny.

'He certainly is that,' said Roxy, a very experienced 46-year-old usherette at the Essoldo.

'Anyhow,' said Tommy, 'ee seems a nice lad.'

The handsome blond-haired, blue-eyed Billy smiled and chatted in his lovely best French accent to everyone he was introduced to, and showed no sign of getting sick of it.

'Oh Christ, young Carter's got him cornered,' said Den.

'Nobody'll ever get them two mixed up, eh? Here, let's away over and have a listen,' said Wilf.

'... Whey it is, Billy,' ranted young Carter, 'as aa keep sayin', but those useless, rotten bastards from Birtley Big Brass are still snatchin' our shows, and they're doin' nowt else other than knockin' out that bloody bang-and-wallop shite!'

'No, it cannot be for people to want to hear such bang-and-wallop,' sympathised Billy.

'Exactly. But mind, we'll never stoop t' that, never. We've got the groove, y'see, and we'll never leave it, not for money or 'owt like that; it's art t' us, Billy, and yer can't put a price on that, no, not us, we'll hold true for as long as we draw breath. And another thing...'

'Is ee off on one wi' the new lad?' whispered the newly arrived Stan, taking his wringing wet cap off.

'Ee's windin' up for one,' said Colly.

'Best get in and rescue the poor bugger, eh.'

'Aye,' said Wilf, stepping in to make the introduction: 'Billy, this is Stanley, our band leader and number one trombone player at the deaf school.'

'Hello Billy, aa'm pleased to meet yer, son.'

They shook hands warmly and had just enough time to know they liked each other before being separated by Roxy, pushing the mesmerising tension of her blouse buttons between them.

'Evenin' Roxanna,' said the completely ignored Stanley to the back of her thick red hair.

He smiled at Wilf telling Lenny, Billy could be in trouble before asking: 'So where's Lester, anyhow; was ee not supposed t' pick Billy up at the station?'

'Aye, but they never got back about times and what-not.'

'So how did ee get here then?'

'Says ee walked,' said Den, joining in at the other side of Stan.

'Walked! Christ, that's a good ten-mile.'

'Like aa say, we couldn't get t' speak t' that Mr Fromelle.'

'Seems strange, that. D'yer not think that seems strange, Len?'

Lenny didn't hear because of the champagne cork thumping into his eye and making him drop his pint. The shouts of Olé! filled the bar and brought Sally with a dustpan and cloth for the mess, and smart Alice with her nurse's skills for the eye.

'How's it lookin', Alice, Pet?' asked Stan.

'Ee'll have trouble if ee doesn't stop rubbin' it.'

'That's what ee's landlady says,' said Wilf.

She let a smile stretch her thick red lips, before slapping Lenny's hand and pulling it away. 'Ee'll live', was her diagnosis. 'What's the cork off, anyhow?'

'Connie Flowers opened that bottle Billy gave them. Mind, ee told them t' give it an hour but she's took no bloody notice, as usual.'

The pub filled and the night got better as it always did when the drinks began to untie the social straps. By ten o'clock Lester had finally stopped smoking like a Grand National winner when his new Harris Tweed suit had dried out in front of the fire.

'Come on, Lester, lad, get yersel' sat down here,' coaxed Tommy. 'What the hell are yer scratchin' at, is yer eczema flared up again?'

'No, aa think aa might be developin' a sensitivity t' wool.'

'That thing's wool is it …?'

'Eh?'

'… it's just that yer took the skin off me hand when yer brushed past.'

'What the hell's possessed yer t' buy that thing for, anyhow?' pressed Colly.

'Aa didn't, me Auntie Sadie dropped it off last night, one of her lodgers must've left it, but anyhow, she says yer can tell it's proper quality by the weight in it when it's hangin'.'

'Are yer sure she wasn't talkin' about the lodger?'

'Christ.'

The bright coal fire added to the reddish low light in the room that was softened again by the filmy blue cigarette smoke. Billy sat and chatted and saw things he thought he knew about the English disappear from his views, as he watched big men with little reserve do what little women with less told them to. His peaceful reflection was shattered by happy loud cheers.

'What the hell's ee got on now?' said Den, nodding to the front door.

They turned to see Duggie sauntering in, as proud as a strutting cock, in a light green pinstripe suit with a dark green regency collar, a yellow satin shirt, white tie, and a pair of black ankle boots with bright white spats.

'What's on ee's hair?'

'That's the new hair oil aa sold him: Joe Louis uses it,' pitched Colly.

'What for, slackenin' rusty nuts on ee's punchbag?'

'Evenin' Duggie, lad, just sayin' how smart yer lookin' tonight,' said Tommy the tactful.

Duggie winked and pulled his baccy tin out of his trouser pocket before sitting down. The immaculate Herbie, in his plain dark suit and tie, with a brand-new collar on his white shirt, followed him with two pints of foaming Black Bess. They all said their hellos before Herbie smiled and pointed he was going to sit with old Joe and Cissy for a bit.

'The new hair oil looks like it's got some slick about it, eh, Dug.'

Duggie let his pencil moustache stretch a little, lit his cigarette, blew a channel of grey-looking smoke to the ceiling, picked a piece of tobacco off his tongue and flicked it on the floor.

'The lasses are givin' yer the eye, Dug.'

He straightened his tie and turned in his seat to look confidently at them. They looked away and tried not to let him see them laughing. With a quick wink at the lads, he stood, pulled his jacket into shape by the lapels and picked up his pint to sashay over to their table, taking his chair with him.

'Ee never gives up, lad.'

'Has ee always been a lady's man, Tommy?' asked young Carter.

'Sort of, son, but aa can't say ee's ever had 'owt t' do wi' ladies.'

'They'll probably be drawn t' him by ee's style, eh,' checked Carter.

''Cause they think ee's blind, yer mean?' checked Wilf.

'Or has ee just got the gift of the gab, y'know, a silver tongue?'

'Whatever tongue ee's got, Carter, son, it'll have a bit baccy on it, and remember, this is Duggie we're talkin' about; smooth talker he is not. Mind, ee can put a lot of meanin' int' the way ee asks lasses if they want a battered rissole on the way home.'

'Hey-up lads, Lenny's ready,' said Colly.

Lenny sat at the old but perfectly tuned piano tucked into the alcove between the bar and the blackened stone fireplace. His puffy, half-closed eye made it look like a child had drawn a monocle on him with her mammy's lipstick. It was 11 o'clock and everybody in the bar knew what it was time for: Tommy was clapped and coaxed out of his seat to start it off with his well-loved *Little pigs make the best Pork*. He sang the humour into the lovely late atmosphere of the pub, to make it even nicer for the serious singers to give everybody the finish to the night they all wanted. The last song always went to old Joe when he was in, who'd be led up to the piano by his daughter, Cissy, a slip of a girl at 66, and it was always *'Scarlet Ribbons for her hair'*, because, alongside Lenny's playing, it couldn't be sung any better by anybody, anywhere, and it never ended with anyone's eyes being drier than they were at the start. They all loved being in the Townley Arms on a Saturday night.

'On the piano is good in the band, yes,' said Billy.

'Ee is, son…'

Before he could get another word out, Stan was turned around by a big heavy hand on his shoulder.

'Have yer seen old Joe's stick, Stan?'

'I have not, Vanessa, mons Pet, but for vous I will look and I will find. You just stay here, sweetheart.'

She smiled after him and turned to Billy, who was being pestered by Ronnie Slack to buy some French cap badges from the war, and who was getting on her nerves. Luckily for him, the rubber end of Joe's white stick lifted under her nose.

'There yer go, Pet, Lester found it down the back of the long seats again.'

She took it and bent down to kiss Stan's glistening bald head, before going to get Joe and Cissy. She always walked them home to make sure they got in all right.

******

Vernon locked the pub doors and turned the big lights off. Stan and most of the rest of the band went through into the lounge to watch Lester kickstart life into the bike that was taking Billy to his new lodgings at big Margaret's.

'Ee's puttin' him on the back.'

'Not much choice with ee's bag in the sidecar.'

'Billy's got all the seat, look; Lester's on the tank.'

'It's like a bloody circus act.'

'Aa saw a monkey ride a bike once, in France it was, and it was smokin' a tab when it was pedallin'.'

'It'll have been a little Frenchman with a beard.'

'No, no, it was a real monkey, on his own little bike as well, mind, and with a bell.'

'Had yer been drinkin' out the petrol cans again, Royston?'

'Aa can't remember that, but it had a little blue and white hoopy Tee shirt on.'

'Whey aye, bound t' have, and a beret and onions?'

'No idea; there was a lot of smoke.'

'Christ.'

'Hey-up, they're off, look.'

They caught a glimpse of Lester's leaky rubberised bike suit before it was lost to the eclipse of Billy. The sight left them long before the racket.

'And there ee goes, our little Tweedy bike-hound.'

'So what d'yer reckon about the new lad, then?'

'Seems a nice lad t' me.'

Wilf winked at the others. 'Aye,' he began lazily, 'looks like ee'll be able t' hammer seven bells out of a drum kit, that's for sure.'

Young Carter sat looking at the dreg of beer in his glass.

'And ee's only goin' t' get bigger wi' Margaret feedin' him up,' went on Wilf. 'Christ, we'll all have t' play up t' be heard, eh.'

They hid their smiles and watched Carter roll his glass on its base a bit quicker.

'Mind,' said Wilf, a little bit louder, 'givin' it some clash might get us some of our slots back from that Birtley lot, eh.'

'Never,' burst Carter, pushing his glass away, 'who the hell would want them back t' play that bloody rubbish? Only bloody nuggets, that's who – nuggets that wouldn't know proper swing from a monkey's arse; and that's not us, is it, Stan? And, aye, ee's a nice lad, but if ee thinks ee can get away wi' just bangin' on, then ee's got t' be put right, or sent back.'

'Aye, Carter, steady, son, we'll keep an eye on him, eh,' calmed Stan.

'We've got to, Stan. And aa know we're gettin' nearly three pound each, and it's a hell of a lot t' give up, but if we let the rot in we might never get it out: the music's got t' suffer if all we want is just t' be bangin' away at somethin' every Saturda' night...'

'That's why we all joined, son.'

'... and then, look at what Top 'C' Turvey said in *Blow it Hard* monthly just before ee died...'

'Ee's dead?'

'Aye: popped a blood vessel when ee was givin' it full throttle in Pinky Chubb's club in New York; that's a year ago, now, mind, but, anyhow, ee said, "that it don't matter whether you're palming a pair of toms, or got a hot horn on your lips, it's the 3 Ts has got to come first"; that's Talent, Touch and Timing.'

Carter told them like a teacher who knew the class had forgotten: 'The Snipes'll always have the 3 Ts, won't we, Stan?'

'We will, son, and these daft buggers are just windin' yer up, bonny lad.'

Carter looked at them, smiling at him, and a pint of Bess slid beside his empty glass.

'We'll hold true, Carter, lad,' winked Den.

'There, listen t' Mr Frogman,' said Tommy, ruffling Carter's hair to make him smile.

'So, Billy's away down t' big Margaret's, eh,' said Wilf, as if he was doing Carter the favour of taking him away from the upsetting subject somebody else had put his way.

'Christ, out of the fryin' pan... Hey-ho, six pints please, Vernon, and just the five rum 'n' blacks.'

'Just five?'

'Aye, it's givin' Wilfy the gleets.'

Chapter 3

On Monday night three of the band turned up for practice wearing new silk shirts that somebody near the Co-op in Oxhill was selling cheap. Billy thought he'd seen the material somewhere before, but couldn't put his finger on it.

'Right,' said Stan, 'this Saturda's a big one for us – one of our band's gettin' married, Billy – now it's a posh do and we want to be at our best, so aa've got the vicar t' let us have the hall every night this week.'

'That's not like him, mind.'

'No, it was that new little chaplain fella stayin' with him who sorted it.'

'Who's ee, like?'

'Is ee from London?'

'Aye, ee is. Anyhow, aa want us at it every night so we can knock the rust off, and Billy can have a chance of learnin' the tunes.'

'And get a bit groove, eh, Carter,' winked Wilf.

'Who of the band is now to be married?' asked Billy.

'Young Ned, but he's not in it now.'

'Will he come back no more?'

'Aa don't think so, son, ee was never that keen really, and ee had a nasty do a few weeks back that knackered his arm good and proper, and now with bein' married … no, aa think ee's finished now. Anyhow, never mind about that,' said Stan, turning to the band, 'let's see if we can get the ball rollin' fer Billy. So who fancies what first then?'

'How about '*Flip, Flop and Flam*'?'

'Easy, Colly, lad, easy, give Billy a chance t' get worked in for Christ's sake. What say you, Len?'

'Aa'd go for '*Kick the Cat*'.'

The happy Stanley nearly pushed the slider out of his trombone. 'Tip-top, Leonardo, lad, aa'd never have thought of that little beauty, especially for Billy t' get goin'. Right, you just play yer way in, son, she's a steady 6 : 8, and we'll see what's-what, eh.'

After the usual shuffling, shifting, squawking and twitching they were ready to look at Stan. 'Right, then, is we is, or is we ain't, ready?'

'We is,' replied the chorus.

'D'yer not have t' thumb yer slider back in, Stan?'

'Aa've heard ee's had to a few times.'

'Never mind me slider, yer cheeky buggers. Don't listen t' them, Billy, lad, and just feel yer way in. Right, ready: a-one, a-two … a-one-two-three-four.'

From the empty echo of single voices talking under the vaulted wooden roof of the bare village hall, the band exploded to fill it with the richest sound of the fullest of full-bodied music. It filled every single inch of space and spilled out and up into the heavens above, the only place it could ever have come from in the first place. The tea-break came after half a dozen numbers and let them make their mental notes on Billy heard:

'He's got a bit class this lad.'

'There's hope,' said Carter cautiously.

'Sounds stiff,' said Wilf butting in.

'Well played, Billy, lad,' said Stanley, returning from the tea urn, 'you're keepin' these wayward buggers in time.'

'That's just what we were sayin', Stan. Mind, if we had somebody up front who could count t' four and play trombone, we'd never stray.'

'Harsh, Dennis, lad, very harsh.' He smiled.

'Time's no good without groove though. Look at what Mild-Mustard Petard wrote in '*Horned Up*' last month, and ee's got t' be the best beatster around for layin' stick on …'

'Hang fire, Carter, son,' interrupted Stan, 'aa want t' have another word about Saturda' night.'

'Well played, Stanley,' whispered Den.

******

Landing back at the Townley Arms after practice, the lads were sorting out seats around the two tables they always pushed together, when two strangers in dark broad-brimmed hats pulled their overcoat collars up, and left without finishing their drinks.

'Just shout them up, lads and Sally'll bring them over.'

'Will do, Vern. Mind, wi' service like this we might come again.'

Vernon shook his head and went back to poking the fire.

'Just the 11 pints of Bess and a bottle of Mackeson, Sally, Pet.'

'Who's havin' the bottle?' asked Vernon without looking away from the fire.

'Lester's takin' it steady 'cause ee's runnin' Billy down on the bike. Well done, Sally, Pet. Just stand the tray down there and I'll sort them out for yer,' said the ever-helpful Tommy.

'Christ, I needed that,' said Roy, bumping his half empty glass on the table. 'Been a long time since we've given it some toot like that, eh.'

'Aa couldn't blow a candle out now,' agreed Colly.

Tommy and Wilf looked at their reddened finger ends and tried for some sympathy, even though they knew they had absolutely no chance of getting any.

'Aa've got just the thing on the van for finger soreness like that,' pitched Colly. '*Blistomatic*: a healing blend of herbs, wi' rare medications from the Hindu Kush. It's a special formula for angry redness, and at a shillin' a tube yer can't go wrong.'

'We'll survive, Colly, lad.'

'Nogsey said it was good stuff, mind.'

'Nogsey? What the hell's he buyin' stuff for when Alice can get it for nowt at the hospital?'

Seeing there was no chance of a sale, Colly shrugged his shoulders to say he hadn't a clue, and headed for the bar.'

'Anyhow, Stanley, that's somethin' aa've been meanin' t' ask about for donkey's years now: how the hell did Nogsey Bland manage to land smart Alice?'

'A long story, lads, a long story...'

'Aye, aye,' smiled Tommy, 'it always is, but crack on.'

'Well, it all started that time when them up at the Sandy Lorran got them proper bailiffs from up in Northumberland, t' come down and sort the poachin' out. They reckon they paid a fortune for them.'

'When was this again?'

'Oh, about six-year ago now. Anyhow, they collared Nogsey's mate, little Frog, in here one night, who'd given them the slip a few times, and by Christ they'd have crippled him if it wasn't for Nessa, bless her.'

Stan sat smiling, and they all sat watching him.

'H'way then, Stan, out with it.'

'Aa was just thinkin' of the look she gave me. But, hang fire and aa'll put yer in the picture. There was two of them goin' at little Frog – nasty buggers they were – whey me and Vern gets up, but Nessa's straight in and tells them t' leave him be. Whey one of them turns round, all hard-lad like, and says, "if yer don't want a slap yersel', yer fat slag, yer'd better fuck off" and that's when she looked at me, y'know; that look she has when her back's up.'

'Like the last peep of light before the thunder clouds of hell roll in, Stan,' said young Carter.

'Christ.'

'It is, son, that's the one. So, she steps up and hooks him, and aa'll tell yer what, lad; he went down like a chopped tree and never moved a twitch, mind.'

'What about ee's mate?'

'Ee got one under the heart and doubled up like a stuck pig.'

'Winded, aa'll bet.'

'Oh aye. The poor bastard had t' have a bloody big needle pushed int' ee's chest for a collapsed lung.'

'That's our Nessa.'

'So what happened t' the first one?'

'Not sure, son. They took him back t' wherever the hell ee came from, and rumour has it ee was in a coma for a month or two.'

'Christ.'

'Aye, and when ee came round he was never the same again; aa heard ee ended up in one of them religious cults.'

'Serves him right for what ee said t' Nessa,' said young Carter to make the others smile.

'So where the hell does Nogsey and Alice fit int' all this, then, Stanley?' asked Tommy, pretending to be confused.

'Oh aye, they got crackin' on when he was visitin' Frog in the infirmary.'

'Is that it? All that t' get t' them just chattin' on in the hospital?'

'Whey, sort of, but it was only after Frog let slip about Nogsey's deformity, when ee was talkin' in ee's sleep, y'know, when Alice was on nightshift and heard him, that they seem t' have clicked.'

'What deformity?'

'Y'know, down there.'

'Never.'

'Oh hell aye, ee's like a skinned rabbit.'

'Christ.'

'Nogsey Bland, who'd 'ave thought it, eh? Ee can only be eight stone with his top coat on.'

'Looks like two stone of that's ee's hanger.'

'Alice 'n Nogsey Bland, eh.'

'Christ Almighty.'

******

The next morning the two strangers who were in the Townley Arms, stood in a service lift as it dropped far below the streets of London to a special operations bunker. A thickset security guard left his seat and yanked the squealing cage door open for them to follow him along the narrow, brightly-lit passage to the black steel door at the end. The echoed noise of their steel-tipped heels on the concrete floor, shattered the claustrophobic silence of the corridor, making it deafeningly quiet when they stopped. The guard knocked on the door and a small red light came on above it. Two minutes later it changed to green and he opened it for the men to go in. The head of Military Intelligence, Group Captain Johnny 'Knackers' Bernhard, stood erect behind his large oak desk:

'Well?' he asked unpleasantly.

'Contact made, sir.'

'Definitely Bundt?'

'Yes sir; as their exchange drummer from Belgium.'

'Right. And Bembrage?'

'We've all of his despatches to date, sir.'

'Good. Keep to fortnightly reports and quarter-point surveillance.'

The Group Captain sat down, put his half horn-rimmed glasses on and read a short memo. The agents waited.

'Right. Thank you, gentlemen. Dismissed.'

Chapter 4

Tommy stood with Duggie, Wilf and Lester, who were having a smoke in the yard at the back of the Sandy Lorran manor house; the venue for Ned's wedding do. The kitchen door opened and Sally came out with four bottles of Brown Ale and a dozen ham and peas pudding sandwiches on a silver tray.

'Yer a good'un, Sally, Pet, but we're a bottle short now Lenny's here,' said Tommy, nodding towards the approaching big-bellied figure, and making it sound as though Sally had forgotten: 'And seein' as yer comin' back wi' Lenny's, yer might as well fetch another five, just t' save yer legs, Pet.'

Sally rolled her eyes, smiled and vanished.

'Aye, who'd've thought it, Lenny, lad,' began Tommy, as soon as Lenny reached them, 'our little Lester here, left all alone up Waldridge Fell all those years ago, a lost little mite he was, Len, and picked up by a band of roaming gypsies.'

Lenny smiled and lit his tab; he knew just to wait for whatever it was they had coming.

'Aye,' went on Tommy, trying to sound like the wearied voice of heartfelt concern, 'one of ee's auntie Sadie's lodgers took him up bilberrying on the bike ...'

'Not one of yer "uncles",' said Lenny with a smile.

'Aye, it was, Len, and one who buggered off and left him t' the mercy of them wanderin' gypsies,' answered the safeguarding Tommy. 'Mind you, they took our little Lester in and nourished the lost little soul. Oh aye, Lenny, they fired up the skillet and fried him a trout.'

Lenny laughed.

'They did,' appealed Tommy on Lester's part.

'My arse,' said Lenny.

'They did,' insisted Lester.

'When was this, then?'

'When Lester-on-Tweed was only just a little spud of six,' answered Tommy.

'Var-nigh 50 year ago and we've heard nowt about it?' said Lenny, doing nothing to hide he was having none of it.

'Aa've repressed it,' explained Lester.

They all laughed.

'Repressed what?'

'Me childhood trauma.'

They all laughed.

'Hang on, hang on, they didn't fiddle with yer, did they?' asked Wilf.

Lester stood silent.

'They interfered with yer!'

'Sort of.'

They all burst out laughing.

'What the hell does "sort of" mean, anyhow?' said Wilf, wiping his eyes: 'Can yer not remember one minute thinkin' "this is a lovely bit trout", and the next wakin' up in a field wi' yer shorts round yer ankles?'

'No, no, nowt like that,' said Lester. 'It was what aa saw.'

'What the hell did yer see?'

'It was a woman, but wi' no clothes on.'

'And that traumatised yer?'

'Aa was just a bairn; aa'd never seen 'owt like it before.'

'Full belt, like?'

'Oh, aye, stark bollock, and just about a foot away.'

'Lucky bugger.'

'No, terrifyin',' said Lester, meaning it.

'Any tentin' in the shorts?'

'Aa was six.'

'She'll have been puttin' somethin' nice on t' try and get a few coppers for takin' him back yem, aa'll bet.'

'She did, she got a thrupenny bit off me auntie, and aa got a crack around the head.'

'Second of the day, eh.'

'So where the hell was "uncle", then?'

'Ee was in the house havin' ee's tea,' answered Lester like a prosecution witness.

They burst out laughing again.

'He'd forgotten about yer? Christ Almighty, Lester.'

'Are yer sure they didn't keep yer and twiddle yer up for a day or two before any bugger noticed you were gone?'

'So how come "uncle" left yer there, then?' asked Lenny, thinking he might as well have the full story.

'Ee was away pumpin' old Dolly blue,' answered Tommy.

'Bugger-me, old Dolly blue.' Lenny smiled.

'Aye, a grand old lass, bless her. Gone but not forgotten, eh, Duggie,' winked Wilf.

Duggie smiled and pulled a piece of baccy off his tongue.

'Hey-up, here's Stan and the rest of them, look. Sup these off and we'll head in for a couple before we set up.'

They left with Tommy throwing a massive right arm over Lester's shoulder as they walked around to the front of the manor house.

'Who's that wi' Billy, Lester?' asked Wilf.

'That's that chaplain fella.'

Chapter 5

August – Saturday, 14th

'Where the hell's ee at?' said Denny to vent the worry they were all feeling in the dressing room. 'And nobody's seen him since Monda' night?'

Nobody had.

'So what did Margaret say again, Lester?' asked Stan.

'Nowt, just that he was away off somewhere on Wednesda' mornin', campin' for a few days, which was nowt unusual for him, 'cause he kept tellin' her ee wanted' t' see as much as he could while he was here, like.'

'Aye, but not t' be back for this,' said Den dismally.

'Might be stage-fright, eh?'

Stanley shook his head.

'Christ, no drummer, tonight of all nights,' said Roy, shaking his head.

'There's always Wilf, ee's better than nowt.'

'Cheers, Colly, lad.'

'There's a bit time yet,' said Stan, but the others knew he was only saying it for them.

The silence of their collective contemplation was broken by a knock on the door that brought the head of Norman, the chaplain, in. He saw the disappointment they couldn't hide. 'Still no sign, then?'

'Not yet,' said Stanley with a weak smile. 'Is your friend here?'

'He is. We're up in the balcony, and I'll make sure he knows about this last minute let down if Billy doesn't show up.'

'You're a good'un, padre,' said Tommy through a jutting jaw as he tried to fasten his bow-tie.

Fifteen minutes later nearly 600 people in Firstwood's packed Essoldo theatre sat looking at the immaculate band, and watched Wilf shifting and pulling about bits of the drum kit. Stan waited, winked at him, and lifted his trombone to start *Kick the Cat*.

After the show the dressing room had a strange atmosphere. It came from the mixture of a quiet satisfaction from knowing they'd done their best, being tinged with regret from thinking of what could have been if Billy had turned up. The door opened without a knock and the little chaplain came in with a short, stocky, tough-looking man in a camel hair coat.

'This is Mr Wiseman,' said Norman, looking at Stanley.

'Hello, I'm Stanley South.'

'Adel Wiseman, Mr South,' he said confidently, taking the offered hand.

'Stanley, please.'

'Yes. Well, you know why I'm here tonight, so without any nonsense my decision is, yes, I would like to offer you a contract to record yo...'

Nothing else was heard above the happy commotion that filled the room and drowned Mr Wiseman's words in a wave of helpless joy.

'I'll see you tomorrow, Mr South,' shouted the executive into Stanley's ear.

He left with Norman because they could see the celebration wasn't theirs.

*****

Monday, August, 23rd (practice cancelled)

'London? When? For how long? All of yers?'

'Aye, a week on Wednesda', but only for a couple of days, Vern.'

'But what about yer drummer? Mind, aa'd love t' know why ee buggered off like that.'

'We all would, Vernon, lad.'

'But Wilfy can play them though.'

'Of a sort.'

'Christ, yer want t' hold back wi' the praise there, mind.'

'You're doin' a grand job, Wilf, lad,' said Stan honestly.

'So it'll be, Wednesda' the first of September you're off, then,' said Vernon distractedly as he checked his leek-growers' Almanac, 'and will yer be back on the Frida' or Saturda' d'yer think? – Frida's the third and Saturda's the fourth.'

'We might not get back 'til the Sunda', Vern, but aa'm not sure what date that is,' said Wilf, who couldn't resist.

'Whose round is it here, anyhow? Aa'm at the mercy of me hyperclampseemia from being bone dry around the neck joint again,' said Tommy.

'It's Wilfy's.'

'It's the fifth, Wilf,' said Vern, holding up the almanac.

'Christ.'

'Listen t' this, though,' said Lester, panting from his run down the car park, and pushing in between Tommy and Colly on the bench seat so that he was in the middle of everything: 'Billy's been back.'

They looked at him not knowing what to say in the two seconds he gave them before going on:

'Aye, early on this mornin', just for two minutes, mind, but ee landed at Margaret's with ee's fatha t' get ee's stuff.'

'Never.'

'Aye. She says ee looked as sick as dog.'

'So did ee say 'owt, then?'

'She says ee muttered on about havin' t' go home 'cause ee's mother'd been taken int' hospital, and he had t' stop there with her, and she died the day before yesterda', and just for Margaret t' say goodbye t' everybody for him, that's all. He left her a five pound note under ee's pillow.'

'That's a lot t' leave.'

'Aye, ee's a good lad.'

'But, yer'd think ee could have let us know before, like.'

'Poor bugger'll have had a lot on ee's mind.'

'Whey at least we know ee's alright, eh.'

'Aye.'

******

Monday, August, 23rd (London)

'Well?' demanded Group Captain Bernhard.

'Well, there may be a slight difficulty with Bundt because of the psycho-suggestive exchange in ...'

'What?'

'They may find he was holding back, so to speak, sir.'

'Holding back what, for God's sake?'

The scientist looked frightened.

'Well?' ordered the Group Captain.

'Gaea syndrome, sir.'

'What?'

'He developed an attachment, sir.'

'To what? Speak up, man!'

'To Lester Churchwarden, sir.'

'Oh, for God's sake, tell me this isn't happening.'

'He must have thought very highly of him, sir, and, er, well, we think this may have caused a resistance, or a latency problem in terms of ...'

A glimpse of the Group Captain's face quickly changed the content of his explanation: 'We hypnotised him too much, sir, and he projected it onto Lester.'

'What?'

'We had to go deeper than the Germans, and it, er, found another vent, so to speak.'

'What the hell are you telling me?'

'Bundt has tendencies we hadn't factored in, sir; sado-masochistic homosexual ones, and his transference object appears to have been Lester, for some reason, we're not entirely sure why. It may have been the genital-sensory stimulation caused by the rampant throttling of his motorbike, for which Mr Churchwarden is well-known, but whatever it was, it brought him to reconfigure authoritative love...'

'If you don't start talking in plain fucking English, I will personally horse-whip you from arsehole to breakfast time.'

'Yes sir. Bundt fell in love with Lester: he may have thought his undercover work here could harm him.'

'I see. And is Lester a homosexual?'

'No, we have his file here. In his lifetime, all of his sexual relationships have been with women; three in this country and, oddly, over a hundred in France during the war ...'

'Good God, what did they have in France?' asked the Group Captain with a knowing smile.

'Tolerance, sir. Lester has complex orientation needs; he subscribes to an excessively specialised sexual practice that very few women, in Britain it seems, will accommodate.'

'And what the hell is that, dare I ask?'

'Well, there are variations around the broader theme of his pathologically presented misogynous dysmorphia... I mean,' recovered the scientist, 'he can't stand the sight of the naked female form.'

'So he has to leave some clothes on them, what's so special about that?'

'Well, it's more than that for Lester, sir: the woman has to be behind a solid partition of some kind; a sheet of wood, or a thin wall, or in a box, with a hole, you see, for ...'

'Yes, yes. Christ Almighty. And he's allowed out, is he?'

'I'm afraid so,' smiled the scientist. 'This is a photograph we had taken last week of his latest lady friend.'

'Good God, has she crashed her motorbike?'

'She doesn't ride one, sir.'

'Then what's happened to her teeth and nose, and why the crash helmet?'

'That's her hair, sir.'

'Good Lord. Well, at least the partition makes more sense.'

The Group Captain meditated on the thick white cigarette he was tapping on its silver case before using it to point the scientist to the door. Pressing a button on his desk he told his secretary to call the Minister for War.

******

'It would work as a poster warning women not to ride motorbikes,' said the Minister, dropping the photo on the desk. 'And this attachment, you say, came about because your boffins made an arse of the hypnosis, is that right?'

'Yes, sir,' admitted the Group Captain, hating the failure.

'I see. But the lovely coal-house band plays on?'

'Yes, they're in place.'

'And the recordings?'

'All of the public house and practice session recordings have been edited.'

'Correctly, I hope,' smiled the empty Minister.

'Might I ask how long now, sir?'

'Yes, he'll invade Poland in a few days and we'll have kick-off on the 3rd. Now then, Bernhard, if that's all, I really must dash.'

He left for a pressing engagement with a grapple coach from Wigan and a Turkish midget porn star called Itsa Proppakok.

Chapter 6

August – Saturday, 28th

Lester pushed his way into the middle of them standing at the bar in the Townley Arms, and pulled the fly-zipper down on his rubberised motorbike trousers:

'Here, have a look at this.'

'Not again.'

'Look away, Sally, Pet.'

Lester looked at her self-consciously and pulled a black leather wallet out of his inside trouser pocket. 'It's Billy's.'

'Billy's?'

'See if there's any money in it,' said Colly.

'There's not,' said Lester, 'it's not a wallet, it's a book that looks like a wallet. It's all writin' and numbers, look.'

He gave it to Stan who opened it to let them see the busy mess of small black characters.

'Where d'yer get this from, Lester?' he asked.

'Down the back of the sidecar seat.'

'It must've slipped out of ee's pocket, eh,' said Royston.

'No, it'll have had t' have been put there,' dismissed Lester with authority, 'and it wasn't there the last time aa had the seat out.'

'When was that?'

'The last Saturda' of the month, aa always strip her down fer a good clean on the last Saturda' of the month.'

'Did Billy know yer did that?'

'Oh aye, ee helped a couple of times.'

'So ee must've known yer'd find it then.'

'Aye, but aa don't know why 'cause it's all bloody mumbo-jumbo t' me. Some of the numbers are back t' front, look.'

'Christ, d'yer think it's a code?' said Colly, peering over Stan's shoulder, 'like Billy was a spy or somethin'?'

'What the hell is there t' spy on around here?' scorned Wilf.

'Whey, there's got t' be some reason for him writin' it.'

'And leavin' it for Lester t' find,' said Den.

The conversation stopped as if it had run out of air. Colly opened another window to bring it back to life. 'Get a look at Duggie's new spats.'

'By Christ, Douglas, they're Bobby-dazzlers, lad,' began Tommy as soon as Duggie reached the bar. 'And has that colour got a name then?'

'Aye, it's in the Doggarts catalogue as electric white lightnin'.'

'Very nice.'

'They're hurtin' me eyes,' said Wilf.

'Never mind him, Duggie. What d'yer reckon t' this; it was Billy's?' said Stan, giving him the wallet.

'Some kind of code, eh? What about lettin' Dinsey have a look?'

'That's the one, Dug, lad; that's the best idea. Fancy scuddin' over t' his place before yer get settled, Lester?'

'Aye, just hang fire 'til that rain eases off a bit.'

Tommy put his empty glass on the bar. 'Sally, Pet, spats lightnin' here wants seven lovely pints of Vern's ambrosia.'

She smiled and wrapped her little, hard-worked, red hand around the thick, shiny wooden Black Bess pump.

The night wore on into the quiet early hours, when only the late lock-in regulars were left in the pub. Duggie lay sound asleep on the bench seat under the window. His urine-stained spats were on his head and fastened under his chin – he looked like a perverted cross-channel swimmer who'd been caught in a sewage spill. Young Carter, Den, Herbie and Lenny were at one end of the two joined tables, talking music and having some mild dispute about trumpet tone. Vern was asleep in front of the flat red bed of the unfed fire, and Tommy sat with Stan, watching him push the horseshoe ring of hair further back from his barren crown with both hands. He knew his friend.

'Are yer thinkin' about Billy, Stanley?'

Stan nodded.

'About him not sayin' ta-ra?'

'Aye, but there's things just not sittin' right wi' me, here, mind, Tom, what wi' that book and what-not. And where the hell did Lester get to, anyhow?'

'Ee's under there.'

Tommy pointed to the upturned log basket with a size five brogue sticking out.

Stan smiled but it didn't last long and was gone before he went on: 'Aa just think we're gettin' pulled int' somethin' here, mind, and aa've got a bad feelin' about it.'

Tommy was watching him rub his tired eyes when the front door opened. Nessa came in, with her hair pushed under a black beret, wearing her dad's army great coat over her nightdress. Stan looked like he'd seen a ghost.

'Yer mother's had a bit of a turn, Stan,' she said calmly, 'it's nowt t' worry about, but she's askin' for yer. Me mother's over there with her now.'

Stan fished his blazer out from behind the bench seat and pulled it on. 'I'll away up now, lads.'

As they were saying their goodnights, he put his hands on Nessa's shoulders and stood on tiptoe to kiss her cheek and thank her for coming to get him. 'You stay and have a drink, Pet, and aa'll see yer tomorrow.'

He left in a hurry.

'There, yer heard the man,' said Tommy, 'so sit yersel' down and aa'll pull yer a nice pint, Pet, and aa might as well join yer, just to be sociable, like.'

She couldn't help but smile.

'And would the debatin' table fancy a fresh one?'

'No ta, Tom, we're off now, young Carter's about knackered. Are yer in for a couple at dinnertime?'

'So long as me close harmony psalm singin' hasn't taken too much out of me.'

They smiled at the same Saturday night reply they'd had for over 30 years, and said their goodnights.

'Is she puttin' it on again?' asked Tommy, sitting beside Nessa with two pints.

'Aye, she'll have woken up and been shoutin' for him and he hasn't come. Mind, aa'm surprised he's stopped out so long; ee's normally back about midnight.'

She started to smile.

'What?' asked Tommy, smiling at her.

'It's just that every Saturda' when he knows aa'm workin' the door, he walks right round by The Majestic and waves from across the road.'

'Ee'll just want t' see yer.'

'Aye, but ee tries t' act all casual, like, as if ee's just passin', and aa know fine well ee's trying t' see if aa'm all right.'

'That's just Stan,' said Tommy affectionately.

'Aye. So ee must've fancied a drink tonight, did ee?'

'Not so much, Pet. It's this thing wi' Billy that's got him all chewed up.'

'Is that why ee looked like ee'd seen a ghost when aa came in?'

'No, no,' smiled Tommy. 'It'll have been yer standin' back in the dark, there, with yer beret on and the trench coat; yer looked just like yer fatha, Pet.'

They both sat quietly looking at each other.

'And mind, ee was a good-lookin' lad if ever there was,' said Tommy with a wink.

She pushed him playfully and they looked at each other. Tommy soon had her settled to listen to his usual happy chip-chap summary of the night they'd had. Half an hour later he let her wrangle him into his coat and lead him to the front door with her steadying arm through his. The heavy latch clacked loudly as it closed behind them, and called the deadly silence into the sleeping pub.

'Not so tight, Pet,' muttered the dirty spats.

Chapter 7

September – Wednesday, 1st

'Get a look at Royston's bus.'

Nearly all the band, and a few others mooching about in the Townley Arms car park in the early morning sunshine, gathered to look at the scrubbed-up 20-seater reversing down the patchworked tarmac slope to the front of the pub. A lovely new paint job of rich mustard yellow ran brightly to the top of the windows to make a handsome match with the contrasting maroon roof.

'She's lookin' grand, Roy,' said Den looking at the SNIPES – LONDON route sign above the big split windscreen.

'Nowt but the best, lads. Best bus Bedford's ever let roll on a road, that is.'

The approaching howl of Lester's sidecar-free Bantam eased off when he dropped his shoulder to turn into the car park. This time he dropped the bike as well as his shoulder, and sent it scudding under the bus in a shower of sparks, while he scattered the band and hit the front door of the pub with a thump – it was in E flat because Tommy's double bass was strapped to his back.

'Me bus.'

'Me bass.'

'Me bike.'

'Christ.'

The laughing little crowd watched Lester twisting and kicking like a beetle stuck to a Guinness bottle. Wilf and Stan unstrapped the case and got him up.

'Must've been the weight distribution that got me off guard,' said Lester, rubbing his knee.

'Course it was, yer bloody nugget.'

'Me bass is alright, anyhow,' inspected Tommy.

'No harm t' me bus, either,' said Roy.

'Are you alright, Lester?'

'Aa'm fine, Stan. Aa just hope aa haven't hurt anybody, y'know, makin' them pull a muscle laughin' at me dice wi' death.'

They started laughing again.

'Hey-up, here's Colly. Has ee been for them, Stan?'

'He has, and fingers crossed they all fit, eh.'

Colly's van free-wheeled to a stop beside them. Before he got out the back doors were opened and young Carter was inside passing out 11 slim white boxes to be taken into the pub and stacked on the bar. The band followed them in.

'Right then, Mr S. South, 48/Short,' said Tommy, passing Stan the first box.

'Take it through the back and put it on, and then come out and give us the first good look, Stan, eh,' urged Vern.

Stan smiled and knew he had to. Taking longer than they thought it would, he came out wearing a beautiful white tuxedo jacket, with a white silk collar running down to the single black button fastening it. A thin, black bow-tie spanned perfectly across his throat, and although he tried to look non-plussed, they could see he was as happy as a little girl with a new frock. The whistles and cat-calls came as he knew they would.

'Come on then, yer cheeky buggers, let's everybody get them on 'cause Mr Malcolm'll be here soon.'

'Who?'

'The photograph fella.'

Tommy handed the boxes out and Sally stopped cleaning the bar to fix their bow-ties.

'Feels a bit snug when it's buttoned,' said Tommy, running a hand over his massive gut.

'Snug? That button'll blind some poor bugger if ee sits down.'

'Here's the photo fella, Stan.'

They filed out into the sunny car park carrying their instruments and leaving the bar looking like a ransacked music shop.

'Up to the main road, please, gentlemen,' urged Mr Malcolm.

Working his composition on the pyramid principle, he had Tommy in the middle at the back, holding the neck of his bass, and the others positioned in cascading order from it. Stan was at the front, with the photographer struggling to make his mind up how to have him hold his trombone.

'What's ee on about now, for Christ's sake?'

'Somethin' about Stan's slider.'

'Nowt but trouble, that slider.'

'Can ee not rest it on Duggie's shoulder?'

'Wouldn't be the first time, eh, Dug.'

'Gentlemen, please. We do have a difficulty to overcome and I really must apply myself if I'm to keep Stanley's instrument from covering Duggie's face.'

'Not again, eh, Duggie.'

'Would it be better if Duggie was on his knees, Mr Malcolm?'

'Christ.'

'No, no, thank you. I'm afraid that wouldn't work with the framing I have in mind; that way his slider would appear to be resting on Douglas's head.'

'Ee's used t' it.'

'Just let it hang loose, Stan,' suggested Carter, 'like Frogmouth Slack on the cover of Earl Thanet's '*Trumpet Thunder*', y'know, the one aa showed yer when we played Ned's wedding.'

Stan smiled and nodded but hadn't a clue.

'Like this, Stan,' helped Carter, 'look, just stick a finger under the coil and let the full length of your 'bone hang over it.'

'What the hell kind of photo is this?' came from the back.

Stan let the trombone drop on the pivot of his left hand to show the mouthpiece to the sky. Mr Malcolm was very happy with it, and disappeared under the broad black cloth hanging behind the polished wooden tripod. With one last call to hold still, the picture was taken.

'So is this for the record cover and posters and what-not, Stan?' asked Lenny.

'It is, and doesn't that sound good, lads.'

'It does. It's lookin' like we're on our way, Stanley, and aa think we deserve it, mind.'

'No arguin' wi' that, Colly, lad,' beamed their happy leader.

******

'What's wrong, Sally, Pet?'

'It's Nessa, Stan, she said she'd be down for 10.00?'

'It'll be that new deputy, ee's a nasty bugger by all accounts. Tell her not t' worry and we'll see her on Sunda'.'

'Aa will, but she'll not like missin' yer.'

'Aa know, Pet, but we're late as it is.'

'That's it loaded, Stan,' said Royston, pushing his black sea captain's cap back to wipe his brow, before hopping up the steps to get in his cab. Stan smiled at Sally, rubbed her shoulder and got on the bus.

Vern followed him onto the first step. 'There's two pints in every pop bottle, right, and there's 24 bottles in each crate, right, and there's three crates, makin' 72 bottles, right, but, think on, that means 144 pints, right, so steady on.'

'That should get us t' Doncaster.'

'Will do, Verny. See yer Sunda'.'

Vern stood back, and after a long, asthmatic struggle, all 38 of Royston's horses were finally kicked into life. A thick fumy cloud of dark diesel-stenched smoke was blown into the pub through the windows Sally had opened to let some fresh air in. The gear-stick squealed painfully into a puritanical first gear, and the bus shuddered up the car park to the little crowd on the path in front of the Post Office at the top. The lads saw Norman, the chaplain, waving with the rest, and waved back from the hellishly vibrating bus.

'Change friggin' gear, Roy,' warbled Colly.

'It'll explode them bottles.'

'For Christ's sake, Roy, it's slackenin' me teeth.'

A skilfully swift double declutch got it into second gear and eased their suffering. A mile later, sitting just behind Royston to look through the windscreen, Stan saw Nessa and half a dozen of the pit lasses at the top of the bank. Some had laid their long-handled shovels against the colliery wall, and a couple leaned forward on theirs. Blackened gloves and dark leather hats with protective neck flaps lay on the path, but they all wore the same heavy boots and brown leather trousers, with thick broad belts for their folded-up skirts to be tucked into. With their sleeves rolled up to try and keep them clean, the deeply grooved strength in the arms of these women would soon be lost to a history that men didn't bother to write.

'Can yer stop at the top, Royston?'

'Can yer get t' the top, Royston?'

'It's all power this engine, lads; plenty pull, like an old Bull.'

'How old?'

'We could hop off here and nip in the Punch Bowl for one, and walk up the bank and wait for yer at the top, Roy.'

'By Christ, there's some cheeky buggers in this band, lad,' said Roy to his rear-view mirror.

The bus trembled its smoky trail up the bank and seemed mightily relieved to stop at the top. Royston stood up and used both hands to pull the handbrake on before he let Stan off.

All the sliding windows were opened for the incoming crack with the coal lasses.

'Ee's still bloody nimble on them feet,' said Colly, watching Stan skip across the road.

They saw Nessa step back.

'She'll not want t' get coal dust on him.'

Stan said something to her.

'Does ee have a clean shirt with him, Tommy?' shouted Nessa.

'Two, Pet.'

And with that she wrapped him in a loving hug before pointing him back to the bus. He got halfway across the road and turned to run back to rub her shoulder while he was telling her something. She smiled and nodded, and he nipped back to the band.

'There's plenty spare seats in here if any of you lasses fancy a bit of a pleasure trip,' said Wilf through a window.

'Oh, aye, and what pleasure would that be, like?' came back quickly.

'No, yer right, Pet, aa wasn't thinkin'; it 'ud be hell for yers sittin' next t' such specimens of manhood and not be able t' take advantage of us.'

The lasses laughed.

'And why not, like?' asked one.

'Whey, 'cause we've got t' keep our strength up for London.'

The lasses jeered. 'By all accounts, Duggie's not much cop at keepin' 'owt up.'

The lads laughed.

'That's 'cause this thing takes some liftin',' defended Duggie.

'Takes some findin' more like – aa heard yer slipped it int' Shelly Pinkerton's hand at the pictures and she said she'd just put one out.'

The lads laughed, but stopped when the panic started. The bus was rolling back. Royston jammed a foot on the dashboard to try and heave the handbrake on further. The bus stopped.

'Thank Christ ee got some brake,' said Den.

'Did he buggery; Nessa stopped it with a copin' stone off the yard wall.'

'God Almighty, have yer seen how steep that bloody bank is when yer sittin' up here like this? Certain death that, mind.'

'By, yer a cheery bugger, Wilf.'

'Just drive the friggin' thing forward, Roy, for Christ's sake,' pleaded Colly.

The bus juddered away from the stone, making the bank disappear in a night-time of smoke, while the lads waved and shouted nice things to Nessa and the lasses. Stan knelt on the back seat in his new thunder cloud shirt, and as they started down the other side of the hill, the last big black hand held high in the air was Nessa's. He watched it until geography took it away. Roy called Tommy down to see if he could get the handbrake off.

'Is there any point?' asked Wilf.

He managed to crank it off and the bus lunged forward.

'Feel that thrust there, lads?' said Roy proudly.

'Thrust, my arse.'

'Gravity, more like.'

'Can somebody thrust a bottle int' me red-raw handbrake hand,' said Tommy.

Royston smiled at them in the mirror, and settled down to let his pride and joy take them all the way to London.

Chapter 8

At half-past one in the morning, Royston was stacking house bricks behind the back wheels of the bus, while the others woke each other up to shuffle semi-consciously into 'The George' guest house in Southwick. Stan and Roy unloaded the bus in the driving rain.

The dull heavy thump of the guns killing his dreams faded into the knocking on the bedroom door that pulled Stan out of a soaking cold trench and put him where he was.

'Howay, Stan, shake yersel' or you'll miss yer breakfast,' said the door.

He entered the breakfast room at half eight, to be greeted by nine fresh-faced band members.

'What the hell have you been drinkin', Stanley? It's done yer no good at all, lad.'

'Ee's got a point, mind, Stan, yer lookin' a bit rough, old lad,' said Tommy.

'Just takes one dodgy bottle,' pronounced Den.

'You've not been up wi' the gleets, have yer?' asked Wilf.

'No, no, just a bit weary,' said Stan. 'Where's Royston?'

'Ee'll be lookin' for more hand-bricks.'

'Ee'll have enough t' build a friggin' bungalow by the time we get back.'

'Here ee is,' said Lester.

Royston strolled in, rubbing his black hands on a dirty old oily rag. 'Just havin' a look at the brakes there.'

'It's got some, has it?'

'Aa think there might be a calliper nipped.'

'Nipped?'

'Has ee knocked a kiddie wi' polio down?'

'Aa'll need the wheel off t' have a proper look, like.'

'Aye, yer'd best have a look, Roy, lad.'

'When's dinnertime here?' said Wilf, rising with the rest of them to leave.

'Aa'll just struggle on mysel' then, eh?'

'Aye, but we're off at 3.00, mind.'

Just after three o'clock a brand new red bus pulled away from the guest house, with one excited band member standing next to the driver for all of the 20-minute journey.

'And here we are, gentlemen,' said the straight-laced driver, trying to sound more friendly than he was.

With everybody off the bus and gathered on the pavement, he led them from the pristine front of the large town-house to the grotty, run-down rear. Going inside, they had a minute to look around the empty, high, windowless space that smelled like a hospital, before a small thin man in an evening suit clicked his way across the marble floor to introduce himself as Rylance Tweedy, their recording engineer. He was posh and unaffectedly polite, and welcomed each of them with a handshake.

'Please follow me, gentlemen, your instruments will be taken to the studio for you.'

Leading them into a large service lift, he dragged the squealing cage door closed before pressing the bottom button.

'Christ, how far down is this?'

'It's what we have to do these days to escape the wretched noise of London,' explained the engineer, 'and the vibrations, goodness me, the vibrations; did you know the vibration from one of those beastly omnibuses can put a double bass out of tune with the other instruments?'

'We're used t' that,' said Wilf.

'Oh, you have trouble with buses as well then?'

'No; we've just never had a bass that's been in tune with the other instruments.'

Tommy smiled. Wilf was about to tell him about the damage Royston's bus would do to the building never mind the recordings, when he was stopped by the engineer yanking the high-pitched door open. He led them along a long, bare, brightly lit corridor to a door with 'recording suite' written above it, and opened it for them to go through into the dimly lit, non-music looking room, that had two rows of wooden chairs facing a large white screen.

'Please, take a seat, gentlemen,' said the engineer, 'we'd like you to watch a short instruction film on how the recording system works, which is important because a whole session can be lost to such a simple thing as clipping an instrument on a stand, or just fidgeting. Now I'm afraid we can't afford for that sort of thing to happen, you see, because there's simply no time for retakes.'

The lights went out. In the darkness they could hear shuffling behind them.

'Sounds like they're bringing the instruments in, eh,' whispered Lenny.

'In the dark?' said Wilf in full voice.

'No, there's a light behind the curtains, yer can see it on the ceiling, look,' said Lester.

'Oh aye.'

A sharp metal clank shot the room into a hard white light that made them squint at the erect uniformed figure standing in front of them. They looked around at the heavy black curtains forming the three other walls, and at each other for any thoughts on what was happening.

'Remain seated and be quiet. My name is Group Captain Bernhard, and I ...'

'Aa don't care what yer name is, lad,' interrupted Tommy, standing up with intentional disrespect.

'Sit down!' ordered the Group Captain.

'Bollocks t' yer,' said Tommy. 'What's with all this shite, eh?'

'I insist you take care not to ...'

'You're insistin' on nowt,' said Duggie, standing at the end of the back row of chairs.

'I see,' said the Group Captain bitterly. 'Sergeant Snaith!'

The heavy-set sergeant came through the curtain at the back of the room and stamped straight up to Duggie. He pushed his face right into his, and screamed his well-rehearsed obscenities about him being a child-molesting ponce, his mother being a whore, his father a crying coward, and how he was going to kick seven colours of shit out of him if he opened his nasty little nancy mouth again. Duggie looked down sheepishly and fiddled with the lid of his Golden Virginia baccy tin. A little twist of his thumbnail popped it open, and in the split second the sergeant looked down, Duggie broke his nose with a head-butt. Reeling back with blood spilling through the fingers gripping it, he sprang forward furiously with his baton raised. It dropped from his lifeless hand to rattle and roll on the wooden floor just before he fell beside it, unconscious, with his jaw broken in two places. The six foot, three inches of broad shouldered, tight-bellied Herbie stood in front of Duggie, watching for any movement, and showing both iron hard fists weren't there to be released.

'Good lad, Herbie,' said Tommy quietly.

Duggie moved forward but was stopped by a big broad hand coming over his shoulder to rest on his breast.

'Easy, Dug, lad,' whispered Tommy calmly as he gently pulled Duggie to him.

A loud buzzer sounded and a dozen khaki soldiers rushed from behind the back curtain to line up with their batons drawn, and their comfortable expectations of soft old musicians being dashed by the sight of their sergeant.

'Three front, two out and sides, Stan.'

'All square: Three, two and sides, Tom.'

The soldiers tried hopelessly to match the menace looking at them. The band moved forward with the most unequivocal promise held in that one ungodly look that can never be unseen or unknown by any human eye: the will to kill. They were stopped by a small, slightly built, uniformed figure in an officer's cap appearing between them and the soldiers. Standing with his back to the band, he addressed the soldiers:

'Attention! I'm going to stop this fight to save your lives. I'm saving your lives because I need you to go and die somewhere else, for your country, and very soon.'

In the heavily wrung silence one of the soldiers stepped a parade ground pace forward. 'Permission to speak, Sir.'

'Speak.'

'With respect, Sir, we'd 'ave 'ad 'em.'

'No, you wouldn't.'

'With respect, Sir, that's what we're trained for, for combat, Sir...'

'Yes, yes. Well, I'll say these few words, then your permission to speak is denied. These men behind me went into German trenches to kill the enemy with weapons they'd made themselves, and they were the best the British Army ever produced.'

He pointed to the projectionist seated in a balcony box above the soldiers and a 16 x 16 foot image filled the screen behind the band. The soldiers looked at a photograph of the men standing in front of them, showing them young and strong, sitting on upturned wooden cases or just the blackened earth cleared of the snow covering everything else. Shattered black spikey stumps of trees and twisted grey staves of barbed wire sticking out of the lumpy white blanket, stretched away into the distance. Tommy was easy to recognise, with a thick sleeveless leather jacket over his topcoat that was belted around the middle, as was Duggie who sat on one side of him, smoking, with Lenny and Wilf on the other. Stan stood behind, smiling, with his arm around Den's shoulder, and Herbie sat right at the front with his long legs stretched out, beside the massive figure of a man, who wasn't in the room, wearing the same sort of leather jacket as Tommy and holding what looked like a medieval mace across his lap. Some of them wore woolly hats under their steel helmets, some smiled, some smoked, some looked weary and some looked like they'd been hurt, but they all looked straight into the camera.

'Little Geoffrey took that photo,' said Lester.

The band turned to look at it, but only for the moment it took them to turn back to examine the little uniformed figure, now facing them with a wide smile and a twinkling eye next to the black oval blind covering the other one. The happy noise of genuine human affection surrounded little Geoffrey in an instant, and came from the deep and lasting friendship that hell on earth had given them.

'Just a minute, lads,' said Geoffrey, turning back to the soldiers. 'None of you will be so lucky again: I'd fain see a yappy spaniel pup rip the throat out of my mastiff, than you stand against these men. Now get him to a medic, and when he can hear you, tell him I'll say thank you to Tommy for him; for stopping Duggie clipping his neck.'

While the unmanned soldiers were taking their curtain exit carrying the sergeant, Geoffrey returned for more handshaking and pats on the back. He was soon turned around again and had his cap removed so they could have a look at the back of his head:

'Christ, it's still a canny old dint, Geoff, lad.'

'We weren't even goin' over when ee got it,' said Den.

'It was Herbie that found yer bit of skull. That right, Herbie, lad,' said Colly...

Geoffrey and Herbie smiled at each other.

'... And Wilfy strapped it back on with some tapes we got from somewhere.'

'We thought yer wouldn't get by that one, Geoff,' said Roy.

'Well, it probably looked worse that it was. The nurses did tell me one of you would land up there just about every day asking about me.'

'Curiosity, Geoff lad, curiosity,' smiled Tommy. 'Mind you, Stan always said yer'd make it, didn't yer, Stan.'

'Aa couldn't do any other after ee only missed a fortnight after havin' ee's eye picked out, and not much longer with ee's arm.'

'Is it just about knackered there now, Geoff?' asked Lenny.

The freshness of remembering them as the closest friends he'd ever had came back in the straightness of their words:

'It is, Len. It was never right after the knock; it's not much more than something to fill a sleeve, now.'

Tommy put his hand on Geoffrey's shoulder. 'Aye, but it was a canny old knock though. Still, serves yer right for bein' so keen to get in first. Yer should have waited for Mickey.'

'Yes,' said Geoffrey softly, 'it would have been the end of me that night if it wasn't for Michael.'

They eased themselves away from the heavy silence of their thoughts by looking at Michael, sitting with the mace across his lap, looking at them from the life they had still in the photograph.

'Can yer see Vern, look, in the background, there?'

'Aa thought it was him. What the hell's ee doin'?'

'Ee'll be by a fire, aa'll bet.'

'Ee is, look; fittin' ee's kettle on it. Can yer remember that kettle Roy made him?'

'Aye, ee'd rather have lost a leg than that bloody kettle. So who's that with him, then?'

'That's them two lads from Kent.'

'Oh aye, good lads, both of them, poor buggers. They didn't get t' drink much tea after that photo, eh.'

'That nurse that Captain Toomer caught Duggie with was from Kent,' said Lester.

'Oh, I see,' said Geoffrey, pretending to be surprised, 'I wondered why Duggie was so keen on visiting, and there's me thinking, "what a caring chap", and all the while it was only to flesh out the nurses.'

'By Christ, ee fleshed that one from Kent, mornin', noon and night,' put in Wilf.

'And that other one; the big lass from Preston wi' the club foot, aa heard she took some fleshin' in the back of one of the ambulances,' said Den.

Duggie let the pencil moustache stretch.

'Is that where the tapes came from, then; that we strapped Geoff's head with?' asked Lester.

'No,' said Stan certainly.

'Aye, aye, Stan?' asked Tommy.

'They were Nessa's; her ribbons from her Christenin'. Michael brought them with him. He had them put away in ee's breast pocket wi' nowt else in – said they were what ee was fightin' for – nowt else.'

'These,' said Geoffrey, holding up two neatly folded ivory silk ribbons with faded, time-locked, Burgundy stains. 'Here, give them to Nessa, Stanley.'

Stan took them and looked at them reverently and said nothing. Geoffrey fastened the brass button underneath his martial ribbons with one hand.

'I'm sure this is all very touching,' interrupted Group Captain Bernhard nastily.

'Hey-up, it's Capt'n Heart-burn.'

'Can I remind you, Sir, that there is business to attend to here, and that…'

'No, Group Captain,' said Geoffrey, cutting in with both natural and military authority, 'you can't. Now if you'd be so kind as to leave us, I would like to talk to my friends in private.'

The Group Captain glowered his apoplectic rage at Geoffrey, who smiled and told him to leave the key to the boardroom on his way out. The slammed door was the only reply.

'That told him, Geoff, lad. So what's all this about then?' asked Tommy seriously. ''cause there's no way we're down here to make a record.'

'Follow me. But have a look at this one first.'

He raised his hand and a new photograph came on the screen. They all laughed at Lester, sitting on his Triumph H, covered in mud from head to toe, with only his eyes wiped clean, looking at them and laughing like a little boy.

'Look, there's Davy Herdie and Clipper.'

'And little Ronnie Miles wi' young Pod in the back, there.'

'Aye, all gone.'

'But not forgotten, eh.'

They followed Geoffrey away from their remembrances and out through a door behind one of the curtains, along a short passage into a large well-furnished room. Taking their seats on the bottle green leather settees arranged around a long low coffee table, they saw Geoffrey whisper to his batman, who left to return with a dozen glasses and two bottles of 20-year-old *Callum Beg* whisky.

'Thank you, George, that'll be all. Tuck in, lads, it's good stuff and there's plenty of it.'

The shuffling and stretching for glasses was stopped by Stan. 'Aa think we'd rather hear what's going on first, Geoff, if yer don't mind, like, 'cause aa'm not sure we're in the mood for drinkin' just now.'

'I understand, Stanley. Well, tomorrow we'll be declaring war with Germany.'

'You've got t' be kiddin', surely t' God.'

'I wish I were, Wilf, but it's happening.'

Geoffrey waited for the noise of their disbelief to die down before going on: 'We know it will be big, they think years again ...'

'But what's this got t' do with us: we're too old t' be fightin',' said Stan.

'No, no, nothing like that. As I said, it will be big, but it'll be a very different war from ours; it'll be at a distance, with new guns and machines, and all the latest inventions, and it'll catch the civilians this time, and this is where you come in: we want you to work for us; to help keep up morale.'

'Geoff, lad, this sounds like a load of donkey bollocks t' me, mind,' said Tommy.

'Well, if you want nothing to do with it, we'll have a good night on the grain and you'll be back on the bus home tomorrow. How about that?'

'Don't bloody start wi' any of that clever stuff, again, mind, Geoff. Remember, lads, one minute he'd be tellin' us we'd be havin' meat and beer, and the next he'd be takin' the last few tins of 'owt we had t' swap for bullets. We know you, Geoff, lad,' said Tommy.

'All a long time ago, we were young and daft,' said Geoffrey with a smile.

'You were never daft.'

'Well, the plan they...'

'Just hang fire, here. Why the hell have we been tricked int' comin' all this way on this cock-a-maimy recordin' shite then? Why the hell didn't yer just ask us?'

'I understand, Dennis, but our field spotter reported that such an approach simply wouldn't have worked.'

'And what makes yer think we'll do it, just 'cause you've got us here, like?'

'Who's this field spotter?' asked Lester.

'That charming Group Captain,' said Geoffrey, ignoring Lester's question, 'was to give you the King and country speech, show you a film, and use it as evidence to put you in jail if you refused to do this.'

'Bollocks.'

'A film about what?' asked Lester.

'About this chappy.'

Geoffrey handed a large manila envelope to Lenny and told him to take the photographs out and pass them round. They were pictures of Billy in full SS uniform. Geoffrey measured his silence as they looked at each other in a way he'd seen many times before.

'The photographs would go with recordings they'd made of you in the pub, and edited to show you were working for the Germans, and they intended to blackmail you with it.'

'And they rigged up a young lad from Belgium t' look like a German, eh,' sneered Wilf to harness their contempt.

'As a matter of fact, they didn't,' said Geoffrey. 'Billy is a German spy, there's dozens of them over here just now; posing as exchange teachers, tourists, musicians, all sorts, working to map out places to land troops, or hide ammunition and supplies and suchlike should they invade. He was called back for their first push into Poland.'

'So how long have you known about all this then, Geoff?'

'One hour, Stanley. I found out in a briefing just before you saw me. When I saw who you were … well, it will be stopped immediately, if you don't want to do it, that is, you have my word.'

'And you can do that can yer, Geoff?'

'I can, Stanley, I'm the Chief of Staff, and I will.'

They accepted his assurance and he accepted their touching comments on him being a good lad and having done well. He smiled modestly and asked if they should try a little 'sharpener' now. Stan ignored the invitation to ask:

'So if you hadn't known us, Geoff, we'd have been blackmailed int' this thing, then.'

'Yes, you would.'

'Why, though? Surely there must be plenty of bands who'd genuinely want to do it.'

'Well, maybe for radio, but there isn't actually that many that can travel and do live performances, they've only managed to land about 12, I think. There's either too many in the band being conscripted, or they're just not playing the kind of music some clever Dick decided was best suited to lifting spirits. You tick all the boxes, you see; old men playing jazz music.' He smiled.

'Swing,' corrected Carter. 'Jazz has nowt t' do with us. It hasn't got the life of what we play, it's lost its heart, or t' put the fact on it, it's been murdered by them that want t' show how clever they are – aye, just for that, they've cut the throat of the nightingale t' see how it sings – it's bloody sinful, a cryin' shame …'

'Easy, Carter, lad. Ee's passionate about the music, Geoffrey,' excused Stan.

'I can see. I meant no offence, young man, I'm just an ignorant old soldier, but that's what they want, you see, your kind of music, played with all that passion, to keep the spirits up and help push us on to victory.'

'Is anybody else havin' any of this shite?' said Wilf.

'You're wastin' yer breath wi' that old flannel, Geoff, lad,' said Tommy.

'Who's this spotter fella, then?' asked Lester.

'But t' call us a Jazz band,' interrupted Carter, 'is like sayin' Dipidee Hardup can't play lead horn off the back of a three-part harmony; it's bloody ridiculous, it's just not on…'

'Aye, hang fire, Carter, son, so let's have this plan then, Geoff, we might as well have all of it seein' as we've come all this way for nowt.'

'You do have it all, Stanley. But, never mind, that's the end of it, I'll arrange for transport back to the guest house and you can be home tonight if you want.'

'Have yer seen Roy's bus?'

'And I want you to know, it wasn't "nowt" for me. I'm heartily pleased to have seen you all again.'

'We're sorry, Geoff, it's just not for us; we can't just up and off, anyhow.'

'Well, you can actually,' said Geoffrey calmly, 'but no matter.'

'What's that mean, then?'

'No, no, honestly, it's of no consequence now, but I was told you'd have had all of this explained to you by your spotter…'

'Who is this fuckin' spotta?' asked Lester, irritated at not knowing.

'It's him,' said Geoffrey, pointing to the little chaplain entering the room.

'Him? And you're supposed t' be a man of the cloth. My arse! Goin' about lyin' t' people and trickin' them. You knew how much this meant t' us, yer rotten little bastard.'

'Just a minute, Wilf, Norman has done nothing wrong,' said Geoffrey.

'He has though.'

'No, he's been taken in just like you.'

'Bollocks,' said Wilf angrily, ''ee had t' know about it, ee had t' be in on it wi' that producer feller – that Wiseman fella – from what records was it, Carter?'

''Rumpin' Tumpin', and Adel Wiseman is the boss, mind.'

'Aye, so how's that, then?' pressed Wilf.

'Ah, yes,' replied Geoffrey smoothly, 'Mr Wiseman did agree to let them use his name, but you, and Norman, only met a secret service agent. Norman didn't know it was a set-up. All he knew was that you'd be *asked* to help with the war effort in the way I've explained, *after* recording your record, and he understood the decision would be entirely your own. He's not to blame for any of this, he's only trying to help his country, just like you did in France. I think you owe him an apology.'

The silence wasn't an angry one, but was sufficiently uncomfortable for the relief to be felt when Lenny broke it: 'Whey, t' be fair, mind, if we got turned over like this then it's just as likely a young church lad could, eh.'

The band were persuaded but remained silent.

'So what's this about us being able t' just up and off, then, Geoff?' said Stan.

'Well, part of Norman's job was to see what help could be given if you did want to do it; basically, there's money available.'

'What kind of money, Geoff?'

'Good money, Colly; full compensation for loss of earnings and a yearly gratuity. The lads at the pit, or in other jobs, will have double their wages paid, and if you have your own business, they'll pay the wages of whoever you want to cover for you while you're away, at £12 a week. On top of that you will each receive a one-off payment of £100 for each year you're with us.'

'Christ, that is good money, Stan,' said Colly.

'It is, it's government money,' reassured Geoffrey. 'And as well as that, you will each be paid a gratuity of £1,000 a year for every year this war runs…'

He was pleased to hear the whistles say how impressed they were, and picked his perfectly timed moment to tell them:

'… which means, if it runs for four years again, on average you'll each have £6,496 in the bank.'

'Christ.'

'Tax?' asked Colly above the excited muttering.

'Gratis,' said Geoffrey with a wink that wasn't lost on Colly, 'these are special payments, they'll be tax-free and completely private. And, there will be nothing for you to pay for travelling, digs, food and everyday stuff like a good drink. You can even claim for new instruments if need be.'

'Just for travellin' around playin'? Come on, Geoff, we're not that bloody daft.'

'I know you're not. The fact is, they want you to travel abroad mostly, so you can act as ambassadors; winning goodwill for Britain by playing in different countries, and encouraging them to fight for us and not against us.'

'So it's danger money, then?'

'Absolutely not. They've set a great deal of importance to this plan, and you will be kept away from danger. The money's so good because they judge it to be a fair reward for the time you'll be away from home and family, and to help persuade you to do it, of course.'

'Aa'm persuaded, Stan,' said Colly.

'And me. Christ, we'll never get another chance t' make money like this,' said Den, 'and aa think it'll be a good laugh as well, like.'

'Aa think we need t' have a talk about this, Geoff,' said Stan. 'Can we just leave it there for now and let yer know what we decide afore we leave in the mornin'?'

'That's fine by me, Stanley. How about I send Norman round at 07.00? There is just one thing to bear in mind: they insist it must be the whole band, all or none. Even I know it takes the whole band to make the thing swing, isn't that right, Carter?'

'It most certainly is, Mr er, Field Marshal, Geoffrey, Sir …'

'Has ee promoted yer, Geoff?'

He smiled with them at young Carter's innocence before asking: 'So, can we have that snifter now, Stanley, or do you want to wait until we meet again?'

'We'll keep it 'til we meet again, Geoff, if that's all right,' half apologised Stan.

'Always the sensible one, Stanley, and rightly so; there's far too much money at stake for it not to be taken seriously. Yes, indeed, financial security for yourselves and your loved ones needs proper consideration, especially to turn it down, but listen to me wittering on like an old mother hen. I'll say no more and wait to hear from you on the 'morrow.'

He stood to let them know their meeting was over and returned their good-natured, if slightly more reserved, bonhomie. His batman led them to the lift and out through the door they came in by, to be met by a different driver waiting with a taxi van. Their instruments had been returned to the guest house as soon as they'd entered the building. Back at the guest house the discussion ran into the early hours of Friday morning, with all things being weighed-up from every conceivable angle. When the sun came up, they were stuck at 10 to 1 in favour of doing it. Stanley was the one standing out because of his mother. He pleaded his case, insisting Geoffrey would arrange to take them without him, and how he would go back and tell him that Duggie could lead, and that they would easily be able to find another trombone.

'It's not that, Stan, and yer know it's not.'

'Aa know, Tom, but aa can't leave her now, it'ud kill her.'

They heard the sadness in the unwanted reply, and knew he knew what they had to go back to after this last big chance of a recording deal had come to nothing. They knew he was well aware that little Geoffrey was offering them their last real chance to get sorted out against the grinding hardships that would be coming to them soon enough, when they were too old or too knackered to work. They knew he knew his mother would be in good hands with Nessa and her mother looking after her, and they knew he knew all these things because of the tears in his eyes. Tommy looked at Wilf and they looked at the lads.

'Aa'll tell the little chaplain in the mornin',' said Tommy softly.

******

'I was only there a minute, Sir. They seemed sorely downcast at the decision, but said it was final; they're not going to do it, Sir.'

'Oh well, that's that, I suppose,' said Geoffrey with a casual smile. 'Would you like some eggs and coffee, Norman? Take a seat. Was it Stanley and his mother?'

'They didn't say, Sir.'

'No, of course not. Well, I'm sure he'll have a change of mind. Go on, tuck in.'

******

After ten slow-moving hours in his own dejection at being the cause of the despondency laying so heavily on his friends, Stan got off the bus to their true and kindly 'goodnights'. He walked through the open front door of his shop to see Nessa and her mother sitting together. They'd been crying. His mother had died in the night.

Chapter 9

March, 1940 – Norway.

General Drubil sat bored and cold in the backseat of his car, waiting for the passengers on the North Sea ferry from Newcastle to disperse. Pulling the collar of his heavy dark grey overcoat tighter around his neck, he listlessly swept his binoculars to a lanky figure waving at a battered old van driving away. He watched him until it was gone.

'Drive on, Gunter.'

They eased along Stavanger docks to the lanky figure.

'Nice to meet you, Mr Elvin.'

'Montague, please.'

'Then it is Henri. Please, join me in the car, Montague.'

Drubil smiled as he removed a kid glove to shake hands and exchange the manicured pleasantries of their trade as the car pulled away. After a 15-minute drive and a lonely four-hour wait in a cold empty office, Drubil returned with a tall, superior looking man:

'This is my friend, Count von Leibernitz, and he would very much like your help, Montague.'

'I'm very pleased to meet you, Sir, and how can I help?' said the MI6 agent cheerily.

'There is something we would like from you,' replied the Count in an equally pleasant manner.

'Of course, you know I'm here to help, but you must understand, my involvement is very much restricted to...'

'May I ask, Mr Elvin,' interrupted the calmly controlled Count, 'do you have the book?'

'A book? Well, I hope you believe me when I tell you I know nothing of any book. But, I can assure you that all and any such information would have been passed on directly through the appropriate channels.'

'It hasn't but it needs to be.'

'Of course.'

'And you will attend to this personally for us, Mr Elvin?'

'I most certainly will, and on that you can depend.'

'Then I must thank you for your kindness,' said the deliberately insincere Count.

He took an expensive silver cigarette case from his inside coat pocket as he strolled across the bare room to the door. He opened it for Drubil to lead them into the small, freezing cold, candle-lit cell of a room next door. The sickening stench was explained by the horrific sight of Billy's eviscerated corpse lying on a stainless steel table. Nonchalantly flipping open the hood of his gold cigarette lighter, the Count lazily rolled its wheel to spark a wide wobbling flame that was simply put to his thick white cigarette.

'We will leave you now, Mr Elvin, but Henri will call in the morning to hear what you are going to do for us perhaps.'

Drubil locked the door behind them.

*****

'No, Minister, we've nothing on him as yet, other than Drubil met him,' answered the Group Captain.

'I see. And the jolly northern brass?'

'They're in place.'

'Well, that's something, I suppose. You don't think they'll try to pull him, do you?'

'No, sir.'

'Very good. Let me know when he surfaces.'

*****

From a mezzanine balcony in the typically wood-cladded Norwegian guest house, Tommy and Stan watched Wilf heading for the front door.

'And where d'yer think you're goin', yer little rascal?' called Tommy.

'For a pint,' answered Wilf as though he'd been asked if the sun was hot.

When he reached the front door, Tommy was by his side and Stan was on his way to see what the others were up to in the dining room.

'So who are you in with, Lester?' asked Den.

'Young Carter, ee's still up there sortin' ee's music magazines out and stickin' pictures on the wall.'

'And Duggie's in wi' Herbie, and Lenny's in wi' Colly.'

Lester knew three of those four had gone out, so he spilled the beans.

'Where to?' asked Stan.

'Just across the road there t' that big place we seen comin' in.'

'With the red lights on?'

'Aye.'

Stan took a piece of paper out of his pocket. 'If that's called the *Det Røde Huset*, we're playin' there this Saturda' night.'

'Suppose we'd best have a look over and see, eh,' suggested Den.

Lester went to get Carter.

'So that means we're just missin' Royston, then. Anybody seen him?'

'Aye, ee's out the back wi' that numb landlord.'

'Doin' what?'

'What d'yer think? Ee's lookin' at that bloody old van thing ee picked us up in.'

'Yous just head over then, and aa'll fetch him.' Stan smiled.

Dug, Colly and Lenny had only just got seated at a big round table in its own horseshoe-shaped booth, when Wilf and Tommy came in. They sat on the thick, red velvet seat beside them and looked around the wooden decor of the high vaulted club.

'It's like somthin' off them Wild West films.'

'It's a size, mind.'

'That's a nice balcony runnin' round.'

'Whose round is it, anyhow?' asked Tommy.

'It'll be Carter's,' said Wilf, seeing them come in, stamping the snow off their feet and brushing it off their heavy coats.

'The daft buggers have been snowballin'.'

As the usual bumping, shoving and shuffling into seats settled down, a very pretty young waitress in a traditional red and black dress, fastened up to her throat, came over and asked for their order.

'Nine spraken Norwegian, Pet,' said Tommy, smiling.

'Ah, English,' she said, with a fall-in-love smile.

Duggie fell first, but the others were close behind.

'Would you like some beer?'

'If yer insist, Pet. We'll try nine of yer best, just t' be sociable,' Tommy replied and looked like he was the only one who could speak any language at all.

'Nine,' she repeated, holding up nine fingers.

The smiling nod and wink from Tommy sent her away so she could return holding the handles of five brim-full stein glasses in one hand, and four in the other. As soon as she put them on the table, they drew Tommy with a force that made gravity look like an idea. Picking one up like a pint at home, instead of by the handle, he held it up to the light. 'It's the same colour as that stuff we had in France, but by Christ, it's a good measure.'

'It's a steiner,' said Carter.

'Tasty,' said Tommy, putting his half-empty glass down.

'Ah, you like beer, yes.'

'Passable, Pet, very passable, and aa think aa might be tempted t' try another,' winked Tommy.

She smiled. She liked him and could feel her senses telling her he was a safe and good man. 'I am Aude. I am your waiter. Would you like some cheese and some bread?'

'Not for me, Order, Pet, aa wouldn't want t' let me boyish figure slip,' said Tommy, proudly patting a massive barrel gut.

She looked at him not understanding what he'd said, but she knew it was nice.

'It is very good cheese to have,' she tried.

'Well, go on then, twist me arm, aa'll try a nibble with a slice of bread, just t' keep yer happy. And on yer way back, Pet, just t' save yer legs, could yer fetch another pint of stein while aa'm waitin' for this lot.'

He handed her his empty glass, handle first, and she flitted away with her smile.

'What a lovely bit lass.'

'She is that.'

'And a little belter.'

'She is.'

Before Stan and Royston had a chance to sit down, Lester asked Stan what he thought of the stage. They all looked across the open space of what they could see would be used as a good-sized dance floor, to a raised platform about two feet high and 12 feet square.

'It'll be tight.'

'We've had tighter, eh, Duggie.'

'Looks like it's geared up for a canny crowd, eh.'

'Definitely.'

Tommy looked at Aude's pretty face looking at him from the serving hatch at the other end of the room. She was waving a long paper tube at him, so he went over. The lads watched him take it off her and tap her on the head with it to make her laugh before she disappeared behind the bar.

'What d'yer reckon?' he asked, rolling their playbill poster out down his front.

'Looks good.'

'Very good, professional, aa'd say.'

Tommy rolled it back up and dropped it on the table when Aude appeared with a tray of bread and cheese, and Tommy's beer.

'Just t' save yer legs walkin' back over, Pet, Wilfy wants another 11 pints of stein,' winked Tommy, and she was off again.

The only trace of four brown loaves and three pounds of bright yellow cheese was the prairie of crumbs across the table.

'Christ, aa'll be bound fer a week.'

'The steiner'll slacken it.'

'Hello, Order, Pet. What can we do yer for, sweetheart?'

'Would you like more things?'

'Oh aye, but no more cheese or it'll do damage. Right, let's have a look, who's for another? Righty-O, Order, seein' as we've got a few casualties, that's just the eight Steins, Pet.'

'Eight,' said Aude, checking with her fingers before nipping away.

'Aa'm sure they're nice lads and tryin' their best up there, but surely t' God they could just try t' put a bit music in. The lad wi' the trumpet might as well be blowin' a stone jug,' said Carter, shaking his head.

An hour later Stan smiled as he watched Carter clap as loudly and as kindly as the locals when the little band took their bows. This time seven brim-full steins slid onto the table and 12 empty ones were clinked into two little fists.

'Just a minute there, little Miss Order, not so fast. Yer've got one more try, remember, and if yer don't get it right this time, we'll have t' think about takin' our custom elsewhere,' said Tommy as seriously as he could but she laughed.

'Right,' he continued, 'aa'll point yer round, ready?'

She nodded and he aimed the poster at Royston, moving along them as soon as she began: 'Royston… Lenny … Wilf … Carter …'

She named them all and got the loud claps and cheers that made her put down one of her fistfuls of glasses to hold her side when she leaned forward laughing.

'Well done, Order, Pet. And now we can start t' teach yer some proper Firstwood English.'

'Yer a lucky lass,' said Wilf.

'And if you will learn some from me and try good.'

'That's a deal, Pet.'

'Lenny's always wanted t' be fluent in Norwegian since ee was a kiddie.'

'Ee'll be bilingual.'

'Nowt t' be ashamed of, Lenny, lad.'

Chapter 10

Stan put his hand in the air to bring *'Sheep doop dee baby'* to a loose and disheartening end. It was the third song they'd tried. He looked around the empty mid-afternoon club, and then at the band looking at him as he pushed both hands over his head to clasp his neck with woven fingers.

'What's your thoughts, Carter, son?'

'It's just like there's a hole where the music should be, Stan; it's nowt but organised noise at the minute. Aa'm thinkin' of that Frankenstein film me and Wilf went t' see; it's alive and walkin' about, but wi' no life in it.'

'And what d'yer think's causin' it, son?' asked Stan.

Carter said nothing but looked his reason back at him. With only the odd chink of glasses being washed, or a far-off word being muttered, the quietness of the club seemed to amplify their troubles.

'Aa'm sorry, lads,' said Wilf, 'aa know it's me, but aa can't do it any more. Aa've stuck at it as best aa can since Billy, but it's just gettin' worse, havin' t' be bangin' these friggin' things.'

'It's not, Wilf...'

'It is though, Stan, me heart's not in it, aa know it's not. Aa can put everythin' int' me guitar, but these bloody things, Christ, they're just the opposite, aa'm sick of it, lads. Aa'm sorry, but it's bloody purgatory sittin' hittin' these for hours on end.'

They could see he meant it this time, and although they tried to cheer him up, they knew he'd had enough.

'We're the ones at fault here, Wilfy,' said Stan, 'we've been takin' a lend of yer as well, mind. Aa promise we'll look for a drummer when we get back, but can yer play us through 'til then, though?'

'Course aa will, aa'll play the bloody things for as long as aa need to, but aa had t' say somethin', 'cause aa know it's me settin' us back.'

The others felt bad for him, not themselves.

'Hello Tommy. Hello Stan. Hello Herbie. Hello Duggie. Hello Lenny …' Aude continued through all their names while they smiled down at her from the stage.

'Hello Order,' they all said at once, before breaking out into solo praise of her remembering them.

'Yer in early, Pet.'

'To work to be ready for this night because you play.'

'Are yer expectin' it t' be busy, then?'

'Oh yes. I say to all that have come that you play tonight, and that you are the best band of big swing of ever.'

'She just touches yer heart this little thing,' whispered Lenny to Herbie. Herbie's smile showed he agreed.

'You practise now, yes?'

'We need to, we're not at our best just now, sweetheart, because of me.'

'What is wrong, Wilf?' she asked simply.

'Ee's gone off the drums, Pet, ee wants t' be back playin' ee's guitar,' answered Tommy.

'Aa was never *on* the drums, aa just had t' stand in, 'cause we lost our drummer.'

'How is this?'

'Ee packed it in, Pet,' answered Stan quickly.

'So we're stuck, y'see; we've only got Wilfy and ee hates playin' them.'

'I will do it if you would like?' she said.

'Do what, Pet?'

'Drums,' she said as if she'd been asked her name.

'Oh,' smiled Stan, 'we'll see, eh, but we'd better stick with Wilf for now, what with one thing and another, eh.'

With a little shrug of the shoulders to accompany her parting smile, she tripped off to get ready for work. They all looked at each other and smiled at the thought of it. At 10 o'clock that night the band were on stage, shimmering under half a dozen spotlights in their immaculate white tuxedos, waiting for their long-winded introduction to the packed house to finish. Stan winked at Wilf. The moment the compere clipped the microphone back on its stand, they burst into *Kick the Cat*. They played it well and got better as the night went on. They enjoyed themselves more than they had done for a long time, and were cheered for two good encores, which let them enjoy the rest of the night in their booth until the bar shutters came down at 2.00am.

'Is Tommy still in the neuk [toilet]?'

'No, aa'm here. Aa've just been up t' the bar t' say night-night to young Order, there.'

They looked over and saw her waving her little red hand. They all waved back and shouted their "night-nights" on the way out.

'She puts a bloody good shift in, that lass.'

'She does that,' said Tommy to himself.

******

'So, at last, you're back, gentlemen. Mr Jesperssen and I have been waiting for you to join us in this little repast we've prepared; we thought you may be peckish after all your on-stage exertions.'

'Well done, Monty, lad, just the ticket.'

With the little late supper table devastated, the first moves to bed began, but were interrupted by Monty asking for a minute. They settled back for one last smoke.

'I've only just received confirmation this evening that we're to make a little road trip. We have five venues in three towns to cover, no more than about 40 mile in the round, so nothing too bad in terms of travel, anyhow.'

'By bus?'

'Yes, Royston, by bus, and I'm sorry I don't have the vehicle specifications to hand.' He smiled. 'But the bad news is that we have to be up and out on the road at an ungodly hour.'

'What time, Mont?'

'10.30 in the am, I mean, is there really any need.'

'Soldier on, Monty, lad.'

'So, will it be Thursda' we get back here, then?'

'May be a little later; we have two nights in both Kleppe and Torgen, so possibly Friday.'

'But we're back t' play over the road there next Saturda'.'

'Oh yes, it's booked. And now I really must rest this sweet head if I'm ever going to hear that horrid bell alarm me.'

******

'Where the hell are we now, then?' asked Tommy, yawning and stretching, having just woken up on the back seat of the bus.

'It looks like the docks,' said Lester.

'The docks?'

The bus slowed to make a tight turn and rudded down a steep cobbled road to stop at the bottom. The driver left his cab and pulled the passenger door open. Monty hopped up the steps and stood in the aisle at the front.

'Everyone awake? Good.'

'What are we here for, Monty?'

'A change of plan, gentlemen, we're going home.'

'Now?'

'Yes, so please remain in your seats.'

'What about all our stuff at the guest house and that?'

'It's all taken care of. Just remain seated, I'll be two ticks.'

He disappeared and left an odd atmosphere. They were happy to be going home, but weren't happy about not saying goodbye to Aude, who they'd all taken to, and who they all felt worried about without saying anything to the others.

'How the hell did he get here, anyhow? Did he not say ee was stayin' on at that last place for a day or two?'

'Ee did, but ee left just after us.'

'H'way then, Lester?'

'Aa just clocked him gettin' int' a car across the road when we were pullin' away.'

'Whose car?'

'Who with?'

'What car?'

'It was a big black one with a driver and somebody else in the back, but aa didn't get a look at him.'

'God only knows what he gets up to. Oh, hello Monty, lad.'

'Right, we're clear to go, so just sit still; they're going to drive the bus onto the ship this time.'

'Christ.'

'So I'll say ta-ta for now, gentlemen.'

'Are yer not comin' with us, then?'

'No, not for a day or two; I've a few odds and bobs to sort out first. Would you like me to pop over to the red club and tell your little friend you've been called away suddenly?'

He knew it was a winning offer, and smiled at the competition to get their honest and touching messages to her.

'Would you give her this, please, Monty?' asked Carter sheepishly, and who felt more unsettled by the absence of the whistles and cracks he thought would be coming his way.

'Was it a love letter, son?' whispered Lenny when the bus pulled away.

'No, no, nowt like that, it's our song list; she asked me t' make her one when we were havin' a break the other night.'

Lenny told the others as soon as they were on the ship because he knew they'd have to know. They smiled at the thought of her having it.

'Whey, it'll be somethin' t' remember us by, if nowt else,' said Wilf, throwing his breakfast into the North Sea.

Chapter 11

'Tommy not in, Vern?'

'Oh, aye, ee's in the lounge, there.'

Stan wandered through with his pint and looked at the large lone figure sitting with the Daily Express covering the table. He smiled as he made his way over. 'New specs?'

'No, they're Vern's,' said Tommy, taking them off.

'Anythin' interestin', then?'

'A bit, aye. Here, have a look at this.'

Stan sat beside him and watched the heavy finger make its way down the column titled 'Western Seaboard Coast'. Tommy began reading: 'It says Norway, *"is of vital strategic importance to both German and Allied forces"*, and, *"control of the North Sea is crucial to the supply of both"*. They're worried the Gerrmans'll nip the place in a pincher movement from top t' bottom, 'cause they want all the iron ore for weapons and what-not. And it's sayin' the Norwegian army is no good on their own, and even the king's been tryin' t' chuck the towel in and claim neutrality 'cause ee wants nowt t' do with any fightin'. That's why they're on about sendin' troops from here and France and all over the place.'

Stan sat far enough back to stop Tommy seeing him smile at his strategic review of Norway. It was funny because when he actually was in a war, the only things he ever bothered about were nicking tins of jam and getting stood down for a drink.

'It's not lookin' good over there, Stan.'

Stan knew what his big-hearted friend was worried about, but couldn't bring himself to mention her.

'Pssst.'

'What's up, Verny?' whispered Tommy, playing along.

'That little chaplain fella's just come in askin' for yers. Should aa tell him yer in here or just t' piss off?'

'Hello, there,' said Tommy to the chaplain standing beside their table.

'Mornin' vicar,' muttered Vern and left.

'A good night last night, ay?'

'It was that, padre. So what can we do yer for, then?'

'Just this.'

He gave Stan a small brown envelope.

'D'yer know what's in it?'

'I do, but I'd rather you read it yourselves. It's nothing bad. Bye for now.'

'H'way then, Stanley, chop chop.'

As he read the few words on the telegram, the look on his face made Tommy sit up.

'We're goin' back, Tom, tomorro' night.'

******

The crossing was long, rough and freezing cold. When the young sailor wound the big steel wheel to open the door to the gangplank, they felt it was a lot colder.

'Christ, aa'd forgot about that,' said Den, pulling his overcoat collar around his face.

'What time's it, son?'

'Twenty-two hundred, sir,' said the young sailor.

'Ten bells, eh,' winked Tommy to make him smile.

They made their way down the cleated wooden gangplank with their instruments, knowing their other stuff was being taken care of. They were getting used to the administrative efficiency wrapped around them. Back at the guest house they said their hellos to Monty and the staff, dropped their instruments off in their old rooms, and headed over to the red club. It seemed different. Asking for Aude before ordering any beer, they found none of the waiting staff knew where she was and that a lot of staff had left in the last couple of weeks.

'If she's not here, she'll be away somewhere safe, Tom,' said Stan.

Tommy smiled as best he could, but without much hope of seeing her he was pleased when they finished their drinks and crunched back through the frozen snow to the guest house.

'You're back, gentlemen. Mr Jesperssen and I have been waiting for you to join us in a little collation tardive we've prepared: we thought you may be peckish after all that time at sea.'

'What the hell was that ship carryin', Monty? It stunk t' high heaven.'

'Oh, but isn't that always the way with dirty old seamen.'

'Christ.'

'Monty?'

'Yes, Stanley.'

'Aa don't suppose you've heard anythin' about the little waitress across the road there, have yer?'

'Heard what, Stanley?'

'Ee means, do you know what's happened to her?'

'My goodness, what has happened to her?'

'No, ee means, do you know where she is?'

'Now?'

'No, ee means ...'

'Boys, boys,' said Monty, 'I do know what you mean, I'm just teasing you. I know, I know, I know, you're all thinking, "what a rascal", but it's always the same when we lads are together, isn't it just.'

Despite themselves, they couldn't help but smile at the polar opposite sitting in front of them who seemed to fit.

'Yes, well, the good news, gentlemen, is that she is still here. You've probably heard how people are leaving, well this means less work for her at the club, you see.'

'So she's just on a night off, then?'

'From the club, yes. However, in order to make ends meet she has taken another job.'

'Where at?'

'At Hendriksen's fish factory.'

'Where's that, Lester?' asked Tommy, knowing he'd know.

'It's that big place just back off the main road as yer comin' in.'

'So we could have a walk up in the mornin' t' see if she's in, eh,' said Tommy.

'Well, I'm afraid it might not be tomorrow,' said Monty apologetically, 'you see, we're to leave here first thing for a week or so. Things are becoming a little more pressing for us now.'

'Surely we'll have enough time t' nip up and say hello t' the lass,' said Wilf.

'Yes, of course, I meant she may not be there.'

'Like a day off, or on a different shift?'

'Yes, exactly that, Dennis.'

'We can give it a try though,' said Tommy who was going to.

'What time are we off, then?'

'Can you believe 8.30? The middle of the deadening night for goodness' sake.'

They smiled.

'So it's gettin' a bit serious over here now, Monty.'

'Well, I really can't pretend it isn't, Stanley.'

'So how come they've brought us back then?' asked Wilf.

'I'll let you into a little secret …'

They knew enough to know he'd have been told to tell them.

'… you're needed. They checked on how things went before, and were shocked at just how well it's working. That's why you're back, and that's why they've appointed me as your permanent co-ordinator for the duration, how about that? For my part I am heartily pleased; I just know we'll do something good.'

'D'yer really think so, Mont?'

'I do, Leonard, I do. Look at it this way: if you play and make one Norwegian happy one night, and he goes out and punctures a tyre on a German's motorbike, and that German can't ride to give a message to his commander, and that commander can't organise his troops quickly enough, and those troops are surprised and defeated, then that will move us one step closer to victory, and that would be in no small part, the result of what you, and me, we, have done. Can you do anything but agree, gentlemen?'

'That's little Geoff talkin' there, mind.'

'It is,' said Monty honestly with a smile.

'Do you know where he is now, Mont?'

'I do, as a matter of fact; he's soon to be heading up into Northern Norway, to a place called Narvik.'

'Well, aa'll tell yer somethin' now, Monty, as sure as God made little green apples, that'll be where the fightin' is.'

Monty raised an eyebrow at the intuitive correctness of their knowledge.

'Oh my goodness, look at the time, I must lay this sweet head down if I'm to be up and at it on the 'morrow. Goodnight, one and all.'

He stood up and swished off, leaving a couple of them thinking he was dodging something.

******

'There it is, look.'

'That's the place, driver.'

Stan and Tommy got off the bus and went into the factory through what looked like a missing wall. Two minutes later they came back out and got back into their seats.

'We've just missed her; she's workin' nights.'

'Poor little bugger.'

'Aye. We'll make sure we catch her when we're back,' said Tommy, meaning it.

'Or, we could pinch a minute or two and drive to her house,' said Monty, expecting to be cheered, but he wasn't. No one knew what to make of it and wondered about how he knew where she lived, or if it was a good idea to just drop in on her when it could be awkward for her for all kinds of reasons.

'Whey, just drop me off and aa'll say a quick hello and then we're away,' said Tommy finally.

They knew they had to go. A rather reserved Monty sat by the driver for the five minutes it took to direct him to a little wooden bungalow set back from the main row of houses like a planner's after-thought. It was painted sky blue with white trimming fascias and porch posts, and they could see it had once been a very pretty little place, but the peeling paint, broken panels, and rotted front door showed those days were gone. Tommy stepped up the two porch steps, knocked, and stood back off them to be the head of the friendly little herd that had gathered behind him. They listened to the rattling bolts and bone-dry locks being worked loose, before the pulling contest with the stubborn door ended and let them see each other. Aude dropped her keys and pushed the single fist she'd made from two cold red hands in front of her mouth. She stood stock still, looking at them as though she would wake up if she blinked, and then they'd be gone.

'Hello Order, sweetheart,' said Tommy, making himself smile.

Without saying a word, or moving her blended fist, she walked to the end of the porch towards him, which made them just about the same height. He looked into the glassiest black eyes that had ever shone on earth.

'There, there, Pet', he said, rubbing her shoulder.

The others tried looking about them to stop their watery old eyes from saying too much. Taking the moment she needed to control herself, she waved and smiled as best she could, and went through their names to make them smile and try to look as happy as they felt to see her. Monty called from the bus, making Tommy and Stan talk quickly to tell her what they had to do, and make sure she knew they were coming back in a week. She tried all she could to smile at them all again as her eyes filled.

'I will look for you to come back, yes.'

'Yes, Pet, we will be back soon.'

Seeing Carter waving seemed to remind her: 'I have now from 'Ali Bongo' to 'Fettle me metal', Carter – they are good and I will now go on all the way to 'Zambeezee baby', yes?'

'Yes,' said Carter, knowing he'd be in for a grilling on the bus this time.

They left with her waving at them waving at her, and everybody feeling a thousand times better than they had been five minutes ago.

'She looks a bit rough, there, bless her,' said Colly.

'Aa think she's havin' a hard time of it, the poor little thing,' said Lenny.

'Bloody night-shifts here and late shifts there; it's no bloody wonder,' said Wilf.

'Aye,' added the far-away Tommy.

'There was next t' nowt in that house, mind: did yers see in when she came out?' asked Lester.

A few nodded.

'We'll do somethin' for that bit lass, Tommy, lad, have no doubt about that.'

Coming from Wilf, it took him by surprise, because nine times out of ten it would be Stan saying things like that.

'Anyhow, young Carter, bonny lad, is there somethin' yer wantin' t' tell us?' diverted Stan.

'Aye, aye, Carter, let's have it, from the top, son.'

He tried to look calm and collected, but began like a choir boy in confession, reminding them of the playlist he'd given Monty for her, and going on to add the detail he knew they hadn't had out of him last time. He confessed that when he'd asked her why she wanted it, and she said it was so she could practise them, that he hadn't taken her seriously, and only did it just to be nice.

'But, what she's just said there must mean she is workin' her way through them, 'cause aa put them in alphabetical order.'

'Never in the world.'

'Play the drums? No, it has t' be somethin' else, somethin' lost in translation, mebbees, eh?'

'Whey, aa don't know what,' said Carter.

'So have you got a copy of the list yer gave her, son?' asked Stan.

'Oh aye, and wi' spaces for stars.'

'Stars?'

'Aye, aa've got a star system t' rate how we play them, y'see: 5's good and 1's shite. If yer fancy we could go through the list and rate how much we still think of them, or like playin' them, just t' pass the time, like.'

'H'way then.'

'You write the stars on, Stan.'

Stan smiled and took the paper and pencil, and started them off: 'Right then, eyes down for a full house: How many stars for *Ali Bongo*?'

'5'

'4'

'3'

'2'

'Shite.'

'Here we go,' laughed Stan.

Chapter 12

Friday, 29th March.

'Whey at least we're back now.'

'You've got some busy roads about the place now, Mr Jesperssen.'

'Hei til dere alle.'

'Ee hasn't got a word of English, that lad,' whispered Den to Wilf.

'Ee might just be a bit simple, poor bugger, 'cause ee's the only one of them that hasn't,' replied Wilf in full voice.

'Feels like comin' home a bit now, y'know, gettin' back here, like,' said Lenny.

'A bit.'

'Anybody seen Monty? Lester?'

'Not since last night when ee was away in that fancy car again: the big black one.'

'With the same fella?'

'Couldn't see. Did you get a look at him, Roy?'

'Eh?'

'That car we saw Monty gettin' in.'

'Oh aye, a '38 Daimler, 4 litre, straight 8 wi' overhead…'

'No, man, the fella wi' Monty, did yer see him?'

'No.'

'Is Mr Elvin here, Mr Jesperssen?' asked Stan slowly.

'Ah, Mr Elvin, yes. For you.' He gave Stan a letter from his apron pocket.

'It says ee's arranged for the stage across the road t' be set up so we can practise when we want… and that, er, ee has some news … and we've got t' see him at 10 o'clock tonight. That's it.'

'Mat?' said Mr Jesperssen, pointing to the dining room.

'Oh aye, aa wouldn't mind a bit mat, aa'm famished.'

'Lead the way, Lenny, lad, yer little linguist.'

******

Seeing them all head over to the club, Mr Jesperssen made his way back through the dining room and up the stairs to the private second floor. In a cluttered little room tucked away at the back of the building, he took a long-handled pole from behind a pile of boxes and pulled a loft hatch open to let the ladder down.

'Ah, Roger, all quiet on the guest house front, I take it.'

Roger Harling smiled and sat on a little round-topped stool beside Monty and took off the glasses he didn't need to wear. Monty slid the black lolly-pop headphones from his head to hang around his neck, and turned from the radio to watch him light his pipe.

'So, you're telling them tonight, then,' said Roger between puffs.

'Yes, that was confirmation just now.'

'Handy. How about lobster with that lovely little Chardonnay, 7.00ish Ok?'

'Oh my word, yes. That walnut shag smells divine.'

******

'Well hello, gentlemen, look what Mr Jesperssen and I have done for you tonight; it's a little soiree legere moyenne we've prepared. Now tuck in and I'll see you when you're all nicely snug and very happy chappies, ay.'

He returned half an hour later wearing a full-length red silk smoking jacket over his gold silk pyjamas, and brown leather mules.

'Lookin' swish, Mont, lad.'

'Oh, just some old thing to relax in after the trials of the day, Dennis. So have you spoken to your little lady friend this evening?'

'Oh, aye, but not for long; she had t' get away t' get some kip before startin' at the fish factory,' said Tommy.

'I see. Then am I right to assume you still haven't heard what she has been telling you?'

He could see they hadn't the foggiest idea.

'Tellin' us about what, Mont?'

'Well, here's a clue, Wilfred; what links oil, ear, and kettle?'

'Tinnitus.'

'I beg pardon, Lester?' said Monty smiling.

'Easy, you've got a bad *ear*, so yer boil some water in the *kettle*, warm up some olive *oil* and run a drop or two in, and there yer have it, tinnitus relief.'

'So you think I'd presume your young lady friend would be talking to you about tinnitus?'

'For Christ's sake, Monty, what the hell are yer on about?'

'Drums, Thomas, drums.'

They looked at him.

'Well? Has she not spoken to you about drums?'

They looked uneasy.

'Ah, so she has and you haven't listened.'

'Monty, she's a lovely little thing and we all think the world of her, and yer right, she has said about playin' drums and even got our songs off Carter' (Stan smiled and shook his head slowly) 'but please Monty, she's just a bit lass and believe it or not they do take some playin', it's specialist stuff y'know and we'd never want t' hurt her feelings ...'

'Well, I'll stop you there if I may, Stanley, and start my work tonight.'

He took a notebook from the inside pocket of his smoking jacket and sat thumbing through the pages of his handwriting, in his own little world, until he found his place. 'Here we are, now where to begin: The past or The present? I'm not entirely sure, but The past I think, yes. You must excuse me while I read out some unfamiliar names: Paul Whiteman, I'm informed is one you will know' (they nodded) 'Art Hickman?' (a couple of nods) 'and Gene Krupa?' (same couple of nods) 'Carter?'

'One numb band leader and two of the finest beatsters that ever put stick t' skin in a swingin' rhythm section.'

'Yes, thank you. And you may know that the "beatster" they profess to have inspired them more than any other is Mr 'Sweetmeat' Steve Stevens.'

'Beat, Monty, Beat, 'Sweetbeat' Steve Stevens,' corrected Carter.

'Oh, I see, I did think it a little intrusive.'

'That's the maestro, Monty, the top of the tree, every drummer wants t' play like him.'

'Apart from Wilf.'

'But ee just disappeared off the scene in about '27,' continued Carter, 'nobody knows why, but they say ee was bumped off by Al Capone 'cause he'd shafted one of ee's dames, and was slung off the Brooklyn bridge in Chicago with a concrete boot on t' sleep wi' the fishes.'

'Yes, indeed,' resumed Monty, trying not to smile at the young man's facts, 'disappear he certainly did, and there may have been a romantic twist to it, but as for any involvement of Mr Capone, I can tell you there was none. I can also tell you that Mr Stevens not only left the music scene, as you say, he also left America and returned home, here to Norway, under his real name, Sven Svensen.'

Monty saw a level of attention in his audience that would have stopped any one of them feeling a pin prick, and went on: 'Yes, he returned to his hometown of Bergen, which is only a few hours north of us, and where we'll be playing Tuesday next by the way, but, yes, Mr Svensen married a …'

'So Order's ee's daughter?'

'No, Lester, she is not,' said Monty flatly, not wanting to be interrupted. 'Mr Svensen married and settled to a line of work I can only describe as reindeer hunter-cum-meat merchant, which caused him to travel to the far north of the country from time to time. Now I just want to digress for one tiny moment; to pick up on a very insightful observation Douglas made on his very first night here, when he noted that the women were all blond or fair and that Aude was the only one who had black hair. Do you remember, Douglas?'

Duggie nodded.

'Yes, well, one day Mr Svensen returned from one of his trips north with a half-starved little girl of about four years old...'

'Order?'

'Yes, it was Aude. She's a Sami, you see.'

He could see they didn't. 'She's a Lapp, a Laplander; one of the people who live in the far north and move about like nomads with their herds of reindeer. Now we don't know why, but Aude had been left without her parents and was having a difficult time of it straggling along alone. Mr Svensen took pity on the girl and arranged with the tribe leaders for him to take her and look after her. And this he did; he looked after her with great kindness and care.'

'Good lad.'

'Yes. Now the woman he'd married was a widow with a son of her own who was about ten years old when he brought Aude back, and he seems to have resented her; maybe a jealous rival for his mother's affections, who can say? Now his poor treatment of her became worse after his mother died quite suddenly about a year later, and he wasn't the only one making her life unpleasant. You see, there were many others who put the mother's death down to Aude, because of the superstitions and prejudices they held against the Samis, and it became so bad that Mr Svensen had to leave, and he moved here with the two children. Now I'll draw your attention to another observation Douglas made after a few visits to the club; he pointed out how Aude didn't seem to have much to do with the other staff working there. Well this is why: she faces the same old, deep-rooted rejection daily; a lot of people over here don't like the Laplanders.'

'Christ.'

'Poor little thing.'

'Yes, exactly, Leonard,' said Monty sincerely.

'So where's this Sven and sonny-boy now, then?' asked Tommy.

'Dead. The fishing boat they were on went down in a storm about five years ago. All of the crew died.'

'So she's been on her own all this time?'

'Yes, since she was just turned 14. Now, one more thing: Mr Svensen seems to have been pressed into taking to his drum kit once more when he came here, most likely because of the loss of his meat trade, the money from fishing not being enough, and him having to do whatever else he could to pay the bills.'

'So ee's showed Order how t' play.'

'That's right, Stanley, and despite the repeated and reported torments of her mean-spirited step-brother, she stuck at it, and I am reliably informed she has become a remarkably proficient player.'

'How d'yer know all this, Monty?'

'Now, now, Wilfred,' deflected Monty coyly. 'So, gentlemen, what do you intend to do with the information I have worked so tirelessly to collect for you? But, no, don't tell me right away, I'll leave you to have a good old chinny-chat and you can tell me at breakfast, ay?'

'What time would that be, then, Mont?'

'Oh, say about 11.00ish.'

'Crack of dawn, eh.'

'Goodnight, gentlemen,' bowed the likeable, strange man, pushing his notebook into his pocket and leaving with a comical flounce.

The chinny-chat he left them with lasted until the crack of dawn.

******

'Well played, Montague.'

'Thank you, Roger. Do you think that lovely little Burgundy will have caught its breath by now?'

Chapter 13

Aude could sense there was something up with the band when she came in but couldn't work out what it was.

'Order, Pet,' began Stan carefully, 'we were just talkin' last night, there, and feel a bit bad about not listenin' t' yer when you've been tryin' t' tell us about playin' the drums.'

Her tired face still couldn't put the faintest first shadow over the beauty of the smile coming up to see them.

'So, we'd like you to give it a go for us, sweetheart,' he blurted out, 'just if you want to, mind.'

'Now?'

'Well, we've asked the manager, there, and ee says yer can. We thought it might be better for you doin' it now, Pet, before you have t' get all yer skirts and what-not on for work, like.'

She smiled at the innocence and took her big overcoat off and laid it neatly on the floor beside the stage while they got sorted around for her.

'What?' She smiled, looking down at herself.

'No, nowt, Pet, it's just trousers, y'see, lasses don't wear them in England, apart from in the pit yard, like.'

'No? In what?'

'Oh, it's just a place that's different, sweetheart, but yer look smashin', mind,' said Stan, as he leaned down to help her onto the stage.

She took his hand out of politeness but hopped up like a bird and went straight to the drums. As she sat fidgeting and moving bits about while sporadically thudding the bass pedal, they looked from her to each other with a sense of anticipation they hadn't expected.

'So have yer been practisin' the songs on the list, Pet?' asked Stan kindly.

'Yes, I am up now to *Lollipop lovin.*'

'And how d'yer know the tunes, Pet?'

'On the records for the gramophone, or by music on the sheets I have, or to take from the store of books.'

'The library?'

'Yes.'

'Right,' said the impressed Stan. 'And is there one that yer'd like t' have a go at first?'

'Mmm, yes, *Jam it up.*'

'Christ, that's a fast one, sweetheart, would yer not like a slower one to ease yer in a bit?'

'No thank you, Wilf,' she said respectfully.

'Righty-O, lads' said Stan, 'let's have this tight and full throttle from the get-go and we'll see what's what with this old pumper.'

They steadied and readied themselves, sliders were slid, stoppers were stopped and all manner of mannerisms were twitched before the eyes settled on Stan. He knew they were ready and looked at Aude who looked back at him as calmly as she did waiting on their table.

'Right. Seein' that we is ready, then it's: a-1, a-2, a-1,2,3 …'

The instant the fast last fourth was counted, the band exploded into life and the music burst with a force that surprised them all. It was touching them again, on their hands, their lips, and on the backs of their necks, and they knew it was the drums bringing it back as they rolled where they needed to roll, thundered where they needed to thunder, and swung where they needed to swing. Stan watched a tired little waitress turn into a highly accomplished musician, lost to the abandoned pleasure of what she was making. He didn't know whether to laugh or cry as he looked from her to his old friends, 'playing up' as they hadn't done for so long, and all because of her, taking them back to a place he thought they'd never see again. Turning his back to them and bending down low, he blew himself back up to full back-arching height, with a top C that pulled them into the perfect full stop. It was perfect and when he turned to face the band he saw his friends, beaming, bright-eyed and young again, calling him over to the drum kit with them. He took his turn to pat and rub Aude's shoulder, and get a kiss on the cheek from her, as she stood with the sticks in her hand. He thought she must have been sent by an angel to give them their hearts back. The manager came up to the stage, clapping along with the rest of the few others in the quiet afternoon club, and spoke to her in her own language.

'I must now go as Anna will not be to work from now.'

Stepping off the stage let the tiredness return to her face, like a cloud killing the moonlight that had been lighting its beauty.

******

'She was better than good, mind, and aa mean miles better, way beyond really bloody good. Did yer hear those off-beat pedals working against the toms in the chorus? Christ that takes some doin'.'

'And the transitions wi' them ghosts in the sixteenths?'

'Oh aye, she's somethin' special all right. And what about old Stan, there; did yer see him blowin' that big C.'

'If you mean the tall boy, Christian, Wilfred, then I'm afraid the rumour of him being so heavily privileged is really just that.'

'Where the hell did you come from, Mont?'

'Oh, I'm here, I'm there, I'm everywhere from time to time, a butterfly on the petals of life, now, tell me, did the practice with your young friend go as well as I heard it did?'

'Whatever yer heard couldn't even start t' tell yer how good it was, or more t' the point, how good she is.'

'I see, Wilfred, and I am very pleased to hear it.'

'I think, er… we might want t'… well, aa think we …'

'Of course we can have a chat about it, Stanley, just rap a tap on my little knocker and I'll be down in front of you in a flash,' said Monty with a straight face before gliding out of the room.

'Ee's a funny bugger, lad.'

******

'Well I don't see why not,' said Monty, 'and I'm sure they will view it positively, simply because it will contribute to the plan.'

'So will you put it to them for us, then?'

'Of course I shall, Stanley, but I do see a problem. Now don't look so forlorn, it isn't a problem with London, I think it's one for yourselves.'

'How come?'

'Well, to put it simply, does Aude want to do it?'

'Oh, she will, aa'm sure, eh, Stan?' said Tommy.

'I should tread very carefully here, gentlemen. It may seem to you she has nothing to lose by leaving here, and everything to gain by going with you, but just remember, this young lady has had very little from life and what little she has had has been here in the love of her father. So please heed my words and approach her softly, with small and gentle steps.'

They heard the uncharacteristic concern in his voice.

'We will, won't yer, Stan.'

Chapter 14

Wednesday, 17th April.

'Tonight's the night, then, lads,' said Stan, returning from Monty's room.

'What's ee say?'

'Ee says Order's workin' at the club 'til midnight and she's got a day off tomorro', and that we can arrange a bit of a do for her here and nab her when she comes out. Sounds good, eh.'

'Put some cake and tea on for her, like?'

'Aye, Lenny. And another thing, ee says the Germans are hammerin' the hell out of everythin' put in front of them in the north, and they're on the march up from the south as well.'

'How long before they get here, then?'

'Ee reckons a week at the most, but anyhow, we're away home tomorro' night.'

'Christ.'

'Aye, for safety, like.'

'Can we get some balloons?'

'Aye, Lenny, aa'll see if there's any about.'

'So why's Monty stayin' in ee's room, Stan?'

'Ee reckons a slovenly waiter corked his Pinot Blanc.'

'That's one way of puttin' it.'

'Blanc and blue, aa'll bet.'

'Mind, ee does look rough. Anyhow, aa wondered if anybody fancied comin' shoppin' t' get Aude a little present, y'know, in case she doesn't come with us and we can give her somethin' t'

94

remember us by.'

Stan's thoughtfulness cast a shadow. He knew it would but had to do it because Monty's warning that she might not want to leave was growing on him. Carter, Lenny and Royston went shopping with him, and they ended up buying two beautiful necklaces; one for Aude and one to take home for Nessa. When they got back to the guest house the preparations for the party were well underway.

'Have the Germans been through here already?' asked Roy looking about the room.

'Christ Almighty, who the hell's hangin' them balloons like that? She's just a bit lass for Christ's sake.'

'That one's "The Nogsey" and this one's "The Monty",' said Colly.

They all laughed.

'H'way then, Stan, get us organised, lad, or we'll have t' tie Lester up wi' the streamers again.'

He smiled and got Lenny to show them Aude's present first.

******

'Here's Tommy and them back.'

'Aye, but she could still have another hour, washin' up and what-not.'

'We've got Carter watchin' for her comin' out.'

'Are yer sure yer want me and Herbie t' go over for her when she does?'

'That's the vote, Stanley, old lad, we're nowt but fair that way.'

'Hello, Monty, how yer feelin? Yer still look a bit green about the gills, mind.'

'Yes, rendered fragile by something I've swallowed ...'

[Coughs.]

'... but you know me, Wilfred, I'm a fighter.'

'Absolutely, Mont.'

'I've only just popped down to wish you luck with the young lady, and to press you to take much more than a little care with her. Don't rush at her with your wishes, take time and listen to hers. Be patient, all of you, let Stanley introduce the subject, and remember, she is still but a child, albeit she has had to grow up a lot more than many of her tender years. Have you listened to me, gentlemen?'

They nodded like school children.

'Good, because if you don't heed my words, I fear you may very well jeopardise the thing you all seem to want most, and I would be saddened on your behalf for that to happen. Now the hour cometh and I must leave you to it; goodnight, gentlemen.'

They said their goodnights and Monty left.

'There she is,' said Lester.

'Where?' asked Carter, straining and craning as the failed look-out.

'There, just by the side of the door, fastenin' her scarf, see.'

'Oh, aye.'

'Aa wouldn't worry about it, Carter, son; that little bugger's got eyes like a shithouse rat, always has had, and a bloody good job for us in days gone by, eh.'

'Right,' said Stan, 'me and Herbie's off, so knock the lights off and when yer hear me cough, switch them on and let's have a nice surprise for Order, eh.'

'Yer on, Stanley.'

With the lights off they could see clearly across the new clean white sheet covering the street, and watched Aude smile as she went to meet them. Herbie stood tall and still as Stan started pointing and shuffling about until she put her arms through theirs, as if it was the most natural thing in the world, and let them walk her to the guest house. They heard Stan cough. He coughed louder.

'Who's gettin' the friggin' lights?'

'Wilf.'

'Bollocks,' came the barely whispered defence.

'Christ, aa'll get them. Where the hell are they?'

'Here.'

The lights came up to show Aude what she would remember seeing until her dying day. All of the balloons had been re-arranged into less disturbing clusters, and hung with brightly coloured streamers. The long table in the centre of the room had been beautifully presented by Mr Jesperssen, with a round white cake in the middle with a little blue drum kit on it made by Carter from inedible plasticine. They all clapped and cheered and blew their party hooters, without any of them noticing the lowing expression darkening over her. She covered her face with her hands and instinctively turned to bury her head into the broad protective strength of Herbie's chest. He looked down with a caring smile and gently patted her shoulder. The noise left the room and they waited in blissful ignorance for what they thought would be the end of her happy tears. Stan began to realise something wasn't right.

'What's wrong, sweetheart, it's just a little party, that's all.'

They heard something muffled into Herbie.

'What is it, Pet?' said Stan like a parent to a crying child.

Monty's warning words were in his ears, and now he heard what they meant for the first time. None of them could have heard their meaning before, because they could never have grasped it came from things they could be doing to hurt her. Stan felt the ice-cold penny drop and turned quickly to the lads. They knew the look and it chased the smiles from their faces. Tommy instinctively stepped forward but was stopped by Stan's raised hand.

'Order, sweetheart, we would never want t' do 'owt t' make yer feel bad, Pet, so… well, aa mean…'

'Of course you wouldn't, Stanley,' said Monty, in an unusually bluff voice as he entered the room. 'So, I take it this is the young lady you tell me can play drums, dear me, whoever heard of such a thing; a girl playing drums, whatever next? Well, hello there, my name is Montague, what's yours?'

She mumbled her name into Herbie.

'I'm so very sorry, my dear, but you will need to speak up a little as I have some limitation with my hearing.'

The decency of Aude brought her head away from Herbie to say it clearly.

'What a most beautiful name. Now tell me, Aude, what have these horrible men been doing to make you cry?'

She spun from Herbie and pointed her clenched, white-knuckled fists straight down the side of each leg of her trousers to almost shout at him: 'They are not horrible men! They are to me kind.'

They could see the panting breaths lifting her shoulders with a passion to take away the words she didn't have in English. 'They are leaving me,' were the only ones that came quietly as the fists turned back into hands to catch her head as it fell. Not a single word could be found by any one of the band.

'Tut, tut, young lady,' bluffed Monty, 'I must protest; they are not leaving you, my dear, they are being sent away, and I think you will find there is a difference.'

He shot them a look demanding they remain silent for him to go on. 'As a matter of fact, you should know I'm the one sending them away.'

He waited for her head to lift out of her hands. 'Or, rather, I should say, it is the British government making them go.'

They all saw the lost look on Aude's face, but before any of them had any thought of what to do, Monty had her by the hand and gallantly handed her into a comfortable chair where she sat and looked at him vacantly. The lads took their cue to sit down. Monty began again:

'The world is soon to be eaten up in war, my dear. Your friends in the band are too old to join the army now, or are unable to because of medical reasons, but they have agreed to help by playing their music for those standing up against the Nazis. Do you understand, Miss?'

She nodded but looked as though she was dreaming.

'Well, in order for them to help like this, they must travel to where they will do most good, and this is why we are here in Norway; but now the danger is too great and this is why we must leave.'

Aude looked at him.

'I see you may not be fully aware of the situation here, my dear. Well, your armies have been defeated and we think it will not be long before the Germans reach here.'

He looked at her meaningfully and she gripped her hands together.

'Yes, it is a very dangerous time. But, as long as you stay close to your parents and family, I think you will manage; it's the isolated individuals we fear for. Now, if you do know of anyone like that, then you must tell them to leave immediately, and the best advice we have is for them to head to Sweden.'

Monty flicked a look at Stan telling him to keep the others quiet. It wasn't easy for him as they could all see the sickening work of fear pull the last bit of colour from Aude's face.

'Leaving you, indeed,' said Monty, affecting a little laugh. 'Do you know why these silly fellows are having this party tonight, young lady? Well, believe it or not, it's so they could ask you to go with them.'

Her eyes filled like stormy pools and she hung her head in her hands.

'I know, I know, I warned them not to. I told them your parents would never agree to it, but, would they listen? I can only apologise on their behalf for upsetting you like this.'

'No,' she said quietly, trying to clear the heavy tears with her fingers. Lenny put a napkin on her knee.

'I'm sorry, I don't quite understand, Miss, what do you mean, "no"?'

He glared at them to stay still, but didn't need to; they could see what was happening and that there was a master at work.

'I have no …' she faltered.

Twelve hearts went out to her and only one was brought under control to continue talking to her.

'Am I to take it, young lady, that your parents have already left and you're to join them shortly? Well, in that case, the sooner the better I'd say; the thought of those Germans finding you alone here, goodness me. Can we contact your friends and help arrange for you to travel with them?'

She shook her head slowly.

For the first time she looked at them, and saw them looking at her to tell her what every human heart needs to hear. Monty looked at Tommy to go to her. She could see the tears in the big man's eyes as he knelt by her chair to put his massive hand over hers.

'Please, Pet, come with us. We'll look after yer and make sure you're safe, and we'll not let anybody hurt yer, will we, lads?'

Out of the 'nos' and 'nevers', Duggie sat forward: 'No bugger'll ever hurt you, sweetheart.'

She took Tommy's hand in both of hers and pressed it to her cheek. They looked at each other but couldn't see.

******

'Well played, Montague.'

'Thank you, Roger. Just the old, love and fear rigmarole, nothing too extraordinaire.'

'Very good. How about a naughty little gin-sling for a change?'

'Lead on, you splendid man.'

Chapter 15

Colly's van rolled along the street to big Margaret's house, and they weren't the least bit surprised to see her standing at her open front door waiting for them. By the time Stan and Den got out the back, Aude was walking around the van behind Colly towards the thick folded arms of an impressively imposing woman.

'This is Order, Margaret,' said Colly, standing aside.

'Watcha, Margaret, Pet,' said Aude, holding out her hand.

Margaret let her arms unfold and spread a big hard-worked hand between her collar bones as she laughed her head backwards. Aude looked around puzzled at the lads smiling at her, and waited with her hand out until Margaret took it kindly and gently in her great hard mitt.

'Mind, you're a bonny little thing,' she said in a way that allowed no debate, 'and aa see these sackless buggers have been learnin' yer to talk proper, eh. Eee, "watcha Margaret, Pet".' She made herself laugh again.

'Has this bairn got some bags, there, Stan?'

He nodded and came from the back of the van, holding one.

'Is that it?'

He knew he was in trouble. 'It is, aye, but we wondered if yer might help out in that way, Margaret, Pet.'

'Oh, yer wondered, did yer? Aa'll bet yer bloody did. And don't you, "Margaret, Pet" me, Stanley South.'

She snatched the bag off him.

'What the hell d'yer think yer at; bringin' this bit lass all the way over here from Scandian-Navian, wi' nowt but a scrat of stuff, eh? Aa'll tell yer what, lad, yer want yer arses kicked, the lot of yers.'

She turned and spoke gently to Aude: 'Aa'll tell you what we'll do, sweetheart, me and you'll look through yer bag and see what yer need, and then we'll go up t' Stanley's shop, and see little Cynthia and get the things we need, eh... How about that?'

Aude smiled at Margaret's kindness, and the lads smiled at Margaret being the same as she always was.

'Just tell Cynthia t' put it down and aa'll sort it out, Margaret,' said Stan helpfully.

'"Just put it down"? Aa'll put you down, yer cheeky little bugger, if yer start wi' that. "Just put it down," ee says. You think on, lad; this bit lass needs her things if she's t' live properly in my house, right.'

'Absolutely, Margaret; that's why we brought her here,' said Stan honestly, but with all the charm he could muster.

'Right. So aa'll be needin' a few other bits and bobs for her bed and what-not, like, just so it's nice fer her. Right.'

'Naturally, Margaret.'

Stan didn't mind her chiselling him for a few things for herself because he knew Aude was in the best place.

'Come on in, sweetheart, aa've got some nice stottie and corned beef hash in there for yer; yer look like yer want for a bit feedin', bless yer. So what time are yers pickin' her up, then?'

'How d'y'know we are, like?' asked Colly unwisely.

'Aa'll tell yer what, lad, if yer weren't so bloody thick, aa'd come over there and give yer a knock. Who the hell would have t' wonder where you's lot'll be on yer first night back, eh? Come on in, Pet, afore aa lose me temper and have t' clip these nuggets.'

She winked at Aude when the lads couldn't see and led her into the house.

'Good job Margaret likes her.'

'Aye.'

'And she's in a good mood.'

'Oh hell, aye.'

'Can yer pick me up about half seven then, Colly and we'll swing round for Order, eh.'

'Half seven it is.'

******

'At last,' said Tommy when Lester told them Colly's van was pulling into the Townley's car park.

The bar was fairly packed and good-natured cheers and whistles went up for Colly and Stan when they came in and stood awkwardly side by side. Word was out and all eyes were on them.

'Well, aa know you'll know by now, so we've brought our new drummer t' see yer,' said Stan.

They stood aside just like they'd rehearsed at Margaret's while they were waiting for Aude to finish her supper.

'This is Order, everybody.'

The volume of the bar dropped from 10 to 2, as brains crashed at the sight of a woman wearing trousers on a Saturday night. Sally came from behind the bar, drying her hands and stuffing the tea towel into her apron pocket.

'Hello, Order, I'm Sally,' and held out her clean red hand.

'Watcha, Sally, Pet,' said Aude, taking it warmly.

The volume hit eleven and Sally laughed with the rest of them as the friendly crowd let her know she belonged there. The introductions started and Aude was absorbed into the life of the locals in her new home.

'Alright, lads.'

'Nessa, Pet, where've yer been? We've been waitin for yer, but Lester said we had t' start without yer.'

'Aye, aye.' She smiled. 'Me mother needed a bit help wi' old Gideon.'

'How's ee doin'?'

As she shook her head to say he was in a bad way, she was made to stop unbuttoning her jacket by the little red face with sparkling black eyes in front of her, holding a hand out to shake. If their hands had been paws it would have been a bunny rabbit meeting a bear.

'I am Aude.'

'Hello, aa'm Nessa.'

Aude took Nessa's hand in both of hers and turned it palm up to feel the calloused hide. She examined it closely, let loose of it and disappeared. Nessa looked at the lads smiling at her. Chucking her coat behind the bench seat on the window wall, she turned to find Aude in front of her again, holding Vern's cracket. Putting it down and hopping on, she put her hands on Nessa's shoulders and kissed her on each cheek twice.

'A double, Nessa, she likes yer,' said Tommy.

She kept her hands on Nessa's shoulders and stood as tall as she could on the stool to look at her. Nessa cast an awkward glance at the lads who were enjoying the show. She put her hands on Nessa's head and let them slip down each side until they came to the bottom of her shoulder length hair, and gently patted it up.

'You have nice hair, Nessa.'

She did the same to her own hair which was about the same length.

'Do you like my hair, Nessa?'

The glance went again to the smiling table.

'Well, aa do, yes, it's very nice.'

'Thank you, Nessa.'

She lifted the pretty pendant on Nessa's new necklace.

'It is very beautiful, Nessa, and the blue is for you in the eyes. It is a lykkeamulett, for the good luck always. Do you like mine, Nessa?'

She lifted it for her.

'Well, aa do, yes, it's very nice, and the silver suits yer.'

'Thank you, Nessa.'

The human bird hopped off the stool, returned it to Vern and disappeared.

'You sit down here, Nessa, Pet and Wilf'll get yer a pint,' said the ever-thoughtful Tommy.

By half eleven, jackets were off, waistcoats were undone and top buttons on blouses were loosened in the packed hot bar of Vulcan Vern. The lads were settled into half a dozen different conversations on their joined-together table, but always switched on to what the others were talking about. Aude's fleeting appearances worked like a magnet to draw them together before she vanished again.

'Oh, hello,' said Tommy in mock surprise, as she sat on Herbie's knee, 'are yer stayin' long enough for Wilfy t' get yer a drink, Pet?'

'No, I am going back now for Joe to feel me.'

No one hearing her even thought of making a smutty remark to get a laugh, as she nipped over to sit between Cissy and smart Alice. With old Joe across from her, sitting beside Valerie and Gina, Cissy stroked Aude's hair back and the lads could see her asking if she was ready. When she nodded, Cissy took her dad's hands and put them to Aude's face. She sat, trying not to smile, as Joe's fingers mapped the features of her face with a gentleness and preciseness of touch only the blind have.

'Now the world's just turned int' a bigger mystery fer me, Pet,' puzzled Joe, 'as t' how such a bonny young lass has ended up wi' these sackless old buggers?'

In the lovely chat it brought from the friends around them, Cissy called Lenny over and pulled him down by the tie to whisper in his ear. He winked to the lads on his way to the piano, while Cissy put Aude's hand in her dad's to lead him to the piano. Smart Alice set a stool for her to sit by him. Lenny played the beautiful big chords that let Joe know it was time to take them to where the mountains of Mourne swept down to the sea, and to tell them of the beautiful, black-haired girl, wearing scarlet ribbons in her hair. He sang to Aude as though she was in his vision, and if ever the words 'beauty' and 'music' meant anything, it was in that tiny piece of time in the Townley Arms that night. The song finished in a perfect moment of emotional silence before the applause lifted to let the night come down once more.

'We'll have t' get her back, it's late now, mind,' said Stan.

'Come on, Order, sweetheart, time fer home.'

'But I am not yet sleepy, Tommy.'

'No, but we'll catch it from Margaret if we don't get yer back when she said.'

'And that's a thing t' avoid, Pet,' put in Wilf.

She smiled:

'Then I will go to save you.'

'Good lass.'

They all got their goodnight kiss and she got loud goodnights from the whole bar as she left with Stan and Colly.

Half an hour later Colly and Stan came back into the bar.

'Yous have been a canny time, mind.'

'Aye, Margaret wasn't happy.'

'So yer had t' wait 'til she'd finished bollockin' yers, then.'

'Oh aye. Here, Nessa, she sent this up.'

'Smells minty.'

'What's it for, Pet?'

'Just a knock, but it stops the ache, like.'

'She knows her stuff does Margaret,' said Tommy, deciding to go on. 'Aye, aa remember the time aa pricked me finger with a boning knife, and the doctor had t' stitch it, but a couple of days later it was up like a black puddin'. Old Mrs Campsell saw it and landed back in the shop wi' Margaret. Anyhow, she has a look and did off for an hour or two, and comes back wi' this yellow paste. And get this, mind, she gets me bonin' knife and as quick as a flash, cuts the stitches and pulls the bloody cut wide open again, oh aye, and starts rammin' this stuff in and then binds the whole finger like a bobbin wi' me jointin' string. Two days of jip that was, but there it is, lad, as good as new...'

He stuck the middle finger of his left hand up.

'... Aye, and, years later, aa was havin' a bit crack wi' this doctor at Doncaster races, and ee said it sounded like the doctor had arsed it up and gangrene had set in, and that she'd more than likely saved more than me finger – me life aa think ee meant.'

'Whey ee didn't mean yer friggin' bass playin'.'

'No. Mind, aa've had t' pay for it ever since, wi' two tubs of potted meat a week, but worth it, eh.'

'Debatable.'

'Aye, aye,' dismissed Wilf. 'So did yers get pumped fer fine detail about Order's night out then?'

'Oh aye, naturally.'

Colly started to laugh:

'It's poor bloody Vern she's after. She says aa've got t' tell yer, Vern; that if she finds out you've been givin' her Bess, "when she's just a bit lass who's never grown up with it", she'll come up here and shove yer pump handle up yer arse.'

'Christ,' moaned Vern.

'Relax, Verny, she knows you were just givin' her shandies,' said Tommy.

'How's that?'

''Cause yer pump handle's still on the bar.'

Chapter 16

'A a'm not gettin' far wi' this stuff, mind.'

Stan looked his questions at Dinsey.

'It's definitely a code, or more like a mixture of different ones. But one thing's for sure, whoever put it together knows what they're about, mind; nowt runs through this, and every time aa think aa'm unravellin' a bit, it just breaks off and aa'm back t' square one. Anyhow, aa've got one bit goin'.'

He looked at Stan seriously. 'It's detail on you lads.'

'On us?'

'Aye, it was yer dates of birth aa stumbled on, and when aa worked off them some other bits came together. Clever stuff this, mind, very bloody clever. Aye, aa found your heights in metric, and they've used symbols for chemical materials t' give the colour of yer eyes, and ancient hieroglyphs t' mark out tattoos and birthmarks and scars and such. Put it this way, Stan, if somebody wanted to, they could find any one of yers wi' this.'

'Christ.'

'Aye, but the real meat's behind that, mind, and aa'm nowhere near it yet.'

'Will yer stick at it, Dinsey?'

'Course aa will, it's drivin' me mad, but aa'm determined to crack the bugger. Mind, aa'm careful t' do it when aa'm on me own, and aa don't think any of you should be lettin' anybody know about this either.'

'Right, keep it hush-hush.'

'Stan, lad, aa think there's somethin' big here, this isn't kids stuff, aa can tell yer that. Yer need t' watch what yer doin'.'

'We will, Dinsey, we will,' said Stan, trying to hide his worry.

******

Stan hung up the phone in the 'Buffs' working men's club.

'H'way then, what's ee say?'

'We're away next Thursda', and yer'll never guess where.'

'North Africa?'

'Sunderland?'

'No, we're away back t' France.'

'Yer jokin'.'

'No, but not where we were before, it's down in the south this time. Ee says the Germans have took it …'

'Took France! Already? Did they invite the fuckers in, then? Maginot line, my arse.'

'By all accounts these Germans know what they're about, mind.'

'Course they do, they did the last time, they only lost 'cause they were fightin' the rest of the friggin' world.'

'Aye, but after what happened the last time, why don't the French know what they're about, eh? Did no bugger think t' say, "just a minute here, lads, ease off tendin' the grapes and let's do a bit soldierin' just in case those bastards come back"? Christ Almighty.'

'Whey, that's what's happened, anyhow. Monty says they've done a deal wi' Hitler and the Germans are only goin' t' occupy the north and leave the south as some kind of zone for some Frenchies t' look after for them. That's where they want us t' go, anyhow, 'cause they reckon there'll be a stack wantin' the Germans out, and yer can understand that.'

'So will we be travellin' around the south of France then?'

'Aye, aa think so, Den, ee didn't say exactly, but it'll be all arranged, no doubt.'

'No doubt. H'way then, Stanley, out with it,' said Tommy, knowing his friend.

'Whey, d'yers not think this might all be a bit awkward for little Order there, and aa suppose for us as well, like, y'know, wi' rooms and things?'

'Like gettin' changed?'

'And washin' smalls?'

'Definitely Duggie's.'

'And what about Wilfy's wind?'

'Aa think yer gettin' it, lads,' sighed Stan.

'It just means we've got t' think about things a bit more, eh.'

'Aye, but yer know fine well it'll be different when we're over there, Tom, and wantin' t' be out havin' a drink and what-not, and what about the lass then, eh? She's still just a bairn really, and aa know we think the world of her, but we're no babysitters.'

'So what d'yer reckon then?'

'Whey, the only thing aa can come up with, is for her t' have a travellin' companion.'

'Christ, Stan, you're not sayin' we're takin' big Margaret?'

'D'yer not think the poor buggers over there'll have enough on wi' the Germans?'

He smiled with them.

'No, there's only one who'd do for me.'

'Nessa.'

'Aye, they seem t' have hit it off, like, and Nessa seems a bit happier in hersel' – she does t' me anyhow.'

Colly laughed.

'Little Order was up takin' Nessa and the colliery lasses some of that apple juice stuff she likes the other day, there, and anyhow, they got her puttin' the empty sacks on the rail for them. Whey, she went back as black as the roads and there was all hell t' pay when Margaret clocked her. Poor Nessa got both barrels again, bless her.'

'Aa would have liked t' have seen that, mind; little Order comin' out the pit.'

They laughed at the thought of it.

'So what's the chances of her mother lettin' her go then, Stan?'

'Whey she wasn't keen at first...'

'So yer've seen Mary then?'

'Aye, just yesterda' afternoon when Nessa was at work. When aa started explainin' about how we're kept from all the trouble, she started t' come round a bit.'

'So she'll let her go?'

'Whey, she was sayin' she wanted Nessa t' do somethin' for hersel', y'know, see a bit life outside Firstwood sort of thing, so aa think she might.'

'And we could see Monty about gettin' her paid, eh.'

'And if they won't, we could divvie a bit off ours for her.'

'Well said, Carter, lad, we're all up fer that,' seconded Den.

'Mind, that doesn't mean we shouldn't press the buggers for her own money though.'

'It doesn't, Colly.' Stan smiled. 'And aa will.'

'So how are yer puttin' it t' her, then?'

'Aa thought mebbees on Sunda' night, a bit later on when it's quiet, eh?'

'Champion. And yer can rely on us t' go steady so we don't put the kyebosh on it for yer, Stan.'

'Ta, lads.'

******

Vern pulled the curtains shut in the bar on Sunday night and ambled off to see if there was anybody left in the lounge.

'All clear,' he reported back, dropping the latch on the front door.

'Anybody for a fresh one?' asked Lenny as he made his way to the bar, picking Tommy's empty glass up on the way.

'Six pints, five rum and blacks, a bottle of Mackeson and a box of matches, Sally, Pet.'

After delivering the drinks, Lenny took his pint over to the piano and softly played heavenly pieces of Beethoven's 9th.

'Is that *Ivory Deeks*?' asked Carter, who'd wandered over to sit beside him.

'No, son, it's a bit before his time.'

'Sounds canny, though.'

'Aye, canny,' smiled Lenny.

'Aa hear yer got a good bullin' off Margaret the other day, Pet,' said Tommy, sitting central on their big table.

'Aye,' said Nessa, 'anyhow, aa saw her this mornin' and she says yer's have got somethin' t' ask.'

'Christ, how the hell does she do it, lad?' said Wilf.

Nessa looked at Stan.

'Well, Pet,' he began uncertainly, 'it turns out we've got a bit of a problem, and we think yer might be able t' help, but only if yer can, like.'

'Aye?'

'Well, we were thinkin' about young Order, there, and it got mentioned about how she's a lass …'

'Oh, there's nowt gets past us, Pet,' said Tommy.

She smiled.

'And we thought,' continued Stan, 'how it might be a bit awkward at times, y'know, with us bein' old cheps and young Carter, there, like what with her havin' t' be on her own, y'know; no room mate, and for gettin' washed and changed and what-not…'

'And Wilfy's wind.'

'… Aye, but, y'know, by hersel', like.'

'What yer sayin', Stan?'

'Ee wants t' know if yer'll come with us t' keep Order company, Pet,' pushed in Tommy.

Stan saw a look of excitement come over her before it vanished like steam.

'Aa can't. Aa can't go the way things are here.'

'Ah, but, hang fire, Pet, yer can if yer want, 'cause Stan's sorted it all out for yer.'

'What d'yer mean?'

'Whey, aa've spoken t' yer mother, sweetheart, and she says she wants yer t' go, if you want to that is, 'cause she thinks it'll be good for yer to get away and do somethin' for yersel', like. And she says she'll be here when yer get back. And we've spoken t' the fella who's our manager and ee's arranged for yer t' get paid.'

'Good money, mind, Pet,' said Colly, 'it'll work out about one thousand two hundred pounds a year, for each year the war's on and we're doin' this stuff.'

'It's fantastic money; enough t' sort yersel' and yer mam out for good, eh,' said Tommy, 'and Duggie and Herbie's been up t' have a word wi' that new deputy of yours and made sure yer job'll still be there when we're finished, if yer want it, that is.'

Nessa smiled at them.

'So are yer comin' then, Pet?'

'Give the lass a bit time t' think it over, Tom. But we want yer t' do it, Pet, and aa know we said it's for Order, and it is, but we'd never want anybody else there with us.'

'And little Order thinks the world of yer, Pet,' added Wilf.

'Speak t' yer mother before yer make yer mind up and let's know as soon as yer sure.'

'Aa will. Margaret says you're away on Thursda' t' the south of France.'

'How the hell does she …'

'We are, Pet,' said Stan.

Nessa left with the eternal beauty Lenny's *Ode to Joy* in her ears, and let it carry her all the way home.

'Looks promisin', Stan,' said Den.

'It does, thank God.'

'Sling another round over, Sally, Pet,' said Tommy, happy the serious bit was over, 'and get one for you and Vern, and come round and have sit down and a bit crack with us. H'way, Wilfy, lad, get these drinks paid for.'

Chapter 17

France

General Drubil sat uncomfortably hot on the soft leather backseat of his open top car. He was scanning the disembarked passengers from the British navy auxiliary ship from Southampton, and counted 13 instead of the expected 12 getting on the private coach to Toulouse. The extra one only added to his growing resentment of what he was having to do to make some anonymous aristocrats even richer.

'Drive on, Gunter.'

The sports car eased along the length of the port, baking in the Bordeaux sun, and drove away to a small café on the outskirts of the town.

'And so we meet again, Montague. Did you enjoy your drive down?'

'I did indeed, Henri. And how are you? Well, I hope.'

'Yes, yes, there are worse places to waste one's time, don't you agree?'

'I do.'

'So, what tit-bit do you have for me to feed to our friend, the Count?'

'Well, we do have a new recruit.'

'So I see.'

'Yes, a sturdy girl, but pleasant and as equally uninquisitive as the rest.'

They smiled.

'But tell me, Montague, what am I to tell him about this book he so desires?'

'Ah, well, there you can assure him I have cast my little book fly all around, but not a nibble as yet. I do believe they know nothing of it, and you can take it from me, Henri, they simply don't have it in them to keep secrets.'

'Do we really have to do this, Montague?'

Drubil smiled unpleasantly at the cigarette case he was opening, lit his cigarette, hung his head back and pushed a thick column of thin blue smoke into the open air.

'So,' he began slowly, 'you don't think Lester Churchwarden, the baritone saxophone player in your band, who drove Bundt around for four months in the sidecar of his Bantam motorbike, may be at all relevant?'

'Ah, now there's a point. Of course we did go there first, I mean, who wouldn't? And we even dismantled the ruddy thing, but to absolutely no avail, a total non-starter, Henri, unlike the nasty motorbike.'

'I see.'

'But believe me, the search goes on.'

'Not for so long, I hope; the Count is very much used to getting what he wants, and I would not like to be the one he chooses to blame for not having his book. Well, no doubt we will speak in Lyon after your little sojourn in Toulouse. Goodbye, Montague. Oh, here, you will need these. Drive on, Gunter.'

Monty stood looking into the dusty buff cloud, holding an envelope the same colour as it.

******

The clapped-out old pied blue Citroen bus trundled through some of the most beautiful countryside ever ignored by human beings. Eight of the band were asleep, four were playing cards, and one was standing at the front trying to talk to the driver about buses. The card players listened to Royston struggle on with the half dozen phrases he'd picked up twenty-odd years ago: two of them were, "how much?", and "can I leave my boots on?", to which the driver had replied: "32 horsepower" and "most passengers do".

Five and a half hours after leaving the port, it crunched over the bone-dry gravel drive of a large detached, red brick house, set in four acres of its own grounds.

'Have yer seen the clip of him?' said Lester.

They folded their cards and watched Monty stalk up to the bus in a light green safari shirt tucked into a pair of short white shorts, with light blue socks pulled up to his knees. Brown sandals, a yellow cravat and a Panama hat completed the outfit.

'Christ, ee's like a cross between a cowboy and a heron.'

'Aa've never seen legs that skinny all the way up.'

'Must be strong enough though; t' carry that packet.'

He greeted them with a genuinely friendly welcome as they stepped stiffly off the sweltering bus, taking Nessa and Aude's hands to his courtly lips. 'Now leave all of those bags and boxes there for now, I've something nice for you around here.'

They followed him around the house to look onto the most lovely country garden they'd ever seen, with a picnic table carefully arranged in the centre of its rich camomile lawn.

'Oh, it is so perfect, Monty.'

'Thank you, Aude, my dear, one does try.'

A gentle breeze blew the red and white chequered tablecloth into a can-can dance along the length of the table, and made every flower seem to jostle to hold up colours that the greatest painters just couldn't quite reach. A thick, high laurel hedge in front of a cedar tree copse screened it all from the collapsing man-made world outside.

'So whose shorts are those yer've got on, then, Mont?'

'There's not some kiddie missin' ee's gym class is there?'

'Gentlemen, I'll have you know these are hand made by my tailor, Mr Roderick, and he assures me they are quite simply the very rage on the riviera.'

'But we're in a back garden tryin' t' have a sausage roll, Mont.'

'Well, I'm pleased you're so taken with them, Wilfred, because I've taken the liberty of having a pair made for each of you as my welcome-back-together present.'

'Seriously?'

'Yes, of course, "seriously", why wouldn't I do something nice for my friends?'

The feeling in his words made them feel a little ashamed of theirs.

'What a lovely thought, isn't it a lovely thought, lads?' rescued Stan.

They kindly said it was.

'But, d'yer not think they're a bit – er, snug, like?'

'Oh, yes, very snug, Thomas, that's the style, you see; you'll like them when they're on.'

'Mebbees when they're on Lenny,' muttered Tommy to make the lads laugh.

'Mind, they look like they've got good sized pockets, Mont.'

'I beg pardon, Wilfred?'

'Just lookin' at the apples yer carryin'.'

'Really,' affected the blushing teen Monty, 'you really are rascals, absolute rascals.'

They sat out smoking and chatting in the warm fresh air, and strolled about the place, and picked through the picnic with tasty delight in the mellow early evening light, until Monty called them together to give them a tour of the house.

'So, is everyone happy with their rooms?'

'Champion, Mont, lad.'

'Good. I kept the room-share allocations the same as Norway, if that's alright, but change if you wish. Now all the boys are on the first floor and the girls are above in the garret. The girls have their own rest room and the boys have two to share…'

'There'll be no rest for us after Wilfy's been in.'

'Well, a little co-ordination perhaps. Now, I do have something I've been hiding, but simply dying to show you.'

'It's nowt t' do wi' shorts, is it?'

'He's hidin' nowt in them.'

'Yer've knocked Lenny off fruit.'

Monty smiled as he led them into the large kitchen and gathered them like a museum guide at the top of some wide stone steps.

'Mind your heads coming down.'

A pull-cord at the bottom lit the place up and showed him how pleasantly shocked they were to see the freshly whitewashed cellar that had been kitted out as a music room, with drums and piano waiting.

'Bloody hell.'

'It's fantastic, Monty.'

'And cool.'

'Yes, I am rather pleased with it,' said Monty.

'So yer should be, Mont.'

'Is there any sticks with the drums up there, Wilf?' asked Stan.

'No need, I have my new sticks, see.'

Aude took them out of her bag and gave them to Tommy.

'They're heavy, mind, for bein' so thin. Where d'yer get these then, Pet?'

'Off Ernie.'

'Old Ernie across from Margaret?'

'Aye,' she went on, slipping into her first full tints of Firstwood, 'he had them for so long ago from Africa when he went there in a war. And, I heard...'

They smiled at the mini-Margaret creeping out.

'... he married a girl called Sambrina, and she died and Ernie had a broken heart and the sticks were for her love of him, and they have charms for good and watch over who will have them.' She laughed and pushed her head back with her folded hands under her chin.

'And yer'll have the names and addresses of all of Sambrina's family, the name of the ship Ernie sailed on, and the Captain's National Assistance number, eh, little Miss Margaret,' said Tommy.

'Yes.' She smiled, giving him a rap on the gut with a drumstick.

He showed her his loaf of a fist to make her laugh as she darted off.

'Christ, that really friggin' hurt.'

'It's what aa keep sayin',' said Carter, 'it's timin' and touch, not power.'

'Whey, yer right, son.'

Once the drum kit had been pulled and pushed, and bits lifted and lowered, the bass pedal thudded with unsettling speed, Lenny picked up the left hand of the nippy *Jelly Roll*. Aude beamed at them as they stood smiling at her, and rolled out the magical pulse of their music as she went swinging in to join him.

'Yer want t' stop them two buggers, Stan, or we'll be redundant,' warned Colly.

'So, did aa hear yer mention somethin' about beer before, Mont?' said Tommy.

Monty smiled and led them back to the living room, where he left them to it so he could get up to his room and start stitching the silk labels from Drubil's dusty envelope into the lining of 26 new pairs of shorts.

The next morning, Tommy and Stan sat comfortably in the living room.

'So is Order out with Nessa, then?' asked Tommy.

'No, she's away up the bakery wi' the cook lass.'

'Madame Brouche.'

'Aye. Nessa's out runnin' wi' Herbie.'

'Aa'm not sure her heart's still in her boxin'.'

'No, but she thinks too much of Herbie t' pack it in.'

'She does, she's a good lass. So where's the rest, then?'

'Duggie, Wilf and Colly are away fishin'...'

'What with?'

'Rods, out of that garage; there's all sorts in there, mind.'

'Monty's room's above that, isn't it?'

'Aye. Lester says there was a light on in there after 3.00 this mornin'.'

'Christ. So where's the rest of them then?'

'Lester and Royston are arsin' about with an old car in there, and Carter's got Den and Lenny downstairs workin' on somethin' for one of the slow numbers.'

'So all present and correct, eh,' said Tommy, standing up to stretch. Pushing his hands up to the ceiling, he angled out a hip, lifted a heel, and farted like an elephant in a rhubarb patch.

'Goodness gracious, Thomas, there could have been flames,' warned Monty, rattling a box of matches as he came in.

They all smiled.

'We were just wonderin', Mont; about what we'll be doin' here, like.'

'Well, to tell the truth, Stanley, this trip is more of an acclimatisation for our main placement, which, by the way, has had to be put back for the time being.'

'Where's that, then?'

'Lyon, and it will be for a longer spell, I'm afraid.'

'How long?'

'About two months, initially, but it may be longer.'

'Christ.'

'Indeed, which is why they're arranging work placements for you when you're there.'

'Jobs?'

'Well, let's say an interesting few hours to break up the long days, but only if you want to. I must say, I think it's a good idea; boredom is not to be sniffed at, and we all know the devil makes work for idle hands.'

'Aye. So when are we off there then?'

'They're keeping an eye on things, but early August has been mentioned.'

'So have we not got much t' do here then?' asked Tommy.

'Oh, yes, quite a lot actually, we've about 12 shows as it stands. You're playing at the ZimZam Club on Saturday; very popular with the bright young things of Toulouse, so I'm told. Alrighty-tighty then, I must be off now if I'm to be back for the great shorts show after dinner, toodle pip.'

'Christ, ee's not goin' t' let them bloody shorts go, is ee?'

'No, we might as well just get it over and done with.'

'Lenny in shorts? Dear God.'

******

'Right,' said Monty, standing in the living room after dinner holding a small hessian bag, 'who would like to be first?'

'For what?'

'Now, now, Dennis, you know what for. Can't you see my bag here?'

'Haven't been able t' stop seein' it since yesterda', Mont.'

'Tut, tut, Wilfred. My bag is to draw the names of who goes and tries my present on, and then return resplendent to give us all a lovely big twirl. Now won't this be 'reet gud fun'?'

They smiled nicely for him trying to speak their English.

'So who would like to draw the first name?' pressed Monty.

'Go on, Lenny, lad, Monty's got ee's bag out for yer.'

Lenny was pushed out of his seat.

'Now, Leonard, in point of fairness, close your eyes for a truly lucky dip.'

Blind Lenny's hand went into the bag Monty held in front of his waistband, and shot back as though he'd been bitten by a snake, making him lash a thick pink link of sausage across the room. It hit Duggie in the face with a wet meaty slap and dropped onto his lap.

'Jesus Christ', was all they heard from Duggie above the laughter that Lenny made louder when he told them he really thought it was Monty's nudger.

'Good one, Monty,' said a few of the lads.

Monty was happy; he felt he was being accepted and he liked it.

'Look away, lasses, it looks like blind Duggie's got little Dug out,' said Wilf.

Everybody looked at the link on his lap and the laugher rose again.

'H'way, Duggie, there's a time and place.'

'Me friggin' eyes are stingin', what the hell did ee throw?'

'Sausisse de porc et oignon,' answered Monty.

'Jesus, the "et oignon" must be ripe,' said Duggie, rubbing his watering eyes with both fists.

'Well how about, by way of apology, we let Douglas decide who goes first?'

'Lenny,' said Duggie.

Lenny smiled and shrugged his shoulders. 'Should aa wait until Duggie Link can see?'

'Aa'll be fine by the time yer wrestle that arse of yours int' them shorts, Lenny, lad.'

Lenny smiled and left to get changed. Strolling in again two minutes later in his socks, vest and new shorts, he managed to disappoint them.

'Whey, they're a good fit; proper shorts, not them stranglers you've got, Mont.'

'I've only gone and got you again, haven't I.'

They could see how happy he was; clapping his hands and giggling like a little girl to infect them with the same good humour.

'I know, I know, I've been on top form tonight, it's in me you see. Oh yes, I was always pranking in my dorm at school, and roundly flogged for it many a time, I can tell you.'

'Aa'll bet.'

'Well, you've got us good and proper, Monty.'

'Just boys together, Stanley. Now how about everyone nip to their rooms for a quick change, and we'll all come back for a few shorts in shorts, ay.'

They did and all landed back in the living room in their comfortable new shorts.

'Nice material, mind, Monty, lovely and smooth when they're on,' said Colly.

'Mr Roderick knows ee's stuff, eh, Mont?'

'Oh yes, he is a very special man.'

'Whey, aa think ee's made a mistake readin' my chart, 'cause these are nippin' a bit.'

'I hate to say it, Thomas, but I'm afraid you may have put on ...'

'Aye, aye, mebbees an ounce or two wi' not graftin' so much these days, but aa'll bet ee's just scrimped on material.'

'Tommy, lad, there's enough material there for a couple of scout tents.'

'Only for the ten kiddies in each, mind,' added Wilf.

'Worry not, Thomas, we'll trim you up with healthy living over here.'

'It's Denny's aa'm worried about,' said Wilf, 'it looks like ee's got a bloody hernia the way somethin's layin' in there.'

They all stared at him when he came back from the toilet. He checked his fly.

'What?'

'Nowt, Denny, lad, just lookin' at the cut of yer shorts.'

'And wonderin' where yer won that coconut.'

The evening passed pleasantly. Royston had fixed a dartboard he'd found in the garage on the living room wall, and four teams were playing a round-robin of very competitive doubles. A welcome break in the game came with Herbie and Lester bringing in a mountain of buttered toast and two big pots of fresh coffee for a late snack.

'No milk and sugar, Herb?'

Herbie lifted a finger and went back to the kitchen.

'The lasses are missin' a nice bit crack gettin' t' bed early, eh.'

'Aye, but they did look tired, mind.'

The whole contented quiet feeling of them all being nicely settled to enjoy the lovely tastes and smells of the coffee and toast in the soft, warm gaslight of their new home, was violently shattered by a loud slamming bang – as if a paving slab had hit the front door. Before anybody moved to see what it was, four men in black uniforms and pill-box caps were pointing revolvers at them. Monty stood up, bringing the leader forward to push his gun to an inch of his forehead.

'Can I help you, Captain ...?' inquired Monty in fluent French, and with charming courtesy.

Instead of the Captain's name, he got a well-practised nasty smirk that irritated him.

'Vous tous dehors. Dehors. Stand up!' demanded the Captain.

Nobody moved. The guns became agitated: instead of the cowering fear they were used to seeing, they saw 11 pairs of eyes look steadily into theirs. It cut the elastic on the malignant smiles stretched behind the barrels, and Monty raised a finger to tell the band to remain still.

'I'm afraid there appears to be some mistake here, Captain ...?'

Again the invitation to give his name was rudely rejected.

'Well then,' continued Monty politely, 'may I suggest you take a moment to look at these, please.'

'And why would I want to look at anything from a ridiculous British spy like you, or from any of these other dead men?'

With total disregard for the gun tracking his temple, Monty picked up his hessian bag and unzipped a side pocket.

'Oh, just something that might keep you alive, Captain,' he said with unnerving composure. 'Now, I'm sure you recognise the name written here, but if I could just draw your attention to the name of the commanding officer on the next page, just here, and now this one: I'm sure you will know the name, but will not have seen the signature; well this is it, and yes it is his signature.'

Monty enjoyed the damp fear seeping from the Captain.

'Now, if you don't mind, would you please replace your guns before you leave us, thank you.'

'I am so very …'

'I'll just stop you there, Captain. On whose orders have you come here tonight?'

There was no reply.

'I see. Then may I ask who it is you thought to impress?'

There was no reply.

'I see. I'll mention it to the first name I showed you.'

The Captain's eyes flashed and Monty smiled his satisfaction.

'You need to leave now.'

They filed out to jeers wishing them "bonsoir filles". Monty followed them to the kicked-in front door.

'There is just one thing, Captain, I really must have your name.'

'Lavat.'

'Goodbye, Mr Lavat,' he said with understated menace.

Back in the room, he calmly replaced his papers.

'What the fuck was that?'

'A silly thing, Wilfred, something that never should have happened; a stupid action by a stupid man, and a thuggish one at that, thinking he could do something he couldn't. We have permission to be here, you see.'

'And he didn't know?'

'No, but he will.'

'Christ, aa thought that one on the end was goin' t' have a go when Duggie spat ee's bit baccy at him.'

The lads laughed and Duggie let the pencil stretch.

'Mind yer a nervy bugger, Mont.'

'I beg pardon, Dennis?'

'Ee means you've got a bit about yer, Mont; yer not frightened by little bits of things, like a gun t' the head.'

'Well, I have been known to cut up rough,' he minced.

They laughed with him.

*****

Four hours later a surgeon in the Saint Simon general hospital in Toulouse stood looking at the ferociously beaten body of Captain Lavat lying on his operating table. He couldn't decide where to start; whether to extract the front teeth so they could remove the snooker ball forced into his mouth, or to turn him over and remove the courgette that had been hammered into his rectum. He decided to turn him over.

'Dear me, the lengths these gardeners will go to win 'best in show',' said the witty surgeon holding the courgette.

'It does not become you, Dr Mosca, to joke about the violence and harm this man has suffered.'

'No, of course not, Antoine, you are right, it is no joking matter. Did you ask the police where the attackers got it?'

'Sorry?'

'It's just that they seem to have found a cracking greengrocer, even though you wouldn't get many of those to the kilo. Perhaps I'll try the one beside the billiard hall.'

Chapter 18

'They reckon there's thousands been killed on the beaches.'

'Whey, there will be if the poor buggers are just sittin' there.'

'How come they can't get them away in some navy ships, for Christ's sake?'

'Very awkward planning around a logistical nightmare, I'd imagine,' offered Monty.

'More like a piss-up in a brewery,' offered Tommy.

'Indeed, and that may be nearer the mark in this case, sadly... Oh, I say, what do we have here, Douglas?'

Duggie had wandered into the living room in his skimpy brown trunks with their snappy white belt.

'Just in fer the sun oil; it's a scorcher out there.'

'You gave me quite a start there, Douglas, I thought I'd glimpsed the muzzle of a grizzly bear.'

The lads laughed.

'Would you like me to rub a little oil on your back, Douglas?'

'No, yer alright, Monty, Madame Brouche's waitin' t' give it a go.'

He winked at Tommy and Lenny, and made a sharp exit.

'Douglas has a very athletic build, don't you think?'

'Aye, ee's not very big, but what's there's all meat and muscle.'

'And do you think that's from working down the coal mine?'

'Whey, it doesn't hurt.'

'And am I right in saying Herbert, Dennis, Wilfred and Carter are also coal miners?'

'Aye, but yer just say 'pitmen', Mont. And Colly was until a few years back, and ... er, aye, a canny few.'

'And me, Monty,' said Lenny. 'Tommy's tryin' t' say aa was a pitman as well, but aa couldn't do it anymore – when we got back from France, like – aa couldn't go back down anymore.'

Tommy gripped Lenny's knee and squeezed it to make him twist and laugh.

'Days long gone, Leonardo, bonny lad, long gone. H'way, then, let's away outside and soak that sunshine up wi' grizzly Dug.'

Monty smiled at Tommy's kind-hearted distraction tactic and decided to help him out.

'So,' he began, winking at Lenny, 'will your shirt be coming off, Thomas?'

'No, no, aa'd best leave it on, Mont; aa'm not wantin' t' deflate the lads wi' me picture of manhood in the flesh.'

He clapped both hands on the barrel of his gut and rolled his sleeves up past the elbows.

'It's just I was thinking, a bigger bottle of oil, perhaps.'

'Harsh, Monty, lad, harsh. Now aa'll need a glass of somethin' t' heal that cut.'

They headed out into the garden where nature seemed to be doing everything it could to show them what life should be like; even the thick high hedge stopped them thinking about the horror beyond it.

'Would somebody ask that Greek God layin' on the deck chair, where Stan is?' said Tommy in full voice.

The little, bald, red, sweaty, pot-bellied God on the deck chair smiled.

'Bloody hell, Stan, lad, aa didn't recognise yer there in that bronzed condition.'

'Tell him t' lay down, Stan; ee's throwin' a hell of a lot of shade over here.'

Tommy lay down on the grass beside Stan. Stan knew his lazy Sunday was over.

'How come aa'm thinkin' of Moby Dick?' asked Colly, looking at Tommy.

'Aa think Madame Brouche might be thinkin' the same thing over there, mind,' said Wilf.

'Where the hell did ee get them trunks anyhow?'

'Out of that catalogue Stan gave him.'

'Stanley, Stanley, Stanley, always in the thick of it, lad.'

'You wouldn't happen to have a spare copy handy, Stanley?' asked Monty.

Two minutes later Stan was struggling to collapse his deck chair to move it away from the industrial snoring lying beside it.

Enough of the heat of the day had stayed behind to let a sultry evening bring them outside for their late dinner. The smell of the kitchen in the garden was gorgeous.

'So how have you managed to press poor Herbert into cookhouse duties again then?'

'None needed, Mont, ee likes cookin'.'

Tommy set the carving knife to work as tureens of potatoes, carrots and green beans circulated until they were empty. For a little while the glass and china birdsong was all that could be heard clinking from the table, before the rising accompaniment of quiet conversation. In due course it was silenced by Nessa and Herbie bringing a wide white dish and two steel jugs from the kitchen.

'It's not, is it?'

Nessa smiled, and a full-bodied cheer went up for Herbie's jam and apple sponge with custard.

'Herbert, lad, when aa'm standin' at the pearly gates havin' a bit crack wi' St Peter and ee's sayin', "please, Tommy, please come in, lad, we need angels like you up here", aa'll say, "Peter, son, if we're havin' Herbie's sponge and custard on Sunda's, aa'll join, but if yer not, yer can lock that gate, and aa'll away downstairs wi' Duggie and Wilf".'

The corks popped, laughter gathered, and the chatter began to lift to make some part of every one of them know they were in a perfect place.

'Now, what have I got in my bag tonight, gentlemen and ladies?'

'Christ, not ee's bag, again.'

'Yes, yes, my little bag of tricks…'

'Little?'

'… Now would anyone like to try their hand for a nice surprise?'

'Go on, Lenny, lad, you're the expert.'

Lenny smiled and shrugged his shoulders. Monty held the bag for him the same as before.

'Do aa have t' close me eyes again, Monty?'

Duggie crawled under the table to make them laugh.

'No, not this time, Leonard, just dive in and tell us what you find.'

'Balls, Monty, smooth, heavy ones.'

'There's not a hole in that bag, is there, Len?'

The happy Monty held up a shiny steel ball, and had them follow him to the crumbling dolomite path at the top of the lawn. He dropped a white ball about 15 feet from them and gave Duggie and Wilf four steel balls each.

'Now, we take turns to see who can throw their balls closest to the white one.'

'French quoits, eh,' said Wilf.

Duggie pitched the first ball an inch from the white, only to see it kicked five feet away.

'Bollocks t' that. We want t' be playin' on the grass there, Mont.'

'No, no, Douglas, that's the point, you see, the game is to negotiate the lumps and bumps; you've to work out where to pitch to get to the white. And you can bash one off against one of Wilfred's balls if you want to.'

'Christ.'

'Fair enough.'

'Now your turn, Wilfred.'

Wilf tried to be clever and pitched beside Duggie's for it to kick back across. It kicked six feet the other way to make them all laugh. By half past ten they were just about playing in the dark, completely hooked on boules, with teams and round-robins formed into a match-play petanque league, with a cup, prizes and a cash bonus for the top scorer.

******

'Are yer sure there's no turps or 'owt that'll do it, Roy?' asked Tommy, looking at the bright red fingernails Aude had painted when he was asleep on the lawn.

'Not a drop,' lied Roy.

'What the hell is it, anyhow?'

'Jeplac.'

Royston knew because he'd given her it.

'Jeplac. Christ, how long will it take t' wear off?'

'Not long; a week or two.'

'Two weeks! We're playin' this Saturda'.'

'Nobody'll notice, Tom.'

'Not notice? Aa'm playin' the bloody bass, Roy; standin' on a stage wi' one hand in the air, and lit up by a bloody spotlight, aa think one or two in there might notice, eh.'

Royston couldn't hold it any longer and had to laugh, and so did Tommy.

'That little bugger. Mind, if one of Monty's lot comes and gets me, tell him t' be gentle, eh.'

'Aa will, Tommy, lad, aa will,' said Roy, wondering when to tell him about the gallon of turps in the garage.

******

'Ah, here they are. And what have you two been doing up there?'

'Just in for me constitutional, but Madame Fifi there's been washin' ee's nails.'

'And well worth it too, such a lovely vermillion, Thomas. Now, while we're all together, it's wash day, so remember to leave your washing out for Madame Brouche to collect before we go. May I suggest you wear your spare shorts over your bathers while the others go to the laundry.'

'Aye. When's the bus comin', Mont?'

'Half an hour, and we'll all be beside the seaside in two.'

'Champion.'

Chapter 19

'Four bloody days, and aa'm still droppin' sand out the crack of me arse,' complained Tommy, in the cramped changing room of the *Chatte Chaude* nightclub.

'Goodness gracious, Thomas, I do hope no one was thinking of using that towel,' said Monty, entering the room.

'It's that bloody sand, Mont, it's lodged.'

'It's lost, not lodged.'

'And I see you've removed your fetching nail colour.'

'Aye, Roy found a drop of turps just before we came away.'

Tommy looked at his finger ends, unaware of the smiles around him.

'Christ, it looks like aa've been hangin' from a ledge for two or three hours.'

'Never mind Fifi's nails, how's it lookin' out there, Mont?'

'Very good. It is absolutely cram-packed, gentlemen. Is Aude upstairs?'

'Aye, she's with Nessa and Madame Brouche.'

Nessa knocked and asked if they were ready. Monty wished them good luck and left to take Madame Brouche to their table, closing the dressing room door behind him. Aude started drumming on it until Tommy opened it, smiling.

'Once those sticks are in your hands, yer little bugger, yer after trouble.'

She continued drumming on his gut and made the three of them laugh.

'What have yer done with yer hair?' he asked, while Nessa was fixing his bow tie.

Aude stopped drumming and gave him a twirl. 'Madame Brouche has put it more up for me to be as a man in the band as well.'

He saw how confident and happy she looked.

'Do you like my hair, Tommy?'

'Aa do, sweetheart, it really suits yer. Hang on, Pet.'

He dipped back inside to tell them to make a fuss about it. When they came out, immaculate in their white tuxedos and black bow ties, they all did and made her smile and say thank you to each of them by name. It made them think of Norway. Tommy came out last, fastening the button on his tux, and nodded for her to go in front. She stretched up to hug and kiss Nessa and skipped off to catch the others.

'Are yer comin' t' the side of the stage, Pet?'

'Aye.'

'Good lass. Aa'll get some drinks shipped over, eh.'

She smiled and looked as if she wanted to say something. Tommy stood quietly and looked at her. She could see his kind old eyes searching to see if she was all right. She smiled and he did what he didn't often do; he put his arms around her and kissed her cheek.

'You're always our special lass, Nessa, and there's nowt can ever change that, sweetheart; your happiness is the only thing that matters t' us.'

He rubbed her shoulder and they looked what they wanted each other to know. She smiled a more relaxed smile and kissed him with her heart.

Den was first back into the changing room at half time and took a bottle from the two crates of beer waiting for them.

'Christ, it's hot up there, lad.'

'Aye, but mind, it sounds fantastic, doesn't it, lads,' beamed Carter.

'It does, son, it really does,' said Stan, who never tired of Carter's love of music.

'And Order and the rhythm lads are pushin' it on a treat, eh.'

'They are, son, and aa think we're doin' a canny job keepin' up.'

'Oh you are, Stanley, you most certainly are,' said Monty coming in. 'I think you sound like the very 'swing cats', and you must be lighting up the whole mood of France. There's no doubt everyone out there loves you: I've been mingling, you see, and picked up one or two little things.'

'Old habits, eh, Mont.'

'Now, now, Colin. Yes, the best band they've had here is the Consensus, and knowing you're English can only mean they accept you. Gentlemen and ladies, a toast to a plan working.'

He raised his glass and the hot, sweaty players drank their beer all the same.

'Do you know, I think you've turned me to swing.'

'Oh, aa think somebody got there before us, Mont, lad.'

'Tut, tut, Dennis. Well, I must return to the heaving throng once more, and I'll tell you all the good things I hear on the way home.'

'Five minutes, Messieurs,' was called outside.

'Champion, time for another. D'yer want some more lemonade, Order, Pet?'

***

******

'But how much longer, though?'

'Aa don't know, Tom, how can aa know? It's just a case of havin' t' wait.'

'But for how long though?'

'Ee's got a point, Stan, we've been sittin' here for well over an hour now.'

'Aa know, but what can we do? It's a hell of a long way back and we can't just leave him.'

'Whey, should we go and look for him then?'

'Where though? Ee could be anywhere.'

'Aye, but ee could be in trouble.'

'What the hell time is it anyway, Lester?'

'3.00, but it could be a few minutes ...'

'Aye, aye, so about quarter past, then. Stan, aa think we might have t' just get back and see about gettin' some help here, mind.'

'That's a point: what if 'owt did happen to him, what are we supposed t' do, y'know, who to get in touch with and that sort of thing?'

'Aa don't know, Wilf, but yer right, we should get somethin' sorted out.'

'There ee is,' said Lester.

They could see Monty staggering down the street with the help of the buildings, and saw him fall like a rag doll in an open doorway. Duggie and Wilf were first to him and turned him on his back. His dead eyes opened and he tried to speak but couldn't, they closed again and his head rolled to one side.

'Get him up, lads,' said Wilf.

'We'll have t' get him to hospital,' said Lenny.

'No, we can't; ee made me promise if 'owt like this happened, we wouldn't take him,' said Stan.

'Why the hell not?'

'Aa don't know, but ee's right, lads, ee told us both that,' said Wilf.

Herbie carried him onto the bus. Raymond, the driver, calmly accepted the emergency and put his foot down. Grinding to a noisy emergency stop on the gravel, he sat still in his cab to let them get Monty out and into the house as quickly as possible. He tapped Wilf on the arm and put a small glass tube in his hand, gesturing to make Monty drink it all. Wilf nodded and ran into the awakening light-life of the house.

'Hub-bye, lads, hub-bye.'

'What? Hang fire there, Wilf, what the hell's that?'

'It's off Raymond.'

'But it could be 'owt for Christ's sake.'

'Give him it, Wilf,' said Stan.

They watched for the eternity it took for their anxious silence to pass through the four long minutes into the fifth that released a change in Monty's breathing. Slowly, each breath stepped further out of the shallows, while Madame Brouche wiped his bloodless face with a wet cloth every time she blinked herself out of her worry. It was 20 minutes before the lids lifted on his scary looking broken doll's eyes.

'Hello, Hilda,' he whispered, 'and how are you liking your first time out, ay? I was your age once, in Russia, you know. Yes, well,

well, yes, the shorts, of course ...'

'Ee's alright,' said Wilf with a smile that sent the green light to let them feel the relief they didn't want to show.

'Chuck a blanket on him, Hilda, Pet, and Herbie'll carry him to his room,' offered the ever-helpful Tommy.

******

'I'm truly sorry, Hilda, if I have compromised you. How do you feel about your position here now? Have I spoiled it?'

'No, sir, in fact it seems to have worked in our favour.'

'Go on.'

'In terms of my acceptance; they're having fun calling me Hilda, and some do seem to be more ... well, rather less reserved than they have been.'

'I see. And no one saw you inject me on the bus.'

'No, and Derek gave them the prop cure.'

'Good.'

'What do you think it was, sir?'

'I'd say the sodium thiopental they're so keen on these days. But never mind, I'll look to that. And for yourself, you're sure you can stay with this?'

'Yes, sir.'

'Good girl. By the way, that was very nice soup, thank you.'

Hilda Clegg, a French teacher from Pontefract, left his room with the empty bowl on the obviously paraded lunch tray, and headed to see Derek Duggan, the special forces commando posing as Raymond, the handyman driver.

******

'Here ee is,' said Tommy loudly.

Monty smiled at the comfortable, happy band as he strolled into the living room on Sunday night, and squeezed onto the big chair beside Stan. He lazily sorted out the folds on his silk smoking jacket, as he steered his way through their questions with an ease that effectively dismantled any suspicion or alarm. He calmly convinced them his Martini must have been spiked by mistake.

'Lucky in the end though, Mont.'

'How so, Wilfred?'

'That Raymond had some of that special stuff.'

'Oh? Did he give you a little glass vial by any chance?'

'Aye, just that.'

'Ah, yes.' He smiled. 'It's what the locals call pee-pee; little more than sugar syrup really, but they swear by it for what we'll call over-indulgence.'

'It looked like you'd have died without it, mind.'

'No, no, Wilfred, comatose for a while longer perhaps, and with a much more disastrous headache to greet me, no doubt, but no more.'

He brushed cigarette ash off his robe to imply the everydayness of a spiked nightclub drink, and knew he had them accept it.

'Anyhow, aa don't mean t' be nasty or 'owt, Monty, but what if somethin' did happen to you, y'know, what would we do then, like?'

'Well, Stanley.' Monty smiled nicely. 'If ever such a situation should arise, you'd never be left alone, I can assure you of that.'

'How though?'

'Well, because you are involved with people who are very good at what they do. I can't say more than that, you understand, but you are in very safe hands, and if you weren't then I, Montague Arthur Kennilworth Elvin, would not be here; I'd have no part of it, you see. Now, let me change the subject and talk to you about going home.'

The simple tactic worked a treat and any thoughts of them standing on the cold thin ice of very deep trouble, comfortably slipped back onto the thick warm hearthrug of home.

'Is it not gettin' t' be risky for us travellin' about these days, Mont?'

'Yes, it is, Colin, very risky, so two things will be happening. The first is to cut the amount of it, which will mean extended placements...'

They nodded.

'... and the second is to vary the way we travel. We can't assume it's safe to sail back because we sailed here.'

'But we'll have to, Mont; Tommy'll never make the swim.'

'No one needs to swim, Dennis … when we can fly.'

Aude screamed playfully and clapped her hands in the background hubbub about flight, height, fright and excitement.

'When's this then, Mont?'

'Tomorrow.'

'Tomorro'?'

'Yes.' He smiled. 'So we need to be up and at it. I did of course try for a more civilised hour, but they insisted we leave at 11.00 in the am.'

'The wicked buggers.'

'My thoughts exactly, Wilfred.'

'Monty, er...'

'Yes, Royston,' he said, winking at Tommy, 'but before you go on, could I ask a little favour of you?'

'Aye, aye, Mont, lad,' was the disappointed reply, thinking he'd missed his chance to ask for the favour he wanted.

'Well, I was wondering if you'd be so good as to spend an hour with one of the flight engineers, and have a good look at the engines before we take off...'

Roy jumped to his feet and put his hands on his head. 'D'yer mean it, Mont, really?'

'I do, Royston, I do.'

Monty glowed in the middle of the noisy cheers for Roy being given just about the closest thing to his heart's desire – and they liked Monty all the more for it.

Chapter 20

B y quarter to 11.00 the bus was packed with suitcases, instruments and large paper carrier bags filled with a very wide selection of things they honestly thought would be nice presents. Everyone was in the house saying goodbye to the tearful Madame Brouche, who was touched by the large flat present they'd wrapped in brown paper and tied with string for her. Monty translated she had to open it before they went. Tearing away the paper, she hid her happy face in her hands as Roy turned the life-sized photo of Duggie in his trunks around for them all to see.

'Now that's for yer mantelpiece, Hilda, Pet; to remind yer t' keep yer coal scuttle full.'

'Good job she doesn't speak English.'

'Oh, I think she may have an inkling of the import this time, Stanley.' Monty smiled.

She could see Duggie had no idea about the picture, and gave him a hug. Ten minutes later, with the others watching from the bus, Monty and Hilda shook hands and kissed each other in the customary French way, before he hopped on to let it crunch away with plenty of tooting and waving. They watched their lovely red brick house shrink in the sun.

'H'way then, Monty, how many hours will we be sweatin' our bricks off on this bloody thing, then?'

'None, Thomas, we're here.'

They all looked their surprise at each other just before the sudden bouncing began. Through the shaky front window they could see they were driving across a baked brown field towards what looked like a toy aeroplane at the end.

'And here we are,' announced Monty. 'Now, the aircrew will load your stuff, which will take a little while, so stretch your legs and attend to nature, perhaps down by the river; and have no fear, I'll come for you in plenty of time, once I've managed to ease Royston away from the heavy pistons those handsome mechanics will be showing him.'

'Christ.'

******

'There, all done, that's everyone in, very good. Now everything's arranged for when you land…'

'You're not comin', Mont?'

'Not just yet, Stanley, a day or two more for me here.'

'A few bits and bobs, eh?'

'Exactly, Dennis. Yes, as I say, there will be a bus waiting to take you home when you land, so just tell the driver where to go and he'll be happy to oblige.'

'So where are we landin' then, Mont?'

'Oh, goodness me, they don't tell me things like that, but it will only be about an hour on the bus. Now have a wonderful time and enjoy yourselves, and don't do anything I wouldn't do.'

Happy to have their jokey cracks coming his way, he wished them bon voyage and stood down to let a mechanic shut the door. When the second of the two propellers finished coughing up its choking black smoke, and start spinning for joy in the fresh air, the plane pulled forward. They could see Monty and Raymond waving after them until they were lost to the shuddering speed making them close their eyes to a fairground effect way beyond anything they could have imagined.

******

At seven o'clock on the morning after their flight, Tommy stood in his navy blue and white striped apron, flashing a large wide blade around a sharpening steel as only a butcher of 40 years could. The loud clattering knock on the shop door made him smile when he saw big Margaret standing in the early morning sunshine with her arms folded. He turned his open/closed sign and let her in.

'Mornin', Margaret, Pet, are yer desperate for me sausage?'

Despite herself, and having heard the same old line for as long as he'd been sharpening his knife, she couldn't help but smile. She liked Tommy.

'Are you bloody desperate for my hand around your ear?'

He laughed. He liked Margaret.

'So is the little 'un havin' a lie in, then?'

'Whey not likely, she's up wi' me. Good little thing she is; done the toast this mornin' and took some over fer Ernie. She's away up t' Nessa's there, they've got some bits of things for the lasses in the coal yard.'

Margaret ran her finger and thumb carelessly around the curve of her present. 'Is young Billy out back, there?'

'No, no, aa've given him a shift off; just t' keep me hand in, like. So d'yer like it, Pet?'

'Eh?'

'The necklace?'

'Oh this, aye, aye, it's a canny bit thing, but aa'd told her not t' be spendin' 'owt on me. What the hell are yer grinnin' at now, lad?'

'No, nowt, it's just she must've took no notice, mind.'

He could see she had no idea what he was talking about so he went on. 'Yer necklace is pure gold, Pet, 24 carat. She said aa hadn't t' tell yer, but it cost a fortune, and that was with Colly workin' on the jeweller. Have yer felt the weight of it?'

She nodded her mild shock and he smiled.

'And, the little bugger made the jeweller change the catch on it.'

'That'll be fer me big hands. Christ, aa'll have t' get it off and put away.'

'No, Pet,' he said good-naturedly, 'it had nowt t' do wi' yer hands, and the last thing she wants is for yer t' take it off – she wanted yer t' leave it on all the time and the strong clasp's only there t' stop it snappin' or 'owt. And don't tell her aa told yer, but she liked that yer might think of her when yer looked at it.'

He saw her sharp old grey eyes go shiny and the heavy fingers touch the golden band gently this time.

'So yer've got t' leave it on, Pet, or yer'll be in trouble, and she's a fiery little bugger wi' them drumsticks, mind.'

He could see she was trying to smile but was struggling with the kindness she'd been shown. The clasp was never opened again.

'Anyhow, what brings yer up so early, apart from wantin' t' glimpse me figure of manhood?'

The characteristic sneer was enough to let him know she was back to herself.

'And, jokin' apart, mind, there's supposed t' be all kinds comin' wi' this rationin', so try and get a bit stock in if yer can.'

'Aye, aye, we'll manage, son.'

He had no doubt she would.

'Aa'm up t' tell yer there's been a few knockin' about the last few days askin' about yers. Aye, and they've been in the Townley. Mind, they've got no bloody chance of gettin' 'owt out of Vern; ee's a numb bugger is Vern … aa tell yer what, lad! If yer don't stop standin' there grinnin' like a Cheshire cat when aa tryin' t' put yer right, aa'll come round there and knock some bloody sense int' yer.'

He did all he could not to think of Vern and look told off.

'Aa haven't got time t' be standin' round flappin' and gabbin' on, so d'yer want t' hear or not?'

'Aa do, Pet, aa'm sorry, aa must still be half asleep.'

'Half a bloody nugget, more like. It'll be all down t' this foreign malarkey and bloody aeroplanes t' Richmond …'

'How the hell d'yer…?'

'Never you mind, but wake up and use the bit brains yer've got in there, 'cause there's a need here, Tommy, son, aa can tell yer, there's a rabbit off.'

He knew when Margaret was serious.

'So are yer goin' up t' tell Stan?'

'Aa'll tell yer what, lad! Aa'm aa goin' up? Aa've been up, yer sackless sod, and put him right wi' a lot less bother than tryin' t' get through your bloody thick skull.'

He laughed and asked what Stan thought.

'That's fer him t' tell yer, not me,' was her final word. 'Anyhow, by-the-by; the bairn wants yer to come down fer a bit supper one night, so it's up t' you if yer want, aa'm not fussed either way, but it'll make her happy.'

Although she offered as carelessly as she could, Tommy knew she'd have dragged him down if he tried to refuse, which he certainly didn't want to. He told her honestly he'd love it.

'Whey, we're having a bit leek puddin' and stewin' steak on Thursda' if yer about, like.'

He couldn't help but laugh kindly at her and she couldn't help but smile either; they both knew it was his favourite. She left with a couple of free chops and a half of dripping for old Ernie. Tommy called to her at the door and told her truthfully how lovely the necklace looked on her. He saw her eyes say how happy she was to hear it, before his ears told him he was a cheeky bugger who was asking for a clip. He went back to sharpening his knife, thinking different thoughts to the ones he'd been enjoying before opening the door.

Chapter 21

Saturday night.

'Oh, the word's out all right,' said Sally, 'they're all comin' down t' see yers, it'll be a grand night, eh.'

'It will, sweetheart, provided aa don't have t' suffer wi' the hyperclampseemienia around me parched drinkin' tract.'

She smiled her lovely wide smile and asked if he wanted a pint.

'No, no, no… none of that stuff fer me, aa want t' keep me voice clear fer the psalm singin' in the mornin', Pet.'

She laughed and put the pint of Bess she'd already pulled on the bar. He emptied half of it at a swallow.

'Aw, Christ, now look what yer've done, yer like that lass, Eve, wi' the apple; yer've only gone and tempted me away from me close harmony singin'. If that little chaplain comes down aa'll have t' cast yer up fer puttin' temptation in me way, Sally, Pet.'

'So yer'll not be wantin' these other two pints of temptation for those two, then?'

'Whey, seein' as they're pulled, "waste not: want not", as the good book says, and yer might as well top this one up, Pet. Where's Vern, anyhow?'

'Ee's havin' a bath for tonight.'

'Christ, that'll be two already this year and we're just int' July.'

'Ee's just over the moon yers are back, it's quiet now and not the same.'

'Well, we're back now, Pet,' said Stan, coming up to the bar with Wilf, to nip the melancholy bud.

They made their way over to the big table Vern had already pulled together for them, and passed a quiet hour with Den, Carter and Colly before the others started to land.

'So did yer have a good night on Thursda' then, Tom?'

'Aa did, aye. It really was a good night, mind, aa mean, aa knew the grub would be good, but it turned out t' be a really good night. She had Mary and little Cynthia down, and old Ernie was there as well, like.'

'Aye, little Cynthia was as happy as a sand boy yesterda', she couldn't stop talkin' about how much she'd enjoyed hersel', and how you and Margaret kept makin' her laugh wi' yer stories.'

'Aye, it was a good night. Hang on there, lads,' said Tommy, sniffing the air. 'No, it's not Lily of the valley.'

He sniffed the air with more exaggeration. 'Aa think aa'm gettin' a hint of pine forest comin' through... Hello Vern, lad, aa didn't see yer there. And is that your aftershave aa'm smellin'?'

'No, it's what the lasses gave me last night t' put on fer best tonight.'

The scrubbed up landlord stood proud in his new white shirt and collar, and best black waistcoat.

'Mind, that's good of them, eh, Verny.'

'So what's it called then, Vern?'

'Whey, there wasn't a label on the bottle, like, but Alice give me this cuttin' out the catalogue.'

He innocently handed it to Den, who read it loud enough for everybody in the bar to hear: '*An irresistible masculine fragrance to enhance the natural essence of the male. Specially formulated by the finest perfumers in Paris for the man who wants women to know he is ready for attention*'.

'By Christ, Vern, if that stuff kicks in, yer could have yer hands full, eh.'

'Aye,' he said like a gentle child, before Sally called him away to change a barrel.

'What the hell have they given him?'

'God knows. Is our stuff in the van, Colly?'

'Aye, it'll be fine there for now.'

'Christ, get a look at him.'

Walking down the car park in the soft eight o'clock sunshine of the warm summer evening, Duggie challenged the beauty of nature with his yellow pinstripe waistcoat, a shocking pink shirt and tie, and a pair of baggy light blue trousers flapping around the newest of his bright white spats. Herbie was immaculate, like most of the Firstwood men on a Saturday night, in a white shirt and collar, and a sharp dark waistcoat and a tie.

'No, aa'm tellin' yer,' insisted Tommy loudly, 'ee's not wearin' a shirt; that's an inflammation.'

'It's not, it's a pink shirt,' argued Wilf, playing along.

'Get away. Ee's just got a waistcoat on, Herbie must be bringin' him back from the infirmary … Hello Duggie, lad, aa didn't see yer there; aa was just sayin' what a lovely shirt yer've got on.'

Duggie smiled with them and pulled his baccy tin out of his trouser pocket. Herbie pointed his rotating finger at the table.

'If yer insist, Herbert, lad, we'll try one just t' be sociable.'

He smiled and turned to Sally who was already pulling them. The distant drone dawned on them and soon reached its inevitable disruptive pitch.

'One of these days aa'll burn that friggin' bike.'

'Ee's got Roy on the back wi' the other stuff.'

'Champion. Two more, Sally, Pet.'

'Here's the lasses comin' now, look.'

On the path outside the post office a little crowd formed to cross the road.

'Aa see them tight skirts below the knee must be all the rage over here as well then, Stan.'

'Aye, they're tryin' t' save material by all accounts, and gettin' rid of pleats.'

'Wouldn't know about that, Stanley, but by Christ we've got some good-lookin' lasses drinkin' in here, eh.'

'Oh aye: look at Alice; she's like a bloody film star that lass.'

'Nogsey friggin' Bland, can yer credit it?'

'No bugger could.'

'There's Nessa and little Order in the middle, look.'

'Right, lads, brace yersel's.'

The friendly fire began as soon as they came in, and the lads knew fine well it was a battle they were never going to win, but did their best to make a bit of a fight of it. They were slaughtered in two minutes and the victors were happy to lay the lash of their tongues to rest so the cuddles, rubs, pats and kisses could happen. By ten o'clock everything was exactly as everybody thought it should be, and the lads felt as though they'd never been away. The lasses had made sure they watched whenever Vern ventured out from behind the bar, and took turns pretending to be drawn to the sexual magnetism he'd got from the bottle they'd given him, and then snapping out of it, mystified about what had come over them. Each and every time they did it, Vern froze, turned bright red and flummoxed an excuse to get back behind the bar. Everybody in there thought the same: on the whole of God's green earth, it could only be Vern who hadn't the sense to twig what was going on.

'So what's in the bottle, then?' asked Wilf.

'Bed pan cleaner.'

'Eau de colon, eh.'

'It might be worthwhile tippin' a bit on Lenny's stool.'

'Christ.'

The front door bumped open and Colly and Den struggled in with a big cardboard box. They put it in the space cleared for it on their table. Everybody was watching. Cissy was telling old Joe what was happening, and Nessa and Aude were telling the lasses what was coming.

'Ladies and gentlemen of the bar,' said Tommy the barrister, standing with his thumbs in the armholes of his waistcoat. 'From our time away, overseas, answerin' the call of duty t' help wi' the war effort …'

He waited for a dip in the jeers and cracks about paid holidays before going on: 'We've come across a few bits and bobs we thought yers might like as little mementos of our travels…'

'Presents?'

'Aye, Connie, presents, so come up when yer called, but yer've got t' open it for everybody t' see, right.'

'Crack on, Tommy, lad.'

'Right. Now there's only one man can be first; come on, Vernon, lad, come and get yer present.'

As he walked up to the table the lasses looked longingly at him, and fanned their faces as they bit their bottom lips. He looked away and put a concentrated focus on his gift. In the middle of the friendly encouragement, he began to pull the paper gently until he held up a cloth loop in his outstretched arms, and let a large white apron drop from it.

'It's a proper French bar keeper's apron, Vern.'

'Try it on Verny, lad.'

He hooped it over his head and looped the long string tapes right around him to fasten back in front of his belly. He turned to let everybody see and enjoyed the wolf whistles and cracky comments filling the bar.

'So what's the embroidery say then, lads?'

'Well, Vern,' said Tommy to the whole bar, 'yer can see that's yer name, so the top bit says "my name is Vernon", and the bit underneath says "and I am happy to serve you".'

'It's bloody fantastic, lads, thank yous very much, mind, and aa will look after it …'

'No, no, Vern, lad, never mind that, we want yer t' wear it all the time, and use it for what it's made for, eh.'

'Aa will then, but aa'll still look after it, mind.'

'Good lad, Vern.'

Within two minutes everybody in the bar, apart from Vern, knew it said: "My name is Vernon and I have a tiny penis".

'Come on, Sally, Pet, you're next.'

She followed the same friendly path to put her beautiful white frilled mousseline apron on.

'The writin' on yours, Pet, says "My name is Sally and I'm the best barmaid in the world".'

Sally smiled but couldn't help looking for Nessa. Nessa winked to let her relax and beam her happiness at the lads and her lovely apron. The calls were kind and warm as they watched her quietly run her little red hands gently down her new apron as her eyes filled up.

'Poor little bugger,' whispered one of the Susans to Lorry Mallet.

'The bastard'll probably take it off her and sell it for drink.'

'Aye, whey if ee does aa'll make sure it'll be the last time,' promised Little Angela, as she stood to go over and bring Sally back so they could make a fuss and tell her how lovely she looked in it. She got a big hug off all of them, but always squeezed Nessa a little bit tighter.

The rest of the presents were handed out. All the lasses were given a neat little basket full of creams, soaps, perfume, lipsticks, hair pins and silk stockings that Hilda had put together, which they opened and showed and swapped and promised to lend and borrow. Bottles of cognac were passed out to the lads, and cartons of Gitanes were divvied up across the sexes. By the time Vern closed the curtains, the Townley Arms smelled like the Moulin Rouge.

******

Monday night.

Stan could see the concern on their faces that none of them had ever tried to hide from the others. 'Look, lads, aa've got yer up here tonight 'cause there's a couple of things we need t' think about, and t' be honest, aa just want yer t' help me think them through, like.'

This worked to ease them a little, but they stayed quiet.

'Is it locked, Carter, son?'

'Aye, and aa'll stand by the window.'

'Good lad. Right, Dinsey reckons ee's got another bit of them codes cracked in Billy's book; about directions this time.'

'What for?'

'To places. And he followed one and ended up by a wall in Teesdale.' (laughs) 'No, lads, no, think about it; there's hundreds of miles of walls up there, and there must be millions of stones in them, but this code took him t' this one exact stone, mind, and ee got this out of it.'

He showed them a cigarette sized steel tube.

'And this was inside it.'

He showed them a very thin piece of metal foil about two inches wide by three inches long. 'And it's covered wi' more code.'

He passed the tube and metal paper to Tommy sitting beside him.

'Dinsey reckons the book has codes t' these places so that somebody can use them get t' these new ones, and then go on to whatever the hell's at the end of it all.'

'Christ.'

'And ee's got no idea what that is.'

'Aa can't see 'owt on this bit foil, mind.'

'Hold it up t' the light, Wilf, see the tiny holes?'

'Oh aye.'

'So Dinsey thinks the book's the starter key?'

'Some good machine work on this tube, Stan.'

They all looked at Royston and wondered about him.

'How many places has ee found these then?'

'He's only cracked that one, but reckons it could be dozens.'

'So, what are yer sayin' about what we're doin' then, Stan?'

'Whey, aa don't know, Den, aa'm just showin' yer that there's somethin' goin' on we know nowt about.'

They knew he was worried by the sharp reply.

'Aa'm sorry, Den, aa didn't mean t' bite yer head off. But d'yers not think we're gettin' pulled int' somethin' here, like?'

There was an uncomfortable silence and they instinctively looked to Tommy to break it.

'Aa get what yer sayin' about the book and Billy and codes and that,' he began, 'but aa still think yer over-thinkin' it, mind. Aa mean, h'way, Stan, d'yer honestly think anybody in their right mind would think a few pitmen and shopkeepers from Firstwood, are goin' t' be doin' 'owt wi' their secret bloody codes, eh? And it'll just be about them landing places little Geoffrey was on about.'

They could see Stan took the point, even though he didn't look happy about it.

'It seems t' me the only one that's been pulled int' 'owt is Dinsey, poor bugger; ee's the one who's got the book and crackin' codes.'

'Aye, aa said that t' him yesterda' but ee wouldn't have it. Ee says ee's fine and got things sorted, like.'

'Ee will have; ee's no mug.'

'So should we not tell Monty then, Stan?' asked Lenny.

'No. Dinsey says ee's the last person t' say 'owt to, and when yer think about it ee's right, aa mean, one slip from him with some of the people he must mix with and that could be us, and Dinsey, in trouble.'

'And it could get Monty int' trouble as well, like.'

'Yer right, Len, especially if this stuff's as big as Dinsey thinks it is.'

'Aye, but that just says t' me that we need t' keep our mouths shut and go on the way we are, then.'

'Colly,' began Stan, with a sign of exasperation, 'aa'm not sayin' we should stop. What aa'm tryin' t' do is just get yers t' think on it, and not have us runnin' blind int' a full trench.'

They knew he was more worried for them than himself, and tried to help.

'Stanley, yer a little worrier, lad. But d'yer honestly think aa'd go on and let Nessa and little Order get pulled int' somethin' aa thought could hurt them? No, so here's what we're goin' to do t' put yer mind at rest.'

Stan couldn't help but smile with the rest of them as they waited for Tommy's wisdom.

'The first thing is not t' say a peep about that book, right, lads. Right, Lester. The next thing, and t' my mind more important, is that we can't stop doin' what we're doin' and put the sweet little children of Firstwood at risk.'

'Oh aye?' asked Den, knowing there was something coming.

'Whey, aa couldn't face bein' blamed for the nightmares them kiddies would suffer from havin' t' see Monty here lookin' for us in ee's shorts.'

'Christ.'

'What is it, son?' said Stan.

'Just little chaplain Norman headin' back up the path,' said Carter.

Chapter 22

The mood on the bus wasn't good. It was one o'clock in the morning, they were sitting in the middle of a field, and home had pulled hard on the strong strings it had stitched around their lives. Aude was missing Margaret and could still see her standing in the middle of the road, in the faint streetlight, waving after them and using the bottom of her pinny to wipe her eyes. Nessa saw a large tear roll down her cheek and splash on her folded hands. She covered them with one of hers.

'She'll be there waitin' when we get back; it'll not be long.'

Aude wrapped her arms tightly around Nessa's neck and tried not to cry any more.

'Here's the driver back,' said Lester.

Getting them off the bus and leading them over to the plane, he stood with the flight crew and watched the lads stand back to let the lasses get on first. He agreed with the pilot who credited them as being the most gentlemanly lot they'd flown. But, like the pilot, he was blissfully unaware of the real reason for their chivalry, which was nothing more than them taking the last chance to "drop their guts" before being locked in an airtight container for hours. Wilf was last in. Holding either side of the door frame, he squatted back like a Grand National jockey and pushed one through, just as the unlucky bus driver had wandered behind him and caught both barrels.

'God Almighty. I'm no doctor, son, but that's fucking woeful.'

Wilf pulled himself in, smiling. Ten minutes later he was fast asleep and the others were suffocating under his relaxed sphincter. Just before dawn, with the engines switched off, they landed with a bump on the same French field they'd left, and bowled along in juddering silence to the dark little group waiting. When it finally stopped and the door was opened from the outside, the lads insisted Nessa and Aude got off first so the painful pressure of their bottled gas could be let off.

'Good God, Nigel, what is that?' asked the pilot.

'Cattle?'

'Only if they're dead and rotting in a Bombay cesspit.'

'Oh, God, breathe through your mouth, Philip, and get out.'

They jumped from the plane to face their smiling audience.

'That's an absolute fucking disgrace,' snarled the pilot.

The lads laughed and turned back to saying their hellos to Monty and Raymond. Monty approached the flyers, fanning his face, and set about placating them with his usual panache. It didn't quite work this time and he left them with words like 'sewer' and 'animals' cutting past him to reach the ears they were intended for. He tapped his watch as he walked back to press them onto the bus – he felt the flyers were on dangerous ground.

The bus pulled away, leaving the air crew flapping their jackets at the plane as though they were trying to chase away a giant, stinking bird.

The lads laughed and Monty couldn't help but join them. He'd missed them and they were pleased to see him, and they chatted on happily to let each other know until the old blue bus crunched over the bone-dry gravel and hissed to stop in front of their big red house. The sun had lifted just enough light to let them see how gorgeous it all was. Mooching through the rooms, checking the drinks cabinet, the dart board, the boules set and all their other little games and fixtures, they made their way out into the garden. Everything was just as it was, and the lovely noise of quiet nature floated perfectly above the murmur of their chat. The strings from home began to loosen, and the coffee, croissants and kisses from Madame Brouche helped.

'Now just take your suitcases up and have nice little 40 winks before tonight.'

'Tonight?'

'Oh dear, I really must protest. Once again, I'm afraid, your little chaplain fellow appears to have been remiss in communicating what he should have.'

'About what?'

'About being booked for tonight, but let's not dwell on it. Now, tootle off and have sweet little naps and we'll call you for a late dejeuner au soleil. How about that?'

'Champion, Mont, lad, Lenny always says ee loves nowt better than a late dejeuner au soleil.'

'Very good, and I'll put my hand to unloading your instruments while you're asleep.'

'Christ.'

******

Two weeks later.

'But couldn't we just stop here and travel, and just stay there on the nights we play?'

'No, no, it's far too far for that, Thomas; it's over 300 miles and it really would exhaust you, and, well, I fear it would spoil our happy times. Besides, we do have our orders to move, so move we must.'

'So have you been t' the place we're goin', then, Mont?'

'Lyon?'

'No, the new house.'

'Oh goodness me, yes, I chose it.'

'They let you do that?'

'Well, not usually, Stanley. They allocate accommodation as a rule, but the ones they ear-marked for us simply weren't suitable for our needs, and I merely pointed this out, although now I think about it, I was rather bullish ...'

They smiled at him being bullish.

'... which ended in them telling me, rather rudely I thought, to find something myself. So I jolly well did, and insisted they undertake the necessary alterations I saw fit. And, I can tell you, we've an absolute peach, the 'bee's knees' as Carter would say. And guess what? Madame Brouche, or should I say, Madame Hilda, and Raymond, have made arrangements with their employers to come with us. How about that?'

'Sounds tip-top, Mont. So, when are we off?

'Well, it's a long drive, about six hours with a following wind, and to do it in the heat of the day would be quite unbearable, so better travel in the cool of the night and maybe even sleep the journey away, ay? I've arranged for Raymond to be ready for us at that most ungodly of hours: 3.00.'

'Fair enough. But we will be comin' back here again though, won't we?'

'Oh, yes, of course, Thomas, on that you can be sure. So, have a lovely restful day while I attend to matters pressing. Ta-ta for now.'

The day passed quickly with them happy to be doing just what they liked best. Wilf, Colly and Duggie went fishing and came back with half a dozen big brown trout for Madame Brouche and Herbie to cook outside for their dinner in the garden. It was perfect enough to make the evening carry a pleasant sadness from knowing they'd soon be packing to leave.

Chapter 23

The welcome cool of the night was being squeezed out of the bus by the strengthening heat of the day, even though the little sliding windows and open passenger door were doing all they could to hold onto it. At about half past ten, Monty called their attention to a picturesque little village nestled at the bottom of high rising hills, and told Raymond to pull over.

'It's called Lavage sur Rhone, and it's our new home.'

'Looks bonny, Mont.'

'It is, yes, very bonny, Carter. Now it's about another six miles to Lyon itself, which is a big city, not that much smaller than Paris really, so have a good look about you as we drive on, and try to get your bearings with roads and houses and the like. Onwards, Raymond, please.'

Struggling around a tight turn onto a narrow, rutted track, they bumped along until they came to a wall of conifer hedge. Monty got off and disappeared into it for a minute before hopping back onto the bottom step for Raymond to drive on through the hidden heavy iron gates Monty had opened. They rolled along a dusty driveway bending through the mangled trees of an untended cherry orchard, and stopped again at another set of gates built into an imposing, high grey stone wall. These ones were newer and opened easily for Monty to let Raymond pull inside and park up.

'Alrighty, everyone off and bring only what you can lay your hand on,' said Monty. 'My, my, we do have some stiff old bones this morning.'

'It's just the cut of these shorts, Mont.'

'Dear me, Wilfred, and we're barely in the grounds. Now follow me and I'll show you all the lovely things we've got for ourselves in our very own petite Chateau.'

They headed past the screening laurel bushes and saw what he was holding out his hand to show them.

'Christ, it's like a little castle,' said Carter.

Tommy, Wilf, Lester and Stan walked behind Lenny, who was having trouble with his shorts. Each time he stopped, they did as well, and watched him turn out an ankle to hitch them up.

'Christ, it's like two sandbags on a rope,' said Tommy.

'Aa can hear yer, yer cheeky buggers,' said Lenny, setting off again.

'It's like a camel chewin' a toffee,' said Wilf, pointing to the mobile shorts.

'Aa can still hear yer.'

The "hanging baskets of Lennylon" hung motionless when Monty reached the heavy looking front door, studded with black iron rivets and cut into an arched stone doorway in the middle of the building, just like the one in the church at home.

'This'll be a spooky bloody hole,' whispered Colly as Monty led them in.

To their relief it wasn't. Turning off the entrance passage into a big, light, open, modern living room that smelled of clean new things, Monty watched them spread out on their little journeys of discovery, and call attention to anything they found worth a note. At the other end of the room was an open doorway to a second living room towards the back of the house. They went in to find it was also well-furnished with nice new things, but more practical and less elegant than the 'front room' they'd come from. Tour guide Monty led them out of the 'back living room' and into the big square kitchen, with a huge stone fireplace facing them with its spits and roasting hooks hanging around waiting for heat and meat. The long dark table in the middle of the yellow flagstone floor caught their imaginations and caused comments about feasts, roast boars, goblets of wine, and fair maidens.

'And how are we liking our new home so far?'

'Fantastic, Monty, it might even have the edge on our red house.'

'Thank you, Colin. And what say you, Thomas?'

'It's neck n' neck for me wi' the livin' quarters. Aa'll pass me final judgement once we've had a look at the bedrooms and seen what's-what outside there.'

'Then walk this way,' invited Monty.

The beautifully appointed grand old bed chambers were on the top two floors, and each one arranged around two double beds, dark polished furniture and an en suite bathroom styled with emerald green and primrose tiles.

'Christ, this is somethin' special though, Tommy.'

'It is, Carter, son, it certainly is.'

Den, Wilf and Royston came down from their rooms on the top floor.

'Christ, this is somethin' special though, Tom.'

'It is, Royston, lad, it certainly is,' he said, winking at Carter.

'We're like the bloody gentry here, mind,' said Colly, coming in with Lenny.

'Ah, here you all are,' said Monty, 'now follow me; we've permission to visit the girls' room.'

He led them across the landing and up a spiral staircase onto a rounded wooden landing just big enough to take them all. He knocked on the only door on it and it opened immediately.

'Hello, lads, are you coming now to see our room is the best one?' beamed Aude.

Tommy took her chin on the way past and gave it a gentle shake to make her laugh. 'By Christ, yer not wrong, Pet,' he agreed.

'And have yers got one of them, 'on sweets', Pet?' asked Lenny.

'Oh yes, come to look.'

She got behind them to push them forward like sleepy sheep. They smiled at her happiness and, as always, did exactly what she wanted.

'Hang fire, here,' said a concerned Lester, 'there's only one bed. Where's the other bed, then, Monty?'

The awkwardness of Lester's elephant was definitely filling the room. Stan tried to kill the silence feeding it.

'The lasses said they were alright t' share, Lester.'

'Whey, it's not alright though; we don't have t' share beds so why should they?'

'No, Lester, it's alright, honestly,' said Nessa, feeling for the others looking at the floor or above the wardrobes.

'No, no, Nessa, Pet, leave this t' me and aa'll get it sorted for yer ...'

She had to smile with a few of the others.

'... so, how about it then, Monty? How comes the lasses are sleepin' together, and me and young Carter aren't?'

For the first time in his professional life he was lost for words.

'It's just lasses bein' lasses, Lester,' helped Tommy, 'they like t' share beds and have their bit chip-chap on a night-time and what-not.'

'Seems all t' hell t' me, like, and not fair. Whey, just hang fire a bit, me and Herbie'll bring my bed up for yer, Nessa, Pet, 'cause me and Carter's got carpet down in our room, and aa'm fine wi' a bit carpet t' kip on, so we'll have it up before lights out, like.'

Tommy put his big heavy hand over Lester's shoulder and pulled him close to kiss the top of his head. Lester never wondered why he did it because he'd been doing it for 30 years. Tommy winked at Nessa and she went up to Lester to tell him that she'd definitely let him know if it did need sorted. It worked to ease him down from his misguided ledge, but it cost her a smiley tear she had to hide when he reached up and rubbed her shoulder and said protectively:

'Just so long as yer do, Pet.'

'Come on, lads,' said Tommy, giving Lester a squeeze and turning him to the door, 'let the lasses get sorted, and we'll nail Mr Tweed's bed t' the floor in case ee starts shiftin' it up here in ee's sleep.'

Back downstairs Madame Brouche had the teapots, coffee pots, cups, sugar bowls, jugs of milk, and two plates of biscuits set out on the kitchen table covering the dozen chairs around it.

'Now, when we've had our little cuppa and the girls are here, I'll take you across the yard and show you something I think you'll really like,' said Monty.

'Hear that, Lenny?'

'Tut, tut, boys.'

With Nessa and Aude in place, Monty led them across the black cobbled courtyard to a long, single-storey building they all thought would have been the stables once over. To one side was a double fronted door with small glass window lights along the top.

'Is this where your room is, Mont?'

'No, no, I'm in there,' he said, pointing to the matching circular tower opposite Nessa and Aude's. 'And Hilda and Raymond have rooms in the other wing of the house. Now, what do you think of this?'

He pulled the door open effortlessly on its new runners, and they went in to yelps of excitement and cheers as they gathered to stare into the solid blue slab of the swimming pool.

'My God, Monty, how've yer managed this?'

'How deep is it?'

'Five feet deep all over, Leonard.'

Stan nudged Monty to watch Tommy creeping up behind Aude. Mesmerised by the flashing silver angles falling from the wide skylight windows onto the tropical blue water, she barely felt the clamp around her waist before she bombed in. By the time she surfaced, Lester had been slung in, and before she could splash the laughing Tommy, there was only him, Stan, Monty, Herbie and Nessa on dry land, but getting soaked by the splashes aimed at them. Monty soaked up the happiness of it all with feelings he thought he'd never have again, until Hilda came in with a tower of towels.

'So what's behind the doors at the back there, Mont?' asked Lester, stripped to his shorts and drying his hair.

'Well, there's something very lovely behind each of them, so which would you like to try first: left or right?'

He was prepared for the inevitable split decision and showed them a shiny new half-crown:

'I propose we take turns to see who can land closest to the edge of the pool from here, and I'll mark your toss with my pencil, and the winner can choose the door and keep the coin, how about that?'

'What happens if it goes in though?'

'Then the tosser's out and has to go in to get it.'

'Easy, Mont, ee only asked.'

The happy cracks matched the playful tension as it came down to a tie between Royston and Lenny. Accompanied by a chorus of

'Ooohs' and 'Aaahs', Lenny's toss finished about a foot from the edge, but Roy confidently overcompensated and the 'Ooohs' and 'Aaahs' reached their loudest just before his coin plipped into the water. He was flung in after it, and all of them put it in the memory bank of the band.

'Well, then, Leonard,' camped Monty, 'which door would you like me to take you in first?'

'Not that old chestnut, eh, Len?'

'H'way, Lenny, lad, left or right?'

'How about left, eh?'

Monty obliged and opened the door, flicked the lights on and stood aside to usher them in. They couldn't believe what they were seeing. Half of the large room was set up as a rehearsal space, with the drums and piano from the red house already in place. The other half had a settee, comfortable seats, a full-sized snooker table, dozens of books and music magazines that drew Carter like a moth to a flame, a dartboard, and a well-stocked bar with a hand pump for beer. They were genuinely overcome with it all.

'Christ, Monty, it's like we've died and gone t' heaven,' said Tommy, feeling the pump handle.

'Have a look at this, Carter, son,' said Stan, holding one of the neatly racked records beside the brand-new gramophone. He gave it to him when he went over.

'What is it, Carter?' asked Wilf.

'It's only a first press of Little Tommy Tucker's, *Easy Slider* – the one with Nutty Ted Stodge on piano; ee sprained ee's wrist once, y'know, Len, aye, givin' it some tump in the Green Lane sessions.'

'Did ee, son?' Lenny smiled.

Carter's fan-struck state didn't transfer to anybody else in the band, but they always made out it did because they knew he liked to think it did. Monty had become well aware of their selfless generosity to each other, and knew it was as natural to them as breathing.

'Here, Herbie,' said Lester, hidden behind a screening partition near the back of the room.

Herbie went up and looked around it to see him boxing a heavy bag. They'd all followed him up and saw the little boxing gym, neatly kitted out with gloves, skipping ropes and dumb-bells. Herbie smiled brightly and looked for Nessa to come beside him. She did and he pointed to one thing and then another for her to speak it out so he could nod and show his thoughts to them. He was stopped from shaking Monty's hand by a jab in the kidney that made him turn to see Lester, the contender, bouncing, bobbing and pawing with the massive brown gloves on. Herbie smiled and put his hand on Lester's head, which he played up to and started swinging wildly at the space between them to make them all laugh.

'But this lot must be costin' a bloody fortune, Mont,' said Colly.

'Well, I'm very pleased you like it,' he deflected; 'now, how about we take a peep through the other door, and then we can unload the bus and get ourselves nice and cosy for a spot of lunch. How does that sound?'

'It sounds fantastic, Mont, lad.'

He smiled as he led them to the last door.

'How about we let Royston, as runner-up, do the honours this time, Leonard?'

'Aye, you do it, Roy,' said Lenny in his naturally good-natured way.

Roy stopped three feet into the room and blocked the way in for the rest of them. With a little help from Den, he was bundled far enough forward to let them get in to see what had stood him still. It was a garage, a big one that easily housed the new big black Peugeot car and the two motorbikes parked behind it, a dozen bicycles stacked on a rack, and sixty, 5-gallon steel canisters full of petrol. It was a fully equipped working garage, with bench machinery and hand tools that Royston could see had been put together by somebody who knew what they were doing. He looked his gratitude at Monty because he couldn't put it into the words he didn't have. Monty smiled and told him kindly he was very pleased he liked it. They could see he meant it and liked him better for it.

Chapter 24

Lounging lazily in the last suntrap of the day behind the swimming pool, they watched Monty work himself into a seat in the middle of them.

'Now, before I begin, I would just like to thank Madame Hilda and Herbert, and their little helpers, Douglas, Aude and Lester, for yet another truly Michelin quality dinner…'

'Mine didn't taste rubbery, Herbie,' said Wilf.

'… Yes. Now, you may recall me mentioning a little plan to fend off that nasty chappy, boredom, remember? By doing little jobs such as cleaning, packing, farm work, bar work, shop work, handyman, fruit picking, and the like; well, the time has come.'

He passed Stan a sheet of paper.

'You can have a look at what's on offer and if there's anything you fancy, just let me know how many hours you want to do, and we'll see what can be done. But please to remember also, there really is no compunction to do it if you don't want to, although I do think it is a good idea and it would be fun for you to try new things.'

He turned the encouragingly light tone off to go on: 'As well as it helping to combat the serious matter, of course; that if you do become bored and start wishing you were home, then all of what we're doing could simply fall apart. Still, money isn't everything, as they say.'

The neatly played money card wasn't lost on them, and the chatter about jobs they could, would, couldn't or wouldn't do, began. For the next few days the list made its way from one little group to another and was never far from any of their conversations.

'So what's wrong with a bit motorbike work, deliverin' stuff, then, Lester? Christ, yer've done it all yer life,' said Wilf.

162

'Aye, but that's just it, y'know, like Monty says; it might be nice t' try somethin' different while we're here.'

'Like what though?'

'Whey, that's me dilemma...'

Wilf smiled at the characteristically conflicted Lester.

'... so what've you signed up for, anyhow?'

'Marketin',' said Wilf confidently.

'Marketin'?'

'Aye, just for a few hours on the two market days.'

'Doin' what?'

'Just strollin' about with an advertisin' board for a greengrocer.'

'And yer fancy that?'

'Oh Aye,' Wilf replied calmly as he blew a thick cloud of smoke around Lester's head. He was out to tempt him to do it with him because he knew it would be better if he wasn't on his own.

'Aye, it was Monty sayin' it was a good little number that got me.'

'How come?'

'Whey, good money and bein' able t' slope off for a drink or two as yer wander about sounds like a good number t' me.'

He could see Lester thinking, so sat silently and covered him in smoke again.

'Good money, eh?' said Lester.

'Aye, two and a half francs an hour, and mebbees four or five hours a day.'

'That's var-nigh 25 francs for two half days.'

Wilf made his move. 'It is and aa'm happy t' take yer on if yer want, like, 'cause Monty says there's another place but it'll go sharpish.'

'Right, let's away and tell him we're doin' the marketin'.'

Wilfy smiled as he followed Lester out.

By the end of the week just about all of them had made their choice and Monty had made arrangements to get them started. Tommy and Royston were the first to start; Tommy in a butcher's shop and Roy in a garage not far from it in the centre of Lyon. Monty caught up with them having their dinner-break together.

'I'm hearing very good things already, gentlemen; the garage owner can't believe he has someone who actually prefers working on old buses instead of rich people's sports cars, and the butcher is simply raving about your meaty Firstwood treats, Thomas. Indeed, I'm reliably informed your potted meat is set to take the nation by storm.'

'My potted meat and the Nazis, eh.'

******

Two weeks later.

The dimly-lit smoky cellar bar in the Café *Coin de Route*, had customers sitting at about half of the 20 small round tables set comfortably apart on the bare stone floor. They heard the front door flung open with a clatter, and watched two little unsteady figures swerve in and slalom down the stairs, laughing loudly and speaking a strange foreign language. Both were dressed the same in well-worn black velvet suits, blue and white hoopy tee-shirts, knotted red polka dot neck ties, and large, flat, black berets. It was Wilf and Lester, wearing the costumes they had to for their marketing job, promoting a greengrocer's authentic French produce.

'Two bieres, there's a good lad,' ordered Wilf, rummaging through his pockets.

'Stick a couple of them Pernods on, Wilfy, we've a bit time yet. Aa'll get us a table.'

'And two Pernods, son.'

'Any idea where the neuk might be?' asked Wilf, standing the drinks on their table.

'It'll be that little door at the back there.'

Wilf couldn't see any door, but made his way to where Lester had pointed.

'Another one wi' just a hole in the floor and twenty bloody feet away from a door wi' no lock,' he complained when he got back.

An hour wore away as quickly as the three bieres and five Pernods they had each.

'Whey, it's midnight by my watch and it's only losin' the five or ten minutes a day now, like,' slurred Lester with the usual pride in his hefty timepiece.

'Aye, best head out in case ee's waitin', eh.'

Lester agreed and they shouted their "bon soirs" to everybody as they made their way unsteadily to the stairs.

'Christ, this friggin' bladder,' said Wilf, 'aa'll see yer outside.'

Lester pulled himself up the banister to the front door, and wobbled out of the café to quickstep sideways across the pavement. He was leaning on a lamppost on the corner of the street, thinking about where he could still get a croissant or a bag of 'freets', when a tall, half-naked woman ran straight into him. She would have knocked him into the middle of the road if she hadn't managed to grab his collar, which spun him around as he was pulled back to face her heavy bare breasts, hanging pendulously six inches in front of his eyes.

'Please give me your coat, Monsieur, I am in need of it. Please.'

Hearing him murmur, 'Holy, mother of God', she realised he was English and asked again in his language. He started riving at the buttons and wrestled the jacket off for her to slip on and make it look like Coco Chanel had spent a hundred hours measuring and tailoring it to fit in the most perfectly seductive style imaginable.

'I am forever in your debt, Monsieur, and I hope one day I can thank you.'

She looked uncertainly at the trembling little man, with his face turned up to the sky and his eyes nipped shut. At first she put it down to his painfully English embarrassment on her behalf, but her look of pity turned to anger when she saw his hand jerking in his trouser pocket, as if he was trying to catch a bad tempered ferret. She was just about to slap the beret off him, when he pulled out a crumpled five franc note.

'It's all aa've got, Pet, but yer might could do with it, eh.'

The kindness took her by surprise, but was lost in a heartbeat to the sound of fast approaching footsteps. She grabbed it, turned and vanished into the night. Hearing the lessening clip-clap of her high heels running away, he opened his eyes and gasped out his release from the crippling spasm her nakedness had caused as he collapsed back against the lamppost. While he was trying to find the tabs and matches in the pocket of the jacket he wasn't wearing, he didn't hear the other footsteps stop behind him. He felt a pain. At first it was dull and queer, but it grew quickly and it became crystal clear he was being strangled. The last of his thoughts told him he was dying.

******

The big, black abandoned Peugeot in the middle of the road had its engine running, headlights on, and the driver's door wide open. The driver was on Wilf's back, screaming at him to stop while he tried to clamp his frantic woodchopping arms.

'Wilf. Wilf. Wilf! It's me. It's Royston. Wilf. For God's sake, Wilf!'

The steel pole from the greengrocer's *'As nature intended'* sign, finally dropped with a clank on the road and rolled to the smashed off signboard lying in the full beam of the car's lights. They did more than the street light to show the ghastly scene of Wilf falling to his knees in a pool of black blood beside the two lifeless bodies, and taking the head of one them gently in his hands.

'Come on, Lester, lad,' he said lovingly through his panting breaths. 'Cut them, Roy, quick.'

A razor-sharp penknife slit Lester's braces above the buttons fastening them at the back of his trousers.

'Get him on his back. Cut this one, Roy.'

Roy did.

'And this one.'

Roy did.

'Hold ee's head up so aa can get them off. Keep it right back, Roy.'

Wilf nipped Lester's nose and fell on him like a famished vampire.

'Come round here, Roy, sit across him and pump ee's chest.'

Roy did, and together as they pumped and kissed, they gave a couple coming out of the bar a chance to laugh at a crack one of them made about how the English did know how to party after all. The toecaps of Lester's boots moved from quarter to three to five to twelve, but there wasn't enough time for Wilf to get out of the way of the heaving plate of vomit landing on his lap.

'Ee's here, Roy, lad, ee's here. Hurry though, grab ee's feet and let's get him back.'

'Jesus Christ, what the hell's ee been drinkin'? This'll stink the friggin' car out for a month. Has ee been suckin' aniseed balls?'

'Just get him in the fuckin' car, Roy.'

166

******

The heavy kitchen door banged open with an angry thud to let Wilf run in, bent double with Lester on his back and his straight dead arms hanging over his shoulders. His face told the lads who were still up it was serious and Lester wasn't just drunk. Tommy lifted him off Wilf and carried him like a sleeping child to the settee in the front living room. He laid him down and they all looked at the state of his red raw throat. Lester twitched and muttered something about a caravan. They looked at Wilf who was opening a packet of Gitanes. He lit one, inhaled deeply, and looked at Lester without any smoke seeming to come back out. He left the room. They looked at Roy.

'Are the lasses upstairs?' he asked first.

'Aye.'

'Somebody was stranglin' Lester when Wilfy came out the bar. Wilfy was brainin' the fucker when aa got there. Aa think ee's killed him, Tom.'

They received the last bit of news as idly as though they'd been told the sun would come up in the morning.

'What the hell for, though? D'yer know what kicked it off?'

'No. And aa couldn't get 'owt out of Wilf, y'know.'

'Aye, ee'll be quiet for a day or two, so best leave him be,' said Stan.

'Could be robbery, mind,' suggested Roy. 'Lester's coat's gone.'

'Strangle somebody for a raggy old jacket?'

'Well, these are very uncertain times, gentlemen,' ghosted in Monty. 'Does Wilfred say Lester will be alright?'

'Aye, but it's a nasty one,' said Roy.

'Then I'll have a doctor call. Now, I think I'd better pay a visit to where this happened. Would anyone care to join me?'

Tommy, Duggie and Colly said they would, and Royston knew he had to go as the guide.

'No, no, Royston, drink your cognac, I can drive,' said Monty, pulling on his Panama hat.

Spinning the car around in the courtyard and flashing out at a speed that made four pairs of knuckles turn white, soon brought them to the place. They all got out and Monty walked on ahead.

'That's professional drivin', that, mind, racin' car stuff,' whispered Roy.

'Terrifyin', more like.'

'And you're sure we're in the correct spot, Royston?' said Monty politely.

'Aye, definitely, but aa can't understand it; there's the pub door and there's the lamppost; there should be puke all over the place here, and blood all over there by the drain. Aa mean, where's the greengrocer's sign and the pole gone?'

Monty wandered out of the lamplight and stood alone looking up a side street as he twisted the car key in his fingers, like a lonesome cowboy rolling a cigarette.

'So, what's goin' on here, then, Monty?'

'I wish I knew, Thomas, I really do.'

They saw the flicker of his annoyance at not knowing, which oddly seemed to reassure them they weren't in any trouble.

'Can aa drive back please, Mont?'

He smiled and gave Roy the key.

******

'Are yer alright, Carter, son? Yer look a bit rough this mornin', bonny lad.'

'Aye, just not much kip last night, bloody Lester's been at it all night, twistin' and turnin' and coughin' and groanin', aa barely got a wink.'

'But ee's asleep there now though?' checked Stan.

Carter could tell something was up and asked what it was.

'Somebody tried t' strangle him last night, up in the town, there.'

He stood with his cup and the coffee pot like a still-life model, and they could see his shock. Sometimes they forgot to remember he was still only a young lad and hadn't been through the forging fires of hell they had. They hoped to God he never would.

'Ee's alright now, son,' broke in Stan, 'don't worry yersel', ee'll be fine.'

'How? Why, like? Aa mean, Lester's nice, y'know, such a good … aa mean, ee wouldn't hurt anybody…'

Stan could see he was getting upset and let the lads know with a quick look.

'H'way Duggie, lad,' rallied Tommy, 'let's away up and see if we can rouse the little mite and fetch him down. Aa'll tell yer what, mind, Carter; ee likes them croissant things yer make on a mornin', doesn't ee, lads.'

'Oh hell, aye, and ee says ee doesn't like them so much when anybody else makes them either, mind.'

Carter knew what they were trying to do in their own kind, but hopelessly underhand way. He also knew why they were hopelessly underhand, and was pleased they were, which made him happy to do his best to go along and let them think they weren't.

'Right, aa'll get some started, but if ee says ee doesn't want t' come down, tell him aa'll fetch it up, if ee can manage, like. Does anybody else want one?'

They all did. Tommy made him smile, saying he'd be to blame if he ended up with an arse like Lenny's.

'Any sign of Wilf, Den?' asked Stan, knowing the answer.

'No, ee was up and out before sun-up.'

They all knew why.

'Here ee is, look,' boomed Tommy, carrying Lester in like a pile of washing.

When he tried to sit him down, he got a low, hoarse whisper telling him to lay him flat instead. Tommy did what he was told but had to ask why. Lester pulled his head to his mouth. They could see Tommy's shoulders start to go, and watched him having to stand up to laugh in his openly honest and infectious way.

'Christ, Lester,' he said, wiping his eyes, 'there's never been 'owt straightforward wi' you and yer injuries, lad.' He started to laugh again.

'H'way then?'

Tommy put his hand on Lester's, as if to claim friendly absolution for telling them. Lester half smiled and rolled his eyes to say he knew it had to be done.

'The lasses aren't about yet, are they? Good: ee's only gone an' got a ruptured bollock.'

'How the hell? Did ee get a kick at yer, Lester?'

'No, no,' answered Tommy, 'the bastard's pulled ee's braces that hard t' get them round ee's neck, that he's had the gusset rive up and trap a love nut.'

They all laughed with Tommy.

'Christ. So, is it fairly swelled, then?'

Lester made a grapefruit-sized circle with his hands. They all burst out laughing again.

'Christ, it's only Lester could get strangled and end up with cobbler rougher than ee's throat.'

'How is yer throat, anyhow?' asked Stan.

Lester tilted his hand from side to side to say it wasn't too bad.

'What about the sax though?' asked Carter, coming in with a cup of tea and a buttered croissant.

'It'll be painful with a nut like that,' said Colly.

'Aye.' He smiled. 'But aa meant playin' the sax.'

'So did aa.' Colly smiled.

'Monty's got a doctor comin' t' see yer at tea-time,' said Stan.

'By, yer a lucky little bugger, Lester; havin' us t' look after yer until yer can carry that thing around by yersel'.'

He rolled his eyes to make them smile.

'Can yer manage t' tell us what happened, Lester, or not?' asked Stan considerately.

He nodded he could.

'Good lad, so come on then let's have the full story,' said Tommy, rubbing his hands happily.

'Aa honestly can't remember that much,' he began in a whisper, 'aa'd just come out the pub t' see if Roy was there, Wilfy was away for a run-off, and the next thing aa knew, aa'd been clattered by this big lass runnin' like hell up the street. Anyhow, she gets hold of me and says, "can aa have yer coat".'

'Yer coat?'

'In English?'

'Aye, me coat, and it was, but she was foreign and could speak it, like.'

'What d'yer mean, big? Big like Margaret?'

'No, aa mean big like tall; over six foot aa'd say. Why the hell would she be askin' for my jacket if she was like Margaret?'

The listeners smiled.

'So what did she want yer coat for?'

''Cause she had nowt on.'

'Nowt at all?'

'Easy, Duggie, lad.'

'Whey, nowt on top; both her knoxills were out.'

'Hardly likely t' be just the one.'

'Hair colour?' asked Duggie.

'Not black like Order's, but not brown like Nessa's, somethin' in-between.'

'Auburn, eh.'

'Right, so yer gave her yer jacket, then what?'

'Aa remember her puttin' it on and givin' her a few francs 'cause the poor bugger looked like she needed a bit help, like…'

They smiled at his familiar kindness.

'… and then she was away full pelt again.'

'Did yer see where?'

'Was she gettin' chased?'

'Aa don't know, lads, aa wasn't lookin',' he admitted awkwardly.

'Yer weren't lookin'! Lester, lad, yer never miss a single bloody thing. How the hell were yer not lookin'?'

He sighed and knew he might as well get it over with. 'She'd given me a spasm.'

The moment it took to for them to twig what he meant dissolved in the blink of an eye filling with tears of laughter.

'Christ Almighty, we're not back t' that gypsy's caravan again?'

'Aa've tried t' tell yer, it was a bloody trauma; aa was just a kiddie.'

'Settle down, Lester, or yer'll hurt yersel', it's just a daft laugh,' calmed Stan.

'So how d'yer manage t' get any knobbin' done, if the sight of a pair of bangers knocks yer int' a spasm?' asked the genuinely intrigued Duggie.

Lester put his hand on his throat to say he couldn't speak anymore because of the pain.

'Yer a funny little bugger, Lester. But hold still and aa'll get yer some of that honey tea stuff,' said Tommy, heading into the kitchen to find Hilda.

'So the bastard caught yer off guard in yer spasm, eh?'

Lester nodded.

'And Wilfy's come out and caught him chokin' yer.'

'By Christ ee did,' said Roy, 'if that fucker's still alive aa'll eat hay with a cuddy.'

'H'way then, Stan, out with it.'

'Whey, it's just how come there was nowt there when yers got there? Aa mean, it was just 20 minutes after? Does that not seem strange when yer think what Wilf would have done wi' that pole?'

They sat silently with their coffee and croissants in their own thoughts.

******

Monty and the doctor left Lester on the settee and went into the back living room to tell everybody how he was. Monty translated the doctor's replies to their questions before escorting him to his car.

'So, nothing to worry about, only bruising, ay. And who do we think is responsible?'

'They don't know, or at least they haven't given me anything.'

'Nothing at all?' fished Monty.

'Well, there is word of some kind of rift on their side beginning to ripple out.'

'Oh?'

'Yes, it seems the Count has brought a woman in and your man Drubil isn't overly pleased, but I'm afraid that's all I have.'

'Yes, of course, thank you, Gordon.'

Lester's undercover doctor started his car. Monty tapped on the window.

'Just a thought: who do they have down for the clean-up?'

'Vichy boys, definitely.'

'I see. See you Thursday, then.'

He walked slowly after the car and hurried up to his room as soon as it turned out of sight.

Chapter 25

'Oh, hello,' said the surprised Monty, facing a new doctor examining Lester. 'Is Dr Lafette detained?'

The old doctor made it clear to everybody in the room that he'd absolutely no idea who Dr Lafette was, and, luckily, only made it clear to Monty he'd never heard of any doctor by that name. Monty wriggled free with the giggling excuse of being useless with names, and the disinterested doctor got on with his work. After examining Lester's throat, he gave his assessment in a fast spoken, thick, south-eastern accent, still holding a lot of the old Occitan words that made it difficult for Monty to follow. It wasn't made any easier by him trying to work out who the doctor was and what was going on. The doctor ignored him and got back to work, making Lester lie back to have the tartan curtains of his dressing gown pulled open for him to perform the testicle examination. He looked like an unfortunate chef inspecting the rotten beef tomato he'd been given to make a favourite dish for Hitler. Holding it while he rummaged around in his black bag for an old leather wallet and a shallow glass jar with a wide neck, he placed the testicle on the jar and sliced into it with a scalpel from the wallet. Thick dark blood pumped in heavy pulses while he raked about in his bag again for another wallet. Taking a syringe from it and screwing it together, he pushed its long needle into a fat brown bottle to draw a measure of liquid, and send a little jet into the air before injecting the testicle while it sat on the jar. From the same wallet he picked out a short, already threaded needle and made four perfectly neat stiches in the cut as soon as the bloody stream stopped.

'No messin' wi' this old lad, eh,' whispered Den, as they peeped around the open doorway.

'This one knows ee's stuff,' said Wilf.

The doctor closed the curtains on Lester's genital matinee, and smiled at the smiling patient as he shook his hand. He turned to Monty and told him it would be 12 francs.

'Oh, right, can you attend to this please, Hilda. Is everything all right, doctor?' he asked.

'It might be now,' he said meaningfully.

'I see. And can you see him again?'

'Yes, Friday. I'll collect my jar then.'

He gave Hilda the jar of blood when she returned with the 12 francs, to make it look like she'd bought it, and quickly wrapped the notes around the coins and shoved them in his trouser pocket before sorting his bag out.

'Let me escort you to your car...'

'No, no. No need. Professor Chambier asked me to give you this. Goodbye.'

Monty glanced at the address on the piece of paper and casually folded it into his shirt pocket.

'One thing's for sure, Lester, lad,' said Colly, leading the lads into the room, 'you've definitely got a numb nut there.'

'Aye, and it's not the friggin' doctor this time,' said Wilf.

They heard his ancient Citroen getting hand-cranked into life, and all eight horses straining hard to putt-putt him away.

*****

Monty looked again at the piece of paper the doctor had given him, as he made his way through the crowded narrow back lanes of one of the most dangerous districts in Lyon. For the second time he stood at the place where the number of the address should have been. This time the hard prod of a gun barrel in the small of his back pushed him into the derelict building, and up a long winding staircase until he was made to stop on the filthy top floor landing. He counted seven dark, paint-peeling doors on it before the gun pressed him through the farthest. In the little murky light the caked skylight let into the room, he saw a battered writing table and a wooden chair were all it contained. He waited anxiously, knowing Drubil would be trouble for him this time. A side door, hidden in the shade, opened and the slight figure coming in told him it obviously wasn't Drubil, and that he was looking at his hired killer.

'Montague, how are you, you old rogue?'

'Geoffrey?'

Little Geoffrey walked into the light and took his hand. He could feel the fear that had forced its way past the professional training, and could see how hard Monty was working to summon every bit of it back.

'This way.'

He led him through the side door into a bright comfortable room, with four men standing around a table covered in a mess of maps, cups, ashtrays and papers.

'This is Montague, gentlemen.'

Geoffrey waited for their short formal greetings to end and took Monty to the seats set around an upturned tea chest at the other end of the room.

'Take a seat.'

He poured two large whiskys and pushed one to Monty, who couldn't stop himself from downing it in one. Geoffrey smiled and topped it up.

'Still the *Callum Beg* I see.'

'It is,' smiled Geoffrey, who could see Monty was pulling himself together.

'And how can I help, Geoffrey?' he asked urbanely.

'Well, you can cut that bloody nonsense out for a start.'

The glare from his eye said more than the words. Monty apologised and meant it.

'Right. We've a problem: Drubil's been cut out and wants to spoil the show; the idiot's trying to hijack it for himself.'

'He can't have much support.'

'No; the Germans have the police and we've made other arrangements – some interesting work as you can imagine – but he does have some of the local lunatics.'

'Nothing you can't handle.'

'Ordinarily, yes, but a tad more complicated here, Montague. Fucking politics.'

'Indeed. So do you want me to pull them out of the jobs?'

'No, I want you to leave things as they are; we're keeping an eye on them.'

'After Lester?'

'Mmm.'

Geoffrey looked thoughtful.

'What about the French doctor?'

'Nothing for you to worry about there.'

'And the labels?'

'Stay with them for now.'

'Is there …'

'No, we just wanted you to know how the land lies.'

Standing up as he replied let Monty know the interview was over. Geoffrey led him to the door where one of the men handed him a folded newspaper. He gave it to Monty when they were in the other room.

'Photographs of the lunatics. Keep them. What's wrong, Montague? Ah, you're wondering why Gordon didn't give you them? Well, he was supposed to.'

'Oh?'

Geoffrey nodded to make him turn and look into a dark corner. The form of a naked man sitting on the floor, with his knees tied up to his chest and his hands bound behind his back came slowly into view. The clear cellophane bag over his head made the bulging wide open eyes and thick purple lips look grotesquely bigger, but didn't stop him from seeing it was Gordon.

'Nasty thing, war, to traitors and cowards, I mean,' said Geoffrey calmly, as he took Monty's hand to say goodbye.

He could see Monty's relief overflow when he released him to leave, and waited until his hand was on the doorknob to the landing.

'Oh, one more thing, Montague, Frau Plank will be completing her contact soon, so keep an eye on our Romeo, Douglas, there's a good fellow.'

Monty forced a smile and left. As soon as the door closed behind him, he breathed in the deep big breaths of the filthy stale air he needed to stop his legs from folding.

Chapter 26

The old doctor drew the dressing gown back over Lester's scrotal exhibition, and smiled and shook his hand before telling Monty it was eight francs.

'Ask him how ee is, Mont,' said Stan.

Monty did, and was told he was doing very well, even though the testicle was lost. Hilda came in with a 10 franc note and the jar she'd washed. The doctor wouldn't accept the extra money and started going through his pockets to find two francs. Lester lifted his hand suddenly and listened and looked puzzled at the others. They started to look the same way.

'It'll be that cat.'

'Doesn't sound like a cat t' me, mind,' said Lester.

They heard it was closer but not much louder, and that it wasn't a cat; it was a woman, an exhausted, distraught and frightened woman trying to shout. They'd only just started to move to the kitchen when Aude burst in, covered in blood, and throwing herself at Tommy.

'Nessa, Nessa, Nessa,' she gasped, pulling his hand to make him come with her.

Tommy ordered Monty to make sure he brought the doctor. The doctor ordered Monty to tell Lester not to move. Monty ordered Hilda to get Raymond to help her lock the place down. They ran through the outer gate in the conifer hedge to cut through the fields to where the girls were working. Aude's legs collapsed under her and Herbie picked her up and kept running, with her pointing the way. Royston had gone straight to the garage to get a motorbike, and soon caught up with the reason he had; it was Tommy, crippled with stitch and barely moving. Standing on the pedals with Tommy on the seat, they reached the others just as they were crossing the main road to run through the high golden corn in the gently sloping field. Royston rode up to Wilf, who was now bent double with the agony of a stitch, and got him on the handlebars. As they rolled down the hill they could see a group of people under one of the cherry trees in the orchard at the bottom, and the doctor's old car already being driven away by Monty. Dropping the bike a few yards away, they ran to where Nessa lay with her head on a frightened old woman's lap. The doctor was trying to get her to release the pressure she had on her apron pressed to Nessa's face. The old woman paid no attention and kept rocking backwards and forwards, until he shouted at her in her own ancient language that he was a doctor. The half dozen old men and women there helped their friend as best they could; holding her and gently lifting her arms to let him carefully lift the red-soaked white apron off Nessa's face. Wilf's head was only an inch from the doctor's, but he said nothing because he could see he was there to examine and not to gawp. Along the hairline above her right eye and down past the temple to her ear, they could see white bone at the bottom of a valley of dark jelly. Aude slipped from Herbie's arms, started forward and fell lifeless onto her face. The doctor rushed a little brown bottle from his bag and gave it to one of the old women, who knew what to do with it. The lads looked their fear at each other, and Herbie turned and walked away with his iron hard hands clasped white behind his head. The doctor let Wilf know to hold her head up and told the old woman to press again gently. He felt around Nessa's head, shoulders, arms, and body and spoke things out in French that Wilf understood in English.

'How bad's it, Wilf?'

'It's bad.'

He let the doctor know he wanted to examine her head, and he graciously moved aside to let him do it. Feeling over and around one point again and again, with a concentration and care his love for her added to the expertise he'd gained in the War, he finally stopped. It looked as though the devil had reached up and pulled his head down by the hair.

'Wilf.'

'It's broken,' he muttered.

'Wilf?'

He looked at the doctor and the old doctor nodded.

'Wilf. For God's sake.'

'Hospital, she needs hospital.'

Tommy was snapped out of his darkening fear by the old doctor shouting at him to come forward.

'Ee wants yer t' lift her up, Tom,' said Wilf.

Tommy did exactly as he was told, as gently as he could, only to be screamed at by the doctor to do it quickly. The moment she was in a seated position, he applied the brace and bit he'd taken from his bag and drilled into the back of her skull. Tommy looked up to the heavens with Roy. Herbie didn't move from looking at the waving corn, and Wilf watched the drill bite into her head. The doctor had Wilf hold it while he made a deep horseshoe cut around it. He took the drill from him and pulled it. The three of them heard a quiet, watery, suction cluck from Nessa's head, and watched him unwind the drill. He seemed pleased to see the blood running like rich red wine from a Spanish porrron.

'C'est bon.'

He threw the drill back in his bag and went on with his examination. Tommy felt the hot blood paint his hands.

The sharp definite click from her dislocated shoulder being put back in made Herbie shake his head against the terrible noises of pain coming from her. The doctor let Wilf know these things had to be done. Wilf understood and the old man knew he did.

'Ee says t' lay her down, Tom, but hold her head on this side.'

The rumble coming up the orchard from the same direction Monty had driven the doctor's car out, was an ambulance, with him and a nurse sitting by the driver in the front. A medic jumped out of the back with a stretcher and worked with the driver to collect Nessa as quickly as they could. Tommy gently took Aude from the Nurse the old lady had surrendered her to, and pulled her in tightly to kiss her head. He felt her trembling as she looked her vacant, heartbreaking fear into the far distance that showed no future. He wanted the world to stop and go back far enough so he could have gone cherry picking with them that morning. The doctor shouted at him to let her go with the nurse. Herbie let Tommy know he'd go to keep watch and got in the front of the ambulance.

'We'll be up as soon as we're done.'

Herbie knew what he meant. Before he left, and in a language that didn't need words, the old doctor was made to know how much they thought of him for what he'd done. Before the ambulance pulled away, Tommy helped the old woman in the blood-soaked apron to her feet, while two of her friends unfastened the strings to take it off. It was rolled into a raggy red and white ball and dropped behind the tree.

'Please, Madame, drink some of this,' offered Monty.

She took a good pull from the flask of cognac and passed it back to her friends. They did the same and gave him it back empty. He smiled generously.

'Can you help us, please, Madame, and tell us what has happened to our friend?'

They stood silent.

'We are not police, and we have nothing to do with the Unione Corse or Le Milieu, we are just musicians from England who have come to play and to show we are with you in this war.'

The others gave the nursing old woman their permission to speak, and she began, allowing time for Monty to translate:

'They came down that field, two of them. I could see Aude smiling and saying hello to them as she does to everybody, she is such a lovely little girl. But one of them grabbed her here' (she grabbed her own breast) 'and made her cry out. She tried to run but the other one grabbed her hair and was pulling her down ...'

Her friends began to talk over her excitedly. Monty calmed them so he could follow. She went on:

'Nessa came running up from that tree there and hit the one pulling her hair. Oh my God, she hit him so hard, mons dieu!'

Her little group did all they could to make them know how hard it was.

'Tell her friends, Monsieur, tell them now how very hard it was.'

Monty did and they clapped their old hands and said 'yes' in English, to try and emphasise the fact.

'And then,' continued the old woman, 'she went for the one who grabbed her here, but he ran away and she picked up Aude and held her tight, and we went over, didn't we, to see what we could do. And when we were there the others came. There were five of them more, and the coward who ran to get them, and the one on the ground who was starting to move...'

'Seven,' said Wilf.

'... and they had these' (pointing at the heavy cricket stump fencing stakes) 'and other things, and Nessa made Aude get behind her and grab her shirt. I could see she did it and Nessa put her back to this tree.'

Tommy looked up to the heavens.

'They came up to here and stopped; they wanted them to run so they could ...'

The old woman stopped talking but they heard what she was saying.

'... but she did not run.'

Her friends impressed this point on them by saying boldly: 'non, non, elle n'a pas couru, non'.

'They came on to her and she stepped forward, Messieurs, do you hear? She stepped forward.'

She saw they'd heard because they looked like children standing at their mother's grave. An old man came forward with one of the fencing stakes.

'One went to hit her with this,' said the old woman, taking it from him, 'and she stopped him and pulled it out of his hand, yes, and with such force it pulled him towards her, and she rammed it into his mouth.'

'The pig screamed like a girl,' said the old man, taking it back.

'Then they all rushed at her and she stood up and she took many, many blows, but fought like a lion, Messieurs – a lion!'

Tommy dropped to his knees with his fists on the grass, and Wilf and Royston stood in tears beside him.

'We shouted at them and one of them came and hit Marianne, look, on her head.'

The old woman lifted her headscarf to show the angry red mark under her wispy white hair.

'But it was the ugly fat one with no hair that got Nessa: he went around the tree and hit her with the spade.'

She made a chopping motion with her hand to the side of her face.

'It was by the edge, like an axe, and she lost her senses, but turned to grab the tree, to keep Aude safe, like this.'

She showed them how Nessa had penned Aude against the tree and wrapped her arms around it to grab the stake with both hands.

'Then they just kept hitting her until some of the men from the bottom shouted and came running up. But it was the first one she hit, who was pulling Aude's hair, yes, and when she was already unconscious and on her knees he hit her in the head with a hammer; the coward.'

Tommy let out the most wretched groan they'd ever heard, and thundered his fist into the hard green ground.

'Before the men were near they ran away,' she said quietly, to finish her account in tears.

'Like the shit they are,' added an old woman.

Wilf walked up to Monty and asked threateningly: 'Who are these fuckers?'

'Please, Wilfred, not now,' he said, turning to the old woman. 'Thank you for all of your help, mes amies. Please accept this with all our thanks.'

He gave her the small fortune of 20 francs he had in his pocket, and she, and each of her friends, kindly kissed each of them before melting back into the land and the baskets of fruit from their labour. Royston pushed the bike as they walked away slowly under the weight of their own heavy thoughts and fears.

*****

Duggie, Stan and Carter were already at the hospital with Herbie, when Tommy and the others got there. Despite everything, they had to smile at Lester being pushed in by Royston in a wheelbarrow; his legs hanging comfortably over a pillow on either side like bent little oars. They gathered by the large window in the wall of Nessa's room. Tommy and Herbie lifted the wheelbarrow to let Lester have a look.

'Is that little bed for Order?'

Herbie nodded.

'Looks like they're both spark out.'

They looked at the heavy bandaging on Nessa's head and the thick plaster casts on both her arms, from the elbows to the raw, bruised knuckles, and watched the drips from the clear glass bottle hanging above her bed on a skinny metal stand, drain into the orange rubber tube running into her arm just above a cast.

'The doctor's comin' in a bit,' said Stan.

'What's the crack here, Tom?' asked Duggie, blowing his smoke to his shoes and picking the ever-present bit of baccy off his tongue.

Their eyes met and everything was said, before Tommy led them all over to the little waiting area across the corridor and gave them every detail from the field. Seeing the tears in their eyes made him have to stop from time to time. Herbie walked back to the viewing window and put his wide-open hands on it and stared in. They could see the tears run from his reflection in the glass.

'Yer bugger,' said Lenny, barely able to speak, 'she stepped forward, lad.'

He put the heels of his hands to his eyes and hung his head.

'Who's these fuckers, Tom?' asked Duggie.

'Ee's tellin us tonight.'

'Is ee?' asked Royston, thinking he'd missed something.

'Oh, aye,' said Tommy, even though Royston hadn't missed a thing.

The clicking heels of a small man in a white coat walking quickly towards them made them look. His thick black hair standing either side of its centre parting, made him look like he was in a wind tunnel. He didn't expect to see them all stand up and greet him so respectfully.

'Ah, you must be Lester,' he said pleasantly, 'I am Professor Chambier.'

He leaned forward to shake Lester's hand. 'And how are you today? You have a nice carriage, I see.'

'Not bad, not bad, doctor, thank you. Aye, it's canny enough, even though it's nowt t' look at. Mind, when aa say canny, aa mean it can be when Roy puts ee's mind t' pushin' it properly and stops bein' so bloody rough wi' kerbs and what-not. But never mind me, doc, that's by-the-by, how's Nessa and little Order?'

'Yes,' said the lost professor, 'she is now settled at rest here now. We have made some X-ray pictures of her and she has broken bones in her ribs and near the spine, which have been set, and at her shoulder and elbow are dislocated, which have now put back also. Her wrists and arms were shown to be very damaged by violent blows, but they are now set into their casts. We must check at later times on them. The wound on the side of the face has made a big cut and a crack in the cheekbone, but her skin is now together with stiches.'

He stopped to organise his words and was immediately questioned by Wilf:

'What about her head, doctor?'

'Yes. The skull is broken and we have operated. It was in compression and I think we have won this day and will go on to watch carefully. But I want you to know to thank Dr Gambon, who has no doubt saved her life from that terrible blow. We must now wait. The little girl has been attended to and the breast should be normal again soon.'

'Christ. The rotten bastards.'

'Yes. There was much violence in these injuries.'

'Will she be all right, doctor?' asked Wilf.

He knew he was asking about Nessa.

'It will take time to see if there has been no bad effect to the brain, but I think it will not be so, again because of Dr Gambon.'

'When d'yer think she'll wake up, doctor?' asked Stan.

'I cannot know, perhaps in one day or one week? The little girl will wake up tomorrow; we have made her rest with a drug.'

Stan broke the gathering silence: 'Will it be all right for one of us t' stop here, doctor?' He asked politely, but knew it would be happening regardless of any permission.

'Yes, that will be a good thing; there may be little bits of conscious waking-up with such head injury, and seeing a friend is very good medicine, yes.'

'Aye.'

'Can aa go in and touch her, please, doctor?' asked Lester, showing the strain the professor could see in all of them.

'Yes. But would you please to go in at only two at one time, thank you.'

They formed in front of him to take his hand in their deeply meaningful way. He smiled at each of them kindly, and at the end took a small piece of paper from a big pocket on his white coat.

'Who would like to take Dr Gambon's bill? It is for 12 francs.'

Chapter 27

Hilda headed back across the courtyard to the kitchen after telling them dinner was ready, with Duggie following her, wheeling Lester. The dinner passed quietly and before the table was cleared, Tommy asked Monty to tell them what he knew. His only reply was a raised finger to tell them to wait until they were alone; it was important he let them think he was careful about Hilda. She brought the usual glasses and bottle of cognac, and let them see she was pleased to be given the night off, as she wished them goodnight in her carefully hopeless English. Monty made sure they noticed him watching her walk past the window.

'Right, now these are a particularly nasty bunch who are making the most of a bad situation...'

Their concentrated attention caught him off guard.

'... er, robbers and rapists and undoubtedly worse, who are now able to hide in all sorts of groups cropping up because of the war.'

'What groups?'

'Some claiming to be for the Resistance and some supporting the Germans.'

'That makes no sense t' me, mind.'

'Well, it does insofar as it lets them do what they want, and then claim allegiance to whichever side would work as protection from the other.'

'Aye, aye, but what the hell's this got t' do wi' the lasses?'

'Our people think they were targeted for being Jewish, or gypsies, either, it's of no matter, the situation provides for such vile and villainous thugs. I've managed to get my hands on these.'

He emptied an envelope of photographs on the table. 'This is the one who hurt Aude.'

'How d'yer know that?'

'I've been down to the orchard and shown them to the old people. Let me see, yes, this is the one who hit Nessa with the spade, and that's the one who used the hammer. All of the men in these photographs were there.'

He waited for the questions, but they sat silently, needing to listen.

'Now, they don't belong to any of the big gangs down here; apparently they're a nuisance to them, but they put up with them because they come in handy from time to time. Our people know they meet at a place called the Cygne Noir.'

'Where's that?' asked Duggie.

'It's in the northern part of Lyon, a dangerous place in itself, but this place moreso, even the police stay clear.'

'Aye, aye,' dismissed Tommy, 'and what's "our people" say about them being there on a Friday night?'

'They have sent that detail, actually; I can only presume by accident because we have been given a very clear warning to stay away.'

He was made to stop talking by the way they were looking at him.

'You can't go there, you mustn't. Please, Stanley, all of you, you must listen, you could be hurt, or even killed if you go to that desperate place; no, I can't allow it, I couldn't bear for that to happen.'

Because they could see he was trying to protect them, they let him see they understood. Tommy swept the photographs together and stood to leave.

'Please don't go there, Thomas, I beg you, please, don't, I'll help.'

Tommy looked him in the eye and told him he had helped. They all left together and for the first time since he'd known them, the glasses were left untouched. An hour later, just after half past eight, Tommy came out of the garage with his arm over Stan's shoulder.

'Christ, we're not in our twenties anymore, Tom, and they're tellin' us this is a rough hole, so we'll need all hands goin' over, up there.'

Tommy looked down and smiled at the podgy little man who was telling him he was still prepared to die beside his friend.

'Aa'm thinkin' the same, Stanley, so that's why one of us has t' stand down and stop back t' see that the lasses, and young Carter, are all right if it goes bad. And seein' as aa'm the one who's kept mesel' in tip-top condition and not let mesel' slip,' he gently jabbed a finger into Stan's gut, 'then it makes more sense for me t' have a look over tonight, eh.'

Stan knew Tommy was trying to make light of his heaviest final word, and he knew deep-down it had to be Tommy who went and not him; they'd need him there. He stood still and looked at his shoes. Tommy could see he was struggling.

'They'll need yer here, Stanley, y'know they will, lad, and we'll be comin' back, and aa'll tell yer why.'

Stan pushed a hand over his head and kept looking at the ground.

'Because those shithouses nearly killed Nessa, and they will rape Order if we don't stop them, so mark my words, Stanley, we'll be 20 again for one more time tonight.'

Stan put his hand over his eyes and faced away. Tommy stood quiet and waited. Without looking at him, he said: 'Come back, Tom, for God's sake, and bring them back.'

He walked away and Tommy watched him all the way through the kitchen door before he wiped his eyes with the back of his hand and went back to the garage. An hour later they heard the big Peugeot pull into the courtyard with Herbie, Den and Colly. Monty had taken Stan and Carter to the hospital to swap with them, and as soon as they got out, he turned the car around and went into the kitchen to speak to Hilda in French.

'Is the house empty?'

'Yes, they're all in the garage.'

'And Derek?'

'Upstairs locking down.'

'Good. And the firearms?'

'All ready.'

'Very good. Stanley thinks they'll be ready by half ten. Now, we will have some cover up there, but if anything happens to me, you'll have the new schedules by morning. At any rate, listen for the doctors, they're only waiting for us to leave and will be here directly.'

She could see he wasn't himself, and knew he'd faced many more dangerous situations than this; he was worried for the lads, they were his friends. She gently rubbed his arm and he tried to smile his reassurance, but it didn't work. An hour passed slowly for the three of them in the house as they watched the bluey-white welding flashes jump through the little windows in the garage door to cut into the darkness gathering in the courtyard. When they stopped the victorious dark seemed darker. It was half past ten and the garage door stayed shut. Ten minutes later they came out of the swimming pool door and made their way to the kitchen. They didn't speak when they came in. Herbie brought a dish of butter from the pantry and they each scooped a knob out and rubbed it between their hands before spreading it on their hair. They scrubbed their hands with soap, dried them, and held them out for Herbie to cover their palms with salt, which they rubbed into the skin. Duggie did the same for Herbie, all in silence. Tommy looked his question at Monty who was standing by the back door holding the car keys.

'I'm waiting to drive you there,' he replied.

Their little nods lifted his heart.

Herbie and Duggie got in the back rear seat, Colly, Den and Lenny, in the back seat, Tommy sat in the front with Lester on his knee, and Roy and Wilf followed on the motorbikes. It wasn't long before the car rolled quietly to a stop in the dirty backstreet of the Cygne Noir. Lester slipped his watch into Tommy's hand and got out. They watched him struggle the 20 yards to the rotten street door and go inside. After six of the ten minutes he'd been given had gone, the back door of the car opened and Wilf and Roy pushed in. Tommy looked from the watch to the bar door every two seconds as the tenth minute came and went. Lester appeared and limped back as quickly as he could. Tommy lifted him onto his knee.

'Straight in, bar facing, tight right three yards, tight left ten to top table, wide oval not bolted, nine on, all ours, bar up left six, end stairs up, tables t' right, eight, 14 sat.'

'Right. Will yer stay here?' said Tommy, knowing the answer.

'No, Tom, but aa'll not be in yer way.'

Tommy put his hand on Lester's chest and pulled him tight, kissed the top of his head and whispered something, before easing him over to get out. Colly and Den went down first. They ambled into the dimly lit, stinking place, looking carelessly drunk and laughing and talking privately. A little old peasant sitting with three younger members of his class tapped the table with a matchstick. Tommy walked in two minutes later, looking lost, and made his way along the bar as if he was searching for the stairs to the brothel. Duggie and Wilf were hidden, crouching close behind him. At the end of the bar Tommy lifted the elbow of his right arm and they flew past, jumping on the big top table with arms and metal flying into the faces of the men sitting around it. Tommy rushed forward, lifted them up with the table, rammed it forward and ripped it backwards, throwing it behind him on his right side. Herbie whipped past on his left and thudded a club hammer into the temple of the first he came to. Tommy did the same to those on the right with the heavy-headed club he'd had clipped inside his baggy coat. A shot was fired before the life touching the trigger ended in a dark oily mess on the wall. Monty stood by the front door, frantically pulling at his jacket pocket: he could see the barman getting a gun, and desperately tried but couldn't get his revolver out. A shot came and the barman snorted and folded to the floor with a black hole in his head. Monty saw the little peasant look down, as his pointless revolver showed itself to Lester who'd just come in. The hellishly ferocious violence at the top table lasted no more than 30 seconds. Colly, Den and Royston had pelted straight upstairs into the brothel. Lenny stood with his back to the long bit of bar and watched the tables opposite. He heard the gunshots above and saw Duggie scud up first with Herbie on his heels and Wilf on his. Tommy stayed at the bottom, breathing deeply, listening like everyone else to the muffled thuds, groans, and sounds of death coming down. A naked, thick-set, bald, ugly man landed at the foot of the stairs. Tommy saw he was the one who'd hit Nessa with the spade. He arched his back, but his club was stopped by Duggie jumping on his back and whacking the four-inch spike on the brass bar across his knuckles into his face. Screaming with rage and pain, he twisted and turned like a half-skinned eel, and threw Duggie off. In the instant he stood to get his bearings, he saw Tommy's eyes. Before his brain could tell him anything, it had left his skull. Duggie stamped his metal heel on the ooze-covered neck and ran back up the stairs. Herbie was the first to come down from the new silence, carrying Colly on his back. Den brought Wilf down, holding his arms over his shoulders, and feeling the blinding mask of his warm blood on his neck. Tommy watched them go in front of him and walked out of the bar last, less than three minutes after going in. The little peasant glanced at him as he passed and saw the purple patch blotting his midriff. When the front door shut he peeped through a gap in the broken shutters and waited until the car drove off.

'And that, gentlemen, is how it's done.'

'My good God, Sir, where on earth did you find them?' asked one of the Special Forces commandos sitting at the table.

'France,' said little Geoffrey. 'Now to work; we've six minutes.'

******

Monty threw the car into the drive, just missing Dr Gambon's old Citroen, and sounded the horn for Hilda to unbolt the kitchen door. The rush to get everybody in was done quickly and carefully under the watchful eyes of the two doctors. They'd set up a makeshift operating theatre in the kitchen, covering the long table with a plastic sheet and having clean cotton sheets, boiling water, basins, bandages and their surgical instruments all ready. Colly was being carried into the kitchen first when they heard Den and Lenny ride the bikes into the garage to complete the head count. A heavy dark blue curtain had been hung as a screen across the open entrance to the kitchen, but as Hilda moved in and out, they caught glimpses of the doctors working, and saw the white things in there turning red.

'He is done,' said Professor Chambier, pulling off a rubber glove as he came out. 'The bullets have missed main things. He has been shot twice, here and here' (pointing to his shoulder and upper arm) 'and once here' (pointing to his thigh). 'Now to take him through to the beds, please.'

Den and Lenny carried Colly through to one of the mattresses on the floor of the re-ordered front living room.

'Please to come,' was the polite invitation to Tommy.

'No, aa'm fine, doc, see t' Wilfy first.'

'I am afraid you are not fine, and we must attend to that.' He pointed to the bloody blotch and drew the attention of the others to it.

'For Christ's sake, Tommy, get in there; this is nowt but a cut,' ordered Wilf angrily.

Tommy went and was in for a long time. The blood-stained professor came out through the curtain, pulling off his gloves. He saw them looking at the old doctor still working on Tommy.

'He is stitching him up. He was not so lucky and has had more to do inside …'

'Is ee alright, doctor?'

'Yes, I think he is,' he said kindly, 'we have stopped the bleeding and taken this out.'

He showed them the bullet.

'Christ,' said Roy, taking it, 'that's not from any revolver, that's from a rifle, or a machine gun.'

'It is,' said the calm professor, 'the one tonight went all through him; that one has been there for many years perhaps?'

They were looking at each other, thinking of how many times they'd had a go at Tommy for complaining of a stitch, when the old doctor came out and spoke to the professor.

'He is asking where is Lester?'

'Tell him ee's fine, doc; aa dropped him at the hospital,' said Lenny. 'Ee went side-saddle on the tank.'

He smiled and relayed the message to make the old doctor smile and shake his head.

Tommy was carried through unconscious and laid next to Colly. Wilf was next on the kitchen table, having to have his head shaved by Hilda so they could stitch down the large flap of scalp that had been sliced by a machete. Herbie followed to have a wound stitched that ran from the back of his neck across his shoulder, and

Duggie, who had more cuts than the doctors bothered to count, but none of them serious and only a few wanting more than a half dozen stitches, went after him. Plasters, bandages and ointments were put where they were needed on everybody else, and all was done just before the dawn began to break. The doctors left with the heartfelt thanks of everyone there, and were walked into the courtyard by Monty.

'The old lad's earned a few 12 francs tonight, eh?' said Den, coming back from the front living room with a bottle of cognac and a handful of glasses.

'Any crack off the doctors, Mont?'

'Well, they say Colin will be on the mend soon enough, but Thomas will need more time, although there is no need to worry about him unduly. And they said Hilda has been a marvel in there; good enough to be trusted with the nursing duties, so well done, Madame Brouche.'

He lifted his glass to her and the lads joined in to make her smile.

'What time are we off up the hospital then?'

'Goodness me, gentlemen, don't you want to go to bed and get some rest after all that?'

'No; we'd just stiffen up and it 'ud be ten times worse,' said Wilf.

'Really?' said Monty.

A few of them smiled at his innocence.

'Aye, but we'll have a good wash and get changed first, like.'

'Yer not on about havin' a bath are yer, Len?'

'No, no, nowt so drastic. Should aa fetch me cap down for Wilfy so ee's not scarin' the lasses with ee's new haircut?'

Wilf smiled and told him it wasn't a bad idea though. 'That's if they're awake.'

They knew he meant Nessa.

******

Roy trotted across the hospital car park to catch the others up after checking the back doors and boot were locked.

'But they're both goin' t' be fine, though?'

'For Christ's sake, Stan, how many times do aa have t' say the same bloody thing? Yes- they- are- going- to- be- fine- Stanley.'

'Ee's only checkin', Wilf, keep yer hair on, lad.'

'By, Christ,' said Wilf, trying not to smile.

'Here's the doc comin',' said Lester.

'Poor little bugger looks shattered.'

'Hello again,' he said with a smile. 'I think you would like to come with me now.'

He led them into Nessa's room and had them gather at the foot of the bed. Aude was curled on it with her arms around one of Nessa's. She stayed as she was when she saw them come in, but tried to smile as she looked at them with the tired, dark eyes terror had given her. They could see her looking for Tommy.

Stan walked round and put his hand on her shoulder and rubbed it gently. 'Hello, sweetheart. Are yer feelin' a bit better now?'

She nodded for him, but searched for Tommy.

'Tommy and Colly have come down wi' some sort of flu thing, Pet, and the doctors warned them not t' come up in case yer caught it and it set yer back.'

He could feel her looking through him and the lie, but knew he had to go on. 'Mind, there's nothin' t' worry about, sweetheart; they're both fine and'll be up t' see yer as soon as the doctors let them.'

It was only the last bit that seemed to settle her, but he could see her looking closely at all their faces for any truth they couldn't hide.

The professor stood at the other side of the bed and blew softly into Nessa's face. Her eyes opened slowly to let her see the old smiling faces of home and her happiness. After the worrying hell of the night, the relief was too much for Stan, and as he leaned over to kiss her cheek, the hot tears touched her skin before his lips. She looked at him and he managed to smile when he squeezed her fingers, before standing back so they could all come up and do the same and make her know she was loved. Herbie came last because he wanted to. She looked at him as he held her fingers, and he looked at her, and they stayed like that for just a little while longer than the others; long enough not to be able to see each other. Nessa knew what the looks in their eyes, and the pinching marks on their skin and hands told her, and her heart filled for them. She tried to turn her head away but couldn't. One by one the lads slipped out into the corridor and came back in with a chair, and before long they were all seated and chip-chapping away as they always did when they were together. She lay and watched and listened and smiled. It was only Carter who was quieter than usual and she looked at him until she had his attention. She knew they wouldn't have taken him into a fight, and tried to make him see they were doing their best to look after him. She winked and rolled her eyes to say, 'Christ, here they go again', which made him smile. The professor came back after half an hour to tell them politely it was time for Nessa to rest. He offered Aude the choice to go home or stay with Nessa, and much to their relief she wanted to stay. Stan had a quiet word with her about Roy bringing Hilda up with some things for them, and asked if there was anything they wanted. She spoke quietly into his ear and he nodded and smiled confidentially. Prompted by the professor, they all waved and said their 'ta-ras' and went into the corridor to wait for him coming out.

'She's comin' on well, eh, doc?'

'Yes, it is very much a surprise to us how fast she is awake. But she is very strong and this is good. Yet, to be full to recover will not be fast for her head, I mean past the mending of the bone. I have not to worry about this when she has such friends to give this care, and also from her lover.'

A sharp cough came from Lester, who heard the last comment halfway through a good pull on his Woodbine. The smoke around his head looked like his own private cloud. They all stared at him until the doctor started to speak:

'Yes, time is the most important thing for her to heal well, and with no work, or stressful things, and no alcohol ...'

'Christ.'

'... yes, no alcohol,' smiled the professor good-naturedly, 'and, of course, no travelling.'

The lads flicked a look at each other on the last condition and thanked him, each of them shaking his hand for everything he'd done, before they headed off, leaving Lenny and Den at the hospital. As they made their way across the car park, Lester started to chuckle.

'H'way then, Lester, lad, let's have it,' said the smiling Stan.

'It's just the doc there, gettin' a bit stuck with ee's English, bless him; y'know when ee said, Nessa's "lover" and thinkin' it must be meanin' the same as girlfriend. Mind, yer can see how it must be hard fer them, y'know, 'cause a girlfriend can be yer lover, or, just like wi' the lasses, a friend that's a girl. Aye, it's got t' be hard for them bein' foreign, when they've not learned the lingo proper like what we did from school like what we went at. Still it was funny, mind. Wait till aa tell Tommy and Colly.'

Lester walked on, still chuckling. Behind him they looked their smiling disbelief at the off-key world he lived in.

Chapter 28

Royston drove around the beautiful streaming fountain in the middle of Lyon and parked across the road from the art gallery to let Stan, Wilf, Duggie and Lester out.

'Right, aa'll pick yers up back here at half five.'

'Aye, aye, see yer, Roy.'

'We've got a good couple of hours, anyhow.'

'Aye, but me and Lester'll have t' get a bite t' eat before ee comes back though,' said Stan.

'How come?'

'It's our turn at the hospital tonight.'

'So ee's droppin' yers off there when ee picks Denny and Carter up?'

'That's the plan, Wilfred,' said Stan with a smile.

They set off in their shorts and short-sleeved shirts, happy to have a wander around, and to do it slowly for Lester's sake. The sun shone brightly on the gentle bustle of people going about their daily lives, trying to make the fabric of the collapsing world around them feel like it still had a pocket of normality.

'Mind, this is a lovely-looking place.'

'It is that, Stanley, it certainly is that.'

'How the hell did they build things like that so long ago, eh?' said Wilf, looking at the cathedral reaching magnificently into the light blue sky.

'Proper craftsmen, eh.'

'Proper grafters,' said Duggie.

'Aa'm sure aa've seen her before,' said Lester, looking across the square.

'So you're not over bothered wi' architecture then, Lester?' said Stan with a smile.

'Oh aye, it's a grand old church is that. Aa think aa might have egg 'n' chips in the café.'

'By Christ, ee's all culture.'

'Whey, aa said it was grand, aa'm just famished.'

'Come on then, let's get this lad fed,' said Stan.

Three of them turned to have another look at the cathedral, and turned back to see Lester had wandered off in front.

'Looks like the lone ranger wants a softer saddle,' said Wilf, as they moved to catch him up, trying not to laugh. 'What's up, Lester?' asked Stan.

'Nowt as such, but aa'm sure aa've seen that lass before.'

'Old flame from the last time, eh?'

'She'll be a cinder now.'

******

'See, this is better than that other one.'

'There was nowt the matter wi' the other one.'

'No, aa just didn't like the feel of it once we got sat down.'

'Christ, Lester.'

'Can't help it, it's just me sensitive senses; aa've had them since aa was a kiddie.'

'Not that friggin' gypsy malarky again.'

'No, no, nowt t' do wi' that.'

'Oh aye?' quizzed Wilf, even though he knew he should know better.

'A vision,' said Lester seriously.

The laughter brought a waitress to their table.

'Sorry, Pet,' apologised Stan to the smiling young woman, 'er, do you speak English, Mademoiselle?'

'Yes, but a little.'

'Good, lass,' said Lester. 'Could we have ouef et pommes freets, and deux slices of buttered bread, four times, please?'

She looked lost, so he repeated the order a little louder.

'She doesn't understand what yer sayin', she's not deaf.'

'Can I help, please?' asked the café owner, trying to rescue her and his other customers.

Stan politely explained what they wanted, and added four teas and a bottle of brown sauce to the order. The owner headed to the kitchen trying not to let them see his culinary disgust.

'Right, yer vision,' said Wilf.

'Aye, aa had it when aa was ten, mebbees nine, but anyhow it came t' pass...'

'"It came t' friggin' pass"?'

'It did, and aa've told yers about it before, but yer took no notice...'

'About what?'

'Aye, aye, very funny. D'yers want hear it or not? Right, it was about this woman; a real beauty, tall with dark hair, but who was really a witch, and who just appeared behind me and turned me red ...'

'Red Lester.'

'... and lo and behold it came true.'

'Bollocks.'

'It did. The next day we got that new teacher, that belter, can yer remember?'

'Miss McCarthy,' said Duggie with authority.

'Aye, that's her, and what did she do? She comes up behind me, the nasty sod, and gives me such a clap around the head for smoking, it turned me ear red.'

The laughs brought complaining looks from staff and customers.

'Vision, my arse,' said Wilf, 'yer'll have dreamed about it later.'

'Couldn't have.'

'How come?'

'Aa wasn't asleep when aa had it.'

'When the hell did yer have it then?'

'When aa was Ferretin'.'

'Yer had a vision when you were out with yer ferrets?'

'Whey, they weren't mine, they were Teddy Bicker's, aa thought ee'd set them off and that aa had t' wait for them ...'

'But?'

'But ee'd already finished and was away home for ee's tea.'

They tried to keep the laughter down.

'Christ, did any bugger ever bring yer back from anywhere they took yer?'

'Whey, anyhow,' continued Lester, 'it must've been lookin' down that rabbit hole for hours that sparked me vision.'

He waited for the slating he knew would be coming, but they sat in silence, gazing gormlessly over his head. He turned and found his face two inches away from a woman's pelvis. Looking up past the precipice of the full breasts that were perfectly fitted into a tight white blouse, he saw the beautiful face of a tall, dark-haired woman.

'It is you, Monsieur,' she said in English, 'I saw you as I passed by the window and I have come to thank you.'

'What for, Miss?' asked the gaping Lester on autopilot.

'For my life, Monsieur.'

She bent down and kissed him deliberately, leaving thick red lipstick marks on each cheek. As she smiled at the messy smudges her matching red finger-nailed thumb was making trying to rub them off, the lads saw it was a smile that must have wrecked a thousand love-struck ships. She knew it was because it had, and she could see these four little boats were taking in water by their open mouths. Opening a small black leather handbag, she took out a dainty white handkerchief and licked it to clean Lester's face. Duggie moved in his seat. Lester remembered his auntie Sadie used to do that when he was little.

'There, you are respectable again.' She smiled.

Clipping shut the shiny gold clasp on her bag, she stood to her full height and leaned back slightly, holding it in front of the lowest part of her flat tummy, right in the middle of the broadening curves of her tight cream pencil skirt. She smiled at them looking up at her like chicks in a nest, and noticed Lester turning redder than her lipstick.

'Ah, I see you now remember me, yes. But you must not be … er, how do you say, Monsieur … disturbed? by the way we met last. Yes, I was naked, but I am only a woman.'

Duggie crossed his legs, Lester forgot to breathe, and Stan tried to help them all: 'Oh, you must be the lady Lester helped that night?'

'Yes, I am her, and he did help me on that terrible night. Hello, Lester, I am Monica,' she said, holding out her hand with playful formality.

Lester took it automatically and Stan made the introductions for them each to stand up and shake hands with her.

'Here y'are, Monica, have a seat,' said Stan, offering his.

She protested, but was never going to refuse. He came back with a spare chair and the waitress.

'Tell the lass what yer want, Monica, and she'll put it on our tab.'

Accepting only a cup of tea she didn't touch, she used all her professional control to lower herself a lot further down the cultural ladder than she'd been trained for, so she could chat cosily about the completely alien things they brought up.

'And have you always had the biggest leek in the club show, Wilfy?' was a question she could never have dreamed of asking ten minutes ago.

'Most years, Pet, aye, although there's a few who'd like t' take me crown: that useless sod, Sid McElvany for one, and aa suppose they will this year, with us bein' away, like,' he said sadly.

'You boys, how have you to judge the biggest leek as the best one? Do you not know that the little leek can be the sweetest? And is it not for the woman who must cook with it who should be judge?' She looked at Lester to make his blushing tide rush back in.

'Science, Pet,' replied Wilf with comic pride. 'To push the boundaries of what man can do.'

She laughed with them, and they thought it was a proper one this time.

'Christ, it's 20 past,' said Lester, looking at his mighty timepiece.

'We've got t' go now, Monica, Pet; we're away up t' the hospital,' explained Stan.

'Nothing bad I hope?'

'No, no, just t' see our friend who's a bit poorly, like,' he said honestly.

'But tell me please, how I can return your jacket, Lester, and the money you gave me, please.'

'No, no need t' bother about that, Pet, it wasn't my jacket anyways so don't worry yersel' about it.'

She saw he was relieved to stand to go, and knew she'd gone as far as she could for now with these new and very different men of her latest assignment. Making sure her friendly and bonding kisses were planted on their cheeks, she wished them a very good day, and caught Lester's hand to thank him once more – from the bottom of her calculating heart.

'Yer've pulled there, Lester, lad,' said Duggie as soon as they were outside.

'Had-a-way, she's like a bloody film star, what the hell would she want wi' 'owt like me, eh?'

'Fair point,' slipped in Wilf.

'No; ee could be the tasty little leek,' said Stan.

'Aye, mebbees, but she looks like she'll take some feedin', eh, Dug?'

Duggie let the pencil moustache stretch and blew a channel of smoke from the side of his mouth.

'What the hell's Roy got in the back of the car now?' tried Lester.

The little hope he had of it helping him wriggle free was shattered by Wilf telling him with a wink, that they'd see him in the morning.

******

'Never,' said Tommy, trying not to laugh because it hurt.

'Oh aye, and aa'd say she'd be about the same height as Herbie with her high heels on, eh, Dug?'

Duggie nodded and picked a bit baccy off his tongue.

'Little Lester Sweetleeks, eh. Wait 'til the little bugger gets back.'

'Sounds like that's them now.'

It wasn't, it was the old doctor's car pulling into the courtyard. Hilda made the coffee and the doctor and the professor had it with one of Carter's croissants. All the news on the lasses was good, but Tommy thought there was something the professor wasn't saying about Aude. The lads left the front living room with Hilda so that

Colly and Tommy could be examined. Having finished with Colly, the professor left him with Dr Gambon and moved on to Tommy.

'Does this hurt?'

'No.'

'And here?'

'No.'

'I see. And what about this?'

'Jesus Christ, doc.'

'Still tender, yes.'

'Just a bit,' said Tommy with watering eyes.

The professor smiled. 'Yes, but this is still good. Let me see, yes, four days and like this is very good.'

'Then can aa please go t' the hospital, Doctor?'

'I told you on Sunday, no, and yesterday, no, and today I should say no for one more day.'

'Please, Doc, aa think aa need to go.'

'Why do you say such? Your friends are there and the girls know you are well.'

'No disrespect, Doc, yer a smashin' lad, both of yers are – Christ, yer've saved Nessa's life, and mebbees a couple more as well – but aa can't help thinkin' yer keepin' somethin' back about little Order.'

The professor hesitated and looked around the room before speaking. 'Yes, you are right, I am not so happy about the little girl,' he admitted.

Seeing the colour being dragged from Tommy's face, he pressed on: 'Yes. It is not her body, it is well now, but her nerves are not well. They are to worry me.'

He could see he didn't understand and tried to explain: 'You are a man, Tommy, a strong man and a fighter. You have seen war and death, but Aude has none of these things to make her strong. But she was in a war. She was trapped by the enemy, and trapped while they pounded their weapons on her lover, her friend, and the one who is her life. This makes more for me to worry.'

'But Nessa's goin' t' be alright, isn't she, Doc?'

'Yes, but you must hear what I am saying: it is to Aude the harm has been done – it is in the noises, the sounds of them beating

Nessa, the smells, of the blood, the memory and the fear she has had, these are the things that have put their bad effects on her nerves. Dr Gambon says you will know of this from many times in the war, and with strong men.'

Tommy nodded to say he did and rubbed his eyes. 'Then what can yer do, Doc, what can we do?'

The professor's heart went out to him and he was happy to say: 'We must bring her back to home …'

'Home?' said Tommy, thinking he meant Norway.

'Yes, home, here.'

He tapped the middle of Tommy's chest with his finger.

'Here is her home, here she is guarded from the terrible things that now won't let her sleep, or eat, and …' the doctor hesitated again, '… and can make her die. Yes, it is a hard fact, Tommy. Don't cry. This is what I have been keeping from you, but only from you until you could go to her.'

The professor looked straight at him looking wonderingly back.

'Yes, we now can begin to make her better. So go and dress and have Herbert and one other strong man to be at your side, as well as me, of course, and we will go to her,' said the good-natured little man.

Tommy took his soft little hand in his heavy catcher's mitt and held it in silence. The professor never forgot that moment for the whole of the rest of his long life.

'Grand news, eh, Tommy,' said Wilf, leading them in from the back living room.

Tommy let go of the professor's hand and shook his head as he smiled at the floor.

'Get ee's duds, Denny, lad, chop-chop.'

'Should aa get ee's good shirt?'

'Aye. And ee wants a shave.'

'Fetch a basin, Hilda, Pet.'

'Oh, Messieurs,' said the professor smiling, 'there is not to be so great to rush, we have some things to make ready at the hospital before you come.'

'Like what, Doc?'

'Like an ambulance,' he said, holding his smile.

'For Nessa?' said Wilf.

'Yes,' beamed the professor, 'yes, we can do little more different at the hospital now, and she will be more to do well at home. But we must make the plan for her to have her visits from us and nurses to help Madame Brouche, yes.'

'Oh, yes, Doc, lad,' said Wilf, shaking his hand.

While they were saying their goodbyes as the old doctor cranked his little car into life, Royston slipped into the garage. The rest of them set about planning the front living room for the lasses coming back, but without Stan there they flapped about like paper kites in a strong wind. With the quiet steering of Hilda, they managed to get organised: their scruffy field hospital was shifted away and, with an almighty struggle, they got the girl's bed downstairs and set beside the big front window. Hilda had them rig up the dark blue curtain as a privacy screen that could be drawn around the bed, and brought little things down from their room to make their new place feel nice.

'So what time's it now?'

'Half two.'

'H'way, then, let's off.'

'Hang fire, the little doc said we'd knack it if we went sharp, mind.'

'Aye, aye. What the hell's Royston shoutin' about out there?'

Duggie and Wilf went out and came back trying not to laugh.

'What?'

'No, it's nowt, it's just somethin' for Tom.'

Tommy looked at them knowing it wasn't going to be good. Herbie and Lenny pulled him up off the settee to walk him through to the back door. They looked at Roy standing proudly in the middle of the courtyard behind the wheelchair he'd made.

'Come on, Tom, lad, give her a spin.'

Tommy had to smile at the state of it and knew he had to get in. Roy pushed him up and down between the two towers.

'Sweet as a nut, eh, Tom. Just once more t' make sure she's runnin' right.'

Tommy smiled to himself at Roy.

'Where the hell d'yer think ee got them pram wheels?'

'There's always a tip somewhere, and Roy's the boy t' find it.'

'Aye, or there'll be a babby somewhere that'll have t' learn t' walk before it crawls.'

Tommy ended up doing about 20 laps between the towers because they all had to have a go pushing.

'Three, trois, three, maintenant,' called Hilda, holding up three fingers.

'She's comin' on leaps and bounds with her English, eh,' whispered Wilf.

'Right, Royston my man, bring the car around for Lord Gutshot here and we'll be off.'

******

At the hospital the little professor let them into his plan. 'Yes, we are ready, but I have said nothing because to make the nice surprise. But I am here for you to tell us when we can begin our work, yes.'

'Yes, Doctor, thank you,' said Stan.

Herbie wheeled Tommy along the corridor with Lenny beside him. They bent down to sneak under the viewing window of Nessa's room and stopped by the door to pull Tommy to his feet. Herbie looked at him uncertainly.

'Aa'm fine,' he whispered, 'once aa'm up, aa'm fine.'

Herbie nodded and let go of his wrist and arm. Tommy went into the room by himself. His eyes met Nessa's and they locked onto each other until their filmy forms were lost. She tried to blink away her tears, but the little success she had failed altogether when she watched him trying to walk to her as though there was nothing wrong. He saw Aude asleep on her little bed and was shocked by the change in her face. Taking Nessa's fingers and putting his cheek on hers, he felt the heavy cast on her right arm rest on his back. He just stayed there and loved her until she lifted it to let him move to kiss her forehead. He told her he'd come to take her home. She did her best to speak, and he waited patiently, rubbing his hand gently over her head until she could.

'Wake her up, Tom.'

He looked like he didn't want to because it must be better for her to sleep.

'Wake her up, Tommy, she needs t' see yer.'

He looked closely at Aude and had to catch his breath from the fear of the professor's words. Just then the professor came in.

'I have the thought that it would be better for me to wake her up,' he whispered, 'for it to be not so much of a shock from me as from you, Tommy.'

He motioned him back out of her first line of sight and knelt down to lightly touch her shoulder. Tommy saw her eyes open slowly and look forlornly at the professor.

'Are you awake, my little girl?'

Tommy heard the loving care in the little man's voice, and saw a little smile try to show him she was there.

'And are you sure you are awake, my little one?' he teased kindly.

She moved to prop herself up, as if to prove she was, and saw Tommy. She looked at him through what he would always know, were the biggest, blackest, shiniest and most beautiful eyes that have ever seen life on earth. They showed how lost and lonely she was in the swirling world between soft unknown dreams and the hard reality of day. He moved towards her. He could see her propping arm start to tremble. In the moment it gave way, he caught her up in his arms and lifted her to him, squeezing her as much as he dared without hurting her. He felt nothing but the little arms go around his neck as they had done so many times before; the excruciating pain from his wound couldn't get past his love for her.

'Aa've come t' take yer home, sweetheart, you and Nessa, yer both comin' home with us now.'

The arms tightened and her head pushed deeply into him.

Chapter 29

It was four days after leaving hospital and nearly everyone was in the front living room, sitting comfortably, smiling broadly, and trying not to laugh, as they listened to Lester talking to Nessa behind the curtain screen.

'Aa mean aa'm not sayin' mine's bigger than Den's, or even Wilfy's for that matter, aa'm just sayin' it's got a better look about it, see; d'yer not think that's a lovely big head?'

'Oh aye.'

'So have they been in and showed yer theirs, then?'

'Aye.'

'So, would yer say mine's much littler than Den's, then?'

'A bit.'

'But it can't be that much littler than Wilfy's, 'cause aa've seen him washin' it in the sink. Mind, Hilda wasn't happy about that, like, which seems strange t' me, 'cause she must've washed a good few in her time. So did they get yer t' feel theirs?'

'No.'

'D'yer want t' feel mine? Aa can run it up through yer fingers if yer want?'

'No, yer alright, Lester.'

'Sure? It's slippy enough not t' give yer any friction or 'owt. No? Oh whey, fair enough. And there's another thought just come t' me there; when aa say "bigger than mine", yer not just thinkin' about length are yer, Pet?'

'Whey, sort of.'

'That's good y'see, 'cause the way aa reckon it, mine could still be the biggest y'see. Think about it this way, what did Denny have? Twelve inches, say, and Wilfy about ten t' ten and a half, eh, right, whey aa'll accept mine's only a nine, but it's a good nine, mind, but, look at the thickness of that thing though, yer can't tell me theirs is heavier than that, eh.'

'No.'

'Whey there yer have it, Pet, y'see, the girth on mine 'ud fill yer any time yer fancied a bit…'

Colly yanked the curtain aside so they could drop the cushions they'd had pressed to their faces and laugh out loud.

'Oh, it's a fish yer on about, is it?' said Tommy.

'What the hell d'yer think it was?'

Springing up to fight off the laughing smut, he fumbled his trout out of his hands to slap Nessa in the face.

'Christ.'

The panicked Lester shot around the bed to get it and Nessa laughed with everybody else at his honest distress.

'Goodness me.' Monty smiled, coming in with a six-foot plank. 'What's happening to poor Nessa?'

'Lester's tormentin' her with ee's nine-incher.'

'How'd yer like that in yer pan, Mont?'

'Now, now, Wilfred.'

'Aa'm sorry, Pet,' apologised Lester, 'aa must've been grippin' it too tight and that's what's made it shoot across yer face.'

'Christ.'

'Yer fine, Lester.' Nessa smiled. 'Yer've just hurt me ribs a bit though, makin' me laugh.'

She winked to make him stop fretting.

'Sorry, Pet. Mind, as soon as yer get them casts off, yer'll be comin' fishin' with us, eh?'

'Aa will,' she said, and meant it.

'Right, Lester, go and slip Hilda yer fat little tiddler, and get back here so we can get sorted.'

Lester came back from the kitchen to take hold of an end of one of the three planks under Nessa's mattress. On the count of three they lifted and carried her Cleopatra-style into the bright white sunshine of the glorious summer's day. Tommy and Aude carried pillows, towels, suncream and other bits and bobs. He gave her a gentle boof with a pillow and saw the old smile come to the surface a little quicker. He told himself she was getting better and cuddled her close, which he did more than ever now, and knew he would for all of the rest of the life he had left. Aude needed it more than anything medical and Tommy seemed to know it.

'Ready?' asked superintendent Colly when they were on the lawn.

They nodded.

'And down.'

Nessa was set down on the bench seats Roy and Lenny had fettled together, so she could sit comfortably in the middle of the enchanting colours of the quietly humming garden behind the swimming pool. Herbie set Aude's lounge chair beside her, and the others brought parasols, little tables, and other handy things for them to have a lovely afternoon outside.

'Right, you two can have a nice bit sunbathe and a bit of peace and quiet without us old cheps pesterin' yers, eh,' said Tommy.

'Where are you going to, Tommy?' asked Aude.

'Snooker, Pet,' answered Wilf.

Tommy went round beside her and although he tried to hide it, she saw him wince as he knelt down.

'Your hip is still to hurt you, Tommy?' she asked.

'A little bit, Pet, but the Doc says it's on the mend, it'll just take a bit time, ee says it's always the same wi' these muscle twists. But, serves me right for tryin' t' chuck the old bass about like aa used to ten years ago, when aa was 30.'

He winked to make her smile. 'Aa'm just in there, sweetheart, probably takin' money off these buggers wi' me delicate break buildin'.'

He smiled at her, pinched her chin, and gave it the gentle little shake that always made her smile. It did.

'So, just shout up, Pet, if yers want 'owt.'

He knew he needed to make sure she knew he was close by, and that the lads were as well. He was right; he could feel the big black jets burning onto him as he walked away, and saw them looking when he turned to wave before going out of their sight. Half an hour later the quiet music from the gramophone floated through the open doors to where the girls were, accompanied by the distant click and clatter of snooker balls and bursts of laugher. Nessa felt Aude's head get heavier on her shoulder and was pleased to know she was starting to sleep better. She heard the quiet purring of a car roll into the courtyard, but paid no attention to it, or to anything else that would stop the loveliness of feeling Aude's restful breath on her skin. She didn't notice the noise of the snooker balls had stopped while the music played on.

'Hello,' said the tall, elegant figure standing in the open doorway to the snooker room, clutching a small black handbag in front of the lower part of her tummy, and wearing a threadbare old jacket, 'is it possible to speak to Lester, please?'

'Oh, aye, yes, ee's just havin' a sh… a short visit t' the, lav, Miss.'

They fell silent and stared at her. She was used to it, and began the well-rehearsed performance of nonchalant ignorance of the effects her beauty had on men. Stan tried to break the siren spell they were under by making the introductions, which were going well until the noisy rake of a metal chain pulling the noisy flush of a toilet couldn't fail to be heard. The new silence it brought was boosted by the end of the record on the gramophone – it made the singing in the toilet crystal clear:

'Oooh, sheep deep dee baybeeeeeee
Shoo boo biddee doooooo
Oooh, honeysuckle baybeeeee
Ass a runnin' to yoooooo …………. yeah'

A little bolt was waggled open and the whistling Lester came out looking down at the belt he was tugging to fasten in the hole he couldn't find. He stopped whistling to tell anybody who might be listening, about the fine, rude health of his constitution, despite the eye-watering stiffness of a bowel movement he claimed was like a copper's truncheon. Looking up from his fastened belt he saw the gathered audience grinning at him with eyes flicking towards the door. He followed them and froze in the reflected fallout of his crippling embarrassment. Monica pretended not to have heard a thing, and expertly stepped into their simpler world:

'I said I would return it to you, Lester, and here I am.'

She put her bag down on the snooker table, unbuttoned the only fastened button, and made the most erotic show of taking off the perfectly fitting jacket. None of it was lost on any of the lads. Standing in her equally perfectly fitting silver-grey satin blouse and matching tight, dark grey pencil skirt, she made her magnificently sculptured curves move enticingly to pick up her handbag and assume her premier pose.

'She knocked the brown there, mind,' whispered Wilf, 'yer break's finished.'

'Bollocks,' argued Lenny, forgetting to whisper because there was two francs riding on it and he was winning.

She swayed a little and looked to the ceiling.

'Would yer like a glass of cognac, Monica?' said Stanley, knowing he had to do something.

'Aye, sit yersel down, Pet, Herbie'll fetch yer a glass,' said the ever-helpful Tommy.

She seemed happy to take a seat on the couch.

'Here's a glass,' offered Colly, smiling, sitting beside Duggie who was sitting beside her.

Herbie filled it from an old bottle and she took her polished etiquette dry lip sip.

'Thank you, you are very kind.'

'So what d'yer think about the trouble you've caused us havin' t write t' London t' get Lester's name changed,' said Tommy seriously.

She looked genuinely lost and Tommy went on: 'Aye, we've had t' have it changed to Lester Sweetleeks for when ee's in England, and Monsieur Le Petite Leek for when ee's in France.'

Monica laughed with them and realised she wasn't acting.

'D'yer play snooker at all, Pet?' asked Lenny.

They all looked their bewilderment at him.

'Yes, I do,' she said simply, 'would you like me to play the winner?'

They all shifted their bewilderment to her.

Lenny grabbed the brown off the table. 'That'll be me, Pet. Aa'll rack them up.'

He smiled at Wilf on his way to set the balls up.

'D'yer want t' break, Monica, or should aa?'

She nodded to him and he bent over the table to take a long deliberate aim.

'D'yer think we should stamp a branding iron on that thing, Monica?' said Tommy, pointing a cue at Lenny's drum-tight shorts.

She leaned forward as she laughed, and again had to accept she wasn't putting it on.

Lenny stood up. 'This is what aa've got t' put up with every bloody day, Pet.'

'Aww,' she soothed playfully.

'What are yer's playin' for, anyhow?' asked Colly.

'Just keep it t' the two francs, eh?'

'Yer a bloody hustler, Lenny.'

'But I don't have any money, so what will you take from me instead?'

Lenny went as red as 15 balls on the table when the lads started whistling their saucy thoughts to make her smile.

'No, nowt, Pet, we'll just play fer fun, eh?'

'No,' she replied firmly, 'I will have your two francs if I win, and you will have a kiss from me if I don't.'

'Chalk that cue, Lenny, lad,' came out of the cheers.

He did and settled back down to his shot, giving the reds a miscued clatter that scattered them all over the place. He walked away, looking at the blameless tip of his cue.

'Still got it, Lenny, lad.'

Monica walked slowly around the table, looking closely at the balls, stopping every now and then to chalk her cue. The shot was chosen, it just happened to be directly in front of where most of them were standing, and she leaned fully over the table. Elbows jabbed ribs, feet kicked feet, and heads nodded to the fertile form. She knew there would be, and stood up and reconsidered as she chalked the cue while walking to the other side of the table to go down on another shot that let them see just enough cleavage to fire their imagination to heavenly heights. She stood up again, went to her first choice and cleared the table with a break of 108.

'Christ Almighty, Monica, Pet, where d'yer learn t' play like that?'

'Oh, I grew up in a snooker hall,' she said honestly, with a note of sadness; 'my mother had one to run in the town where I grew up in Switzerland, and all of the men always wanted to show me how to play with them.'

'Aa'll bet they did,' just reached her ears.

She didn't tell them the snooker hall was a front for the most notorious brothel in Hamburg, or that her mother was the even more notorious Madame Honig.

'H'way Lenny, lad, get yer hand in yer pocket.'

Monica had no idea what this meant, but, unusually, didn't fear the worst from these men. Lenny pulled out half a dozen coins and offered them to her. She smiled and thought of Lester giving her his money that night.

'No, it wasn't fair for me to take advantage of you, Lenny; so I will give up the game as a cheat and make you the winner.'

She sidled up to him and kissed his cheek, leaving her red oval trademark, before going over to Lester for the handbag she'd trusted to him while she played. She bent down and kissed his cheek a little differently, and took his hand to say goodbye. She felt the nerves in it and smiled nicely as he stood looking up at her.

'Oh, hello?' said Monty, strolling in. 'Aren't you going to introduce me to your new friend, gentlemen?'

'Aye, this is Monica, Monty; the lady Lester helped that night. She's just droppin' ee's jacket off.'

'Oh, I see,' he said, working hard to hide his recognition of Count Von Leibernitz's most trusted spy, Sylvia Plank.

'And this is Monty, Monica; he's like our manager,' said Stan.

He took her hand and bowed to kiss it.

'It is nice to meet you, Monsieur, but you must excuse me as I must rush away now.'

'That is a shame,' oiled Monty, before Lenny stuck a spanner in his works.

'Whey, why not come and have a bite t' eat one night, eh?'

They all encouraged her to accept, and Monty went along with professional enthusiasm.

'I would like that very much.' The winning Sylvia smiled. 'Is there a good night for you to have me?'

Duggie coughed a cloud of smoke out.

'Any night we're not playin', Pet.'

'Well, how about I telephone Monty to make a date, yes?'

With that, they walked her to her car and waved as she drove out of the courtyard.

'Some motor that: fantastic bodywork, and it'll go like the clappers – aa'd love t' give it a good go.'

'Duggie's nearly thinkin' the same thing, Roy, lad,' said Wilf.

'Tommy,' came the quiet call on the gentle breeze.

He walked around to the garden and came back a few minutes later. 'The car door must've woken her up and she just wanted t' know we're here, like.'

They could all see how painfully fragile Aude was, but did their best to make sure Tommy didn't see they could.

Sylvia was back in Berlin that night and sent on to London the following day.

Chapter 30

Four weeks later.

Monty wheeled the desk full of papers he was working on under a table and let the tablecloth fall to the floor to hide it, before he answered the knock on his door.

'Stanley, come in, come in. And to what do I owe the pleasure?'

Stan smiled as he entered and took the seat he was offered.

'It's a couple of things, Monty.'

'Nothing bad, I hope.'

'No, no. Yer know how we're due t' go home for a couple of weeks at the end of next week?'

'I do, Stanley.'

'Well, it's just that we've had a bit of a meetin' there, after the doctors examined the lasses, and we've settled on us not goin' back... not just now, like.'

'Oh, I must say that does surprise me. May I ask why?'

'Whey, it's 'cause Nessa can't go, y'see; they won't let her travel, and that means Aude won't go without her, and then that means Tommy won't go 'cause he won't leave her here, and then Colly would struggle, and then Lester said he didn't feel right goin' when they were havin' t' stop back, and anyhow, it ended up nobody wantin' t' go and leave the others.'

Monty felt his emotions pulled by their attachment.

'But,' continued Stan, 'we still want to touch base back home, y'know, get a few messages back and see how things are, like, so we had a bit of a vote and me and Herbie got picked t' pop back, if we can, like.'

'I see.' Monty smiled kindly. 'But why do you think they voted for Herbert when – and please forgive me if I sound insensitive – when he'd be the one who'd have most difficulty relaying messages?'

'Because ee's sister's not very well and ee's mother's a good age now,' answered Stan simply to touch Monty more.

'I see, and when would you like to go and for how long?'

'Anytime yer can manage, Mont, and just for a day or two, but the sooner the better, if possible.'

'Only two days, are you sure?'

'Oh aye, no more; we'll want t' get back.'

The manner of the reply made him think there was something else coming.

'Well, as there's only two of you, I can get you over on a Lizzie tomorrow night and have you back on Wednesday evening about 7.00. How about that?'

'Yer the best, Monty, lad.'

He noticed the knitted brow settle on Stan and waited.

'There is, er, one more thing, Mont.'

'Go on,' he said good-humouredly.

'Well, two things really. The first one's a funny one, mind.'

Monty watched the puffy little hands push over the bald head.

'It's for you t' make out we've had our time back home cancelled, like. Now aa know this'll make yer look like the bad bugger here, and it's not fair for us t' ask, but it's the only way we can think of t' stop Nessa thinkin' she's causin' us any bother and stoppin' us from gettin' home: she's been through enough without havin' t' feel guilty about us sackless old sods, eh.'

Monty stood and walked to the window. He did it hoping Stan would think he was wrestling with the request, but it was to hide the emotion he didn't want him to see.

'We thought,' continued Stan, 'that mebbees you could make out we've got behind with the playin', and now we've got t' catch up, or somethin' like that. You're better at this stuff than us, Monty, but whatever yer come up with, the lads know to go along with it.'

'I see,' said Monty, looking out of the window. 'How about I mention a postponement after dinner tonight, and a longer

Christmas break perhaps? I'm sure that would seem realistic, and Nessa would see it wasn't too bad for you all, ay?'

'Monty, you're a proper good lad and we'd be lost without yer, mind.'

He had to keep facing the window. 'I'll risk being Mr Nasty,' he said playfully, 'and I'll be happy to do it, Stanley, because we're all friends in this together, isn't that so.'

Now Stan smiled at the unseeing Monty and told him he was right; they were all friends together.

'And the second thing, Stanley?'

'It's a favour for me, please, Mont.'

'For you, Stanley, if it can be done, it shall be done.'

Monty kept his face to the window and listened.

******

'So, what's ee say then?'

'Ee says ee'll come down tonight to do ee's bit, ee was really good about it, mind.'

Stan shuffled the cards, making out he was having trouble with them.

'So, how yer feelin' now then, Tom?'

'Fine and dandy, Stanley,' lied Tommy, 'just a bit listless; age, that's what it is.'

'Aye.'

The silent pause seemed longer than it was while he dealt the cards.

'Wilf says yer were sick again last night.'

'Too much bloody fish that's what that was; thanks t' him and Duggie and little Sweetleeks there wi' their bloody rods out again. Still Hearts fer trumps?'

'Aye.'

The pause was short but the silence felt longer.

'Wilf says yer not right, Tom.'

Tommy was about to throw his cards down to have a go at Stan, but stopped when he saw him trying to hide behind his.

'Stan,' he said firmly but considerately, 'ee's right, aa'm not a 100%, but it's nowt more than a bit gut-rot, or even just not gettin' me nutrients off Vern.'

He saw Stan smile.

'But there's nowt more than that. What's up, like, what's ee been sayin'?'

'Ee's worried sick…'

Tommy knew it was Stan who was worried sick.

'… 'cause ee thinks it's got somethin' t' do wi' yer wound and somethin's not right inside.'

'It isn't; aa would know if it was 'owt like that, and surely t' God the doctors would have clocked it, eh.'

'Aye.'

Tommy could see he wasn't convinced. 'Anyhow, never mind witterin' on about me, what's happenin' wi' goin' back, then?'

'Ee says ee can get us over in somethin' called a Lizzie tomorro' night; 'cause there's just the two of us, like.'

'That's good, mind. And for the two days?'

'Aye, plenty of time t' let them know what's what.'

'Will yer see Dinsey?' whispered Tommy.

Stan nodded.

'Yer'll need yer headpiece screwed on, mind.'

'So we're buggered then,' said Stan to his failing but smiling friend.

******

Monty looked at them as they sat chatting around the dinner table, thinking about Stan's visit, and watching their close and complete indifference to their decision not to go home. He saw Aude sitting between Nessa and Tommy, and noticed how much better she looked and how much worse he did. He watched him sneakily pull a loose hair on her head to make her spin round and slap him happily. He was still smiling at Tommy playing the innocent victim of her harsh injustice when he stood up and tapped the side of his glass with a spoon. Wilf asked Aude if she thought he'd make a drummer. She smiled and said: 'No, Wilfy,' to make them all cheer big-heartedly for her.

'Does everyone have a drinky?' began Monty. 'Good. And is everyone sitting comfortably? Good. Now, gentlemen, and of course our young ladies, I bring news and will endeavour to deliver it with my usual vim and vigour, even though I am myself now struggling under the cloud of shattered ambition on hearing my career as a drummer is over before it began.'

'Now see what yer've done, Order, Pet.'

She laughed with them.

'But, I must go on – adversity forges character and you will see here, standing before you tonight, a character turned as true as steel.'

'Christ, Monty, what the hell have yer got stashed away up there?'

'Life, Colin, only the *joie de vie*, and with it I will press on against the cold, icy winds of outrageous beatster criticism, and pass you the torch of news I have. But, I'm afraid it is not to be good news tonight, yet far from terrible. How could it be? I hear you ask – how could a horrible message possibly lurk within such an innocent and boyishly handsome visage?'

'For Christ's sake, Mont, crack on so we can get outside: we're in the play-offs wi' the boules and Lenny's lookin' at relegation and heavy losses.'

'I will, Wilfred, I will, "crack on" directly. Well, I have received news, or to be more correct, I have received orders to postpone our return visit home next week, which will, of course, mean you won't have the scheduled first two weeks in October in Firstwood.'

The lads made all the right noises, comments and cracks that anyone who knew them would have expected.

'Please, gentlemen, the word to note here is "postpone". We are not being denied anything or, to my mind, being treated unfairly, we are merely being asked to defer for a short time.'

'Why though, Monty?' asked Stan on cue.

'Because, Stanley, we have obligations that have not been fulfilled, and, unfortunately, they must be completed in this first phase. Now you will know I can't say any more about that, but this is the news and those are our orders. And, we must remember that there are contractual commitments underpinning the remuneration detail.'

'Do the work if we want the money.'

'Exactly, Dennis.'

He waited for the well-acted grumbling to die down. 'Now, a couple of things I have been able to do may apply a little salve to the disappointment you're feeling now. The first is to secure more time for you at home over Christmas and New Year.'

He enjoyed the cheers and the "well done, Montys".'

'The other thing, which was a lot more difficult to pull off, is to arrange for two of you to go home tomorrow for two days.'

This was met with the silence Stan had prepared him for.

'Yes, I understand this will seem very odd, and you're all wondering who will go and why, and goodness knows what else. Well, I'll give you my reasons for doing it and if you don't approve, then we can simply forget about it, and you can call me a silly blooming Billy.'

'Easy wi' the language, Mont, it's upsettin' Lenny.'

'My apologies, Leonard. So, as to who will go? Now I simply couldn't bear being the one responsible for forcing you to have to make such a devilish decision, so London drew names from a hat. I have them here, but I won't reveal them if you don't want to do this. And as for why send two people home? I thought you might like to send messages home and have some news brought back, that's all.'

He stopped and watched them while he sipped his cognac. The chatter began and he waited, but only for a minute.

'We think it's a good idea, Monty, but wondered if yer could get a bit bigger plane comin' back, t' fetch a few bottles of Bess.'

'I'll try my best, Thomas.' He smiled.

'So who got drawn out then, Monty?'

'Right. Now, could I please check you're all sure about this?'

They made it clear they were.

'The names were drawn using randomly assigned corresponding numbers, and they are: number 82, Stanley, and number 14, that's one, four, 14, Herbert.'

Good natured cheers and pats on the back greeted the winners.

'Aa think there's a job for yer after the war, Mont: callin' the bingo in the Buffs.'

Chapter 31

The snooker balls clacked and the darts dudded as the mellow music played on the gramophone behind the quiet little pockets of chat that murmured around the music room.

'But aa'm famished now,' said Lester.

'Aye, but we said we'd wait fer them.'

'Aye, but they were supposed t' be back at 7.00 and it's after 8.00 now.'

'They'll not be long now, Lester, lad, yer ravenous little beast.'

'Aa need me grub, Tom, or aa get all feisty.' (laughs)

'Chuck him a bit baccy t' chew, Duggie.'

'Hang on till half eight then, and if they're not back by then we'll get yer somethin' t' keep yer civil.'

'Hey-up, here's a car comin',' said Lester.

'It's them. Right, just stay put the way we are, and when they come in we'll just crack on as if they've never been away, eh,' said Colly.

They heard the car doors open and thump shut and waited. As one they all sat bolt upright, as though they'd been shocked by the same electric prod. Their breathing stopped. They looked at each other.

'It can't be,' whispered Wilf.

Tommy put his finger to his lips and had them follow him single file down by the pool to peep around the open door. They snapped back in a hiding huddle and froze in ambushed silence, listening to a very familiar aggravated voice:

'And what the hell d'yer think yer doin' wi' that now, lad?' boomed the voice across the courtyard.

'To lend you my hand, Madame.'

'Aa'll lend you my hand across the side of yer head if yer don't get yer bloody mitts off it, yer cheeky bugger.'

'Ee's just tryin' t' help wi' the ...'

'And who the hell's askin' you, eh? When aa want your opinions, Stanley South, aa'll ask fer them, lad. Look, ee's still rivin' on. Aa tell yer what; the pair of yers are startin' t' work yer tickets here, mind. Herbert, you carry that one and aa'll come back for this one. And you sackless buggers hidin' ahind that wall there, can come out afore aa have t' come over and give yers all a bloody knock, 'cause that's what yers are askin' for; arsin' about like bits of kids.'

'How the hell did she see us?' whispered Lenny, before he was pushed out.

'Hello Margaret, Pet, aa can't believe yer here.'

'Whey, there's a bloody first 'cause yer'll believe 'owt any bugger else tells yer.'

The lads summoned their smiles and went into the softening evening light to gather around and get their homely little arm-around-the-neck-cuddles from her. She left them all talking to Stan, and headed for the kitchen door as though she'd lived there all her life. Tommy called to her quietly to stop.

'What for?'

'It's just, aa was just thinkin' how much of a nice surprise we got and that it would be grand for the lasses as well, eh?'

Encouraged by her not having a go at him, he went on: 'How about if aa go in and get them lookin' at somethin' for a minute, and then aa'll say there's somebody come t' see yers, and when they look over yer'll be standin in the doorway, eh.'

She looked closely at him while he was talking, smiled faintly and rubbed the back of his arm.

'Right, hang fire a minute,' he said.

He picked one of the little yellow flowers growing by the garage.

'Half a minute, Denny.'

'Hello, lovely lasses,' he said carelessly as he walked in on them playing draughts.

'Hello Tommy. Have you won at the snooker some more?' asked Aude.

'Not so much today, Pet, aa' think me arm's tired from havin' t' carry all that money off Lenny. So aa just happened by the garden, there, and picked this little butter-flower t' see which one of yers likes butter.'

Nessa smiled, she'd had every one of them, apart from Carter, do this to her a dozen times each when she was little. Aude looked curiously at him, trying to work out if it was another one of his tricks coming her way. He showed her the little flower just as Den's bird whistled.

'But before aa test yer both, there's somebody here come t' see yers.'

They automatically looked past him to the open doorway and saw Margaret standing square in the middle of it. Aude shot off the bed and ran to her, throwing herself into the open arms and gripping her as tightly as she could.

'Hello my little Pet.'

Margaret cuddled her closely and kissed the top of her head before looking up and straight at Nessa. Tommy left them alone and herded the watching lads back to the music room. Margaret walked the cuddling Aude over to the bed, and laid her heavy hand on Nessa's cheek to rub it with her thumb, just as she'd done so many times before for so many years gone by. They looked at each other and their glassy eyes shone. Nessa's gave the tears to show the kind of feeling evolution won't be able to change, which made Margaret gently ease Aude over so she could lean forward and kiss them off her cheek. Doing the same to Aude, she looked right into the sparkling black pools.

'The pair of yers are lookin' nice and strong, but for the want of a bit more meat and suet int' yers.'

They smiled brightly in the happy shock of having her there.

'Right, let's have this bandage off.'

With not the slightest reservation, she unclipped the safety pins and unwound the bandage on Nessa's head with a speed they hadn't seen from any of the hospital staff. It was dropped on the bed in a perfectly tight tube, and with the safety pins in her mouth she pulled Nessa's head from side to side, forwards and backwards, with the assurance Nessa hadn't felt from anyone.

'Yer alright, Pet, they've got the back canny and that's the main thing. Order, sweetheart, will yer run across t' where the lads are, and tell Stan t' give yer me little brown bag, there's a good lass.'

She flitted off like she used to in the club in Norway.

'Yer mam and everybody's fine, Pet,' said Margaret to the healing cut on Nessa's face, 'and little Cynthia's stayin' at yours now. Aye, they make the match for each other; yer mother's got little Cynthia t' look after, and little Cynthia's got yer mam t' look after her, so they're both as happy as Larry.'

'That's good.'

Nessa was pleased to be relieved for her mother, and happy for little Cynthia, whom she liked a lot.

'How's she been, Pet?' asked Margaret, nodding to the empty space on the bed.

'Bad, it knocked her all t' hell but aa think she's comin' on a bit now,' she said, looking for some encouragement.

'She is, Pet, she is.'

Nessa knew Margaret would always tell her the truth.

'Here it is, Margaret. And the lads have said for me to ask if they can please to come in now.'

Margaret winked at Nessa. 'Aye, Pet, tell them they can, but say she says she wants no more arsin' about, mind, can yer remember that, Sweetheart? Good lass.'

She took the bag and they smiled at her running off smiling.

'Aye, she's not far away,' said Margaret.

There seemed to be a ton of stuff emptied on the bed before the jam jar she wanted had its lid popped off, and a dollop of thick white cream slid up the thick red gash struggling to close on Nessa's face.

'Yer not doin' a bit stylin' wi' Wilfy's Brylcream, are yer, Margaret?' came from the doorway.

'Aa'll style my hand across your ear, lad, if aa' have t' come over there.'

She sat with her back to them and looked at Nessa as she rubbed the cream around the horseshoe, and its intersecting straight line of stitches in the back of her head.

'This'll give yer a bit jip tonight, mind, Pet,' she warned, 'but yer'll be alright in the mornin'.'

'How many times have yer said that, Duggie?'

Margaret smiled at Nessa.

'Right, aa'll put the bandage back on fer tonight, but it's comin' off first thing, mind: it needs fresh air and a bit sun on it. These useless buggers can get things sorted in the mornin'.'

Nessa could see them smiling behind her.

'So were yer missin' us, Margaret?'

'If aa didn't have me hands full here, Lester Churchwarden, aa'd shy that last nut off yer, lad.'

She still kept her back to them, winking at Nessa and listening to them laugh.

'Christ Almighty, Stan, did yer have t' say about me ... er ... trouser injury.'

'Trouser injury,' repeated Wilf, laughing with the rest of them.

Margaret wound the bandage back on and ten minutes later the settees had been moved and the big kitchen table was butted up to Nessa's bed, and everyone sat down to a lovely rabbit stew Hilda had made as something she could keep warm if the plane was late. Herbie gave Margaret her brandy glass and half filled it with the best cognac they had.

'Are we on rations over here, Herbert, lad? No? Whey get the bugger filled then.'

She winked at him as he filled it and the lads felt like they were home again.

'Nice rabbit stew, eh, Margaret?'

'Aye canny, son, very canny, not enough tatie fer me, like, or salt for that matter, and the onion was over much, especially wi' there not bein' that much carrot on the go, but aye, very canny.'

They tapped each other's feet under the table to make sure they knew she was bound to say something like that.

'Not bad for a French lass, eh?'

'Aa don't know about that, son, but that's a Yorkshire rabbit stew.'

The lads dismissed the remark as Margaret being Margaret. Hilda nearly collapsed on the kitchen floor.

'So where's this Monty, then? Stan says ee's been good t' the lasses.'

'Ee has been and ee is, Pet,' said Tommy.

'Aa asked where he was.'

She wanted an answer.

'Aa think ee's had t' go back t' London.'

'How d'yer reckon that, like, Lester?' asked Stan.

'Just the way ee was off out about 3.00 this mornin' with ee's suitcase, and poor bloody Raymond havin' t' drive him.'

'So, when it is yer sleep again, Lester?'

'Is that bottle empty, Herbert, lad?'

'If it is, Margaret, our very welcome guest, there's plenty more t' whet yer whistle,' said Tommy.

She rolled her eyes at him and Herbie filled her glass. Hilda returned to clear the table.

'You just leave that, Pet; these lads haven't been brought up t' have some poor lass skivvying on after them.'

They knew the look without having to see it, telling them there would be trouble if they didn't move. Hilda stood holding a salt cellar in wonder as they left their seats, collected plates and cutlery, cleared the table, and carried it back into the kitchen with the chairs. Margaret oversaw it all to make sure it was done the way she wanted.

'No, Duggie'll wash and Den'll dry. You two, empty that cupboard and put the stuff over there for now. The cups'll go on the top shelf, Wilf, there's a good lad. Aa want them plates clean, mind, Duggie. Ask Hilda where she's got her clean tea towels – Lester! Are yer deaf, lad?'

With Margaret satisfied everything was as it should be, they settled comfortably in the warm gaslight of the front living room, with glasses of wine and cognac and the gorgeous thick ginger biscuits she'd brought from home. Some sat on the floor with their backs against the settees, and Margaret sat on the bed with Nessa and Aude, rubbing and twisting and pulling each of Nessa's fingers as they chatted on. She'd heard and seen enough of Hilda to know she was a good little worker and liked her for it, and had wanted her to come and sit with them, but she wouldn't. She made her excuses in pitiful English to get back to the safety of her room, as she felt that Margaret could see straight through her French housekeeper's clothes.

'Well, we got that lot cleared away in good style,' said Stan, as a safe opening remark.

'What the hell? D'yer want a bloody medal for puttin' a few pots away?'

'No, no, Margaret, Pet, aa was just sayin' it's nice t' get sat down with a glass …'

'"Nice t' get sat down"? Yer all the bloody same you men when it comes t' the house; if the woman stops pushin' yer stop friggin' movin'.'

'That's so we can keep our strength up fer bringin' in the bacon,' said Lester bravely.

'That's why there's no lass daft enough t' have yer, son; they'd friggin' starve.' (laughs)

'Oh, but hang fire, Margaret, yer might be off the mark there, mind.'

She stared at Wilf to explain.

'Aye there's a bonny French lass who's keen on him.'

'Is she somebody who shouldn't be out by hersel', like?' (laughs)

'No, no, she's sharp as a tack, six foot tall, all red lipstick and nails, and looks like a film star.'

'Then she's trouble, son,' said Margaret, looking at Lester seriously, 'mark my words and stay well clear. Anyhow, what about Donny Kirk's daughter, aa thought yer were doin' a bit courtin' there?'

'Gretchin?' said Wilf.

Everybody stared at the reddening Lester, pulling on a Woodbine like a condemned man.

'By Christ, ee's a dark horse is that little bugger,' said Tommy smiling.

'Gretchin Kirk, though Lester?'

'Never mind curling yer lip like that, Wilfy Watkins, yer no oil paintin' yersel, mind.'

'Aa know, aa'm sorry, Margaret, aa didn't mean 'owt nasty.'

'Aa know, son.'

'Me mother always said Gretchin could crack a Black Bullet with her gums,' said Lenny.

'Been puttin' yer head in the lion's mouth there, Lester, lad.'

Margaret laughed with them while Lester pulled harder on his Woodbine.

'Poor little bugger's always had stick about her nose.'

'About Coco the clown bein' her fatha.'

'Aye, aye.'

'Kids can be cruel.'

'Aye, Carter, son, they can, and yer had enough of it yersel', bonny lad, but little Gretchin got it from other mothers as well, mind. Oh aye, aa've scattered the buggers a good few times when aa've heard them.'

The lads could imagine, and felt their eyes open a little wider to see why they liked Margaret so much.

'So d'yer carry a picture of Gretchin close t' yer heart then, Lester?'

'Christ.'

Fully furnished with enormous detail on all things back home, they drifted peacefully through the evening to accept Stan telling them it was time for bed after he'd noticed Margaret stifle a yawn that made him think about what she'd been through that day. A bed from his and Tommy's room had been moved up to the girls' room for her. Lester insisted Stan move in with Carter and have his bed, and he'd take a cushion off the settee and move in with Tommy to keep him company. Duggie helped Herbie carry Margaret's wardrobe of a suitcase up to her room, and they all sent their goodnights after her as she went upstairs. The lads came back down and talked quietly for half an hour more.

'Is that little Order asleep, Nessa, Pet?'

'Aye, just gone.'

'Right, h'way lads, nice and quiet, let's off up,' said Stan.

'Aye, and we'd better shake up in the mornin', 'cause yer know who'll be on the prowl.'

Chapter 32

The brass rings were sent racing along their polished curtain pole above the big front window, and the patiently waiting bright light of the day was welcomed in. Margaret smiled at Aude lying like a kitten in a basket and laid her hand on Nessa's cheek to make her open her eyes and squint at the sunlight blinding them. Without opening the screening curtain to the living room, she walked around the bed and put her hand on Aude's rising head to softly push it back down onto the pillow.

'Give yersel' a minute t' wake up, my little Pet,' she said, and left them alone.

'What time is it?' asked Nessa.

'Quarter to six,' said Aude, stretching an arm to its limit above her head as she looked at the clock.

Nessa smiled fondly at Margaret's cast-iron consistency.

Going back up to her room for something she wanted for Nessa, she saw Tommy coming along the landing.

'Mornin', son, nice fresh day.'

'It is that, Pet.' He smiled.

'Come and let's see t' these lazy buggers, eh.'

Without any thought of knocking, she bowled straight into Lenny and Colly's room with Tommy close behind. They were met by a large, full moon of an arse as Lenny struggled to free the underpants he'd caught between his toes in the rush to get them on. The pistol shot crack from Margaret's hand on Lenny's lardy white cheek left a perfect red print that looked like aboriginal rock art on a badly bleached rock. Luckily it was the underpant elastic that snapped and not his toe as he shot up. Colly had been standing full frontal drying his hair when she walked in, and was too slow dropping the towel on his modesty.

'Sit yersel' down here, son,' she said in a way that made him think he must have been quick enough, 'and let's have a better look at yer hurts.'

Colly sat down obediently and she pulled, pushed, twisted and turned him about until she was happy she'd seen enough. She cupped the bottom of his face in her big right hand and made him look straight at her.

'Yer doin' fine, lad; yers have all had a canny enough doctor by the look if it, so yer can thank yer lucky stars for that, 'cause aa've seen too many useless buggers among them in my time. Aa want yer t' put this stuff on, and aa'll show yer how after breakfast, right.'

'Right, Margaret.'

On her way out she stopped with her hand on the doorknob and said: 'Canny link, mind, Colly, lad.'

She shut the door, winked at Tommy, and they smiled as they listened to them trying to cough their warnings to the other rooms. He did the rounds with her and was back in the kitchen before six o'clock, watching her pulling stuff about to start the breakfast.

'Here she is, Margaret,' said Tommy, pulling Aude onto his knee, 'yer little helper's ready fer duty, that right, Pet.'

'It is, Tommy,' she said happily. 'I am here now to do all the things to make you to rest on your holiday with us.'

Margaret didn't answer but walked over to cup her little face and kiss her head. Tommy saw her sharp old eyes shining.

Hilda came into the kitchen at her usual time of 6.30 to find the lads busying about like hotel staff. The table had been moved back into the front living room, and Carter and Stan were laying it. She joined in and helped Herbie and Aude cut bread and butter toast, and half an hour later she sat quietly at the table with them, listening to their chit-chat while they finished their teas and coffees with a smoke. Once Aude came back with the bowl of warm water she'd been sent for, Margaret closed the screening curtain around the bed and started rubbing a brick-sized bar of Fairy green bath soap on an old yellow flannel before clapping it on Nessa's face. The feel and smell of it made her remember nice things from when she was little. Margaret thought of what she'd be remembering and smiled as she scrubbed her face and neck, front and back, behind her ears and over her shoulders. She rinsed the flannel and did it all again before taking the towel off Aude and polishing her dry. She pulled Nessa to sit up and gave her the cardboard box she'd gone back to her room for. Handing the lid to Aude, she took out a carefully folded bright pink blouse, with a bold lilac chiffon corsage stitched onto a lapel. Margaret knew it wasn't the type of thing Nessa would normally wear, and that she probably wouldn't like it, but she took it and put it on her without asking. Nessa made no objection at all.

'Little Cynthia made it for yer, Pet. She sat up all night t' do it so aa could get it in time t' fetch over.'

Nessa had guessed as much and looked at Margaret.

'It only looks a touch big 'cause yer dropin' a bit weight wi' not gettin' yer proper grub, and only eatin' scratty bloody fruit and vegetables. Now, aa know it's not what yer liable t' wear much, but aa said aa'd bring it and aa'm not goin' back t' tell the little thing yer didn't have it on, like.'

'Tell her it's the bonniest blouse aa've ever seen,' said Nessa, 'and tell her aa'll always wear it for best.'

Margaret rubbed the top of her arm.

'It's just she thinks the world of yer, Pet, and always has since yers were bairns, mind, so she'll be over the moon when aa tell her.'

The lads could hear unusual shuffling sounds, mixed with little groans and quiet words of encouragement, before the curtain opened to show Nessa, standing by herself, without her bandages, with her hair combed and her handsome face looking wide awake again. They made their way over to her, sending every kind and honest message they could from the words they had. Margaret told Lester and Duggie to get either side of her because they were the best height for her to lean on if she needed. They did, and she rested one cast on each of them as she walked to the settee Tommy was plumping for her. She looked at Margaret.

'Aye, sit yersel' down, but just for a bit, mind, 'cause aa want yer outside in the fresh air, and judgin' by the state of them rooms up there, it'll not be over fresh in here for long.'

'Harsh, Margaret, Pet, Lenny's gettin' t' be a fanatic with ee's washcloth; it's out twice a week now, mind.'

'Aye, aa saw the state of it – what the hell's ee been washin' with it, turnips?'

'No, but heavy vegetables come t' mind now yer mention it.'

'By, yer a cheeky bugger, Wilfy Watkins, lad, yer just like yer fatha.'

As Nessa settled on the settee and the lads got themselves more tea and coffee to keep her company, Margaret strolled behind Tommy and knocked the side of his head with the back of her hand.

'You can get yer lazy arse up and show me this little burn the lasses are on about.'

He rolled his eyes to tell them she'd be bound to want to see every little thing. Without waiting for him she made her way down to the pretty little stream at the bottom of the garden. Tommy smiled at the thought of anybody ever being able to show her anything. She sat on the shiny smooth silver birch log seat and patted it for him to sit beside her.

'Bonny place, and the lasses are right, it is a lovely little burn.'

'Aye. Monty calls it a babbling brook.'

She smiled and looked straight ahead into the far distance.

'Now, aa know yer've got me down here t' ask how aa'm keepin',' said Tommy, 'and that…'

'No. Aa haven't.'

'Whey, don't listen t' Stan, anyhow, Pet, y'know ee's a little worrier.'

'Aa have listened t' him, and aa heard enough t' come over. And now aa've seen yer aa can tell yer ee's got a good right t' be worried.'

Tommy felt the weight of the words but refused to let them pull him down. 'Ee hasn't, Pet, look.'

He stood in front of her and lifted his shirt so she could see the wound he was pushing and prodding to prove his recovery. She looked at it and pushed a solid finger into it, making him bend double and sink to his knees in agony. She sat silently still and looked into the far distance again. Catching his breath he struggled to get back on the seat beside her.

'So, yer fine, eh?'

He sat wiping the wetting pain from his eyes. 'But it's gettin' better, for Christ's sake,' he said quietly.

'No, son, it's gettin' worse.'

'But how though? The doctors have done their stuff and the wound's all healed up...'

'Stand up here.'

She shifted her knees to one side to let him stand with his wound close to her face. She lifted his shirt and put her nose to his skin. Letting go of the shirt she told him to sit down.

'It's rotten, son, it's rottin' away inside yer.'

'So what's that mean then, another bloody operation?'

'No, it means yer dyin'.'

Coming from her, he couldn't stop the shock hitting him like a hammer, but like the strong man he was, he sat silently in the same meditative way as her.

'How long?' he asked finally.

'Months, but not a year.'

After a long pause he straightened his back. 'Aa'll put me shop and savin's, and all the money from this int' your name, Margaret, if yer don't mind, like, so that yer can sort the lasses out, y'know, get them started ...and...'

He put his hand over his eyes and her heart went out to him, but she still didn't move.

'For God's sake, Margaret, look after that little lass; she's got a heart of gold and the poor little thing's had nowt but bloody shite in her life from the day she was born, until ...'

'Until she met you, son.'

'And the lads, they love her just the same.'

She smiled to somewhere far away. 'Are yer settled, son?'

'Aye, aa'm sorry, Pet, for bein' so soft, aa'm alright. Will yer say nowt t' the lads, though.'

'Right. Now shut yer stupid bloody flim-flammin' mouth before aa shut it for yer.'

Tommy looked at her in vacant disbelief, and for the first time since they'd sat down, she turned her distant gaze off and fixed a close one on him.

'Aa needed all that shifted out the road for yer t' listen properly. Now aa've told yer the fact of the matter: aa can see the faeries wrappin' the shrouds on yer, son, and if yer don't listen t' what aa say, yer'll not see the blossom in yer garden next spring.'

He sat sinking in his silent shock and listened.

'Aa've got t' open yer up; it'll be Sunda' by the time aa'm sorted with what aa need, and it'll put yer through two and a half days yer wouldn't wish on yer worst enemy; it'll be bad, mind. After that we'll see if we've got yer back – they want yer, yer see,' she said, nodding to the distant pale blue sky, 'and aa've got t' fight them t' keep yer here.'

Just before the very last prop of Tommy's manhood fell from him, he looked straight at her. 'Then aa'm the luckiest lad in the world, Pet, t' have you fightin' for me in this world or any other.'

He broke and sobbed like a lost child. She held him close.

******

'Aye aye, and where have you two been?'

'Ee hasn't been tryin' t' show yer ee's instrument, has ee, Margaret?'

'No, son, Colly's trumpet was enough fer me this mornin'.' (cheers)

******

'The lasses are over in the house wi' Margaret and Hilda.'

'Right, so what did Dinsey say then, Stan?'

'Not a lot, just that there's not that much more comin', or at least not enough for him t' make any sense of. Ee says it's like workin' with a bucket of worms.'

'Has ee found any more of them places, Stan?'

'Aye, two more for sure 'cause ee's been and got two more of them tubes wi' the foil in. One was in Pontefract and the other in Richmond.'

'Where we fly to.'

'Aye, but that says nowt; it's a big enough place.'

'But nowt else, like, Stan?'

Stan hesitated. 'No, whey mebbees; ee's not a 100% sure, but thinks there's somethin' t' do wi' castles and stately homes …'

'What?'

'Ee doesn't know, but ee thinks one's in Germany.'

'Christ.'

'D'yer not think Dinsey's gettin' carried away a bit, Stan?'

'No, Den, aa don't. But, anyhow, ee warned us again t' say nowt t' nobody, and ee means it, mind.'

They sat silently, making their own ways through the ever-shifting sands blowing in from what they thought they'd just heard.

Chapter 33

By six o'clock on Friday morning everyone was up and doing their best to be seen to be doing something so they wouldn't get flayed by Margaret. Tommy and Duggie had the kitchen fire cleaned, laid and lit, and Aude, who'd brought over two pails of logs, laughed with them as Herbie felt her biceps. The big table and all the chairs had already been moved into the front living room, and Hilda was helping Stan and Carter set it for breakfast.

'Job, jobbed,' said Duggie, flicking a dead match into the fire and blowing his smoke after it.

'Aye, Dug, lad, we should be spared a bollockin' for an hour or two, eh? So where's she now, anyhow?'

Duggie shrugged his shoulders and fished for the bit of baccy that had to be on the tip of his tongue.

'Have yer seen Margaret, Den?'

'No, aa'll ask about.'

Aude came skipping back across the courtyard after putting the pail back in the log shed, and bounced straight into the kitchen, nipping Duggie on the back of the leg to make him hop and all of them laugh.

'Like a bloody wasp sting that, lad,' rubbed Duggie.

'Have you seen Margaret this mornin', Pet?'

'No, Tommy. Might she be tired and to rest in bed?'

They laughed kindly to make her smile.

'There's more chance of Lenny gettin' Lester's shorts on than Margaret havin' a lie in, Pet.'

'Christ, there's a sight yer wouldn't want t' see.'

'She's in the garage talkin' t' Roy,' reported Denny.

'Hey-up, here she comes.'

'Mornin' my little Pet, and what have these useless buggers got yer doin' now, eh?'

'I have been to get this wood.'

'No,' she said in faux disbelief, 'there's too much there fer you t' have carried all that over.'

'She did, Margaret; we watched her, didn't we, Dug.'

Duggie nodded to the truth, but she still wouldn't have it, just to make Aude happy.

'Whey, aa'll be needin' help wi' these, Pet.'

She put her wicker basket on the bench and took out two dozen eggs, most of them waving little downy feathers, and two big brown chickens.

'Where the hell have yer been gettin' them?'

'That little farm just over yonder. Right, let's get sorted here.'

They knew the nearest farm was about two miles away and the old one-armed farmer never seemed very friendly to them.

'So, how much did ee charge yer fer that lot, then?'

'Coppers.'

She dismissed the question in a way to warn them not to ask any more. Duggie waited for Tommy to change the subject.

'So is Order doin' some fryin' then?'

'She will be if you useless buggers shift out the way.'

'D'yer want Duggie t' give them birds a good pluckin', Margaret? Ee's practised.'

He saw a half smile as she rummaged for butter and milk in the pantry.

'No, Nessa's doin' them.'

'Nessa? She'll not be able t' manage wi' them casts on, though,' said Tommy unwisely.

'She'll not, will she not? Aa'll tell yer what she can and can't do, lad. Now shift yersels, the pair of yer, or aa'll put this pan round some bugger's head.'

Tommy and Duggie knew to leave.

'Aa'll tell yer what, lad! Where the hell d'yers think yer goin', eh?'

'Int' the front room?'

'"Int' the front room",' she mimicked, before clashing back into her natural irritated force. 'And are yers expectin' these friggin' chickens t' walk in there on their own, eh? No? So take them in, and tell Nessa aa want them plucked. And you (Duggie) take some paper in t' cover the bed, and this bowl for the feathers. Now shift.'

She turned with a smile and a wink for Aude.

They went into the front living room to see Stan sitting on the bed combing Nessa's hair to cover the reddening cut. He noticed her look past him and turned to see Tommy carrying the chickens by the feet, with their heads swaying like flowers in a breeze.

'H'way, Stanley, lad, yer'll have t' shift yersel', Margaret wants Nessa t' pluck these chickens.'

Stan gave his puzzled look to Nessa first and moved to let Duggie spread the papers across her lap.

'Aa'll put one up for yer, Pet, and leave the other on the floor here,' said Tommy.

She sat up a little more and looked at the heavy, wide-eyed chicken on the paper.

'Oh, it'll be for yer fingers, y'know, t' get the muscles workin',' said Stan, showing he was pleased with himself even though he didn't mean to.

Ten minutes later everybody was settled enjoying their eggy breakfast, including Hilda, who kept slipping out to make more toast and bring more coffee and tea. Margaret stayed in her seat when they'd finished, so they knew they could light up and have a nice smoke.

'Let's see yer handiwork, Nessa, Pet,' said Lenny.

Aude moved her empty plate and cup and put the chicken back on Nessa's lap for her to lift up and show them.

'Christ, yer've got it lookin' like a vulture.'

'Is that for our dinner tonight, Margaret?' asked Lester.

'Ask Hilda,' directed Margaret kindly.

Lester pointed to the chicken and then made a knife and fork mime to bring a smile from her.

'Yes, oui, for dean-aire.'

She saw Margaret's eyes flick away with a hidden smile.

'Mime yer want a bit breast,' stirred Wilf.

'Don't bother, son, aa'll mime Wilf doesn't want any 'cause ee'll be gettin' my fist.'

The cheers went up for Wilfy.

'Right, lads, let's have this lot away and tidied; there's stuff t' be doin'.'

With that she was up and off. Five minutes later she came down from her room with a long, thin brown paper parcel and sat on the bed and gave it to Aude.

'This is for you, my little Pet.'

Margaret winked at Nessa as she unwrapped the drumsticks.

'Old Ernie's sent yer them 'cause they're lighter, and somethin' or other, but for yer t' try them. Now aa'm goin out wi' Roy in a bit, so let's away over there now, so aa can tell him what yer think when aa get back. Mebbees yer can show me how t' play the drums and aa'll come round with yers, eh.'

Aude laughed and said how much she wished for that, and got a kiss on the head. Nessa got another wink. As soon as Aude got her nod of encouragement from Nessa, Margaret put her in front of her to lead the way, and so she could knock Lenny on the side of the head to follow them to the music room.

'So what's this for then?' asked Margaret, sitting at the drums, pointing to the bass pedal.

'It is for you to put on your foot and to press.'

Aude was trying not to laugh, but the heavy boom broke the last of her control. Margaret tried not to smile and thudded another two beats in her own time to bring Royston and Lester in from the garage.

'Sounds like yer a natural, Margaret,' said Roy.

'Now you hit this one with your stick, and do it so you count to four.'

A snare drum got four rapid whacks to make them all laugh.

'It's not a kid yer've caught in the garden,' said Tommy, wandering in with Duggie and Herbie.

Aude managed to stop laughing and the lads could see Margaret was trying to look serious.

'Now you try to go slow and hit on 1 (hit) and 2 (hit) and 3 (hit) and 4 (hit).'

She was just about sitting on Margaret's knee with her hand on hers.

'There, now I will count out loud for you for the numbers to hit, yes, and not the 'ands' for yet. So: 1 and 2 and 3 and 4. Very good, Margaret,' said Aude clapping her hands.

They all saw the return of the beaming happy look they'd so longed for.

'Wasn't it very good, and to have groove, yes, Carter?' She smiled.

'Ah, so there y'are, aa've been lookin' for you, lad.'

'Oh, Christ, is ee in trouble, Margaret?'

'Ee will be if ee doesn't get ee's arse on that couch.'

Before she knew it, Aude was sitting at the drums and Margaret was standing beside her.

'Right, my little Pet, so show me how yer count yer fours and hit the 'ands' as well then, sweetheart, Lenny can play that one ee was on about before, t' help yer?'

To the relief of everybody in the room, apart from Aude, who didn't suspect a thing, Lenny only just managed to cotton-on to what she was doing.

'Was it *Kick the Cat* aa was on about, Pet?'

'Aye,' answered Tommy.

Aude didn't hear the question because she was busy shuffling, shifting and pulling her drumkit about just like she used to.

'Can aa play bass on it, please, Margaret?' asked Carter, to let the lads see him as so much younger than they usually did.

'Aye, son, so long as aa can keep me eye on yer.'

'Is that alright, Tommy?'

'Course it is, son, help yersel'. Mind there's not many aa'd let put their mitts on her, she doesn't give up them sweet tones easily; she only responds to a musician's touch.'

'So yer like us then and never heard them.'

'Count it in, Order, Pet, while aa have t' deal wi' this latest cut.'

They heard the four little clicks of the sticks start them in perfect time. Everything of what three musicians could do with those three instruments in the 165 seconds of time spent on that piece of music, was perfect. Margaret sat forward on the couch and clapped loudest in the little audience that Den, Wilf and Hilda had joined, and who were clapping as joyfully as the others at Aude's return. Aude looked out at them and glanced down at her sticks and then the kit before looking back out, sending her smile to let them know she was on her way back.

'More! More! Encore!'

They shouted to chase away any ghost of apprehension from her, and were rewarded by being allowed to see the happiest drummer in the world. Tommy caught Margaret's eye and she winked.

'How about '*Roll Around*', Lenny?' said Carter. 'It'll sound canny if aa play off the back wi' Order, eh.'

'It will that, son.'

He gave Aude the nod and the stick clicks started before Margaret stopped them.

'Just a minute, there, yer crafty little bugger, don't think yer'll get by me like that, lad. Now stand that thing up fer a minute and sit down here, and don't give me any of that look, or there'll be no more playin' for yer today, mind.'

Carter walked to the settee like he was headed for a noose, and sat down beside Margaret. Everybody watched her put a big hand on his chest and push him to lie back as far as the couch would let him, so she could pull his right leg up by the shin and yank off his shoe, sock and foot. Aude took a breath and looked with wide open eyes at the sight of seeing it done for the first time.

'Not comfortable, eh, lad,' said Margaret, looking closely at the stump and giving it a couple of sharp pats.

'No,' he said quietly.

The lads felt sorry for him because he knew Aude was watching.

'That's because it's like a babby's arse. How many times have aa told yer about this, eh.'

'Go easy on the lad, Margaret.'

'Go easy! Never mind "go easy". And what the hell's the matter wi' you lot, eh? Oh, it's because Order's watchin', is it. Come down here a minute, my Pet.'

Aude did as she was asked, and Margaret took her hand and put it on Carter's stump.

'There, can yer feel what that's like, Pet? Right, now feel my hand, can yer feel the difference, sweetheart?'

Aude nodded.

The stump was like silk and the hand was like brick.

'Whey, that should feel like my hand, and d'yer know why it doesn't? Because ee won't take ee's foot off and do what ee's been told t' do since ee could walk; and that's bloody well walk on it.'

Catching his quick glance at Aude, she sensed his undeserved shame and eased off.

'D'yer think a lovely lass like Order would be bothered by seein' yer wi' yer foot off? Course she's not, are yer, sweetheart?'

'No, I am not bothered, Margaret, and I want Carter to do it for him to have his leg strong.'

'There, now listen t' the lass. And you lot!' Looking at them in turn– 'Yer all want a bloody good clip fer not t' be botherin wi' young Carter here. Aa told yers t'make sure ee walked on ee's stump, didn't aa, eh?'

'Yer did, Margaret,' answered Tommy.

'So how come it's like this, then, eh?'

'It's just that ...'

'It's *just* nowt, lad,' she spat, firing up. 'But aa will tell what it is: ee hasn't got circulation like yous, and if this gets soft and ee gets a bit of a nick and it gets inflamed, ee could lose ee's leg, or worse, mind. D'yers think aa just say things 'cause aa've got frigg all better t' do, eh?'

They mumbled their apologies from a disappointment in themselves, as they felt the guilt of the consequences that hadn't happened, but could have because they hadn't done what she'd trusted them to do. Margaret threw Carter's foot at Duggie to catch.

'Ee only gets that back t' go outside, right.'

Duggie nodded. Margaret let go of Carter's shin and they could see the broad red finger marks on his spindly white leg.

'Right, son,' she said more softly, 'get yersel' up on Tommy's big fiddle there, and let's hear yer play for the bairn t' do her drummin', eh.'

Carter stood up and started to peg his miserable way to the bass he'd left propped against the piano. He felt her take his hand.

'Aa wouldn't want t' lose yer, son.'

She stood up and they caught each other in the full embrace of their adopted grandmother and grandson love.

Lenny heard the clicks from Aude's sticks and the two of them started to play *Roll Around*, but only the first verse in repetition because they'd let each other know to wait until Carter was ready. Ten minutes later, the whole band was in full swing to an audience of four, and Margaret, Hilda, Nessa and Colly enjoyed every beat of it. They played magnificently for an hour and a half, and everybody in the music room felt the thrill of it moving them a good bit further back to normal.

Chapter 34

'Mind, aa like that hat, Pet,' complimented Tommy, who wasn't trying to be funny.

'Old Mrs McCamney lent me it when aa asked.'

He smiled at the remoteness of the possibility of anybody not lending her something she'd asked for, and told her again it really suited her because it really did. The light brown sun hat,with a light blue ribbon joining a wavey wide brim to a low domed crown was perfect for her, but if Aude had it on she'd have looked like an exotic little mushroom.

'So are yer off out for a walk then, Pet?' he asked, watching her touch her necklace.

'We all are, so get the lads sorted. And tell Wilf, Duggie and Lester t' bring their fishin' gear.'

With that she set off out across the courtyard to the garage, leaving Tommy wondering and smiling after her. He spread the word and the house began to move. Shorts and shirts were changed, flasks were filled with everything from water to wine, Hilda and Aude buttered bread and cut cheese, Herbie loaded apples and hard-boiled eggs into little canvas bags and everything was stashed into big canvas bags, and the busy kerfuffle went on for quarter of an hour. When all was done, Margaret walked Nessa to the wheelchair waiting for her at the kitchen door. She was happy for her to say she'd be able to do without it, but still made Tommy push it because she knew she'd need it later on. It was half past twelve and the sun was high in the cloudless blue sky when the little tribe set off at Nessa's pace. Margaret was in the middle, wearing a lovely cream sleeveless frock with big red roses on it, and had Aude and Nessa either side of her holding her hands.

'Where's this chair from?' asked Tommy, taking up the rear.

'She sent Roy up t' the hospital t' get it yesterday,' said Stan, walking beside him.

'There's that mark, look, on the top of her arm,' said Wilf, pushing in between them.

'Oh aye, aa've seen it before,' said Tommy.

'It's definitely a bullet hole that.'

'Aye, aa remember yer sayin'.'

'D'yer not think it is, like.'

'Whey aa can't see it properly from here, aa'll have a better look later on.'

'Aa'll bet that woman's got some stories t' tell, eh.'

Stan and Tommy smiled their complete and utter agreement.

By the time they got to the place on the grassy green bankside where Margaret had decided to set camp, Tommy still hadn't worked out how to stop Nessa rolling away in her wheelchair. She rolled her eyes at Royston to come and sort him out with the brake.

'Nearly all the way, eh, Pet,' complimented Roy.

'Who the hell thought these brakes were a good idea, eh?' said Tommy, pressing the axle.

'Nowt the matter wi' the brakes.' Roy smiled.

'Poor bloody design t' my mind.'

Roy winked at Nessa and easily locked the wheels with his big toe. Two king-size tartan blankets were put down to carpet the chosen spot, and the picnic was unpacked from the canvas bags. Hilda found the cups first to get them all a drink of something as they seated themselves into a comfortable circle. They sat and sipped quietly as they looked down the gentle slope to the silvery brown river throwing blinding mirror slashes at them as it slid serenely by.

'Are yer not havin' a sit down, Margaret?'

'Not just yet, son, Duggie and the lads are wantin' t' show me where the good fishin' is.'

Duggie and the lads had no idea they wanted to, but knew to say nothing and get their rods and boxes, and wait. She picked up a bag and nodded the way for them to go. After about half a mile she stopped to look closely at the riverbank.

'Right, lads, yer'll need them shorts off.'

'Christ, Margaret, Duggie's used t' a bit chit-chat first, mind.'

'Aa'll give yer chit-chat, yer cheeky bugger. Aa want yers across the river there; t' where them reeds are.'

'That's a canny swim, mind.'

'And mebbees a stiff current.'

'So get yer bloody shirts and shorts off and get in, then. Now what's the matter?'

'Aa haven't got any undercrackers on,' admitted Lester.

'Or me,' said Wilf.

'So? What the hell have you's got packed in there that aa haven't seen afore, like?'

'Nowt. But can Duggie not go for the reeds; ee's got trunks on?'

'No ee bloody can't. And who the hell says aa want reeds, like?'

They looked at each other and knew there was trouble coming. They knew it for certain when they saw the big glass jar come out of her bag.

'All of yer have t' go 'cause aa want frogs.'

'Frogs?'

'Aye, frogs, are yer friggin' deaf? They'll be in them reeds, but it'll take all of yer t' catch them: aa want a dozen.'

'Christ Almighty, Margaret, what the hell d'yer want 12 frogs for?'

'Never you mind, just get yer shorts off and fill this jar.'

'Not the first time yer've heard that, eh, Wilfy?'

Margaret smiled with them.

'Is this for Tommy, Margaret?' asked Lester innocently.

She was just about to blast them into order, but relented when she saw them looking at her like three little calves wanting milk.

'It is, son. Now aa'll be needin' yers t' be gettin' a few things t' put him right. Right.'

'Right,' they said together.

'Good lads. Now for the last time, get yer bloody shorts off.'

'Aa can swim wi' mine on,' tried Lester one last time.

'Not in that,' said Wilf, 'the drag on them things'll have us all under.'

'Whey, can yer give us the jar and leave us to it then, Margaret?'

'Oh aye,' she agreed, but stood stock still looking at them.

'Christ. Whey, can yer turn round then; for me modesty,' tried Lester.

'Aye, aye.'

Without a single bush or vine near enough to lend a screen, three shirts dropped onto the grass followed by three pairs of baggy shorts, leaving two little pairs of lilywhite buttocks for Margaret to smile at. Duggie stood proudly in his brown, grizzly bear trunks, finishing the last few pulls on his tab, while Wilf and Lester stood hunched over with their hands as cupping codpieces. They heard her laugh.

'Nice tattoo yer've got there, Wilfy. Did these daft buggers do that for yer?'

'Aye,' sighed Wilf.

'It was at Beaumont Hamel,' said Lester, talking to the river and starting to laugh. 'Can yer remember, Duggie?'

'Oh, aye.' Duggie smiled.

'It was Tommy's idea, mind,' spilled Lester. 'Ee got this French lass t' do it one night when Wilfy was pissed.'

'Lucky it was just yer initials, son.'

'Aye,' laughed Lester. 'Tommy told her t' put one 'W' on each cheek so it'ud say WOW when ee bent down.'

'Whey it works, mind,' said Margaret to make them laugh.

'Right, now get over there and look fer little light brown ones, and none of them bigger than a babby's fist. Take a line over from one of the rods, Duggie, and hook one on so aa can pull it over t' have a look at. H'way then, lads, or they'll be lookin' for us afore long.'

Wilf and Lester were pleased to get into the river and Duggie followed with the line. It was a hard job getting across far enough to get their feet down and feel the relief of the warm mud squeezing through their toes. Margaret lost sight of them, but knew where they were because of the twitching reeds, and soon felt a tug come with a whistle from Duggie. She reeled the line in, and by the time she'd unhooked the pitiful little frog, Duggie was looking across at her from the edge of the reeds. She gave him the thumbs up and ten minutes later they were back with 14 frogs in the jar. Margaret took it while they were crouched in the protective water.

'Good lads. Right, there's a towel up there, aa'll see yers back at the picnic.'

'Thank Christ fer that,' said Wilf as they crawled out like skinny mini-Tritons.

'Where's the towel?'

'Here it is, lads,' said Margaret to their full frontal and quickly hand-cupped discomfort. 'Forgot t' take it out the bag; aa must be slippin' in me old age, eh.'

They could see her laughing as she walked away.

******

'That was a lovely picnic yesterda'. She just gets yer doin' things yer never would have done, and yet they're so bloody easy and good – it makes yer wonder why we don't just do them ourselves, eh.'

'It does that, Den, lad.'

'Aye, mind, aa never would've thought those three would have gone swimmin', though.'

'She'll have chucked them in fer not catchin' 'owt.'

'Aye, more than likely.'

'Where's she now, then?'

'Out in the car wi' Roy, Wilf and Duggie, and Lester went after them on a bike.'

'She's got them roped int' somethin', that's for sure.'

******

At the top of the biggest hill near their little chateau, about six miles away, Royston pulled the car over and Lester rolled his bike up behind it. He throttled it off as he always did and pulled it onto its stand to walk up to Margaret's open window.

'Get in, son.'

He sat beside her, Wilf was on her other side and Duggie was in the front. Taking an old thick book from the bag at her feet, she carefully turned the pages of beautifully coloured plates, each with a protective transparent paper cover, until she reached the one she wanted.

'Right,' she said, tapping the bright picture of a yellow flower, 'this one here, get a good look at it. It'll be down by the water and in bits of shade from bushes; like them over there, see?'

They looked where she was pointing and nodded. Turning the pages again, she stopped at another exquisitely detailed print:

'And this one. Now get a good look at this one 'cause there's a few that looks like it but are no good. Look for the points on the leaves, there, see. It'll more likely be farther back int' the trees over there, see? Have yer got them or d'yer need another look?'

'No, no, we've got them.'

'And yer can ride the bike across them fields alright, son; wi' Wilfy on the back, aa mean?'

'Whey, aye.'

'Ee can, Margaret, ee's better on the bike than ee is on ee's feet.'

'Right. Take this bag and get about a dozen of each, and then just head back and put them in the box aa showed yer in the garage. And make sure yer leave them in the bag, don't faff on wi' them once they're picked or they'll be neither use nor ornament.'

'Right. H'way then, Lester, let's get these buggers picked,' said Wilf.

They watched him whip the bike past the car and set it away down the steep, winding road to where she'd pointed – the canvas bag over Wilfy's shoulder flapping like a ship's flag.

'Right, lads, we want t' be over that way and int' the wood at the bottom.'

'What are we after, like?'

'Mushrooms.'

'That yer need for Tommy as well?'

'No son, for our breakfast, they're lovely wi' butter.'

They smiled and Roy let the handbrake off.

******

'Whey, if yer'll just shift yer arse the pair of yers, aa'll have a look and tell yer.'

Margaret knelt beside the open box in the garage, and opened the bags she'd given Wilf and Lester so she could gently jiggle the plants for inspection:

'Good lads, yer've got some good'uns there.'

Her praise filled them with equal measures of relief and reward. Wilf always said there were more men with VCs than a compliment from Margaret.

'So what's next, wi' Tommy, like?' asked Lester.

'Aye,' she began with uncharacteristic reserve, 'aa've been meanin' t' have a word wi' yers about that. Run and get Roy will yer, Wilf, and fetch him down t' that log seat at the bottom of the garden.'

Two minutes later she stood in front of her little class of four sitting on the log.

'Right, listen: Tommy's insides aren't right...'

Not one of them thought of cracking any one of the thousand one-liners they had in stock.

'Bad, like, Margaret?'

'Aye, son, bad.'

'Christ, aa knew ee wasn't right, didn't aa say ee wasn't right, lads, didn't aa say.'

'Yer did, Lester.'

'How bad is ee, like? Will ee be all right? What's goin' ...'

'Steady on, son, or yer'll work yersel' up and yer'll be no bloody use t' man nor beast. Now aa've told yer it's bad and it is, so just leave it at that and listen. Now, t' get him right aa'm goin' t' need yer help – aa'm goin' t' have t' open him up again and put some medicine in him.'

'Christ.'

'When?'

'Tomorrow, and mind this'll be hard for him, and aa mean pain, mind. And it'll be non-stop fer about 60 hours.'

'Jesus.'

'Aye, son, nasty, but there's no way round it if we're goin' t' get him back. So, ee'll be up in that top bedroom, there, and aa'll get him cut and packed as soon as aa've got the stuff ready; mebbees about one o'clock. From then on ee'll have t' have a couple of yers with him all the time, and when aa say all the time, aa mean all the time, right, t' watch him. And when aa say watch him, aa mean make sure ee goes through all the pain and does nowt t' stop it.'

'Bloody hell, Margaret.'

'Ee'll have to, or else ee'll not make it, ee'll wither away like one of them flowers yer picked. Ee'll rive the wound open and pull ee's insides out, it'll be that bad, and if it means you've got t' put him down, you'll have to.'

'Us, put Tommy down? And when ee's full of hell and pain, Christ Almighty, Margaret.'

'No. Listen, ee'll be as weak as a kitten; ee's life's nearly out of him now and that's the fact of it; that wheelchair yesterda' was doin' more t' keep him up than pushin' Nessa. And what aa'll be puttin' int' him will take most of the rest of it out. Can yers hear what aa'm sayin'?'

They nodded and she watched Lester rub his eyes. She went on with a little more light for them to see it wasn't all dark:

'Look, ee'll more likely be pleadin' with yers for water, and if ee gets it, we've lost him, and if ee doesn't, aa think we'll get him back. So what d'yers reckon? Can yer do it or not? But mark my words here, now, if any of yer have a spit of doubt, say so, and aa'll get one of the others. Mind, aa'd be surprised: that's why aa've come t' yers in the first place.'

She watched them closely and could see the long, strong ties that bound them together, pull tight and force them to sit up.

'What's it t' be then?'

'We'll do it 'cause you're tellin' us it needs doin', Margaret, and that's that.'

Coming from Duggie she knew that would be the last word and that there was nothing more to say.

'Right, now wipe that worry off yer chops and get in there and get the daft bugger laughin' and chappin' on the way ee likes. H'way lads, up and in fer Tommy, eh.'

They couldn't help but smile at how she knew all their things, and they each got a nice squeeze on the log.

Chapter 35

'What is it?'

'How the hell do we know? She just said yer had to drink it at quarter to one.'

'The whole glassful?'

'Aye, and we'll catch it if yer don't.'

'Christ, it smells like Lenny's piano stool.'

'Down in one then.'

Tommy did, squinting and gurning all that needed to be said.

'She says it's t' clean yer out,' said Lester with a smile.

'Oh Christ, a brown bomber.'

The lads laughed.

'So how come she's roped yous in then? Aa thought she'd have had Stan in?'

'No, she says ee's too soft wi' yer, and ...whey, wouldn't cope sort of thing.'

'Aa can't see there'll be that much t' cope with t' be honest, aa mean, aa know she said it 'ud be a couple of days of jip, but that's it.'

He saw the looks of hidden things pass between them, just as the bedroom door opened and Stan's head appeared to stop his questions.

'Margaret said we could come up fer a bit.'

'Enter, Stanley, lad, and park that perky peach.'

He led the rest of them in and could see Tommy looking for Aude.

'She says we hadn't t' say 'owt t' Order just yet; in case it knocked her a bit, like.'

'Good job, 'cause ee's got a brown bomber lit in there,' said Wilf with a wicked smile.

Tommy saw their smiles and they saw his fade quickly behind a cloud of concern.

'Mebbees yer should set off now, eh,' suggested Den.

'Aye, best be on the safe side, 'cause there's somethin' on the mooch in there.'

He made his way into the en suite and closed the door. Standing quietly they heard a single, short, high pitched fart, and before Colly could say "B flat", the first battery opened like a bucket of meaty slops hitting a concrete path from an upstairs window. They heard Tommy say "Jesus Christ", and tried not to laugh, but when the bigger second load that sounded like it was dropped from higher up, muffled the "Christ Almighty" in the middle of it, they had to let go. The short silence of the lav ended with a final clattering splatter and a badly blown conch.

'That should empty the tank,' said Wilf.

Tommy came out, pasty white and sweaty, with both hands holding his gut, and collapsed on the bed. He farted and followed through to break the last of their defences.

'Are yer sure it was the full glass she said, Lester?' asked Roy, wiping his eyes.

'Aa'm thinkin' it might'ave been just a mouthful she said, now yer mention it.'

They laughed and Tommy groaned to good effect.

'Somebody'll have t' fetch a bucket.'

Just before 1.00, Margaret closed the door behind Stan, who was the last to leave.

'How are yer after that, son?' she asked with a little smile.

'Better out than in, eh.'

She didn't answer; she had her back to him and was busy sorting her things into careful order on the dressing table. Satisfied with them, she poured a spirit measure of clear liquid into a tumbler and stirred it with a silver spoon, before lifting it up to the light.

'Down in one, son.'

'Not again.'

'No, no, sup it off.'

He saw the solemn look in her eyes and heard the tension in her voice, and knocked it back. She took the glass and went over to her helpers.

'Ee'll be out in a minute. Now if yer goin' t' keel over when aa open him up, make sure yer don't fall on me, mind.'

They promised they wouldn't and she gave them each a small silver pan from the dressing table. Going back to the bed she took a long-handled, short-bladed knife from its pouch and checked the sharpness of its edge with her thumb, more from habit than ever thinking it might be blunt, and pricked the sole of Tommy's foot with it:

'Ee's over.'

Before they had any inclination of what she was going to do next, the full blade of the knife was stabbed into Tommy, and a deep, straight five-inch split was sliced into the new scar the professor had left on the lower left side of his belly. Placing the knife on the bed as she knelt down, she put both hands, in reverse prayer, into the slit and pulled it open. The noise of the wetting suction and the retching evil smell it released, made all the lads feel the room darkening and their mouths taste the water that begged for them to vomit. They swallowed hard and stood fast, and watched the clean white towels dye red.

'Wilf,' said Margret sharply.

He presented his silver pan; it had six smelly gauze golf balls and a pair of long flat-ended scissors in it. One by one she picked them with the scissors and worked it frantically inside Tommy before dropping it as a gruesome meatball into a bowl on the floor. The last one hit the bowl with a clink because it went with the scissors.

'Roy.'

The contents of his pan looked similar, but with smaller different smelling balls. She worked through them the same way, and Duggie was called forward as the last one hit the bowl with the same clink. His pan had a large metal-ringed syringe that looked like it belonged to an African vet. Pushing it deep into the open wound, the long plunger was pressed to empty the yellowy oily stuff it had taken from a flat brown bottle. It was refilled and emptied four more times.

'Lester.'

He came forward with a thick dark sausage on greaseproof paper in his pan, and knelt down beside her like a choirboy. She glanced at him as she picked it up to start packing it firmly inside the sucking gash. Fifteen very long seconds later she sat back on her heels and wiped her brow with the back of her hand to leave a savage red sign of her work.

'Right, pass that blue tin, there, Duggie.'

She popped it open and took the ready threaded needle before kneeling forward again.

'There,' she said, cutting the thread, 'it's done. Good lads, yer did well.'

'Will ee be alright now, Margaret?'

'We'll see, son.'

'But it went well, like?'

'It did. It was more than aa thought it would be, but we had enough. See if Stan's left them sheets, Wilf. Can yer wipe the thick of the blood off him, Duggie.'

Coming out of the en suite, drying her face and hands, the first thing she saw when she rubbed the towel from her eyes was Aude, staring at her with terror in hers. Wilf had just managed to throw a sheet over Tommy to hide what would have hurt her. Margaret walked straight to her and clamped her to her breast.

'It's all done now, my little Pet,' she said to the ceiling. 'Tommy can start t' get better now.'

She could feel, and the lads could see, the heaving, heavy trembling sobs of the little lost girl who was theirs. Margaret nodded at them to give her a minute with Aude, and they went and sat on the landing.

'Poor little bugger, d'yer think she saw?' said Roy.

'No, she didn't; aa had the sheet opened when aa clocked her runnin' up.'

'She was straight in, mind.'

'Aye, but it was on him; ee was all covered and the bowl's right under the bed.'

'Christ, what a sight that would have been fer her, eh.'

They sat in silence until the door opened and Margaret led the calmed but frightened Aude out. Standing her still in front of her, she cupped her beautiful face and rubbed it tenderly with her thumb as the water began to run back into the deep black pools.

'Now, now, my Pet, no more tears; Tommy was poorly but ee's gettin' better now. Listen t' what aa've just told yer, sweetheart, and think about seein' him better and up and about on Wednesda', eh. Aa want yer t' wait till then. Can yer do that for me, my Pet?'

Aude nodded.

'Good lass, yer a proper good lass, isn't she, lads.'

They stood up and made all the fuss they could without going too far and worrying her more.

'There, now you come downstairs wi' me,' said Margaret lovingly, 'and we'll see Nessa while the lads change Tommy's sheets. And, if yer want to, yer can help me bring them up a cup of tea and some of that nice Madeira cake Hilda baked, eh.'

Aude nodded.

'Margaret told me it was a bit dry and wantin' more marge, mind,' said Lester in a comical whisper, to make her try to smile.

'Mebbees a bit,' said Margaret with a wink. 'Come on then, sweetheart, we'll let the lads get on.'

Chapter 36

The agonising cries of pain and pleading for water had finally taken a break in Tommy's unrestful sleep, which let the three little tings from the carriage clock on the dressing table carry into the dead-of-night quiet of the bedroom. In the very low light from a hurricane lamp, Duggie sat awake on an adopted settee cushion, and Lester and Roy lay asleep on theirs by the bathroom wall. The door opened and Margaret came in with a candle stuck on a saucer by its own melted wax. She was in a full length dark blue dressing gown, with her long white hair enjoying the nocturnal freedom it had to run down her back from its strict daytime bun.

'Yer don't have t' have yer light so low, son, if yer want t' read,' she said louder than a whisper.

Duggie shrugged his shoulders to say it didn't matter.

'How long's ee been over like this?'

'About an hour.'

'Hard work, eh.'

'Aye,' he said, taking his baccy tin out.

The door opened again, slowly this time, and two big white pots of tea came in before Wilf.

'Aye, aye, Margaret. D'yer want a pot of tea, Pet, aa can nip down for another?'

'No thanks, son, aa'm just havin' a look.'

She put her hand on Tommy's brow, bent down and listened to his breathing, pushed one of his eyes open with her thumb, and had a quick look at the cut. 'Right, aa'll be back afore long.'

Turning to go she caught a look at Wilf in the flare of her moving candle and stopped in her tracks.

'What's that about?' she demanded without adding volume.

He put the cups on the floor and tried to look innocent but failed.

'Aa said, what the hell are yer about, lad?'

He gave up the ghost and looked at Duggie concentrating unnaturally on rolling his tab.

'So, ee's got yer all soft and kind and carin', has ee? And yer thought yer'd just give him a little drink of somethin' when ee wakes up, eh?'

'Just a sip, Margaret; ee's pleadin' like a hungry bairn, Christ, it's bloody heartbreakin'.'

'Right! Whey you give him ee's tea and ee's water, and whatever the friggin' hell else yer want, and aa'll take him home wi' me and get him buried for yer, right. Fair enough?'

Every word hit them with the mighty pressure it was meant to. She turned to leave and Wilf stepped quickly forward:

'Ee'll not get a drop, Margaret, not a drop.'

She glowered at them in turn. 'What aa've spent my time puttin' int' him, you'll wash out with a spoonful of water, and he will die.'

'Aa'm sorry, Margaret, we're stupid.'

'Aye,' she said easing off, 'now can yer see why aa didn't pick Stan?'

They nodded they certainly could.

'And make sure Lester and Roy get it as well, mind, 'cause if ee gets liquid, the good stuff'll be away like dust off a step. Just you think on; that's not good old Tommy layin' there wantin' nowt more than a little sup of tea; that's a dead man layin there that we're tryin' t' get back from the grave. So sort yersel's out or let him go t' his maker. Aa'm sayin' no more t' yers on this.'

She left the room.

'Christ, aa didn't think it was like that, mind,' came a voice from the bottom of the bathroom wall.

'Me neither,' said the voice beside it.

'Whey, we know now alright,' said Wilf, lifting the hurricane lamp to see where he'd put the teas.

It showed Roy and Lester holding a big white pot each.

'Did yer not think t' bring a bit cake up, Wilfy?'

******

'Margaret, Margaret,' said Lester, out of breath, 'there yer are, aa've been lookin' all over the place for yer.'

She didn't answer. She sat like marble on the log seat, looking into the far distant dark grey sky.

'Ee's awake, Margaret, properly, like. Ee knows who we are this time, mind ee hadn't a clue what day it was and got the shock of ee's life when we told him it was Wednesda' dinner time – ee thought it was Monda' mornin'. What are yer lookin' at, Pet, them big rain clouds?'

'They're not rain clouds, son.'

'Looks like thunder t' me. Mind, that's a bonny sight, there; the way the light's comin' through the middle of them, eh.'

'It is, son, it is a bonny sight.'

'So are yer comin' t' have a look at him and see if ee's done it then?'

'Ee has, son,' she said standing up and putting her hand on his shoulder; 'ee has done it, ee's come through.'

Not for the first time in his life, Lester looked like he didn't know what to make of her. She smiled and went with him because he wanted her to.

Up in the bedroom she let Tommy's eyelid blink back into comfort, and put her heavy hand on the side of his face.

'So, yer back then.'

He put his hand on hers but couldn't speak the words she knew he wanted to say.

'Aye, aye, son, yer all right. Mind, yer want t' thank yer lucky stars yer've got good pals like these,' she said turning to them. 'Good lads, you've done well. Now aa can see yers are tired, but aa need yer t' watch him one more night, alright?'

They let their tired faces smile to say it was.

'Can the lads see him yet, Margaret?' asked Roy.

'Aye, aye, just for five minutes, mind, ee's got another day t' go yet.'

Lester opened the door to run downstairs to get them, but they were gathered on the landing with Aude and Nessa. They came in slowly, not knowing what to expect.

'By Christ, that was quick,' said Margaret, telling them to behave normally.

She moved away from the bed so they could get to him. Tommy tried to let them know he was alright with a smile, but knew it wasn't enough when he saw Aude standing back beside Margaret, with her hands meshed together into a white-knuckled ball in front of her mouth. She looked frozen, with all her fretful fear falling on Tommy's tired, washed-out face. They thought she wouldn't be able to go to him, even though they knew how much she'd want to. Tommy could barely lift his arm towards her, but he tried and she flew at him like an arrow from a bow, burying herself into him, into his heart, her home, where she knew she belonged. He rubbed her back slowly as it lifted with sobs, and the lads looked away so they didn't have to see the tears rolling from his eyes into his ears. Margaret gave them a minute before she gently eased Aude off and cuddled her in.

'See this little thing, Tommy, she's done just what aa asked her, and sat down there, worried sick all this time, and never been a pick of bother. But these useless buggers,' she fired playfully, 'have been nowt but a bloody nuisance – every hour of every bloody day: "how's Tommy doin' now, Margaret?".'

Her mimicking child's voice made them laugh, and Tommy smiled and blinked slowly.

Stan put his hand in his pocket and got a sly kick off Duggie.

'Aye, good lad, Duggie,' she said in a very different tone as she glowered at Stan, ''cause if aa'd have seen that flask come out, aa'd have knocked yer friggin' head off yer shoulders, and aa'm not playin' either, mind.'

They all knew she wasn't.

'Aa just thought...'

'Right. Everybody out. Out, the lot of yers,' she burst, turning to her helpers. 'Make sure none of these get back in, especially that sackless sod.'

The lads left with her glaring at Stan.

'Christ, poor Stan, Margaret, ee looked like a yarked pup.'

'Aa know, son, but yer know why we can't have him around Tommy: ee's too soft and ee'll do damage. And aa mean it, mind; ee comes nowhere near.'

'Aa don't think there's any chance of that now.'

Lester tapped Margaret's arm and pointed to the bed. They all looked over. Nessa was sitting on it, using her fingers like a giant comb to put Tommy's hair tidy while he held the fingers of her other hand. They stayed still and watched them for a minute until Royston answered a little knock on the door.

'Denny says the doctors are downstairs, Margaret; they're havin' a look at Colly and are askin' about Nessa and Tommy.'

'Right-O, son, we'll be down in a tick.'

Walking with Nessa and Aude into the front living room where the lads and the sad-looking Stan were, Margaret saw the professor, standing in a clean white shirt and light blue trousers, with his arms folded, watching an old doctor listening to Colly's chest. He turned and smiled pleasantly at her. The old doctor said a few words in French to Colly's chest, and the professor replied before telling everyone he was saying everything was going well.

'So when can ee get back t' playin' then, doctor?'

'Yes, I think he is now ready to make the joint to swing, is that how to say it, Carter?' asked the professor with a smile.

'It is, Doctor,' he replied, as pleased as punch.

Margaret liked the professor.

'Good. Yes, and now Mademoiselle Nessa, who I see is doing very well today and on her feet and walking very good, can you come to sit down here, please.'

Nessa sat on the settee opposite Colly. Aude sat beside her and Margaret stood behind them. The professor took Aude's hand in both of his and looked closely at her. She smiled at him smiling at her as he rubbed her hand with care. Margaret liked him more.

'Marguerite! Mon dieu c'est toi. Oh, mon coeur. Oh, Marguerite!' filled the room.

The split second of Margaret's confusion vanished like a snowflake on a bonfire of memories, as the excited little doctor rushed towards her to reach up and cup her face in his hands. She leaned forward with a beaming wide smile to let him do it, and stood still so he could look at her through his overflowing eyes. He embraced her and kissed her from cheek to cheek half a dozen times, before she hugged him and rubbed his back. Standing him off by the shoulders, she looked straight at him.

'Never in the world, Georges; Georgie, yer little bugger, it's lovely t' see yer, lad. Aa never thought aa'd see yer again, son, but thank heaven aa have. How are yer, Georgie? Yer lookin' well, mind.'

'Oh, bon, bon, bon. Oh, Marguerite. Mon dieu c'est toi?'

'Aye, it is, it's me,' she laughed happily, and was caught in his arms again.

The lads, Nessa, Aude and the professor all looked at them, and then at each other, in amazement. The giddy old doctor turned and spoke quickly to the professor as he led the smiling Margaret towards him by the hand. They all saw the smile drop from the professor's face, and his posture stiffen as he looked at her differently.

'This is her,' said the professor, more to tell himself than ask a question.

'Oui, c'est elle.'

The professor stood up like a palace guard and put his open right hand across his chest and bowed his head. 'Madame Marguerite, it is my honour to meet you.'

He took her hand and kissed it with the most honest, respectful courtesy they'd ever seen.

'It's nice to meet you as well, son. And are yer takin' good care of this lovely man?' she asked playfully, but he stood looking at her as though he'd lost the power of speech. She smiled and asked if she could have her hand back.

'Yes, yes, oh yes, pardon me, Madame.'

'Don't be daft, son. Come on then, Georgie, let's have a look at Nessa's casts, eh.'

The old doctor smiled and took her hand again on their way to Nessa. They talked non-stop in their own half-English half-French, with Margaret using most words in French and Georges most in English. Nessa felt her head shoved forward with little ceremony and felt the weighty assurance of Margaret's hand rub the back of it, before the much gentler touch of the old doctor took over. They jabbered away and only stopped when they started to laugh. The lads looked at the professor for an explanation.

'They are reminding each other of a young man whose life they saved in the War. They are telling of the big shrapnel damage to his head, and how, when they did build it back together, it healed to look like he had a doorknob to the back of his head. That is what made them laugh so.'

'Oh, so they worked together in the War, then?' said Lenny.

'Whey, how the hell else d'yer think we know each other, yer sackless sod,' said Margaret, rolling her eyes at them, and taking them back for Georges.

'Le temps pour les coupeur,' she said.

'Aye,' said Dr Gambon, with a tinge of Firstwood, 'time fer cuttin'.'

Margaret smiled at him and he smiled his heart out at her, and everybody in the room smiled at them both as the professor handed the doctor his bag. After the usual rummage around he pulled out a pair of heavy shears. Margaret watched him fit the cutting blade into the top of one of the casts, grip them with both hands, and tremble with the effort to make them cut.

'Crue, Georgie?'

'Oui; blunt as butter.'

'Let's have a go. Mind, they are blunt, aa'll get Roy t' have a look at them for yer when we're done.'

'Merci, Marguerite.'

She split the casts off as easily as running pinking shears down a yard of baize. Aude picked one of the big, dirty white gauntlets up and put it on to make them smile and call her Popeye. Margaret and the doctor didn't notice because they were lost examining Nessa's wrists.

'Doctor Gambon is explaining how he thinks they were so badly damaged because she would not let go of the stick she held around the tree,' translated the professor, 'but they are happy with them now.'

'Right, come wi' me, Georgie, and you as well, lad,' she said to the professor, 'aa want yers t' have a look at Tommy. And you two'll have t' come as well 'cause ee'll want t' see Nessa's arms and little Popeye here.'

Nessa was helped up and hugged, squeezed and kissed, and then left alone by the woman she knew she had to follow.

'So the old doctor's told yer about Margaret, then, Doc?' probed Stan, who'd been delegated to get as much out of the professor as he could, as soon as they saw him come back down from Tommy's room by himself.

'Oh, yes, many, many times. It is a great honour to meet her.'

'Why though? Aa mean, what is it ee's said about her, like? We'er just wonderin', Doc.'

'Ah, I would so much like to tell you, because I can see you really do not know, but she just this moment made clear for me to stay silent, and I think you will agree that it would be a very silly thing not to listen to Marguerite, yes.'

'Oh hell aye, Doc, yer not wrong there, lad,' said Den.

'Whey, can yer say how they met, like?' tried Stan.

'Yes, yes; when they worked to keep their field hospital working all through the time you will have heard of at Verdun.'

'Christ.'

'Yes, and Dr Gambon has for all these years now, never one time changed one word of what happened there, and what she did, and … and I think I must stop, Messieurs, because I do not want to betray a lady's confidence, yes. But I know it is true, and what she has done to Tommy is more to her proof, if ever it was needed.'

The good-natured professor smiled, even though they could see he was as desperate to tell them as they were to hear.

'Well, we might get it out of yer one of these days, eh, Doc?'

'Oh, yes. I will promise now to tell you, one of these days, yes, and I will keep my promise to you. How is that, Colly?'

'Good enough fer me, Doc, lad. D'yer fancy a cognac?'

Chapter 37

Sitting peacefully by the kitchen wall in the Sunday afternoon sunshine with a clean white cloth across his knees, Tommy polished the cutlery in the two wooden boxes at his feet. He heard a car coming and waited to see who was. Roy parked beside the boxes and rolled his eyes at Tommy before getting out to open Margaret's door.

'What d'yer reckon t' this one, Tom, lad?' she asked, opening the boot and keeping hold of the handle to make her look like the Statue of Liberty.

'Christ, where the hell did yer get that?' said Tommy, running his hand along the length of the warm, dead pig, and expertly pressing and nipping in all the right places. 'Nice animal, though. Did yer get the blood?'

'Did aa get the blood? Course aa got the friggin' blood. Aa tell yer what, lad.'

Her natural exasperation made him smile.

'What the hell are yer standin' grinnin' at? Get the lads t' get it in and yer can get it jointed. Roy, get over there and tell them t' shut that racket off and get across here t' see what wants doin'. All the pots, plates and glasses need washed and cleaned, properly mind, so Stan and Duggie can get a start wi' that, and you (Roy) and Wilf can get both the tables through int' the front room and make sure there's chairs fer 18...'

'18?'

'Aye: Georges and the professor, all of us, and wi' yer Monty, Hilda and Raymond, and then this Monica lass comin'; that's 18 by my reckonin'.'

'Christ.'

'Aye, and t' get it all ready fer 7.00, so get yer arses in gear.'

Taking the pail of blood from the car she disappeared into the kitchen, and Lester and Den came scarpering out, looking like they'd had a rocket.

'Christ, does she ever bloody stop, that woman?' said Den.

'Where did she get it from?' asked Tommy.

'Some farm about 20 mile away,' answered Roy, 'but don't ask me how she knew it was there, or that ee had pigs.'

'That'll be the little doc, eh?'

'Aye,' said Tommy, smiling at the pig.

Lester and Den struggled to get it out of the boot and had only made their first steps to the kitchen, carrying it belly up, when Den's leading grip on the front trotters started to slip through his sweaty hands. Lester had a good hold on the back pair and tried to urge him forward by bumping the pig with his hips.

'What the hell's Lester doin' t' that pig?' came loudly across the courtyard from the little group gathered in the doorway with snooker cues.

'Go on, Lester, lad – ride 'em cowpoke.'

'There's a time and place for that, Lester.'

'We've got t' eat that, mind.'

'Aa'm havin' chicken.'

Den laughing didn't help stop him dropping the pig's head on the cobbles, and panic Lester into the brutal mistake of thrusting harder to try and plough the pig into the safety of the kitchen. It didn't look good to the corrupted male mind, and the shouts began again; telling him lots of things about lesser-known criminal convictions, and how they hadn't realised how much he was missing Gretchin. It would have gone on until somebody burst a blood vessel, if Margaret hadn't come out and grabbed a front trotter to lead Lester away.

'Is there nowt between them ears of yours, lad?' she said, half smiling. 'Get it up on the bench, there, and fetch them two buckets.'

Tommy came in smiling and began sharpening a knife on a steel. When it went in everybody went out, apart from him and her.

*****

267

The joined tables in the front living room looked like a clean, white-linened capital T that would have been at home in the Savoy. The cutlery and glasses shone brightly, and seemed to throw off a lot more light than the big window let in. It was quarter to seven and everyone was dressed in their best, having a glass of something as they stood in little chatty groups. Tommy had a pair of Lenny's black braces over his white shirt, and made sure they all got to see the newly slack waistband on his trousers. Georges and the professor looked naturally elegant in their black suits and white ties, while Raymond looked smart but unsuited to his. Hilda came back after 20 minutes away from the kitchen looking very attractive in her long blue dress, before it was hidden under an apron until the food was served. The whistles that had gone up for Hilda, went up for Nessa, Aude and Margaret when they came in together. Margaret looked stately in her black frock, and Nessa wore her promise in little Cynthia's bight pink blouse, with a comfortable grey skirt Margaret had brought her. Aude took everyone's eye as she stood shyly beside them in a simple little black dress they'd been shopping for in Lyon: she looked more beautiful than they'd seen her for a long time. Margaret carefully let the lads know to make a fuss of the lasses, which they would have anyway, even though they thought Nessa didn't like it much. Stan took control of the gauge of their attention towards her, knowing he could leave them to go full steam with Aude.

'Aye, there's a lot of work in that blouse, Pet, aa've never seen stitchin' any finer, mind; she's a clever little thing is Cynthia,' he said honestly.

Nessa smiled, but he could see there were no words coming, and even if there had been they would have been stopped by the gentle commotion caused by Monty coming in with Sylvia on his arm. He was in full peacock mode: the brilliant white shirt, waistcoat and bow-tie were made more resplendent by the scarlet silk cummerbund, and the way his perfectly tailored tuxedo provided the enhancing black frame. Despite the warm evening, Sylvia wore a rich, full-length mink coat that looked like it had been made for a Tsarina. Monty gallantly held up his hands to take it, but the simple, sleek movement out of it to stand in her premier pose with the ever-present clutch bag pressed lightly to her pelvis with both hands, was only done when she was satisfied all eyes were on her.

'Christ,' whispered Den to the back of Colly's head.

Sylvia stood tall in a tight, full length, shimmering silver, backless evening gown, with a low-cut front and a thin pearl necklace making its way down the deep valley of her breasts. With an expertly manufactured innocent expression, her hard-working eyes looked lazily about until Monty returned to escort her into the room.

'Ladies, this is Monica, the young lady Lester helped one evening, and who has since become one of our little circle of friends. Monica, this is Nessa.'

The handshake greeting with Nessa was friendly, and Sylvia managed to suspend every impression of anything she could possibly call tasteful to complement her blouse.

'And this is Aude,' said Monty.

A tiny ripple of something crossed the professionally still waters of Sylvia's face when she took Aude's hand. The ever-watchful Monty smiled, thinking the queen had seen she wasn't the fairest in the land. He was wrong about that, but right about the consummate ease of her control.

'Hello Aude, I am so happy to meet you. And you should know your friends have not told me lies; those really are the most beautiful eyes, my dear.'

Aude smiled politely, but a few of them thought she didn't seem to like the compliment she'd had a thousand times before.

'And this is Margaret,' said Monty.

Their eyes met. Any audible clash of the hidden daggers would have been heard a mile away. Neither gave way or showed anything of what was going on behind the customarily polite masks, and simply shook hands and smiled their knowledge into each other's understanding. Sylvia complimented Margaret's beautiful necklace, but made sure her parting look and deliberately vacant gaze showed the insult she wanted. Margaret smiled after her as Monty took her to meet the doctors, and felt a little hand slip into hers.

'What the hell's ee done t' Lester?' said Carter, to make them all look toward the doorway to the bedrooms. Duggie sauntered in with his head in the air and one hand in his trouser pocket, loving the attention his magnificent outfit was designed for. His brown pinstripe suit over a flame red satin shirt and gold lamé tie, ended in a pair of blue Cuban heeled shoes with bright white spats. His jet-black hair carried a battle axe centre parting and shone with an industrial slick from his new hair oil. Behind the strutting, high resolution Duggie came the lesser unfocussed Lester, dressed in the mirror of his leader, with a light blue pinstripe suit, a lime green shirt and black tie, and a pair of ox-blood brogues with baggy white spats.

'Jesus, what's ee done with ee's hair?'

The Clark Gable look Duggie had tried to style onto Lester hadn't worked.

'Hello, Adolf,' said Tommy, to let everybody know who'd turned up instead.

It looked like the leader of the Third Reich had been caught coming out of a Hoochie Coochie club.

'Get in the kitchen,' said Margaret, pushing him out of the laughter.

Holding his head under the tap she scrubbed a bar of soap over it in the freezing cold water, and stood him up to dry it with a tea towel. He looked up at her, just as he had when he was a little lad. She remembered and smiled, and combed his hair back to normal.

'Here, take the cracklin' in, and mind yer get first pick, son.'

She winked to make him smile and think the cruel world had stopped laughing at him.

'And tell them t' get sat down, and send Herbie, Stan and the lasses through.'

Succulent meat from the large joints of pork or four golden chickens, was added to plates stacked with colour from the vegetable tureens, before Margaret's little navy of gravy boats came to carry most of them home. Tommy sat beside Stan at the end of the table, looking down at the guests. He watched Monica cut small delicate cubes from her chicken leg and Margaret pick hers up and bite it to the bone. It made him smile. The dinner found a comfortable canopy of pleasant conversation that lasted beyond the metal on china music of the table, and only stopped when Margaret stood up.

'Right, Stanley, fill the drinks, and Den, Colly and Carter can help me clear this stuff away, Wilf and Lester bring the bowls and spoons through; Herbert's made us a treat, isn't that right, son.'

She rubbed Herbie's back on her way to the kitchen, smiling at the cheers from the lads who knew what was coming. It came and they settled to the simple delight.

'What d'yer think of Herbie's apple sponge and custard, Monica?'

'I think it is the most delicious thing I've ever tasted, and it would be a very lucky woman who could have it every day.' She said it with a playful saucy kindness the lads liked.

'Play yer cards right, Pet,' winked Colly to make her laugh.

'So are yer workin' in Lyon, then, Monica?' asked Stan.

'Yes, in hotel work; taking bookings and dealing with complaints and all such things.'

'And are they still busy now, like?'

'Oh, yes, a lot of people are still travelling and needing accommodation.'

'So which hotel is it yer work at then, Monica?' asked Lenny.

'I'm in the hotel Terminus just now.'

'Oh, aye, the big one on the corner,' said Lester.

'It is, but I don't expect to be there for long now; my bosses tell me of changes coming, and it is likely I will have to move.'

'Where to, Pet, have they told yer?'

'No, Lenny, it will be a last minute thing, it always is; but I'm used to it, I've been doing this for quite a long time now.'

'It'll be a shame if yer get sent away and we didn't get t' see yer again, like.'

'Well, that's very kind of you to say so, Lenny. I would like it very much to keep in touch, yes?'

'Oh, hell, aye,' said Colly. 'Monty can send yer letters from us, eh.'

'And, yer never know, we might end up playin' in the same place where you are, and could meet up with yer, eh,' said Lenny.

'And we'll make you dinner again and get some apples for Herbie for yer,' said Wilf with a wink.

While she was smiling her practised professional smile, she felt something that was, at one and the same time, both lovely and disturbing to her. It was as if each time the little wave of their innocent kindness rolled into her, it ran a little further up the dry sands of her man-made shore. Only Margaret saw the lady Canute.

With plates and cutlery cleared to the kitchen, six tall, ivory candles were lit in each of the three candelabras on the table. They worked perfectly with the gas mantles to make a lovely atmosphere that dismantled anything standing in the way of their enjoyment. Carter and Lenny brought the gramophone from the music room, and Carter found himself a nice little space picking and playing records. Aude sat with him for a lot of the time, and the others saw them laughing as they tried to teach each other dance moves, or just sit talking about what they knew would be music as they tapped out pieces on the arm of the settee. Monica took her turn on the dance floor they'd made by shifting the tables and settees, and danced and chatted happily with everyone who wanted to dance with her, including Lester, on each of the three times he was marched up to her by Wilf and Den. Monty's close monitoring of her left him in no doubt he was dealing with someone at the very top of their professional tree. All of the women danced with plenty of ready and willing partners, although Margaret danced mostly with Georges, but made the professor happy with a turn around the carpeted floor. When they weren't dancing, they sat or stood in talkative little groups, and the happy round robin of the evening turned the hands of the clock very quickly. It was the cough of a car horn at the silent end of a record that brought them to look about and wonder what it was.

'Oh, that will be my taxi,' said Monica sadly. 'It had to be for now because I'm to leave early in the morning for Paris. Life is not fair.'

She flashed a look at Monty that Margaret didn't miss.

'All good things, eh, Monica, Pet?'

'But is it not dangerous for yer goin' there now?'

'No, no, Lenny, I have no problems because of my work – they need hotels you see.'

'Well, yer still want t' watch yersel' and take care, Pet.'

'I will, Wilfy.'

'And you know where we are, and t' keep in touch, sweetheart.'

'I do, Lenny, I know where you are and I am very happy to think I will always be able to find you.'

Monty returned with the sumptuous coat and held it for her. She slipped into it with the usual graceful half turn to pull it around herself in film star fashion. The premier pose was assumed with the little black bag.

'I have had the most lovely evening. Thank you so very much and goodnight, everyone, and I do look forward to seeing you again.'

The lads all thought she meant it. Monty escorted her away from their sincere goodnights and goodbyes into the middle of the courtyard.

'Have you had a good evening, Frau Plank?'

'Dear me,' said the unshakeable woman, scornfully.

The driver was waiting with the door open, and spoke very quietly to her in German before she slipped into the back of the taxi.

'Goodnight, my de…' was all he managed before she told him to shut up.

'Flaubert's, in Macon, 20th,' was all she said before the door whumped shut and the car drove off.

'Never mind standin' out there watchin' the stars, there's a tea towel in here wi' your name on it, Monty, lad.'

Chapter 38

'Shussh, shussh now, my Pet,' said Margaret to the top of Aude's head, 'it's not for long now, and we'll all be back home before yer know it.'

There was still no sign of Aude leaving loose of her, and she signalled Monty.

'Aude, my dear, Margaret must go now or the aeroplane will leave without her, and I may not be able to arrange another for quite some time if it does. Now I'm sure you don't want that to happen.' He spoke compassionately but firmly enough for Margaret to feel the pressure ease out of the gripping arms. Putting her hands on Aude's shoulders, she bent down to look into the tearful face that couldn't look at her.

'Now yer know aa need yer here, my Pet: t' look after Nessa 'cause she needs yer, and t' make sure Tommy doesn't start on wi' the cognac again, right.'

She saw the first faint flicker of ease.

'And the most important thing for yer stayin' here a bit more, sweetheart, is t' make sure yer get the nice clean air and sunshine t' make yer strong, 'cause aa'm not gettin' any younger and aa'll be needin' some good help at home soon enough, mind.'

The word "home" got through and Aude looked up and tried her best to smile. Margaret could see her own face in the polished jets looking at her.

'That's a good lass,' she said, drying Aude's eyes with a hanky as she craftily took her hand to let her think she was leading her out of the house to the car. The silvery white light of the bright full moon hanging low in the cloudless starry sky lit the courtyard with an other-worldly vapour that looked like it didn't belong to the real two o'clock in the morning night-time. Everybody was out waiting for them.

'Nice night for it, Margaret,' chipped Wilf.

'It is, son.'

They each got the same old quick cuddling squeeze that made them feel genuinely saddened she was going. Margaret held on to Hilda's hand after her cuddle. 'Yer a good lass, but just make sure you look out for these lads, mind.'

The lads thought it was odd for her to say that in English, when she knew fine well Hilda could barely speak a word, but shrugged it off as Margaret being Margaret. Tommy stood back to be last and came forward to wrap his arms around her shoulders. She rubbed his back. It lasted longer than the others and everybody knew why. When he stood back from her it was easy to see his eyes shining in the moonlight.

'Aa'll see yer when we get back, Pet,' he managed.

'Yer will if yer stay off the drink, although here's me forgettin' you're a teetotaller these days, eh.'

Tommy was happy to be able to smile at her.

'Aa've got Georgie comin' down on Frida' t' clip them few stitches out, and then that's you done, son. When ee comes give him this.'

She gave him a little white envelope.

'Did yer forget t' give him it when ee was here sayin' ta-ra?'

'No, son,' was all she was going to say.

'I am sorry to be such a boor,' interrupted Monty, 'but we really do need to be making tracks now.'

'No bother, son. Right, aa'm off. Watch yersels, mind, and aa'll see yers back yem for Christmas.'

They made a lot of chappy noise for her as she pulled Aude and Nessa to her and gave them each a mother's kiss, eying Tommy to make sure he did what she'd told him to do with Aude. He nodded it would be done. Four doors clumped shut and Raymond drove slowly away from the waving little crowd to turn out of sight at the corner of their chateau.

'So when will Stan and Herbie get back then?'

'Tomorro' night, whey, that's tonight really. Monty said they'd be comin' straight back after they got Margaret in the house.'

'The place'll not be the same without her, mind.'

'Yer not wrong there, Lenny, lad.'

'Aa'll be havin' a lie in.'

*****

'By Christ, yer lookin' a bit rough there, Stanley; not much sleep on the plane, eh.'

'None on the way back, that's for sure.'

'Turbulence?'

'Wilf had a touch of that this mornin'.'

'It's them eggs.'

'So Margaret got back alright, then?'

'Oh, aye. Mind, it was bloody cold and chuckin' it down, we got soaked just gettin' her stuff in, and we were parked at the door.'

'Home, sweet home, eh.'

'Look what she's left yers,' said Lester, giving them a large black pop bottle each. 'A pint and a half of Bess. We all got one left in our rooms, apart from Tommy, like, but we haven't supped them 'til yers got back and can have them all together, like.'

'And we can tell Tommy what it tastes like,' said Wilf. 'Lenny can let him sniff ee's bottle if ee wants.'

'Aa'll do no such thing, Tom, lad, tormentin' yer like that.'

Tommy smiled at Lenny not being able to run with the joke because of his kind heart.

'Can we hold off 'til tomorro', lads,' said Stan, smiling at his bottle, 'aa'm knackered and Herbie's got t' be as well, mind.'

'Whey aye, you rest that sweet head, Stanley,' said Tommy standing up and clapping his hands together to show he had pressing business. 'Right, Carter, lad, let's at it.'

Without another word he left the living room with Carter following and smiling at them.

'Yer look like yer've seen a ghost, Stan,' said Den.

'Ee's never going over t' ...'

'Ee is.' Wilf smiled. 'And ee did an hour at tea-time, and ee reckons on puttin' a couple of hours a day in from now on.'

'Well aa'll be buggered, our Tommy, practisin'. What the hell did she do t' him up there?'

'H'way then, let's away over and see what they're at,' said Roy.

Stan and Herbie watched them file out.

'This is lookin' good, Herbert, aa think we might be gettin' the band back.'

Herbie rolled his hands and Stan knew he was saying 'about time'.

******

'Thanks very much, Doc, aa didn't feel a thing,' said Tommy, holding his shirt up to have a look at his new scar now the stiches were out.

'Oui, very good.'

He could see the old doctor wasn't very happy.

'It looks nice and neat, Doc; Margaret's done a good job, eh.'

'Yes. Very best.'

The strength of feeling in the words made Tommy feel sorry for him.

'Aa've got somethin' for yer, Doc.'

He took the little white envelope from his shirt pocket.

'It's from Margaret.'

'Marguerite?'

Georges took it gently and opened it carefully, breaking the brief point of the seal at the end of the flap. Tommy watched him reading and felt anxious, not knowing if it would make him happy or sad. He waited while he read and re-read the short note, and was surprised to have it put in his hand.

'Tell me how to understand, Tommy, thank you.'

Tommy could see the awful anticipation of misapprehension looking at him, and was pleased to be able smile broadly after a quick scan.

'What's wrong, Doc, d'yer not want t' come back with us and see her?'

He saw a smile dare to dawn on the old doctor's face, and work its way into the biggest of unaffectedly happy ones as he looked again at the words he was holding.

'Moi, to England with you, Tommy?'

'That's right, Doc, she's arranged it with Monty t' have yer come back with us, if yer can, like, t' spend Christmas with her, and all of us really. So how about that then?'

He pulled Tommy down by his shoulders and kissed him on each cheek.

'Aa take it that's a "oui", then, Doc,' he laughed.

He watched the little doctor kiss the powder blue notepaper and say, 'Oh oui, yes, yes.'

Chapter 39

December, 20th

Duggie stood in his heavy top coat, in the bit of the courtyard lit by the crude block of light from the open garage door. He watched his freezing grey breath catch his cloudy blue smoke, while he waited for Roy and Herbie to get the portable gas fire sorted out. As soon as they bundled it past him, he turned the lights off, pulled the door shut and ran over to help them get it onto the bus.

'Two minutes, lads, and we'll have a bit heat,' promised Roy.

'Aa mightn't last that long,' said Wilf.

Raymond started the engine and a loud banging hammered on the side of the bus. Roy looked at the ghoulish-looking lads sitting in the pale orange light, wondering what it was, and opened the door to have a look. Aude hopped onto the bottom step.

'Can it be all right for me and Nessa to come tonight?'

The cheer came from nothing more than the pure joy they all felt at the thought of her getting better. She smiled brightly in the red and black shadow of the fire, and saw Tommy looking all of his guarded hope as clearly as a lighthouse in the ten watts of watery coachlight. Wilf and Den stood to give them their seats by the fire but were pressed to sit back down by Aude, who happily made her way up the aisle.

'So what made yer change yer mind, sweetheart?'

'To come to enjoy our last concert for now, Tommy.'

He heard "our" and smiled.

The bus pulled out of the courtyard on its 70 km drive north to a town called Macon.

'Right, Raymondo, give it some boot, there's a good lad.'

******

Stan answered the tap on the dressing room door at half time.

'Is everybody decent?' he asked, looking around.

'Jury's out wi' Lenny.'

'Yes, Pet, come on in.'

Nessa came in with Aude, bouncing and clapping her hands like the biggest Snipes fan in the world she was, and showing the biggest, happiest smile she had.

'It is fantastic, you are so good, it is so very good,' she beamed, and got playful bows from them. 'And, Wilf, you are just so very good.'

'Thank you, sweetheart, aa'll do me best for as long as yer want me t' stand in for yer, Pet, but, aa love me guitar and aa'll say no more.'

He winked and she laughed, much to their relief. Wilf seized the moment. 'So, how about because it's our last one, you play the encore, Pet, and just have a bit fun and enjoy yersel', if yer want to, like?'

All eyes were on her, with Tommy watching like a hawk to take her away from anything that didn't look good. She shrugged her shoulders simply and smiled and said she'd love to. Now it was her turn to make her playful bow to their cheering and clapping – they were her biggest fans.

'But–' she smiled, holding up a finger like a school teacher– 'if I play, then Stan must go to low down to lift all the way up for him to get his very big 'C' in *Jam it up*, yes.'

'That's a deal, Pet,' agreed the happy Stan amid the cheers and whistles.

'And,' she went on, with the old glint in her eye, 'Tommy must once more spin his bass like he did before when you were young.'

A bigger cheer went up as the sparkling Aude leaned back and put the ball of her folded hands under her chin.

Tommy hung his head in mock dismay.

'She's got yer, Tom, lad, see what comes of fillin' the lass wi' stuff about the good old days, eh.'

'I knew I would get you, Tommy,' she laughed.

'Yer have, Pet, good and proper this time. But, for you, sweetheart, and this lot who think aa might've lost a touch wi' me tip-top stage gimmick, aa'll make it spin tonight alright.'

'But only in the encore, yes, I want to play for that in our band.'

Tommy threw down his towel and picked her up by the waist, spun her around to make her laugh, put her back on her feet and bent down so she could grab him around the neck and kiss his cheek. He kissed the top of her head, and while he still had her face in his hands he warned her to make sure she held onto the drum kit when his bass started spinning.

'You will make the hurricane, Tommy,' she laughed.

'Creatin' wind's ee's speciality, Pet,' said Wilf.

'Ee's cleared us off stage with it a few times, Pet,' said Den.

'And the punters off the dance floor in Blackpool that time,' reminded Colly.

'Then I will make sure I hold onto my drums,' said Aude, innocently taking the meteorological reference.

'And yer dinner, Pet,' whispered Wilf to Colly, preferring the medical.

******

'Everybody's decent, sweetheart, and ready and waitin' for yer,' said the hot and sweaty Stan, holding the door open for Aude to come in.

'Here, Pet,' offered Wilf, 'yer can have my jacket.'

'It is all right, thank you, Wilf, Monty has brought my shirt and tie and jacket in this bag.'

'Has ee?'

'Yes, and he has also brought Hilda and Monica and her uncle as well, to see us on our last night to play here. And something else that will come soon.'

As if it had been rehearsed, a solid knock took Stan back to the dressing room door.

'Well, well, well, Wilfred, you shall go to the ball,' he said, showing him his guitar case.

'That is what else he did bring,' said Aude happily.

'What a star that man is,' said Wilf taking the case, 'what's ee not come in for, anyhow?'

'It wasn't him, it was one of the waiters,' said Stan. 'Right, get it tuned, Wilfy, lad, while Aude gets changed in the lavvy there, not a minute to lose, mind, we're straight back on.'

'So where are they sittin', Pet?' asked Tommy.

'Far back on the balcony level and to the left side as you look out from the drums,' answered the toilet door. 'It is a very good view to see us, and Nessa is there, and Monica said she would dance with her uncle if the songs are not so fast.'

The toilet door opened with her last word to let them see her in her white tuxedo and black tie.

'Yer look lovely, Pet,' they all said in their own loose chorus.

'The sticks are on the snare, sweetheart.'

'Thank you, Wilfy, but I have mine here, look.'

She dropped the bag on the floor and clipped her thin heavy sticks together distractedly to make them smile.

'Just get an 'E' off Tommy out there, Wilf. Come on, lads, we're at full-belt now, so let's make some proper noise, eh.'

Three fast and three slower songs later, the dressing room door burst open and the noisy, sweaty, laughing, high-spirited band bundled in, all of them talking over each other, saying the same things but differently in the same excitable way. Aude was hugged and kissed and complimented by each and every one of them, and although she couldn't stop the tears rolling down her cheeks, there wasn't a single thought of her being anything but happy.

'You were absolutely fantastic, Pet,' said Tommy wholeheartedly, 'and no disrespect t' Wilfy, 'cause ee's done a grand job, but by Christ yer were bloody fantastic.'

'And so were you, Tommy, and now I have seen the big spinning.'

'She's not wrong, Tommy, lad, yer were tip-top out there tonight, mind.'

'Thank you, Wilfred. Mind, it nearly didn't happen when aa saw these brassy buggers puttin' the old half turns in. When did yers decide on that then?'

'We didn't, it just happened.'

'That's the groove for yer.'

'It is, Carter, lad, it is that.'

'And what about our Stanley, eh? Turnin' the clock back there, old lad. Look, ee can't speak for grinnin'. How long's it been since we played like that then, Stan?'

Stan smiled and rubbed a hand over his glistening red egg of a head.

'Never, we've never played like that – that was the best we've ever been, it was perfect and aa'll never forget a minute of it as long as aa live … it was just perfect …'

They could see how much it meant to him as he tried to rub the water from his eyes. Aude put her arms around him and made them all feel the moment in the same way. It was only the door being flung open by the exuberant Monty that pulled them out of the lovely warm blanket of their collective pleasure.

'Yes, enter all,' he called over his shoulder, 'there's nothing too disturbing on show. My, my, gentlemen, and Aude, what a show.'

Nessa, Raymond, Hilda, Monica and Count von Leibernitz came into the crowded dressing room.

'Yes,' said Monica talking to Stan, but loud enough for the others to hear, 'this is my uncle, Walter, who is staying at the hotel where I work. He has travelled from home in Switzerland, and has something to say to you that I don't want to spoil.'

'H'way, then, Walter, let's have it,' said Tommy, butting in good naturedly.

'Hello,' he began in a vague European accent, 'I have come here to see you tonight because of what my niece has told me. I am a music producer, you see, and I am decided I would like to ask for you to record your music with my company, and to play some concerts for the radio.'

The silence was just what Sylvia and the Count expected. They watched the lads look at each other, and then at Monty.

'Is there a problem for you to do this?' asked the Count plainly.

'There could be, Walter,' said Stan, 'and t' be honest, aa'm not sure we can do it, like.'

'Oh, I am surprised at this; your manager, Mr Elvin, has just now told me it would be something you would like very much. Please to excuse me if I have not understood things correctly.'

'Have yer told Walter we could do this then, Mont?' checked Tommy.

'Well, perhaps more along the lines of knowing you'd want to, and that I really don't have anything definite to rule it out.'

He smiled professionally but Stan could see something wasn't right.

'Well, how about lettin' us think on it for a bit, if yer don't mind, Walter,' said Stan to ease the situation.

'Yes, yes, of course, but for how long will you take? As you will understand, I must arrange many things.'

'Oh aye. How about we let yer know after Christmas?'

'Yes, I can wait for then, but not so much more into January, I'm afraid. And you will instruct Mr Elvin to inform me, yes?'

'We will, yes.'

'There is one thing, Walter,' began Colly, showing he was caught in a current of thought he couldn't resist, 'we're on good money doin' what we're doin' now, y'know, so we'll not be wantin' t' risk it, like.'

'I understand,' said the Count. 'May I be so rude to ask what it is to be called "good money"?'

'With everythin' in yer lookin' at £1,600 a year, mind.'

'I see.'

The lifeless response worked to hook Colly. The Count saw it had and went on to reel him in:

'Well, I am sure money shouldn't be everything when you want to do good against those horrible Germans, yes...'

'But please tell them, Uncle, tell them what you told me,' pressed Sylvia, expertly playing the part of Monica, the agitated niece trying to help her new friends.

'No, my dear, I think they will decide on all things they need to, and not just for money.'

The skills of their world didn't belong to the band, and they had no protection against the seductive pricks being fired at them. It was unbearable for Colly.

'Aa was just wonderin', Walter, y'know, t' help us make our minds up, like, if yer could mebbees give us some idea about the money, like?'

'I cannot do so exactly because we do not know of the sales of the records.'

'Please, Uncle, I am sure it will help.'

'Well, I do not like to work like this, my dear, you know it is not my way to mislead people. But, if the records are sold less than any band we have, which I am sure they will not, and we come to rely on radio and performance revenues most, then it may fall to £1,000 each. However, I would not expect it to do so; I would expect it to be at least two times this amount.'

'So yer sayin' mebbees up to £2,000 a year,' clarified Colly.

The Count looked at him and laughed awkwardly, waited, and waited a little more, and said: 'A week.'

Monty's groan was kept to himself. Even if it had escaped, it wouldn't have been heard above the whistles and colourfully worded disbelief.

'Jesus Christ, Walter, yer sayin' more than 2,000 quid a week, each! A week!' said Colly in a state of shock.

'Yes, I am.'

Again, the deliberately lifeless response worked well to show them it was nothing out of the ordinary, and by lazily tapping a cigarette on the side of his gold lighter he emphasised the ordinariness of it all. Waiting for the hubbub to die down, he nonchalantly flipped the lid in Monty's direction to light the cigarette he had nipped between his lips, before going on:

'Well, I will leave you to consider this,' he said casually, blowing the smoke to follow the words. 'I must now bid you all goodnight; goodnight, gentlemen, and ladies, of course.'

'But you haven't met Lester, Uncle,' coaxed Sylvia, putting her arm through his as she looked around the room.

'Ee's over there, Monica,' said Lenny.

They all looked at Lester, who was standing in front of the seated Nessa with his fists in her face. In the silence of their curiosity, they could hear the conversation:

'See, so after them rolls, the thumbs are up on top, see, like if aa was boxin' yer, right. Now, if aa turn them t' the side, like that, as if yer were ridin' me bike, then yer in position 2, right. So it goes like this, and aa'll go slow so yer can follow, 'cause aa've been practisin', like. Ready?'

Nessa sat looking resigned with her fists up.

'Right, here we go; thumbs up, thumbs side, roll t' the left, roll t' the right, and thumbs up, and again, Pet...'

'Lester!'

'Hey-up?'

'What the hell are yer at now, lad?'

'Exercisin'.'

'Exercisin' what?'

'Nessa's wrists.'

He replied as though he shouldn't have had to.

'Lester,' soothed Sylvia, who was now beside him, 'this is my uncle, Walter.'

'Hello Walter, pleased t' meet yer.'

'It is I who am very pleased to meet you, Lester,' said the Count, taking Lester's offered hand. 'My niece has told me of that terrible night and how you helped her, and for that I am forever grateful. If there is anything I can do to say thank you, then please to say and I will do all I can.'

'No, yer alright, Walter, anybody would've helped the lass. But thank you, all the same, though.'

'Monica tells me you like fishing,' said the Count.

'Aa do, aye.'

'Well, I have a yacht and a crew you can use to fish in the Caribbean over the holidays if you would like.'

'No, no, yer alright, thank you, Walter. Aa'm takin' Nessa up the reservoir, so long as her wrists don't give her any jip, like. Mind, aa can help her land any biggun's 'cause the sharp pulls could set her back a notch, sort of thing – and aa'd catch it from Margaret if it did.'

Nessa sat looking at him with his wide eyes wondering how to stop a fish from hurting her, while he went fishing with her in the freezing cold at the reservoir six miles from their home, when he could be on a yacht in the tropics. She blinked and looked down at the fists on her knees becoming blurred.

'Well, my offer is there and will remain so, Lester,' said the Count sincerely. 'Come, my dear, I really must get back, or I will be in trouble with your aunt.'

Sylvia put her hand on Lester's shoulder. She felt him tremble as she leaned down to leave her luscious red mark on his cheek. 'Goodbye, Lester. I wish for you to have a lovely holiday and I hope we see each other soon.'

'Aye, yes, Monica, aa will, and you have a nice one too, Pet.'

As soon as the door closed, the band silently pushed their fists into the air and grabbed each other with wildly happy, but muted joy. Monty smiled at their childlike naivety, as the noise slowly came to fill the volume of the room as soon as they thought Walter and Monica would be far enough away not to hear. Aude sat beside the contemplative Nessa and explained the offer to her, while the lads tried to give all the detail to Lester, who'd heard it all but couldn't make them hear he had.

'What's up, Mont?' asked Stan, slipping out of the crowd to join him and Hilda.

'Good Lord, Stanley; rich boys and girls is what I'd say was up.'

'No, Monty, aa can tell there's somethin' up, and no doubt yer'll have yer reasons for not wantin' t' say 'owt, but aa wish yer would, or yer could, because aa'll tell yer now; aa think there's a rabbit off wi' Monica's uncle, but aa daren't say 'owt t' them yet.'

'I simply don't know, Stanley, but you can be sure I shall look into it.'

'And you'll let us know what's what?'

'I will, Stanley, through Norman; he's still with your vicar. I'll do the best I can and I would like to think you know that.'

Stan said he did, but the uncharacteristic feeling in Monty's words made his high adrenaline tide start to turn.

******

'At last! What on earth has happened; did you break down? We've been back ages.'

'Don't ask, Mont,' said Roy, stepping off the bus into the early morning light.

'We've been off the road twice,' said Den following behind.

'Oh, difficulties in the snow?'

'Aye, yer could say that.'

'Aa think aa've slipped mesel' a hernia,' complained Colly.

'Oh, right off the road, ay? And you've had a spot of bother getting back on?'

'Just a couple of "spots of bother" with the ten of us pushin', Mont, but apart from that, not much bother at all,' said Wilf.

'If it wasn't for laughin' at Lenny we'd have froze out there.'

'What happened to Leonard?'

'We got the bus pushed so far back up t' the road this one time, when it started t' slide back on us. This was before the fella with the car and the rope turned up, so we just stood aside, apart from Lenny the log there, who dropped on ee's back, and the bloody thing rolled over him.' (laughs)

'It's these boots,' said Lenny.

'Have a look, Mont – show him, Len.'

Lenny opened his coat and lifted his shirt to let him see the blistered cricket ball on his gut.

'My goodness, Leonard. And the car you …'

'Probably the flange couplin' on the exhaust housin',' interrupted Roy, 'it would've been red hot like.'

'D'yer hear that, Lenny? Roy says yer were dragged by the flange, not the coat.'

'And ee was dragged a canny bit further back than we started from.'

They started laughing again.

'You mentioned a car, Royston?'

'Aye, a lovely black '38 Jag it was, and lucky for us him havin' a rope.'

'Yes, fortunate but not altogether unlikely at this time of year. Did Raymond speak to him?' asked Monty, hiding his concern.

'Oh aye. Mind, ee didn't seem in any big hurry once they got crackin' on.'

'Will Hilda have 'owt for Lenny's gut, Monty?' asked Stan.

'Yes, of course, forgive me, Leonard, let's get you inside.'

'We might as well have our breakfast now, eh, and then hit the sack.'

'Good thinkin', Denny, lad. What about a good old fry up, Herbie?'

Just before nine o'clock, Hilda, Herbie, Carter and Duggie made their way to the big table in the front living room, with their breakfast in one hand and buttered bread in the other.

'Here's the chefs. Come and get yersels sat down and enjoy yer breakfasts,' said Tommy, as though he'd just cooked it for them.

'But before yer sit down, Herbie, can yer take my cup back t' the kitchen before aa stot it off Colly's head if ee doesn't give this bloody money a rest.'

Herbie smiled and settled to his meal.

'Aa'm just sayin', though,' persisted Colly, 'yer talkin' of upwards of 100,000 quid each, in a single year, mind, and for God knows how many years. That's half a million pound in five years, 500,000 quid! For Christ's sake, lads!'

'Colly,' said the mildly exasperated Stan, 'there's nowt of anythin' but words just now, so settle down, or risk a fall, mind.'

'Ee's right, Colly, look how it turned out t' be gobshite the last time.'

'No it didn't, we got this,' defended Colly.

'Aye, but it wasn't a record deal. But yer right, we did get this and it is good money, and aa like it, y'know, travellin' about together and playin', and aa'm not wantin' to scupper it, like,' said Wilf firmly.

'Aye, aa get that, but for Christ's sake, yer can't be knockin' back a chance at money like what Walter's offerin', though.'

'But that's just it; ee's doin' nowt but offerin'. Look, we've got real money here, and a hell of a lot of it t' my mind – too bloody much t' lose.'

'Definitely,' conceded Colly, 'but if we can get a crack at the big stuff and do nowt t' risk this, then it has t' be worth a try, eh.'

'Aye, but wait and see what Monty comes back with, eh?' said Stan to let the steam out.

'So are we all agreed to do nowt t' bugger this, though?' said Den.

Everybody put their hand up.

'Right, let's leave it there, we're all knackered, let's get t' bed so Colly can dream about flashin' ee's fat wad in the Ritz.'

'Christ.'

'D'yer want t' watch me havin' a go wi' me wrist for two minutes, Nessa, Pet?'

'Christ.'

'Aye,' said Nessa, standing up to choke off any smut, 'that'ud be champion, Lester, ta.'

Chapter 40

Lester walked into the music room.

'Right, that's everybody,' began Stan, 'so, me and the lasses have spent what we all chipped in, and this is just t' show yer what we got before we wrap them up. We got Raymond and Hilda a watch. They're not proper gold or 'owt, but they each cost a bit so should be canny for keepin' time. If yer open the cover on this one, yer'll see we got *Best Wishes Raymond, From the band* engraved on. That was Nessa's idea.'

'Nice one, Pet.'

He passed it to Den to start its round for their individual examinations.

'And this is Hilda's,' continued Stan.

He opened a slim black box and held up an elegant gold ladies' wristwatch before passing it to Den to follow Raymond's around the room.

'It's a lovely face on it, like Mother of Pearl instead of bein' just white. Is that what it is, Stan?'

'It is, Len.' He smiled. 'We thought it set the little black numbers off a treat.'

'It does,' said a few of them together.

'And this is what we got Monty,' said Stan, opening a short black box to show them a beautiful gold lighter. He flipped the lid and fired the flame into life.

'First time, eh,' said the unimpressed Wilf.

'Real gold, Stan?' asked Carter.

'Aye, mind it wants t' be for the money.'

'Ee'll love that,' said Tommy.

'Aye, and we got a bit engravin' on as well; if yer look on the back it says *From your Firstwood Friends, 1940*,' and that was Nessa's idea as well.'

She smiled at their generous old ways of telling her how much they thought of her, rather than the engraving. The heavy lighter went on its way after the watches.

'Now aa thought t' give them them after dinner, y'know, when everythin's been cleared away, like, but if the dinner's at the usual time and we don't have t' get the plane until midnight, then there'll be that funny couple of hours; yer know what aa mean?'

'Aye, aa do.'

'Whey, how about we arrange for a late dinner, about half nine or ten, and say it's because we're goin' t' be up all night travellin',' suggested Wilf.

'Aa'd go for 10.00, and get everythin' packed aforehand,' said Den.

'Right, aa'll have a word wi' Hilda,' said Stan, seeing the support for Den.

'Good lad. Right then, who fancies a round Robin snooker doubles? Franc a head, winnin' pair takes the pot.'

They had no trouble letting Tommy know he'd hit on a good time-killer.

'Lenny's handicapped, mind,' said Roy.

'That's what ee's teachers said,' slipped in Wilf.

'Aye, aye, but what about that bloody big thing on ee's belly?'

'Ee's cardigan?'

'Ee's blister.'

'What d'yer reckon, Len; can yer manage wi' yer flange damage?'

'Whey aye, just a bit more off the rest.'

'Right, who wants handicappin' wi' restin' Lenny?'

After dinner, Monty stood at the top of the big table with the lighter in his hand. They could see he was touched by their present. 'I can't thank you enough for this, it really is the nicest thing and I will cherish it for the rest of my days.'

He read the inscription again as if it was irresistible. 'I don't know what to say.'

'First time for everythin', eh, Mont?'

'There is, Thomas, and for once I think I should just keep my trap shut and follow the good example of Raymond and Hilda; say my heartfelt thanks, shake each of you by the hand, and steal a kiss from the ladies.'

'Yer could steal one from Lenny if yer want, Monty.'

'Yes, I'd be happy for Leonard to feel my enormous gratitude pressed onto him' (cheers). 'But if I don't speak up I think I'll burst.'

'Just fire away, Mont, lad, we're used t' it.'

'Oh, well, if you insist.'

He smiled and playfully straightened himself as if to make a formal address:

'Can I begin by saying, I completely understand why you would think such an elegant, handsome and refined gift would be the perfect choice for me,' (cheers and laughs) 'and how it must have made you wonder how I've managed to maintain this athletic physique and these boyish good looks as I approach my 40th year.' (loud happy jeers)

'Have yer been usin' this speech for 20 years, Monty?'

'Dear, dear,' he said with a comically offended nose in the air, 'the hurtful lash of Wilfred's tongue stings once more, but I'll suffer and soldier on to pass my humble words onto you all.'

'That's the way, Mont, soldier on.'

'Yes, well I will try my best, but I must say the truth and admit the plain fact of the matter; that I just don't have the words to do justice to how much I want to express my eternal gratitude for this most beautiful gift. Indeed, knowing that I don't have them really does tell me that the best thing I can do is to follow the very fine example of Raymond and Hilda, and say my simple and honest, "thank you". So, thank you, and I hope you believe me when I say this; that it comes completely from the bottom of my heart – thank you, I will treasure my present forever. And in 60 years from now, when the world turns into the 21st Century, and I'm nearly 100 ...'

'By Christ, ee doesn't give up, lad.'

Monty coughed and smiled. '... And I'm nearly 100 years old, I'll look at this' (holding up the lighter) 'and read these perfect words, and tell everyone, and indeed anyone who will still lend me their ear, that this is what I won in the war: this is the honour that was given to me by the people most special to me, and it is, and will be forever, my honour to have had the greatest good fortune to meet you and to call you my friends.'

He stopped and looked out at them with shiny eyes, and they saw him working to collect himself.

'So a toast,' he offered, lifting a glass to his own relief: 'To Firstwood Friends.'

'To Firstwood Friends,' echoed fully.

Monty emptied his glass in one unusual swig and asked: 'Oh, did I forget to say, "gedoon", gentlemen?'

They all laughed kindly as they always did when he tried to speak their Firstwood for them.

'Mind, if yer really wanted t' impress them in London, Mont, yer could knock back a glass of yer fancy Champagne and say, "gedoon, yer bugger, gedoon",' said Wilf. (laughs)

'I do believe they'd think the world had ended.'

'Aa'll bet they would.'

'Six months ago, you know, and to my eternal shame, I would have been one of them, but no more, my brave new world has only just begun, and it's a world with friends and a better one for it.'

'Even wi' Wilfy in it, Mont?'

'Yes, even with Wilfred in it.' He smiled, and paused thoughtfully. 'I do have so many things I would like to say …'

He stopped and looked at them with his smile working hard to hide a wryly concerned look in his eyes.

'But I did promise I wouldn't prattle on tonight of all nights.'

'I've got a toast,' said Tommy, standing up with his coffee cup raised to help Monty out: 'To Raymond, Hilda and Monty: Hip-Hip …'

Each Hooray rang louder, and ended with a clear signal for them to leave their seats and mingle around the three with gifts to enjoy the little time they had left before the flight home.

******

Monty stood in the open door of the freezing cold plane.

'Now have the most wonderful Christmas time, and a very happy New Year, of course, and we'll see each other soon. Et êtes-vous gentil et sûr, Georges?'

The worried looking old doctor nodded.

'Good, and I'll be in touch as and when.'

'And you're leavin' tomorro', Mont?'

'Yes, yes, all arranged for tomorrow, Stanley, just a few odds and bobs to tie up, and make sure Raymond and Hilda get home safely. You can rest assured, I'll be in London tomorrow night.'

'Try and stay out of them funny clubs, mind.'

'I'll do my best, Dennis. Now please take care Thomas doesn't overdo it in the Townley Arms, although I must say I really did enjoy his bottle of Black Bess.'

'Good stuff, eh, Mont.'

'It certainly is. I really must come up one of these days and we can sup a couple, ay?'

He enjoyed the noisy mix of kindly cracks and invitations coming his way until they were stopped by a powerful propeller starting up and vibrating the seats.

'Righty-O, everyone, Merry Christmas and I'll see you soon. And remember: don't open my little present until Christmas Day.'

They assured him they wouldn't and that they'd make sure Margaret got hers. They all thought about the little brown boxes tied with a red ribbon bow he'd given them, and wondered what was in them as they shouted up their goodbyes and Merry Christmas wishes. Being asked to step back by a mechanic, Monty heard them silenced by the thick rubbery thud of the door being shut, and stood with Raymond and Hilda on the frozen white sheet covering the field. They watched the plane crunch through a trundling turn to line up for its dash into the starless sky, and waved until it dissolved into the dirty dark grey night.

'You're both sure you want to stay with this; it's looking like a tricky road ahead: Hilda?'

'Yes, I do.'

'Derek?'

'Yes.'

'Very good, I'll let them know tonight.'

End of Norman's notebooks.

Chapter 4

'So how much do I owe you then, Charles?'

'Well, the paper was a couple of quid and the printing and binding was £8.60, up at that new place near the roundabout, so call it a tenner, eh?'

'Tenner it is.'

'Still seems a canny bit to pay out when you didn't have to, mind.'

'Aye, but he hasn't got a computer and he'll be over the moon to see it all done like this.'

'Haven't they not got a computer in the office he could use to see the website, like?'

'Mustn't have, or at least not one he can use; he said he couldn't get to one when he gave me the books, but it's done now anyhow. I'll drop it in tomorrow, it'll make his day.'

'Janet always says you're a big softy.'

'Janet's never wrong.' Brendan smiled.

For the second time in his life Brendan pressed the little white button in the functionally neutral foyer of Tipton Grange Nursing Home. This time a smiling young receptionist slid one of the little glass doors open.

'Hello, Pet, I was just wondering if I could give this to one of the residents; he's called Norman.'

'Norman? What's his last name, please?'

'I don't know, Pet, I just returned somethin' he'd dropped – this was back in November.'

'Oh, right.'

She opened the visitor's register on the counter and followed her finger down the list of names.

'No, there's none of the residents here now called Norman.'

'Are yer sure, sweetheart?'

'Yes,' she said honestly, 'but if you tell me your name, I can look up your visitor slip and check who it was.'

'I didn't get one, the nurse just let me in.'

He saw the look on her face tell him something wasn't right. 'Should I have had one?'

'Yes, we haven't got to let anybody in without one.'

She licked her finger and dragged a visitor slip off a photocopied pile and pushed it to him.

'No, I didn't get one. Like I say, she just buzzed me in. I'm sure she'll remember me, though: she's older and quite stocky, but not very tall, with light blue eyes.'

He could see he was making her uncomfortable.

'I'm sorry, Pet, I know I'm in the wrong here, but would you see if she's in?'

'She isn't, and I don't know anybody like that who works here, and I've been here a month.'

'Oh, right. Well could you find out what's happened to Norman if he's not here now?'

'I can get Mr McDermot, the manager, if you want to wait.'

Brendan sat waiting for 20 minutes before the security door opened and a small middle-aged man in dull slacks and a navy blazer came up to him offering his hand. Brendan stood to shake it as he looked at the unmilitary badge on the breast pocket.

'Hello, I'm Mervyn McDermot, the manager here, Elizabeth tells me you visited one of our residents in November, someone called Norman?'

'It is, I did, yes. It was only to return something he'd dropped. The receptionist let me in to give him it back, that's all.'

'Right,' said the manager in a way Brendan didn't like, 'I've checked the register and we had two Normans with us then. Can you tell me where his room was?'

'Aye; straight through to the stairs and up and then left at the top, and straight along. I think it was the second door off the end, on the right.'

'You have a good memory,' he said humourlessly, looking at a piece of paper. 'That would have been Norman Bembrage. I'm in the past tense because he left us on the 28th November. No, not died, he was collected by his sons, Luke and John, to live with one of them at his family home in London.'

Brendan's mind raced uncomfortably around the remembered bits of conversation with Norman:

'Do you have a forwarding address for him?'

'I do, and I would like to make it crystal clear that on no account would I release such information to a non-family member, and certainly not to someone, like yourself, who may be considered a perfect stranger, were it not for the express instructions of the sons to give it to anyone who wanted to contact their father.'

The developing snottiness of the manager wasn't going down well with Brendan.

'So what is it?'

'251a, Green Lane, Woolwich. Now, the member of staff who let you in; did she have dark grey hair, brushed back, and very light blue eyes?'

Brendan nodded. He tried to make a case for her, saying she could have felt pressure to let him in because he wanted to return what he'd found himself.

'No matter,' said the manager.

'So is she in trouble?'

'No, but only because she doesn't work here anymore. And for your information, she left at the same time as Mr Bembrage; to be his private nurse, would you believe?'

Handing the piece of paper to Brendan because it had the address on it, he nodded to Elizabeth to open the door and left without a word.

******

'Don't write to that address, it's a trap,' said Charles.

'Easy, Tiger. He's very forceful that husband of yours, Pet,' winked Janet.

'It has to be; why else would anybody do that? I mean, would anybody in their right mind give out their parent's address for anybody who'd ever spoken to them to know where they lived? Course not. And remember, this is somebody who told Bren he had no family. And these so-called sons just happen to come for him a day or two after he hands over that stuff? The whole thing seems shonkey t' me, mind. So you can't get in touch with that address.'

'He has got a point, Pet,' said Janet.

'So just do nowt?' said Brendan.

'Exactly, don't get drawn into their latest play.'

'That's it, listen to spymaster Charles, there.'

'But what if he's in trouble and needs a bit help, like?'

'Then there's nothing we can do about it; it's horrible but that's the way it is,' reasoned his wife.

'Aye, aye. It's just the thought of the poor little bugger bein' stuck somewhere, frightened and thinkin' there's nobody doin' 'owt to help him.'

Janet rubbed the middle of her husband's back.

'The thing that strikes me about this, though,' said Charles, thoughtfully, 'is that what went on at the old folk's home yesterday seems to lend somethin' to his story. I mean, even the names of the sons: Luke and John? Is that the best they could come up with, for Christ's sake?'

'He definitely said he had no family didn't he?' checked Janet.

'Definitely,' said Brendan, 'and, I mean, I didn't want to jump t' conclusions or 'owt, but I did get the impression he was a homosexual.'

'Gay; that's what they say now.'

'Who says?'

'Just anybody talkin' about homosexuals.'

'Oh, whey, I thought he was a gay, y'know, there was just somethin' behind the way he said things; like the way he said he didn't have any family – kids, like.'

'So that's all the more reason to stay clear of writin' to that address,' pressed Charles.

'But being gay doesn't mean yer can't have kids, a lot of men dally between the two, don't they, Charles?'

'Dear me, Janet, still with this from so long ago?' smirked Charles, feeling the limelight begin to glow. 'It's only because I'm a lover, not a fighter...'

'And the red coat at Butlin's,' she got in quickly.

Charles folded his arms and looked theatrically huffed to make them smile. '1967 that was, getting on for 30 years ago, and for the millionth time, he only ended up in my chalet because I was too drunk after the Beechcomer club to lock the bloody door.'

'Easy, Charles, you don't have to dredge it all back up, it can't be very nice for yer in front of Gloria. What was the red coat's name again?'

'Pack it in, Janet,' said Brendan with a smile.

'How did you know you'd had a red coat in your chalet, Charles?' asked Gloria.

Janet coughed.

'He was still there in the mornin', Pet,' said Brendan, trying to help, 'me and Jimmy saw him comin' out on our way to the breakfast hall.'

'Was it Quentin or Tarquin?' asked Janet.

'It was not,' rejected Charles camply.

'Brendan said yer didn't make it to breakfast,' said Janet, enjoying herself nearly as much as Charles was, basking in the full glow of the limelight.

'Because, O Madame Slur, I was hungover from the cocktails; I've never had a head for those things. Can you remember the rain thing they did in the Beechcomber, Bren? Good technology for the time I'd say.'

'Never mind technology. So you couldn't get up in the mornin' because of a cock tale...'

'Really, Janet,' smiled the attention-loving Charles.

'But yer made it to the fancy dress party in the afternoon. And before yer ask, Gloria, he went as John Wayne.'

'The cowboy?'

'That's him, Pet. The one with the awkward walk, eh, Charles.'

'Charles still has it for when we go to the Caravan, Janet.'

'Has what, Pet?'

'No, no, Sweet Pea, Janet doesn't want to hear about that.'

'Oh, but I do.' She smiled, like a cat to Charles the mouse.

'It's really good fun, Janet; we get dressed up for the Wild West nights and Charles is a cowboy and I'm his cowgirl girlfriend.'

'No?'

In the one unbelieving word she let Gloria know just how much she wanted to hear every single snippet of detail, and Gloria was happy to oblige:

'Yes, we've got different outfits for the different nights they have on, and Charles has his six-shooter and I'm going to get my own rifle, aren't I, Charles?'

'Yes, you are, Sweet Pea, like Annie Oakley,' he said kindly, giving in, and thinking he might as well get it over with.

'Wow,' said Janet trying to keep a straight face, 'your own rifle. And I'll bet you've both got your own special cowboy and cowgirl names, eh?'

'Oh, yes; I'm Cindy-Lou and Charles is Tex Ritter...'

Although she was sitting down, Janet folded in half and her head fell below the level of the table. Brendan tried to make out he was laughing at something else when he saw Gloria wondering what had happened to her. Putting his hand on his wife's back he could feel the heaves of laughter as she used both hands to cover her mouth.

'Somethin's gone down the wrong way, Pet,' he said to Gloria.

'Tex Ritter,' slipped out from under the table.

'Tell her to come up, Bren, Tex and Cindy-Lou want to see she's ok,' said Charles, in his good-natured way to let Brendan see again why he was his oldest friend. Her red face appeared, with shirt cuffs drying her eyes.

'What went down the wrong way, Janet?' asked Gloria.

The unsuspecting concern in the question, and the way she nervously touched the big bright bow on the flamingo hairband Janet had given her for Christmas, made Janet care.

'One of these little buggers,' she said, rattling a handy box of mints, 'would yer like one, Pet? Put yer hand out then.'

Gloria took it and said thank you.

'Tic Tac, Tex?' was the offer she couldn't stop herself from making. Her laughter was joined by Gloria's, who thought it sounded funny.

Chapter 5

2001

'**W**hat the hell have yer got there?'

'It's fer you.'

'What is it, like?'

'Aa haven't a clue but it's a ton weight.'

'Let's have a look,' said Brendan, 'aye, there's a bit weight in it. Where's this from, then?'

'Just off the Posty there.'

'Posty? It's 4.00 in the mornin', Jimmy, there's no Post at this time.'

'No? Whey, it must've been the little red van wi' Post Office written on, and the lad wearin' a Posty uniform that threw me, eh?'

'Aye, aye.'

Brendan looked after the van as it ran away into the barely broken daylight along the bottom lane.

'Whey, aa've never known any post at this time, mind.'

'Me neither, but there it is. Were yer not expectin' 'owt, like?'

'No, nowt.'

'Has your lass not ordered 'owt?'

Brendan shook his head as he looked at his name on the suitcase-sized parcel.

'Aa'll just nip in and see what's what, Jim, aa'll be two minutes, see yer down the sheds.'

In the kitchen, Brendan split the brown wrapping paper while his wife watched, drying her hands on a tea towel, to let them see a plywood box, with a lid fastened with metal toggles.

'Christ, it's tight.'

'It's pinned as well, look,' said Janet.

'Can you get that screwdriver out the middle drawer, Pet.'

The lid finally gave way.

'That bloody thing wasn't meant to come off in a hurry.'

'Who packs stuff with cotton wool these days?'

The perfectly fitted cotton wool sheets were carefully lifted out and laid on the table. The last of them revealed the marbled slab of Oxford blue notebooks in their purpose-made box.

'It's another set of them notebooks,' said Janet, mildly concerned.

'Must be another copy. But who the hell's sent them now? And why? And how did they know to send them here?'

A single sheet of paper dropped from the last cotton wool layer Janet was holding, and glided across the kitchen floor. She read it as she walked back to the table.

'What's it say?'

'"Dear Brendan, please do it again. Thank you. Faithfully, N.".'

'That'll be 'N' for Norman. Christ, d'yer think he's still alive?'

She didn't answer and Brendan went on:

'I suppose he must be. I never thought we'd hear any more from him, mind: it's got t' be five years since we did that stuff.'

'Six.'

'Aye. So why does he want us to do it again then? But I never told him where I lived.'

She could see he was bothered and didn't feel happy about it either. She told him to wait a minute and went upstairs. He listened to her crossing the bedroom floor above and waited for her coming back with the bound copy of Norman's story.

'Get one of the new books out, Pet, and see if it's got a number on the cover again?'

'Aye, I've got number 5.'

'Get the one opposite.'

'Number 1?'

'Aye, read it out from the start,' she said, opening the bound copy.

He didn't read much before she told him to stop.

'I thought it might be; it's a new lot, they're a different set; they'll be the rest of the story.'

'Whey, we did think it was strange for it to finish at Christmas, 1940, when he made out they'd been doin' stuff all through the war. So these'll be t' do again, then. Christ, remember how much work went into the last one.'

'Oh aye, but you're still goin' to do it though, aren't yer,' said his wife seriously.

'We can't not do it now.'

'Yes we bloody well can "not do it now". Let some bugger else do it who's bothered about it, or got more time on their hands than we have.'

'But there must be a reason for givin' it to us; it'll be to do with the website thing and uploadin' and all that stuff, eh.'

Janet had to smile at her 20-stone fish out of water.

'So you're sayin' it's much better for me to be strugglin' on for another five weeks with Rootin' Tootin' Tex and Miss Marble.'

They both laughed.

'I'll give him a ring tonight,' said Brendan carefully.

'He's goin' t' bloody love this. Oh, Christ, not again.'

He smiled at her.

'D'yer want me to shift these somewhere, Pet?'

'No, just leave them there, or Jimmy'll be asleep in the sheds.'

'There's a bit weight in them, mind.'

He knew straight away he'd slipped on a path he shouldn't have been on. She looked at him as she picked the box up and weighed it deliberately with a little bouncy motion.

'Aye, a bit weight, more than yer'd want around yer head.'

'Au revoir, sweetness.'

END

Printed in Great Britain
by Amazon

17694205R00178